An Arcane Shot/Knights of the Boardroom Series Crossover

Ben O'Callahan has worked a long day. The last thing he wants is to find a couple witches and two guys who claim to be "Guardians," aka sorcerer-stye cops, lying in wait for him on the parking deck of the K&A offices. But he has information they need, about a dark witch from his past who may have plans to destroy New Orleans.

Well, screw that. This is his town. Much as he'd prefer to go home to his beautiful submissive and a nice steak, a knight knows when it's time to don the armor and go fight evil. Only in this case, his lady isn't the type to wait at home. Marcie is going to fight for the city, right by his side, with the Guardians and witches who know that love is the one thing that evil can't defeat.

Not if the will is strong enough.

[Note: **Arcane Knight** was previously released under the title **The Problem with Witches**.]

I0552536

ARCANE KNIGHT

An Arcane Shot Series Crossover

JOEY W. HILL

Arcane Knight

Formerly Titled: The Problem With Witches

An Arcane Shot Series Crossover - Book #4

Copyright © 2019 Joey W. Hill

ALL RIGHTS RESERVED

Cover design by W. Scott Hill

SWP Digital & Print Edition publication June 2019

Digital ISBN: 978-1-942122-91-3

Print ISBN: 978-1-951544-20-1

ACKNOWLEDGMENTS

Many thanks to Irene for her help with Russian endearments. Like Raina, I'd be happy to listen to Mikhael talk in Russian all day, even without having a clue what he's saying. However, I thank Irene for making sure those words have the right meaning, lol.

Thank you as always to my hardworking critique partners and line editors for your patience, insights and invaluable friendship.

To my husband, for the gorgeous cover, the book set up, and all those other publishing tasks he handles so I can focus on the books. It would be impossibly difficult to be "storywitch" without the help of "Story Witch Press."

There've been a lot of personal challenges during the writing of this book, a lot of life lessons learned. I hope those experiences have only enhanced the final result and that you enjoy this story. Though it's rare I intersect our contemporary with our paranormal worlds as extensively as occurs in this story, it was a fun ride.

A final important thanks to Kristen. Life's crossroads are far more bearable with the benefit of a kind and listening ear. Since I'm far better at being a writer than a friend, it makes me eternally humble and grateful to have a friend like you. I wish you many well-deserved blessings, dear lady.

CHAPTER ONE

Drip, drip, drip.

Just a leaky pipe, he told himself, shrugging it off. Ben glanced at his watch. He'd told Marcie he'd run late tonight, so when he got home, he anticipated finding her on the small nook balcony of their Garden District home. She'd be nested into the wrought iron garden chair she'd repainted a cheerful blue and placed amid the forest of blooming potted bougainvillea there. She'd have a glass of wine at her elbow, her sneakered feet propped on the rail. Her lovely face would be creased in concentration, strands of her silky blond hair framing her delicate features as she studied for the police academy exams.

He tried to curb his demanding appetites while she was in study mode, which was part of why he'd chosen to work late, but pinning her to the wall and taking her hard before he fixed them a late dinner qualified as restraint for him.

He'd probably want her once more when they finally went to bed, but she wouldn't be studying then. Or when he woke at the 3am witching hour, which he often did. His beautiful submissive would murmur in her sleep, open to him, give him all of herself, as she took all of him, and then slip back into dreams, drawing him with her. His good witch, with her own special magic to counter the darkness of the bad stuff that disturbed his sleep in the middle of the night.

He—

Drip, drip, drip.

Damn it. Ben paused, his brow furrowing. He tracked every foot of the parking deck, looking for the source. It was one thing to hear dripping from the eaves in the aftermath of a rain shower. They hadn't had rain in three days, and this drip was like the leak from a rusty pipe, something heard underground. He didn't like it.

Two vehicles were on the top covered level of their parking deck, the McLaren and Lucas's Outback, since he'd biked home this afternoon, the maniac.

Only two cars, but the parking deck wasn't empty.

Ben didn't carry a gun. He was glad as hell his wife carried and knew how to use the concealed Glock she favored. But he'd learned to fight and survive without one. Had killed without one. The ability to handle a situation with wits and whatever weapons were close to hand was a skillset he'd never abandon. Never wanted to get out of the habit.

It came in handy when a couple of assholes were trying to corner him on his own parking deck at work.

"If you don't come out of the shadows, the security cams can't show me kicking your asses on YouTube. I've had a long day, I've got a beautiful woman waiting on me at home, and a good sirloin. So show yourselves, let's get this done, or fuck off."

The shadows to the right moved. Ben set down the briefcase and put his car at his back. As soon as the cameras did show whoever was approaching him, the alert team Kensington & Associates employed would be on their way to clean up what he left in a crumpled mess on the concrete. The cameras should have already tracked what he was dealing with, but apparently the bastards had knocked out a couple lights on that side.

The big son of a bitch who emerged wasn't what Ben was expecting. He wore a cowboy hat, for fuck's sake. He also carried a white ash staff, very Gandalf-like, that didn't blend with the worn jeans and dark blue button down he wore. But it did work with his boots, which might have been snake or alligator skin but were neither, at least no species Ben had ever seen. The scales were bronze and silver, with tinges of iridescent color. The guy wasn't wearing them as a fashion accessory. They were scuffed, well-used.

His face was lined and rugged. Maybe forty-something, until you reached the steel-blue eyes, and then Ben thought he was looking at someone—or something—way beyond room for candles on his birthday cake. Unless the expanse of buttercream frosting was the size of a football field.

The set of the guy's mouth and jaw said cop to Ben, no matter the odd get-up. Too often in his youth, Ben had been on the opposite side of the law, so that cop-vibe was another instinct that never went away. Yeah, he got the irony. Leland Keller, a Baton Rouge police sergeant, was a close friend, and Ben's own wife was studying to join the blue line. God help him.

Asshole number two stepped into the light a few feet away from Cowboy Gandalf. This one had the same cop vibe, was also tall and broad-shouldered, though he presented himself quite differently. His black suit was a Brioni bespoke, Ben was certain of it, a four- or five-figure investment. No *Lord of the Rings* staff for this one, but there was an odd energy vibrating around him.

His gaze was so dark Ben couldn't detect pupil from iris, as if that wasn't eerie as fuck. The guy's hair was dark, thick and silky, enough to make Jon, their resident K&A pretty boy, trade hair product recommendations with him. But there was nothing pretty boy about the eyes. That darkness ranked up there with vampire movie effects, not so easy to laugh off in the middle of the night.

But he'd faced a lot scarier things.

"Getting bored," he said sharply. "I do have office hours. What do you want?"

"A voodoo priestess named Elagra Bluebird Jones," said Cowboy Gandalf.

Okay, that was one of the scarier things.

It was perhaps the last thing Ben would expect someone to say to him. Yet it wasn't a surprise to hear it, because somewhere way deep down in his gut, he'd always known he'd have to deal with her again.

Out of all the disturbing things that woke him at 3am, one of them actually was a witch.

"She's no voodoo priestess." He knew voodoo practitioners. They'd want nothing to do with something like Elagra. But it was New Orleans, and the bitch had always known how to market herself.

To pull in the unsuspecting.

Drip, drip, drip. If that fucking noise didn't stop…

Just water, he reminded himself. But when he'd been younger, the rust had turned it red. When he woke with the drops staining his skin, she would say it was blood. And smile.

"It comes through the pipes. It is all the blood shed on a New Orleans night. In the dark places, where hope can't exist. It all flows to me, for there is power in despair, to twist a man's heart any way I wish. I can make him abandon his soul. Even if the world, with its unseeing eyes, thinks him the strongest of men, he is a naked, shivering thing. Always."

When she'd told him that, they'd been in a section of tunnels that picked up the sounds of New Orleans through the drains. The rhythmic bump of traffic, the call of vendors and tourists, the salty humid smell of the nearby waterfront. They hadn't been far from the Warehouse District. Back then, he could get to the surface through a grate near Mardi Gras World.

Thanks to an unexpected friendship with the late shift security guard, he'd become a regular nighttime visitor there when he was a kid. He'd slip in, wander amid the floats. Occasionally, a couple of designers would be working late at their drafting tables or computer screens. They knew him, would lift their heads when they saw him, nod, and go back to what they were doing. All of them silent ghosts haunting the dormant Carnival world.

He remembered coming face-to-face with the Grim Reaper float. The towering figure had looked down at him with staring eyes that seemed to follow him. Even when he circled behind the damn thing, he kept expecting the head to swivel around one-eighty. He'd been glad when they'd torn that one down, to build something new. Its eyes reminded him too damn much of Elagra Jones.

Shit. Memory had sucked him in, and he'd lost time and place. The hair on the back of his neck was a prickling, charged field, and his muscles were tense and ready for the fight.

The two men hadn't moved any closer, but that didn't make Ben less annoyed with his distraction. *Way to get yourself killed, O'Callahan.*

"Sometimes my presence resurrects old demons," Brioni Asshole said. Those dark eyes held Ben's. "It is one way I get to the truth of things, sooner rather than later. More efficient."

His tone was resonant, in an inexplicably contained way. Cowboy

Gandalf's was the same. In the mostly empty parking deck, their voices should have echoed, rather than sounding like the notes were filling all the hollow space and drawing decisive lines around it.

For just a moment, the clustered shadows around the dark-eyed male looked like a pair of large, sinister wings. The lights Ben thought had been knocked out weren't, and caused the talons at the joints of the wings to gleam.

Ben blinked again, and the wings were gone.

"You are right. She is not a voodoo priestess." Cowboy-Gandalf brought his attention to him again. His expression was grim. "It's good you already know she's not what she presents herself to be."

Ben's gut was as tight as an overwound spring, his heart cold and still. He didn't tolerate fear, especially not from specters of his past.

"You need to fuck off now," he said. "Give that staff back to the pimply geek you stole it from at DragonCon."

"But the tears of surly teenagers give him such joy."

At the first note of the purring voice, Ben was hit by a wave of far different energy. Whereas the two males heightened his warrior instincts, driving him to evaluate what kind of fight he was facing, this one took him to an entirely different kind of arena, though no less physical.

He had a stronger-than-average sex drive. His wife would declare that an absurd understatement, with fervent gratitude, loving amusement and the right kind of sensual trepidation. Yet he was also a grown man who had iron discipline over when he opened the flood gates on that formidable carnality.

This voice wrapped around that lever—pun impossible to avoid— and pulled it into the On position with the ease of glossy feminine fingernails flicking a light switch.

The woman who came out of the blackness behind Brioni had the kind of shiny ebony hair that had shimmers of blue in certain lights. Her exotic green-gold eyes made Ben think of dragons. She had a dusky complexion, lush lips and an even lusher body, clad in a velvet green scoop-necked top with flared sleeves that draped over ring-bedecked fingers. Which yes, were tipped with glossy nails, painted dark green and sparkling with a black diamond chip on the middle finger and thumb. Her black jeans fit her every bit as well as expected, showing off an ass that would fill a man's hands just fine. The penta-gram around her neck gleamed silver.

She laid her hand on Brioni's arm. The glance he sent her was ten percent exasperation and ninety percent possession.

"We need his mind clear," he said. "Perhaps dial it down."

"That was our thought," said another female voice. "You and Derek are broadcasting 'tell us what you know, or we'll fuck you up.' She was balancing it, so this didn't turn into a fight. Which you already know won't work with him."

This voice had a Lauren Bacall sound to it, raspy but direct. The woman to whom it belonged stepped into Ben's field of vision at the elbow of "Derek," the blue-eyed staff wielder. She was far more func-tionally dressed than the other woman. Form-fitting but well-worn jeans and an Army green tank top outlined a feminine but toned body. Based on the way she carried herself, her obvious situational aware-ness, and the open shirt she wore over the tank, Ben guessed she was carrying.

With her hair pulled back in a ponytail, she'd have looked totally in her element standing next to Lara Croft with matching Desert Eagles at the ready. Though he expected what she had concealed would be something like his wife's compact Glock, easy to hide but just as lethal when needed.

"We were being direct," the dark-eyed male said, tossing her a slightly annoyed look. "And exceedingly polite. For us."

"Could everybody attending this rave step out into the light?" Ben said, with more than a tinge of annoyance in his voice.

"This is all of us," she told him. "And don't worry. Your cameras will see nothing but you getting into your car and driving home."

"I'm not worried. But how is that supposed to reassure me?"

"It's better than your security people wondering why you're talking to the air," she said, with a practical tone that made Derek's lips twitch. The male sent her a fond look.

Unlike the two men, her manner of speaking was far less formal. The way the other woman spoke was something unclassifiable, but definitely not casual English.

A crazy thought crossed Ben's mind. He and the Lara Croft woman might be the only fully human things on this deck.

"Look," she said, "we didn't mean to spring out at you. We just really need to find her, fast. Some bad shit is going to go down in New Orleans, and she's got info about it we need. I'm Ruby. This is Derek." She nodded to the man in the cowboy hat. "Mikhael," she indicated the Brioni, "and Raina."

The sultry woman who emitted pheromones like her personal oxygen supply swept him with a glittering look that trailed heat from the back of his neck to the soles of his feet. No lie, it felt as if her fingertips trailed along that same path. Another minute, and he'd pull Marcie's picture out of his wallet and hold it up, like a priest wielding a cross.

"Derek and Mikhael are Guardians, Light and Dark, respectively," Ruby said. "Their job is to defend the world from the big, really bad stuff."

"Of course," Ben said. "Like auto-tuning and the Fed raising interest rates. What do you two do in this circus act?"

"We're witches. Another class of magic user." Ruby didn't smile. Yet when his glance went pointedly to Raina, she offered a tight chuckle.

"She's got something extra thrown in. She's half succubus. She's not trying to lead you around by your cock, believe me. This is her on her lowest setting."

"Almost," Mikhael said, tossing Raina a reproving look before he brought his attention back to Ben. "It does not matter if you believe we are a cadre of lunatics. Tell us what we need to know, and we will be on our way."

"Lunatics aren't usually this well-organized," Ben said. He sighed and pinched the bridge of his nose. "Hell, I really wanted to get home to my wife and that damn steak."

"I'm not seeing how we will interfere with that," Mikhael said.

"Because finding Elagra isn't the same as giving tourists directions to Jackson Square," Ben said irritably. "On top of that, this is our town. If something's going down, you're going to tell us what it is." Ben pulled out his phone and hit a programmed button.

"Us?" Mikhael exchanged a look with Derek while a smile crossed Raina's moist red lips. Ben made the mistake of looking at her when she did it, which brought on a surge of lightheadedness. Christ.

"I told you," Derek said to Mikhael. "They're warrior class."

"Sorry?" Ben frowned at him. The phone was searching for a

signal. The deck could be a spotty area, but it should go through on the top deck. He'd called Matt from here before.

Ruby answered the question. "Warriors are what we call those who will heed the call if needed, no matter how things change, how modern and separate from magic society seems."

Apparently, they preferred her to do the talking, probably because she came off the most normal of the bunch. They assumed that would make all this sound more *yeah, okay, of course*.

He wasn't the type of person who let himself be fucking handled. However, from the knowing light in Ruby's eyes, he expected she understood that, and was playing it straight with him. Another reason he was pissed.

It would be far easier if they were lunatics.

"Yeah?" Matt's Texas drawl on the other end of the phone had that no-nonsense, head-of-the-pack authority that Ben always appreciated. "We've talked about you working too many late hours. You have a wife now. I can hire you interns."

"Don't threaten me. Plus, she needed study time. But work's not why I'm calling. I need you and the others back at the office. We've got a situation."

Matt's tone sharpened. "What kind of situation?"

"Not a topic for the phone, but I want just the team. No one else. Understood?"

A pause, and then Matt spoke. "Give me about thirty minutes. Lucas a few minutes longer, since he's further out of the city."

"Tell him to borrow Cassie's Harley. We can't wait on him to pedal it in the middle of the night."

Ben cut the connection. Abruptly, because Mikhael had advanced as the conversation concluded. While he pocketed the phone to free up his hands, Ben narrowed his eyes in warning. But the Dark Guardian—whatever the fuck that was, though Ben was still guessing some form of cop—circled the McLaren Roadster. His initial concern that the guy was executing a flanking maneuver disappeared. Ben recognized the light in the male's eyes, the first emotion Brioni Asshole had shown.

Pure gearhead appreciation.

"Nice car," Mikhael said.

"It's my wife's," Ben said. "She's letting me borrow it while my minivan's in the shop."

The first part was a true statement. His Mercedes S 560 Cabriolet had been due for a tune-up and Marcie had graciously, with mischief dancing in her gaze, offered to let him "borrow" the car that had originally been his.

Before he'd worked some of his personal shit out, he'd been drinking too much, being too self-destructive, and it had spilled out over her on one terrible night. Part of his amends had been to give up the McLaren for a charity auction. Eventually, the team had bought it back from Richard Lewis, the business rival who'd bought it at the auction. They'd gifted it to Marcie. His own damn car.

"What's your ride?" Ben asked pleasantly. He nodded toward Raina. "Or do you straddle the back of her broom and wear matching helmets?"

Raina chuckled, a total grip-a-cock-just-right-and-stroke-it sound. Ben made a mental note to stay away from the jokes if he didn't want to embarrass himself.

Mikhael's expression was back to statue mode. "Ferrari 458 Italia."

Nice. But Ben scoffed. "The McLaren will run circles around you."

"We can test that." Mikhael straightened from his study of the McLaren and showed his teeth. "Or rather, your wife can. Since it's her car."

Ben met that dark gaze. "Can't get to my wife except through me. I'm the fucking chasm to Hell."

"I've been there," Mikhael replied. "It's best to visit in winter."

"And he tells me to dial down *my* energy," Raina muttered to Ruby.

Ben heard the comment, but kept his eyes on Mikhael. Yeah, he and this guy were going to have a problem. He could already tell that. Might as well bring it to a head. He preferred that to thinking about Elagra Jones.

"As much as this rabid display of male plumage is making my panties wet, can I interrupt?" Raina drew closer to Mikhael's side, so her breast pressed against his biceps. She rested her long-nailed hand on his chest, caressing him through the dress shirt. With her back mostly to Ben, she offered a premium view of her curvy ass while she looked up into Mikhael's face. "His dick is longer, yours is bigger around, and both of them will scare fish when you're naked," she said. "All right? So can we move on?"

She tossed that last part over her shoulder to Ben, including him in the sensual reproof.

Ben pinched the bridge of his nose again. Fuck, fuck and double fuck. "Let's head back up to our board room," he said. "We'll wait for the rest of the team there."

CHAPTER TWO

$\mathcal{W}$ hen not accompanying her mate on a trip to save a riverfront town from annihilation, Raina ran a bordello populated by her adopted cluster of sex demons. The congregation of incubi and succubi relied on her skills as a witch so that they could nourish themselves on their human clientele without causing them harm, all while repaying their mortal offerings with unforgettable pleasure. A win-win, and one that worked out nicely for her bottom line. She could afford her own Ferrari, if she cared about such things.

Her profession depended on an intimate understanding of the minds of others. Mostly male others, so she had more practice with that gender. Ben O'Callahan was an intriguing study. After their initial bumpy introduction, he'd called in his reinforcements with surprisingly little additional interrogation on his part. When they adjourned to the executive board room, he'd even politely inquired if they wanted coffee or a drink while waiting. Then he'd said little else, moving to the bank of windows and staring out at the distant Mississippi. While it was difficult to see the river in the darkness, the lights following the river front made it easy to mark its whereabouts, particularly from this top floor.

She'd expected the board room of a company like K&A to be intimidating, and it was, with the large table and array of deep-seated, masculine chairs, but there were other touches to it she appreciated. Like several Japanese cut leaf maples, and a quietly gurgling corner fountain, made up of dark, glossy stones. The original paintings on the walls were by local artists. The table was shaped like a lotus pond, pleasing curves that reminded her of a woman. She wasn't sure that was accidental. Power and sex moved hand in hand, and she detected a strong undercurrent of both here, as if this room had been used for more than business dealings.

As she said, intriguing.

Ruby's brisk, direct personality and more human-relatable qualities had gotten their foot in the door. For the time being, she'd portaled back home. She'd come back when needed. So Raina was currently the only female in a roomful of alpha males.

None of them showed the need for random chit chat. Derek and Mikhael wouldn't waste energy sharing information that would have to be repeated when the others arrived. Both centuries old, they'd long ago left behind the need for small talk. Derek had his gaze on the ceiling as he rocked on the axis of his chair, turning it slowly back and forth. Mikhael had removed a deck of Tarot cards from his shirt and fanned them out on the table, studying them. Not to read them, but as a focus for whatever was going on in his head. The minds of Guardians were complex.

But they were also males. With her own senses and specifically tuned radar, she could pick up other things.

Derek missed Ruby, as he always did when they were apart. It gave his aura a yearning blue tinge, and it had taken on a deeper hue since Ruby had borne their son.

For the first few years of Jem's life, he'd intended to take a full hiatus from Guardian responsibilities, but this particular assignment couldn't wait.

A lot of them couldn't. The two new parents were starting to realize that, but they were working it out. Doing things like this, where Ruby tagged out so she could be with their child, was part of it. It didn't mean she or Derek liked the situation. "It sucks hairy-balled, rotten eggs," Ruby had told Raina flatly.

But saving the world was kind of a full-time job for Guardians, and Derek was one of their best. For him, missing a day of work didn't mean a report wouldn't be filed or a meeting would be missed. It meant lives, worlds collapsing, total universe chaos. He and Ruby cared about the world, so though that blue yearning was there, so too was that bold striation that most determined heroes had, the core of who they were.

Her gaze turned to her own mate. Mikhael's aura had that, too, but there was an underlying rich red tinge. It told her of his awareness of her, of the bond between them, even when his mind was occupied. She liked that.

Though he'd admonished her about her succubus power, when she'd upped the volume to help Ben be a little less guarded, he'd allowed it. She could travel outside of her bordello safely, thanks to a part of Mikhael's multi-faceted mind always buffering her, so she didn't have to carry the full shield load. Helping her tone down her energy was almost second nature to him now, such that she didn't often have to ask when she needed it.

He was a gentleman, her Guardian. Even as he'd have her over his knee in a blink and be far less of a gentleman if she pushed him the right ways.

His mouth quirked, a frisson of heat crossing his gaze even as he kept it on the cards. He couldn't read her mind word for word, but he came damn close.

She had no doubts Derek and Mikhael were both fully aware of everything happening in this room, every movement Ben made or sigh that escaped her lips. It didn't make them any less capable of solving some other universe problem in their minds while they waited to discuss the plan ahead.

But mechanics and strategy were only part of a mission like this. There had to be a cohesion of effort, a melding of personalities. That was part of why she was still here. She had a purpose similar to that of Ruby's. Keeping that foot in the door of the minds of the people whose cooperation they needed. She moved toward Ben.

The man had his hands in the pockets of his slacks and was motionless. No rocking back and forth or twitches of irritated movement, but the energy coming from him wasn't calm. Not in the least. After speaking to Matt, he'd called his wife, letting her know he'd be late, and that he would explain later. She doubted he would. He wouldn't wish to share this with Marcie; he would not want it to touch her.

That wouldn't matter. It never did. Men could be foolish. Wonderful, but foolish. As Raina came to his side, she felt Mikhael's cocooning energy increase, a heat as welcome as his physical body. With that dampening field, she could stand near Ben without being too distracting.

She already knew this was a man fiercely devoted to his wife. She had a feeling if Mikhael removed the field and she lifted her own, so that Ben's body reacted to her without an emotional desire to do so, he'd cut off his own cock before betraying his beloved Marcie.

Raina had no interest in driving a man to those ends. Especially one as dangerous and handsome as this.

Really?

The note in Mikhael's mind-voice gave her a shiver. She sent him a sultry look under her thick lashes. *Just making sure you're paying attention to me.*

You're going to receive more attention than you desire.

Impossible. There is no quantity of your attention that could be more than I desire.

She received an answering gleam from his dark eyes. He knew her heart. Knew all of her. She was no more likely than Ben to be disloyal to the one who owned her, body, heart and soul. Not because Mikhael had taken them, but because she'd willingly relinquished them. Trusted him with the most vulnerable parts of herself.

Though his campaign to compel her to do that had been very... forceful. Something she appreciated considerably.

"I can guess why they're here. Why are *you* here, other than to try and throw me off balance?"

Ben's abrupt question drew her out of the exchange of provocative feelings with her mate.

"Elagra is a witch," she responded. "There are some elements of that craft that are more intuitive to me than to them."

His green eyes locked with hers, shrewd, penetrating. This one didn't think with his cock, even when it was at full mast. "Yeah, I can see that," he said. "You remind me a bit of her."

He turned back to the window. He hadn't meant it as a compliment. A lot of tension there. She shifted to gaze out at the view with him. "Is that good or bad?" she asked.

"Not sure yet." He slanted a glance down at her. Like Mikhael, he was tall, over six feet. "I don't know you. I know her."

"You accepted what we are pretty quickly," she observed.

"No reason to waste time denying what's obvious. Does he…" Ben stopped, glanced at Mikhael. "You're with him?"

"Yes."

"You belong to him."

Her brow lifted, but before she could answer, Mikhael did. "Yes. She does." Mikhael didn't look up, but the message was clear. *Mine. Touch at your own risk.*

Not that she thought that was Ben's reason for asking. The vibe from Ben O'Callahan was pure sexual Dominant. She wasn't surprised he'd picked up on that nuance of her relationship with Mikhael. Or other things.

She tossed her hair back and leveled an amused look at Ben. "Though I make him work for it."

"I'll bet." Ben pursed his lips, his brow creasing. "Does he…have wings?"

She didn't sense his hesitation was due to feeling foolish for asking the question. It was as if the human male were gauging other issues, the implication of finding out. Determining if he really wanted to know the answer.

"Yes," she said. "You saw them. I thought you did. Only a person exposed to magic, enough to find it impossible to stay within the human comfort zone and block its reality, would have seen them. Which explains why you seemed to accept who we are far more quickly than expected."

Ben shrugged. "Shutting out the truth just gives it the chance to take a bigger chunk out of your backside. Most kids' first experience with magic is Disney. Elagra was mine."

She knew exactly what it was like to be caught in a web of dark magic. But she hadn't expected to see that knowledge reflected in the shadows that rose in the eyes of the man before her. The comfortable room around them disappeared, and she remembered the endless cold against her bare, bleeding skin, the fear, the pain. And worst of all, the terrifying helplessness.

"Don't." *Raina.*

The spoken word had been Mikhael's command to Ben. The second, much gentler but just as firm, was to her. It held her, pulling her back from that edge.

When she focused, she realized Ben had reached out to touch her in reassurance, concern for her momentarily driving out the suspicion. He was a man who took care of women. Her sudden distress, the shudder that went through her, would have come off her in waves too strong to be feigned.

Ben didn't bristle at Mikhael's spoken directive. Despite their initial adversarial stance, a couple of alpha dogs setting territory lines, Ben had correctly read Mikhael's admonishment. Touching her when she was feeling out of sorts was not a good idea. Not when she wasn't expecting it.

She shook her head, smiled at her mate. *I'm all right.* The flashbacks were unsettling, but they were something with which she'd made peace, long ago. Primarily because she'd killed the bastard who'd inflicted those torments upon her. A far preferable manner of overcoming the experience than years of therapy. She expected Ben understood the value of that kind of closure.

She touched Ben's arm, a brief contact she drew back smoothly. "I'm sorry that was your first experience with magic. Magic is a wondrous thing, but it is merely a tool. It can be turned to evil or good, by the ignorant or the wise."

He was studying her in that way that told her he was evaluating that she was okay, not necessarily hearing her words. "You saved yourself with a different kind of magic, didn't you?" she persisted. "Your wife. A love bound in a reality so strong it can't be shaken. Which is why she's going to be joining us."

That caught his attention. The green eyes snapped back to a far less friendly mode. One step from the threshold of deadly. She was used to dangerous men, however, and enjoyed walking that tightrope.

Far too much, woman. Watch yourself.

It landed me firmly in your arms, didn't it?

"No, she's not," Ben said in a deceptively mild voice. "None of our wives are going to be part of this."

"She is already on her way," Raina said. "On her own, so you can rein back that blast of Irish temper you're about to unleash. She didn't like what she heard in your voice."

Another curse and he'd turned away from her, was already dialing the phone. That was easy enough to deal with. She merely sighed, twitched her fingertips, and knew the signal wouldn't go through. A wafting of magic could trounce most electronics.

It wasn't that Ben would be able to change Marcie's mind if she thought he was in trouble; it merely saved the arguing time, something for which she knew Mikhael and Derek would have little patience. That was another thing about Guardians. Both of them were mated to human females—well, she was mostly human—but that didn't mean they had much tolerance for human waffling. For them it was simple. They made a decision, and everyone fell in line. Or were trampled by the inevitability of the choice they made.

She leveled another amused look at her Dark Guardian. Apparently staring at his cards, but now even deeper in her subconscious, reassuring her he was there. Holding her in that never-ending dance they did through the ballroom of her soul. He knew she loved to dance.

Men might be foolish creatures. But vital as well, to the thriving of a woman's heart.

Which was why Raina wasn't surprised when Marcie arrived less than a minute after the rest of the team did.

CHAPTER THREE

*B*efore coming here, anticipating who might become involved in the situation, Derek and Mikhael had done their research and shared it with Raina and Ruby. The five men sitting around the table had been dubbed "Knights of the Board Room" by a female columnist. She was now a successful blogger in Baton Rouge, mated to a police sergeant there who was a close friend to these men.

There were multiple reasons she'd given them the name. Publicly, it would be for their generous charitable donations and their ruthless abilities in business, jousters who rarely met defeat on the corporate battlefield. They also had an old-school, outdated but very appreciated protocol of courtesy, care and protectiveness toward women. Which went along with the unique stamp of sexual Dominant that every single one of them was.

Raina detected all of those latter qualities in their attitude toward her and Marcie, who currently sat with quiet attention to her right. The young woman had given her a couple searching looks since taking a seat, not entirely friendly. Raina couldn't fault her for it. When she'd arrived, Raina and Ben had been standing at the window, Raina's hand still on her husband's arm.

There'd be time to correct any misimpressions. For now, Raina's focus was on evaluating the men of the Kensington & Associates executive team.

A brothers-in-arms camaraderie was there, a bond that their

shared sexual preference had enhanced and taken into some deliciously unexpected places. They'd combined their skillsets multiple times to win the hearts, bodies and souls of each of their women. Because what woman in her right mind could resist that? She'd love to have the whole lot of them at her bordello for a weekend. They could bring their wives. She expected these men were well aware that visiting a house of pleasure could be a delightful couples' activity.

Subconsciously, though, the Knights of the Board Room moniker had also been sparked by what Derek had acknowledged. These men held to the warrior code. They could be counted upon to step up when danger threatened. A simple but vital thing in the world.

While Ben was the head corporate lawyer of the K&A empire, each man brought his own skillset to the team.

Jon, an absurdly beautiful male with black hair and blue eyes, as well as a deep, melodious voice somewhat at odds with his lean but yoga-fit form, was a mechanical and financial wizard, with near-genius level intelligence. His hobby was reading ancient texts, historical records, that kind of thing. What anyone else would consider torment, he considered pleasure reading.

Derek and Ruby had actually met him and his wife Rachel some time ago, a chance meeting when both couples were on a getaway trip. When Derek greeted a surprised Jon cordially, Ben and the others were filled in on that history. It didn't alter the expectant atmosphere by much.

Lucas, with silver grey eyes and hair the color of sun-touched wheat, was the calm eye of the storm. An incomparable man of numbers, he was K&A's CFO, and an amateur competing cyclist.

Peter was the size of a muscular tank, with storm gray eyes and dark blonde hair. The former National Guard captain had served multiple tours in the Middle East and handled the operations end of their many manufacturing interests.

Then there was Matthew Kensington. Both the tip of the spear and the propulsion behind it, he'd turned his father's oil field interests into a global manufacturing company. His chiseled features, well-cut short brown hair and direct, glittering brown eyes only reinforced what he was. A formidable CEO and intimidating man who didn't suffer fools.

"So, everyone at this table knows I was a street kid," Ben said brusquely. His tone said he had no intention of dwelling on any unnecessary details of that part of his life, nothing not directly relevant to the topic at hand. "When I was twelve, I pissed off a couple gangbangers. Turf issues. I managed to get away from them by ducking into the tunnels under the city."

"Tunnels?" Lucas lifted a brow. "We're below sea level. New Orleans doesn't have any tunnels."

"Yes, it does," Jon said, in that remarkably smooth and deep timbre. "Some are documented, some not. At the turn of the century, when civil engineers figured out how to build underground in negative sea level environments, there was a plan for a fairly impressive thoroughfare under Harrah's Casino. It was eventually shut down by historic preservationists and other logistical issues."

"Yeah. What he said." Ben nodded. "At the time I wasn't all that familiar with them, but that was the beginning of a pretty intimate knowledge. I gave them the slip, but I got lost."

He paused. Unexpectedly, his gaze slid to Raina. She knew he didn't mean the kind of lost that required a map to correct.

"That's when Elagra found me," he said. "The underground is her world. Like Pennywise the creepy clown, in that Stephen King novel Peter talked me into reading."

An avid reader herself, Raina agreed *It* was a fantastic story. Reading how the protagonists had overcome the clown's evil had been life-affirming. Fiercely so.

"Elagra offered me refuge in her world until the thing with the gangbangers blew over," he continued, "but like most things, there was a price for my room and board. I collected things for her, stole what she needed. And gave her someone to torment with her mind games. I got free as soon as I could and didn't look back. That's that." He lifted a shoulder. "You're not here for a trip down memory lane. She's a witch. The real deal."

Lucas, the practical accountant, cocked his head, his silver eyes narrowing. "Meaning what?"

"Meaning if she wanted to wave her wand and dress Cinderella up in the fairy tale ballgown, she could. At least, that's what Cinderella would see. Until she got to the ball, looked down and realized her dress was made of rat guts and pig's blood."

∽

A creature made of mud, sticks and pebbles flashed through Ben's mind. A boy's idle creation, no bigger than a hamster, had suddenly come to life, with a touch of Elagra's slim hand. She'd had curved black nails with shimmers of lightning sparking off them. When she touched him with them, the contact would tingle. Or jolt the nervous system like keys stuck in a socket, depending on her mood.

When she brought the mud creature to life, it hadn't looked like his crude rendering. It had looked exactly like he imagined it in his head. A miniature version of a sleek, powerful, and beautiful monster. A guardian at his back. A friend and companion. Someone who would make him feel less alone, and be too powerful to let choices be taken away from him.

Peter was studying him. Ben was close to all the men here, but he and Peter had a special bond. When Ben met the gaze of the blond-haired behemoth, it hit him, almost made him smile. He'd eventually found that creation. And not just in Peter. In the shape of the four men at this table.

Ben looked toward Lucas. Mr. Grounded-In-His-Calculator was still looking to make sense of it.

"So, she's a hypnotist of some kind," he said. "Like an illusionist."

"It would be a lot more reassuring if that was true," Ben said. "You remember when Peter told us that surviving in combat means never getting confused about who your enemy is, or isn't?"

At Lucas's nod, Ben set his jaw. "Then take what I say exactly at face value. She's a witch. She knows how to do magic, and it's the creepiest Freddy Krueger mixed with flying monkey stuff you've ever seen, rolled into one freaky shitstorm. Only it's not smoke and mirrors or Hollywood magic. It's as real as that bad tequila you projectile vomited when we were in Mexico."

He took a breath. "If I could talk myself into writing down directions, handing them over and forgetting these three ever showed up, I would. But one thing I learned about Elagra is this. When she shows up on your radar, you don't turn your back. Until you're sure she's off screen again. Right now, she feels way too on screen to me."

Lucas studied him for another long moment. "Okay," he said.

Peter likewise nodded. "Can't be any harder to swallow than the esoteric crap Jon feeds us about the connectivity of life energy in the universe. How it fuels all worthy endeavors."

"You were listening," Jon said. "Glad I'm sitting down to handle that shock."

"He pays attention because he thinks you're going to give us a quiz on it, and Captain America refuses to fail any test," Ben informed him. "I just ignore you."

He looked toward Matt. Their leader's expression wasn't giving anything away. But Ben knew him well enough to know Matt's steel trap mind was running it through, waiting for the other variables sure to come. He looked like a former star football player, with his broad shoulders and formidable physical presence. But with his piercing eyes he'd been compared to a raptor, the way he waited, watched and collected info before making his move at just the right time. They wouldn't look for him to make a comment until they reached that point.

Unless they got off track and needed a yank back onto the path. Matt preferred the straightest line between two points, in the rare circumstances where a problem's solution presented that as an option. This wasn't one of them.

Ben looked toward their silent guests. "Floor's yours."

As Ben took a seat next to Marcie, Raina saw their eyes meet, the tension in their expressions. He wasn't happy with her being here, but Raina heartily approved of the stubborn jut to Marcie's jaw. Submissive didn't mean doormat. This one seemed very aware of that. Her love for Ben was likely one of the few things that could override her strong natural desire to submit to him.

Her gaze slid to Mikhael. She understood that herself. She'd accepted him as her Master. But there was nothing she wouldn't do to care for and protect him. Yes, he might perceive himself as invincible, but everyone needed someone watching their backside. Since he had a very fine backside to watch, it was no chore to her.

Even though he could regularly be a pain in hers. That, too, was part of love.

Derek leaned forward in his seat, clasping his hands in front of him on the table. "A strong, Dark energy is moving beneath the surface of New Orleans," he said without preamble. "It's putting enough pressure on the magical ley lines to suggest it's very close to breaking free. When it does that, if our estimate of its size is correct, it can initiate an apparent natural catastrophe that will turn the city into a lake. Elagra is the strongest Dark magic user in this area, so she will have knowledge of its nature, what's coming. We seek that intel from her, so we'll best know how to contain, re-channel, or destroy it."

"If Elagra's as evil as all that, will she just give you that information?" Peter asked.

"Dark is not synonymous with evil," Mikhael said. "No more than Light is with good."

"However, as magical tools, they more often align with the purposes of evil or good, respectively," Derek put in.

Mikhael shot him a dubious look, but thank the Goddess they left their eternal argument over it there so that they didn't get off point. They usually preferred to debate it over a bottle of vile Campari.

"True enough," Jon said, appearing pleased to find himself elbow to elbow with those who gave some thought to such questions. Raina stifled a chuckle when Peter tossed him a cross-eyed look and Lucas barely resisted flipping him off.

The double-edged pleasure of men was that the boy in all of them rode so close to the surface. Then Jon directed a more serious question to Mikhael and Derek. "When you say it's close to breaking free, do we have a timetable?"

"Two to four days." As the men shifted and muttered, Derek swept a quelling glance around the table. "In our world, that's often normal lead time."

"Better than usual," Mikhael added dryly.

A grunt was Matt's only reply to that, though that laser gaze suggested they would have been squirming in their chairs if they worked for him and provided such an excuse. But since they didn't, and it was simple fact, not an excuse—plus Mikhael and Derek had a few centuries of experience over him—they matched him with equally impressive stares.

She gave Matt props for matching it with a flinty look of his own. But Kensington had a strong aura, the consistency and color of tempered steel.

The last time she'd been in the same room with so many alpha males had been when her bordello had hosted a SEAL team for one intensely intriguing weekend. Being surrounded with so much focused testosterone was a pleasurable distraction, one she didn't mind savoring. She liked to live in the moment.

Her glance slid back to Marcie. The young woman was digesting the information, all while a very large part of her focus remained on Ben, and his on hers. To Raina at least, it was clear an argument was brewing, just waiting for a trigger to let it erupt. But that conflict couldn't override stronger things. Ben sat beside his wife, his elbow and hand resting on the table. The placement of his arm and cant of his body kept him facing Mikhael and Derek, the arm a subtle barrier between them and his wife. He likely wasn't even aware he was doing it.

"We would have preferred not to involve one of your people at all," Derek continued. He tilted a grimly amused look toward Ben. "But we've been advised that finding her isn't as easy as directions to the nearest tourist attraction."

"It's a one-man op," Ben told Matt. "I would have just done it, but..." He paused, a muscle twitching in his jaw. "Not telling you about it would have left you unprepared. In case things get sticky, I wanted you to have had a face-to-face with these three."

Marcie O'Callahan did not have a poker face. Her deep brown eyes flashed and soft pink mouth tightened. Ben didn't look toward her, but from the subtle tightening in his shoulders, Raina expected he was aware of her reaction. Though Marcie said nothing, Raina didn't think her silence was going to hold long.

"It sounds like you need some backup, man," Peter said.

"He will, because I'm going with him." Marcie said.

"*We'll* take them to her."

Less than ten seconds, in fact.

Her voice reminded Raina a little of Ruby's, a touch of sultry texture in the feminine syllables that suggested both delicacy and strength. It mirrored her appearance. She wore jeans and running shoes, but the soft, flowing sleeveless top revealed arms with sleek muscle tone. She leaned forward in her chair, one knee crooked beneath her thigh, an energetic, ready-for-action pose. Her thick blond hair was pulled up in a tail. Her expression was serious. And more than a little angry.

She wore one item of jewelry, a silver band that hugged her throat, the metal unembellished except for an etching of three flowers on the front. Forget-me-nots. It was a lovely piece, but Raina knew it for what it was. A submissive's collar, likely only taken off when social or work constraints made it necessary. But that evidence of her bond with Ben hadn't stopped her from throwing down the challenge.

As Raina had thought—submissive, not doormat.

Responding as a Master would, Ben's own mien became ice, razor sharp as a broken piece of glass. "You might want to dial back that attitude," he said.

"My thoughts exactly. You were sorry to involve them." Marcie made a brusque gesture toward the other men at the table. "But you were more than willing to keep me in the dark. I'm your wife. Which means I share your life and what happens in it. All of it."

Marcie met Ben's cold stare head on, though it took her a visible act of will. Raina had been there with Mikhael. This discussion was about to get ugly.

As Marcie threw up her chin, Peter reached out, laid a hand on Ben's arm. It didn't break Ben's focus on Marcie, but it was a reminder. A connection to something important.

Lucas exchanged a glance with Matt. A check, to see if the leader of their pack thought they should intervene, defuse this, particularly in front of their three guests. Matt shook his head.

Raina surmised he wasn't concerned about this for the same reasons she wasn't. Marcie's next words combined implacability with undeniable heart. That made all the difference, revealing the core of the relationship between these two.

"You're not scared of anything," she said softly. "And this woman scares you. So I'm going."

"Ben." Raina spoke, drawing everyone's attention to her, particularly when she eased the hold on the shield between herself and her impact on human senses. Even so, Ben turned his attention to her last, and not until Marcie reluctantly broke that challenging eye contact to look toward Raina herself.

"Elagra put her mark on you," Raina said. "It's best to fight the wrong woman's hold with the right one, a female energy more vested in your well-being. It's important that the balance, the mark of the woman you chose to be yours, be there as part of your arsenal against her."

Marcie raised a brow. "I can beat this bitch's ass with girl power? Why didn't you say so? We can send the boys home and get this done."

Raina smiled. She liked this one. The comment made Peter and Jon chuckle, even Matt's serious face creasing in a wry smile. Ben's jaw eased a fraction, though his green eyes still had sparks of temper in them. Marcie's gaze possessed the same, but when she reached out, closed her hand firmly on his, he didn't draw away from her. Though he did squeeze her fingers a little hard.

Matt's gaze moved from Ben, back to Mikhael and Derek. "I trust you'll keep my people safe while they help you," he said. "And advise us on what else you might need, once you find out what the full situation is. We have contacts throughout New Orleans and the state. We can mobilize them for action if you think it's warranted, to protect the inhabitants."

Derek inclined his head. "We intend this to be an exchange of information, not a fight. Though we are always prepared for it." He looked toward Ben. "How long will it take us to get to her?"

Ben frowned, and seemed to be searching for something in his own head. Raina knew it wasn't instructions, but she doubted anyone else at the table knew what he was doing the way she did. When his gaze met hers once more, the naked discomfort flashed there, then was gone behind a smooth expression. A lawyer's face, giving away nothing.

"An hour at most. But to get to her, we'll need the cover of darkness. The later the better."

Derek frowned. "It would be better to seek her out at the height of the day, when her powers are at lowest ebb."

"The best way to slip into her lair isn't a place you can enter when the whole world is watching. It's a tourist hot spot, the old St. Louis cemetery."

"They built out the tunnels that far from Harrah's?" Peter asked. "Under a cemetery filled with vaults because we can't dig graves without hitting water?"

Ben nodded, an ironic twist to his lips. "There were a couple attempts to start other tunnels, farther out from Harrah's. Elagra took a couple of those half-finished places and expanded them, over time, with her abilities. There are things she knows how to do that I can't explain."

"It's complicated spell craft, requiring patience and focus," Raina agreed. "Plus, a certain level of skill, to lock it in place in a way that isn't a constant drain on one's strength to maintain it."

She tapped her fingertips on the table, lips pursing. This was no kitchen witch. Raina had already deduced that from Ben's lasting memories of her. Unfortunately, over time, a practicing witch's skills only increased, and a couple of decades had passed since he'd seen her last. It increased the likelihood that the witch was more than a source of information. She could be involved with the impending disruption. And nothing Ben had told them thus far suggested Elagra would be an ally.

"That confirms it's best to wait until the height of the day to confront her," Derek said. "Particularly on her home ground."

"Can we afford to wait that long?" Lucas asked. "Especially if you anticipate this happening in as little as two days?"

"As you no doubt know from business dealings, the right information can cut response time considerably," Mikhael said. "Whereas the lack of it can lead to utter failure. Derek is correct. Daylight is far preferable when dealing with a dark witch whose intentions are uncertain."

"I can talk to the Archdiocese," Matt said. "Maybe give you a half hour window at noon, Ben, when they could close the cemetery. I couldn't guarantee they'd clear out the caretakers, but at least the tour groups wouldn't be in your way."

Ben glanced at Mikhael. "Can you do what you did with our security cameras to a scattering of people? For about thirty minutes, make them see nothing but an empty cemetery, even if we're in the middle of it?"

Mikhael inclined his head. "I can."

Lucas's expression became dubious, but Ben shot him a look. "Check the security cam footage for the thirty minutes before I called you. You're going to see an empty parking garage, or me getting in my car and driving off. None of which was what happened. A picture saves us all a lot of pain in the ass explanation."

He turned his attention back to all of them. "We have a plan," Ben said. "I get them to Elagra, figure out what the hell is going on, we report back."

Another noncommittal noise came from Matt, but it didn't indicate disagreement. His endorsement held the necessary weight to conclude their business here. But then his raptor eyes turned to Raina, Mikhael and Derek.

"I was not speaking casually," Matt said. "I will have your word that you will protect my people, keep them safe."

"Keeping you and your city safe is why we are here," Raina said with simple sincerity. "They will do everything they are capable of doing to accomplish that. And they are very accomplished at what they do."

Her attention moved to Peter, who she knew was still unconvinced that Ben and Marcie didn't need another person along as backup. "Ben and Marcie's safety will be a top priority."

"We have a suite at the Monteleone," Mikhael interjected. He looked at Ben. "Rendezvous with us there by mid-morning."

"It's best for you to be with us somewhat early," Raina said, before Ben could open his mouth to object and suggest meeting them at the cemetery. "Mikhael and Derek will be in touch with the energies that tell us the most fortuitous time to embark, and that time can shift with circumstances. When they know it's time to go, it will be best that we are already together."

"Fine," Ben said. He shot Mikhael and Derek a narrow look. "Monteleone has a good chef. You two are picking up the tab for brunch."

"A wise decision." Raina chuckled. "Guardians have terrifying appetites."

CHAPTER FOUR

*R*aina stood on the balcony of their suite at the Hotel Monteleone. As she gazed out at the city, she ran her manicure over the railing. Back and forth, back and forth.

She'd told Marcie and Ben they were welcome to stay at the hotel tonight, in case things changed unexpectedly. She'd given them a key card in case they wanted to do that. While she doubted they would, it would take them some vital time to decide.

She needed that time.

Derek had not come back with them. In the lobby of the office building, before they'd parted ways, Mikhael had given him a significant glance. Derek had returned the look, understanding in the steady flint-blue eyes. He swept that gaze over Raina, offered her a nod, and then he had portaled back home. He and Ruby would join them after she and Mikhael visited Elagra. For the purposes of interrogation, the two men had decided it was best to let the Dark Guardian take point.

Raina's body swayed as she inhaled, all her senses reaching out, seeking the way a predator's did, when hunger was stirring and couldn't be denied. She could walk these halls, feet hushed in the soft carpet. Stop at any door, tap, and the inhabitant would open to her. That energy, the nourishment of it, was there, so close...

She changed her focus with vicious will. She registered the lightly pitted texture of the metal under her hands. It came from the passage of years and exposure to the salt-laden, humid airs of a coastal town.

She inhaled again, only this time slow and deep, measured. Closed her eyes. An appetizer would take the edge off.

As a witch, she was always attuned to energy currents. Being half-succubus, there was another, equally absorbing layer of feedback accessible to her, particularly in the heart of decadent New Orleans, in the late hours of night.

On the floor just below theirs, a couple had had a volatile argument followed by a vigorous round of makeup sex. They lay tangled with one another and a snowy expanse of twisted sheets, their balcony doors open to the night. She could tune into their heartbeats, his still a little rapid under the woman's palm. Her lips were swollen from the violent heat of his kisses. Her mouth *and* the petals of her sex, where he'd had his lips and then his cock buried only a short time ago.

Maybe makeup sex was the wrong term, implying they'd resolved the argument and then had sex. The argument had been resolved with sex, a sensual physical battle where both combatants had eventually succumbed to one another, to what the depth of their anger meant. How much they cared about one another. At least that specific couple.

"Cawrawr."

She jumped, then cursed her nerves as a large raven came in for a solid, vibrating landing on the railing. He flapped his wings, spread wide for balance. Tucking them fastidiously around him, he sidled over to her and dropped a long string of glittering green beads over her hand.

She sighed, a smile tugging at her lips, easing her tension if not the cause of it. "What mischief won you those, Cathair?" she asked. "I can smell the beignets on your breath, and you didn't even have the decency to bring me one."

The bird bobbed at her and then launched himself, a shooting low glide through the open double doors behind her. He'd end up napping on the perch stand they'd brought for him, set in the corner of their bedroom.

"The pet policy here is strict."

Relief gripped her, strongly enough it annoyed her. But she usually didn't give Mikhael the razor-sharp edge of her tongue. Unless she craved the pleasure of the punishments he would use to answer it.

"They say nothing about a witch's familiar," she said. "He's very different from a pet."

"Yet he's pampered like one."

She turned to look at him. Cathair had chosen an interim landing on Mikhael's shoulder. When the bird rubbed his head against the side of Mikhael's, he received a stroke of his feathers from those clever large fingers, before her mate sent the bird onward to his perch.

Mikhael considered her with an implacable expression, those fathomless dark eyes with the fall of hair over his broad brow. He had a face that could eclipse every woman's bad boy fantasy, because there was nothing boyish about him. When he shrugged out of his jacket and turned to drape it over the chair in their bedroom, the dress shirt he wore creased in a distracting way over the flex of his shoulders and back.

"I've been neglectful," he said. "I'm sorry. I had to attend to a couple things."

"I'm a grown woman. Fully capable of entertaining myself. On my very first vacation in..."

Ever. It was the first vacation she'd ever taken, in a mortal realm, at least. And she found herself standing by this railing, holding onto it as if she'd manacled herself there. As if she'd wished he had.

Until he'd come into her life, travel was a luxury she couldn't afford. Going into town for groceries was something she'd had to delegate to her other staff members. The energy it took to mute her impact on human senses was too much of a drain, especially when she had the first priority of keeping her sex demons buffered so they didn't kill their clients. For a long time, her world had been limited to the grounds of her bordello. It was a lovely place, the haven she'd built there for all of them, so she had no complaints.

But Mikhael had given her the freedom to spread her wings like Cathair, go where she hadn't gone before. However, being away from home for the first time like this meant her nerves had been consuming her energy in greedy gulps. Add to that the focus required to interact with the mortals in that board room. She'd thrown herself into what needed to be done, wanting to give Mikhael back something for giving her so much.

"You asked too much of yourself tonight," Mikhael said. "If you think joining me on a task like this is a vacation, I need to take you on a real one."

She turned back to look over the city, not sure she could say anything more. She heard him step over the threshold and come to stand behind her, his body only inches away while the heat of him already enclosed her. When he laid his hands on her upper arms, she quivered.

The mild reproof in his tone was a reminder he hadn't asked her to give what she'd given tonight. She knew that. But he was here, it was all right. After having not been free to travel like this in such a long time, she was just unnerved and being foolish about it. Or perhaps her subconscious was cataloging how many hotel rooms she'd stayed in years ago, when her purpose had been so different.

"This *is* a vacation for me. Don't bother to deny it. Cathair's not the only one being pampered." She put effort into keeping her tone light. "It's why you booked this hotel."

"They have good room service," he said neutrally. "The bed is soft."

"You prefer hanging from a tree like a bat, in a deep, old growth forest."

The Monteleone had been built in the 1880s and was infused with the power of age, compared to the newer hotels. That grounding would make it appealing to the two Guardians. But when he and Derek couldn't be home because of their work, they more often stayed in places like the forest she described, or gateway places between portals. While both of them far preferred actual food, they could draw on the magical energy in those interdimensional locations for sustenance, while studying the arcane libraries available to them.

So Mikhael was staying here for her. And she was having trouble keeping it together enough to enjoy it the way she so desperately wanted to.

His arms closed around her, one over her breasts, the other under them, slow coils that tightened, letting her feel the power in his arms. He could crush an enemy in his grasp, but his embrace was always a shelter for her.

When she inhaled, she took in his scent. Soap and aftershave, but beneath that, always, there was the hint of fire and smoke. The good kind. A musky incense burned in a woman's bedroom. Vanilla-scented candlelight. The heat of the sun, the symbol of the Lord of the Underworld he served.

Mikhael shifted one arm to curl a hand around her loose hair. "Do you love me, witch?"

She made an indifferent noise, with effort, but her hand curled over his forearm, the stuff of his shirt, her fingers holding even tighter to him than she had the rail. "You didn't always use the term witch as an endearment."

"Yes, I did. You just couldn't hear it. Why? Do you prefer something different? Should I choose one you like better than *koldunya?*"

"*Koldunya?*"

"The more flattering word for *witch* in Russian. Enchantress, wise woman. Though for you, I think *vedma.* Hellcat, one of the translations.

"How can you be centuries old and still revert back to that language? Even the accent." She had no complaints about it. She could listen to him talk Russian all day without understanding a single word.

"We never forget home. Even when we meet it for the first time. And Russia was my kind of darkness. Cold and endless. The angel who visited my grandmother and conceived my father, must have felt the same. She said his wings were like mine."

"Not white and fluffy, like a swan's?" She smiled, because there was definitely nothing fluffy about Mikhael."

"There are black swans."

"Hmm." She let out a shaky breath as he drew her hair to the side to bare her neck. "You tell me you like me to leave it down, and yet you're always having to pull it out of your way."

"Because I can do this." He put just enough pull in the hold to send a low thrum of sensation pooling in her lower belly. "And because I like the way my hands feel in it, my fingertips grazing your neck, so I feel your fragile pulse. I like the way you draw in an unsteady breath when I set my teeth...here."

She drew in that erratic breath as he gave her the sharp scrape. Her body was all liquid, wanting to rush and churn against his.

"Mikhael."

"I have you, *vedma.*"

She closed her eyes as his mouth worked its way down the column of her throat, along the curve that led to her shoulder. His fingers preceded his mouth, lightly, so lightly sliding along her skin. Every woman's skin was sensitive. Once a man learned and realized that, the smart ones, they could turn a fascination with a woman's response into a lifelong obsession. Become immersed in it and slow down time like, well...this.

The benefit of being with a male who'd had centuries to figure out so much.

Energy was already spilling off her. It had started the second he touched her. The slash and swirl of bright color was like a twisting broad ribbon around them. It would have killed any man it touched, but Mikhael knew how to grasp it, wind it around himself, draw her attention to the sustenance he could provide.

She'd tried to grab it, pull it back, but it was as if her very soul knew the truth he spoke in her ear. "You worry needlessly. You are not losing your infamous self-control, Raina. No matter how long I took to get here, you would have contained it. Because you trust me to be here to nourish you before it is too late." He lifted his head, cupped her face in a firm hand so she was looking up into his serious, uncompromising face. "When I am here with you, you do not have to control anything."

As a succubus, draining sexual energy from another was how she fed. To her prey, her willing capitulation to their sexual demands could easily be misinterpreted as surrender, trust. Yet all she was giving them in exchange for her dinner was her body.

In contrast, when Mikhael had her like this, she was a bird landing in his cupped palms, her wings spread out and draping his fingers, her head resting on the heel of his hand so he could rub his thumb over it, slow, circular caresses.

"Raina. You will tell me you love me."

"I did. I do. With every word I speak."

The shields came all the way down and the urgency behind it surged forth. Along with everything that came with it.

She'd starved for years, kept that way by her Master so when he wanted her to kill, she wouldn't hesitate to do so. Sometimes he wouldn't let her distract the quarry with the drug of sexual pleasure. He wanted his enemy terrified. Riding their loins, she'd watched their fear grow, even as their hands gripped her and they begged for more, to be taken higher. She'd gulped down their fear and desire and felt sick and sated at once.

"Raina." Mikhael had turned her to face him. Both of his hands were coiled in her hair, his thumbs against her parted lips. His dark gaze locked with hers.

"This is why vacations are hard," she whispered. "Maybe it's better when I'm busy, preoccupied with the million things I have to do at *Sweet Dreams*."

Two hours of relaxation she could manage. Two days, and her mind would go to bad places, like this, and drive her mad. Her leisure time might no longer present a danger to those around her, but her own sanity was in jeopardy.

The sudden hard grip of Mikhael's hands on her biceps, the still heat of his breath against her fluttering pulse, snapped her attention away from that thought. His dark eyes had become an abyss, drawing her in.

"You forget yourself, my sweet witch. You forget how deeply I can be in your mind when I choose. You spoke the word that does not belong to him. Does it?"

She shook her head, her body shuddering with need, with hunger. His grip shifted up and he pulled her arms back further, so she felt the restraint of his hold, her breasts lifting against his chest.

"To remind you, I have to be crueler than I intended. But it is what is needed."

She trembled again under the heat of his regard. But with need, not fear. His hands constricted and she felt the glorious strain on her shoulders from his strength. He dipped his head, nuzzled her jugular, set his teeth to it, let her feel the compression, the pounding of blood against his hold upon her. She shuddered, closing her eyes again.

"There are other names for you," he said easing that bite, but only to speak against her skin. His tone was now ruthlessly conversational. "*Kotyonok*, kitten. But I also like *zvezda moya*, my star. Or even better. *Moya edinstvennaya*. My one and only."

When his teeth bit deeper, she surged up against his hold, the slashes of energy becoming the crimson of a dazzling sunset. It formed a haze over her eyes, shimmering over her body. Her canines sharpened, and her fingers curled, evolving into talons with wicked curved claws. If there were a mirror, she knew her pupils would show as dark slits, her green-gold eyes now even more brilliantly colored.

"Mikhael," she said, her voice a rough growl. Pleading, savage.

"I am here, Raina. He was never worthy of that title. You have a fine, noble, fierce heart. Dark and beautiful, like a violent rainstorm. Only your true Master can command it. So tell me who that is."

She, who confidently handled every male in her life, was always in deep water when it came to Mikhael. With him, she could play and tease, unleash the succubus power that could kill a human in a matter of minutes. He would absorb and channel it, use it as a binding upon her, immerse her in her own magic. She trusted him to command her like no other, because he put her needs before anything else. Even recognized what they were, before she did.

Her male, such a frightening force in the world they inhabited, had a heart that never ceased to give when it came to his love for her.

"Settle now. Sshh, *vedma*. Settle." He soothed her, nuzzling her throat with his mouth. "It is not yet time. I would tease you a little longer, build your hunger even higher, now that I am here where I can deny you for the pleasure of us both. That is my right, is it not?"

She was safe. He kept her safe and, even more importantly, he kept everyone around her that way. Calmer now, she pressed her forehead to his shoulder, since she was facing him, held close against his chest. He curved one large hand over her skull, his fingers stroking her scalp, as they stood before the silent city, felt the energy currents from it together.

The hunger was still sharp and there, but the chance to feed was under his control, and close enough she could think straight. Wanting to prove she could keep herself together, she shifted so she stood next to him at the rail. However, she still curled both arms around one of his, feeling the solid upper arm muscles press between her breasts. As she propped her chin on his shoulder, she gazed back into the room. Graceful antique-style furniture, sparkling warm lights from a chandelier. When she inhaled, she took in the scents of a building that had stood for over a century, absorbing the energy and memories of all who had stayed here.

"Thank you," she said softly. "For this."

"You paint too bright a picture of me," he said, brushing his lips along the top of her head, moving to her forehead as she tipped back her face to look up at him.

"Brightness has nothing to do with it." She dropped her touch to his slim belt, fingering it, and gave him a feline smile. "It's in the dark I find things worth grasping."

"Wench." He caught her wrist, but it wasn't to push her away, though he did deny her the touch she wanted. Lifting the hand to his mouth, he bit it lightly before he left her at the railing and moved to the threshold between the balcony and the bedroom.

When he reached it, he stopped. Tilting his head down, he glanced at her out of his peripheral vision. The look was a clear command. He expected her to follow.

Cathair, smart bird that he was, decided to vacate the bedroom. He glided past them and back out onto the wide balcony, taking an eagle's eye view on the railing.

Raina moved to Mikhael. She slid her hand up to his shoulder, his strong neck, stretching her body as she did so. A purr came to her throat when she leaned full into him, arching to press against him, into him. When she dropped her head back, he took his pleasure with her throat again. A leisurely, maddening press, tease, kiss and bite. He gave her the tip of his tongue, the cut of his teeth. All while he stroked the length of her from hip to rib cage, to the outer swell of her breast and back again. Such simple caresses, that created an explosive surge of energy within her, and across every inch of her flesh.

He slid his hands down, over her buttocks, and with a hitch, lifted her so she had her legs around him. He carried her inside, laid her down on the bed, keeping one arm around her as he braced the other, put a hand on the mattress.

"Master," she said softly, reaching up to stroke his mouth. She trembled as more of that energy spilled out over them. She was suddenly too hungry. And though she knew he could contain it, it still startled her a little bit, how much it hit her, took her over. The claws that had receded returned, and she curled them into his shoulder. A hiss came from her when he moved his hand to her throat and lifted his body further, knee pressed between her legs as he watched her body writhe under his hold.

"Stay there."

He stood up, at end of the bed, and began to open his shirt, flicking open the buttons. She rolled to her stomach, gazing at him through the veil of her hair that had dropped over one of her eyes. Though she stayed on the bed, it was a big one, so she lifted onto all fours and prowled across the mattress to him, her body swaying with desire. For years after winning her freedom, she'd kept this side of her so locked down, never letting it out like this so she could embrace her full nature.

He knew what it did to her, denial, teasing. More denial. But behind it, promises he made would always be kept. It made her heart ache even as her lust grew. He knew how to answer both.

Shirt now open and sleeves precisely folded back to reveal his corded forearms, he leveled an even look upon her.

"If I am your Master, then why are you still wearing clothes?"

There was sensual menace in his voice, the embers of hell simmering beneath the deceptively soft tone. That hell possessed a heat she craved.

"Why haven't you made me take them off?" she teased him, goading the beast.

He crossed his powerful arms over his chest, making the shirt stretch over his shoulders in a mouthwatering way. "Take them off. Now."

She rose to her knees, lifted her arms. First, she ran her hands through her thick hair, loving the way he watched the thick silky locks pour through her fingers, fall over her breasts and down her back, nearly to her waist. His hands curled against his arms, and she knew he was thinking of what he said. How he liked to wrap his hands in it when he took her body, binding her to him.

He'd once taken her to a crystal cave in Hell. It had a hot spring that caught the lights of the crystals and turned the water jewel-like. He'd allowed her no covering except her hair while there, and yet he'd ensured her comfort, because the air was warm. And she'd had the heat of his body to cover her.

He attended to her every need, which made her want to do the same for him, and give him the kind of pleasure that only a succubus could. She knew every potent nuance sex could possess, and the key to unlocking it was never, ever to rush the opening of the door. Grasping the hem of her velvet shirt, she drew it off, revealing the green satin lace bra beneath that barely held her generous breasts. The mesh at the top showed a teasing glimpse of areola and a lot of curve. Her silver pentagram fell back to her cleavage as she freed her hair from the neckline and dropped the garment to the floor.

She still had Cathair's green beads looped around her wrist like a bracelet. Now she put them over her head, let them tumble around her neck, rest in her cleavage and over her breasts.

She pierced herself when her mood called for it, let the piercings close when it didn't. Right now, her only one was a navel piercing. It was adorned with a tiny dangling bat, a playful thing he'd given her when she teased him about hanging by his heels from the trees to sleep, his wings folded about him. Though his wings most often seemed like a bat's, or a dark dragon's, their form could morph, even to her magic-enhanced senses. One moment they'd be in sharp relief, black, leathery and possessing sharp talons at the joints, their span a formidable width arching over his broad shoulders. Then they would blur and be like a rippling cape with ragged edges, soft as the softest fur when they folded around her.

She toyed with the piercing, dipping her head so her hair brushed her now naked waist. The jeans rode low, exposing her hip bones.

"Don't play with me, Raina. I will incinerate those clothes, turn them to falling ash around you."

She cocked her head, giving him a sinful look from beneath her lashes. She opened the jeans as she did so, sliding her hand beneath the open zipper to caress herself inside filmy panties that matched the bra.

Now he moved toward her, volatile heat cutting a wide swathe around him. He was no incubus, but she'd often wondered if there was a drop of that blood somewhere in him. He had a way of moving, all dangerous power, that made a female instantly think of sex, and how knee-weakeningly well he would do it. The darkness within him only fueled such imaginings. Especially to a creature of darkness, like her.

His hand slid into the jeans on top of hers, pressing her fingers against herself even more firmly before he clasped her wrist, drew her arm up. As he licked her wet fingers, she quivered at the look in his eyes, her lips parting.

He curled one hand in her hair, putting another at her waist, and lifted her against him. He held her there, brought her mouth to his. Now she whimpered against him, because, Goddess, the man could kiss. He took over, with the right amount of firmness and heat, his lips caressing and stroking, tongue executing an exquisite dance against her moist flesh. She clung to him, and gave him her passion. Her energy reached out for him eagerly, and he bound it even more securely to him. Not until he was ready. He would hold every tendril of energy, until she was insane with the hunger and need.

He turned her so she was on all fours on the bed, and pushed her to her elbows, her backside high in the air. When he yanked the jeans and panties to her knees, her breath caught in her throat.

"No foreplay, Mast—" She strangled on that attempt at a playful question. Before she could get the words out, he'd opened his slacks and shoved his cock into her slick heat, his relentless hands grasping her hips to lift her up further, take his considerable length and girth even deeper. She grasped the covers in her fists, holding on. All mischief fled, because she felt the underlying emotions driving him. He wanted her with the hunger of a beast of the underworld. The ferocity of his demand didn't give her room to even wonder what had goaded him to this level.

Her energy roared forth, saturated the room, swirled and gripped, coiling tight around them, giving every stroke the strength and intensity of a climax. She was already biting the covers, muffling her cries in a pillow. But he was having none of that. He gripped her hair, yanked her head up so her screams reverberated against the walls. Now at last, he denied her no more. His energy surged forth, twining with hers, wrapping around her, soaking deep into her, filling her. Feeding her like a hot, pounding rain fed the earth. And he hadn't even climaxed yet, when his sexual energy would be at its most rich and satisfying. She could probably live on his sexual emanations at their lowest wattage.

She became a simple beast herself, meeting every thrust to show her willingness to take him. Another whimper escaped her throat, a note of trepidation that he answered in the way she needed. She closed her eyes in sheer bliss as those wings she loved curved around her. She shifted her grip to them, to the edges that held the talons. She wrapped her fingers around the hard, unyielding bone, but pressed her forehead to the soft, leathery substance beneath it, giving herself to that cradle as he used her body mercilessly.

As a succubus, her body was always ready to take a man, but her desire for him was far more than physical, which fanned the flames to a level that always terrified her in some strange, addictive way. As she drew so close to release she made a warning noise, he reached beneath her, captured her clit in his fingers and pinched, offering her pain and denying her the pleasure. He released inside her, grunting through the harder thrusts that pushed her against the mattress. She let out a moan, her body shuddering as that energy filled her, sated her, taking hunger away and leaving only her boundless desire for him, a wave she could ride forever.

Because of that, she couldn't suppress a noise of protest as he pulled free.

"What was that?" he demanded, hearing it.

He flipped her to her back. When he grasped her hair, knotting it in his fist, he had his other hand on her throat. He used the hold on her hair to lift her off the bed onto her knees, but the grip on her throat tightened as he brought her face inches from his unholy gaze, the dark eyes possessing licks of crimson flame. His mouth was a hard line she wanted upon her again.

"Nothing, my lord," she said, sweeping her lashes down. Her voice was thready, because she was literally on the edge of climax, but she wouldn't release. Not without his permission.

"My witch wanted foreplay," he said. "And I will never deny her what she truly wants." He put his hand down between them, and she made another tiny noise as he cupped her sex. When she felt the electric touch of his magic, her heart pounded in sensual dread.

"No climax for you," he said, a threat and a promise. "Not until you have experienced all the pleasure I want to inflict upon you. Feeding your appetite isn't enough. I want to overwhelm the woman, give her everything she needs, until the word *Master* has only one meaning to her, now and forever."

He'd promised her cruel punishment for that slip, and his reminder would be sensually brutal enough to drive away the shadow of the past.

"Your nature is to misbehave, Raina," her Dark Guardian said. "My punishment reminds you that you may misbehave all you wish, but that you always, always serve your Master." His fingers tightened on her throat. "That you are always mine."

"Always," she responded. Despite the ruthlessness of his words, the unshakable grip, she reached up and sketched the side of his face with her fingertips, letting her nails leave a faint line. His eyes were wholly dark, the whites gone, an effect that occurred in moments of great feeling.

There was no room now for her sharp tongue or her clever teasing, the things that she enjoyed doing to challenge him. When she was vulnerable like this, she could reach into his soul, see what he needed and wanted, too. Her touch was intended to give him that. She would do whatever was necessary to convince him of the truth in her soul— she wanted what he demanded. And the word Master, when it appeared in her heart or soul, applied only to him, now and forever.

He leaned into the bite of her nails, his lips so close to hers.

"We are no longer alone," he murmured.

"I know. Don't stop. Please."

CHAPTER FIVE

Before they took their leave for the hotel, Raina had given Marcie their room number at the Monteleone.

"Take this for whenever you arrive, whether it's in the next hour or so, or if you decide to come closer to mid-morning," the witch said, pressing a key into Marcie's hand. Her fingertips slid over Marcie's wrist pulse, sending a sensual thrum through the arm and her breast, tightening the nipple. As Marcie stood there, a little mesmerized, the woman played her fingertip over that pulse. "You don't have to knock," Raina said. "It's a connected pair of suites and they both have living room areas. We keep the doors between them open. You can use the unoccupied bedroom."

The witch turned to take the hand Mikhael had stretched out to her. Marcie watched his large fingers close over the female's slim ones. As Mikhael tucked that hand into the crook of his elbow, Marcie noticed Raina gripped his biceps briefly. There seemed to be several things in the gesture. Intimate affection for certain, but a certain level of reassurance. For the witch, as if she was reminding herself he was there, at her side.

Then they were departing, Derek hefting his staff and touching it to the brim of the cowboy hat he'd donned, before following in their wake.

The way Mikhael drew Raina to him showed Marcie a man and woman bonded in so many ways that nothing would ever cut all the lines, especially the one between their souls, a rope twisted by the Fates themselves. Marcie didn't think she was being overly romantic. It was something she recognized.

Which provided her a small measure of reassurance to a worry she knew was foolish for that very reason. When Marcie had arrived, Raina had been standing by the windows with Ben, close, her breast nearly against his arm, her hand upon him as she gazed up into his face. Ben had looked oblivious to his surroundings, in a way that had given Marcie a bad moment. But ruefully she realized when Raina had been touching her, she'd been caught in the same fog, with probably nearly the same look on her face.

She also remembered that, within a second of her stepping across the threshold, Ben's attention had snapped to her, as if the mere hint of her presence had a stronger pull on him than the witch's super-power level of sexual appeal at close proximity.

Ben was at her side now, just behind her. Marcie tensed, but her worries about other things eased slightly when he put his hand at her waist. She leaned into him, and let out a little sigh at the heat of him. The way he dipped his head to brush his lips across her temple. He was always so solid. The wall at her back. She couldn't gauge his mood, but his initiating the contact was an encouraging sign.

When he tightened his grip against her flesh, she tilted her head to look at him. "I was thinking about when I first came into the board room," she said. "I didn't know how to feel."

"I know." Ben met her gaze. "You've got nothing to worry about, brat. She's..."

"Yeah. Ten seconds in the same room and *I* wanted to do her."

The skin around his green eyes crinkled. His smile eclipsed the tingles Raina had given her in a heartbeat. When he slid both his arms all the way around her, she inhaled his scent, the clean starch of his shirt mixed with the heat of the man wearing it. "Can I watch? Sell tickets?" he asked. "Lucas would approve. We'd eclipse our quarterly profits in a heartbeat."

She chuckled, and laid her forehead on his chest, registered his heartbeat. Then she tipped her head back up again. They gazed at one another. "I'd say I'm sorry, too," she said. "But mainly for acting out in front of everyone. Not for standing for you." She curled her fingers into his shirt, pressed her lips together. "I wasn't trying to disrespect you, Master. Just love you."

"Hmm." His mouth tightened, but fortunately, he let it go. For now. "I need to talk some of this out with Matt and the others, now that our guests are gone. Let Matt ask all the questions he wouldn't in front of them. I also need to convince them they don't need to be more involved in this. Why don't you help me with that? I think between the delegation from Hogwarts and your badass self, I've got the backup I need to see Elagra."

Her initial wave of pleased surprise passed, and she studied him narrowly. "If you think it will be easier to ditch me by myself, versus ditching a group of us—"

"I could ditch you, if I wanted to do so," he said evenly. "The truth is, I don't want any of this near you. I would do a great deal to make that happen, including tying you up and locking you in a closet. Which I could do, and there's not a thing you could do to stop me, if I was determined to put you on the ground. You know it."

Her heart tightened in the cold fist created by those words, the flash of ice in the green eyes that said he meant it. Then he confused her, cupping her face in a hand that was as gentle as his eyes were hard. "But I love you, too. And that comes with a burden of trust in your judgment I'm trying my best to respect. But you better damn well understand the distraction of worrying about you when dealing with this isn't helpful to me."

She tightened her jaw. "That's not fair."

"It's not fair, but it's truth."

She crossed her arms, drawing back from him. "Well, you leaving me at home, not knowing if you're hurt, in trouble, when I could be there to help? That's something I can't live with."

"Welcome to the world of being a cop's spouse. Maybe you need to practice walking in the shoes you're so eager to have me wear."

Direct hit. He knew how to fight dirty, in so many ways. He was a lawyer and could twist words, but he wasn't fucking with her head. He meant what he was saying, the simple truth.

The ache in her throat kept her from saying anything, but then he sighed, shook his head. He laid his hands on top of her tense upper arms. He lifted then lowered the touch a couple times, almost rhythmically, something between a pat and a repetition, like he was counting, then his hands closed on her biceps again, and he gripped hard, putting his forehead back against hers.

"Loving you the way you want and need to be loved is the hardest thing I've ever done in my life," he said, low. "And it's the one thing I can't not do."

She squeezed her eyes shut, threaded her hands back between his arms to grip his shirt again, shake him, her knuckles pressed against his muscled chest beneath the soft fabric.

"Same goes."

"Then that's where we are and where we'll stay." He kissed her forehead and drew back, staring into her eyes. There was always so much going on in his gaze at a moment like this, a conflagration of past, present and future.

"Let's get this done," he said.

He'd been right. Between the two of them, it didn't take too long to get things squared away with the team, though Marcie thought the others, particularly Matt, still had his doubts when Ben emphasized that this was just an information hunt, nothing overly dangerous, particularly with the current backup he had.

But Matt trusted his man. And not just him. When the CEO of K&A turned his gaze to her, let it rest there an extra moment before they took their leave, Marcie gave him a subtle nod. She'd have Ben's back, emotionally as well as physically, to the best of her ability.

Ben escorted her to the parking deck with little conversation, and took the wheel of the McLaren. She didn't argue with him over it, knowing that driving would help him think through whatever was occupying his mind.

As she expected, he said little, merely wrapping his hand around hers, bringing it to his thigh and letting her leave it there as he navigated the sportscar through traffic. She curled up on the seat to rest her head on his biceps. She was here, and he was accepting it. That was enough, and the rest would just figure itself out. As it always did in their complicated relationship.

When he didn't turn toward the Garden District, she knew he'd decided in favor of Raina's suggestion that they come to the hotel sooner rather than later.

"Makes more sense to maximize the amount of sleep you can get there, rather than having to wake up at home and get to the hotel in mid-morning traffic," he commented.

She was secretly relieved, because she'd been trying to figure out how to sleep as light as a cat so he didn't slip out without her. It might be a moot point, though, since right now she was wide-awake.

"The dinner staff should still be there," he added. "I can talk the chef into whipping up something for us and the *World of Warcraft* escapees."

"You've been spending time around Nate," she observed, referring to her little brother. "You speak gaming geek."

"Not fluently, thank God."

After they made the turn onto Royal Street, it wasn't long before she saw their destination. With its ornate façade work, the snowy white exterior of the Hotel Monteleone reminded her of an elegant queen presiding over the other historic buildings on Royal Street. The flower boxes crowning the covered entrance were populated by riotous bundles of pretty pink petunias.

Ben turned the car over to the valet with a substantial tip, backed by an underlying warning that likely made the poor kid fear for his future if the car got so much as a scuff mark on it. Then he guided her inside. The lobby had ceiling murals outlined by decorative molding, all of it illuminated by the diamond glitter of chandeliers. Scattered tables and cushioned benches were interspersed with tremendous flower arrangements that changed with the seasons. Today they were lavender flowers with lots of greenery.

It was the hour at which some people were returning from late dinners, while others were decked out in club wear and headed out to enjoy the New Orleans nightlife on Bourbon Street or the jazz joints in the French Quarter. Ben squeezed her hand and left her on one of the sofas before he moved to the desk staff.

She watched him fondly. Ben was an incredible cook, restaurant-chef level, in her opinion, and very particular about his food preparation. While she served him in a variety of ways as a submissive, including helping with the prep of his recipes at home, cooking was entirely his domain.

Though he graciously said she was doing "better" at the things he'd taught her how to cook, she knew that was the power of love. He wouldn't tell her outright she was hopeless when it came to it.

That was all right, though. She had other talents. Like the ability to field strip almost any firearm and put it back together in a matter of seconds. And kick the ass of sparring partners three times her size. With the exception of Ben. But he was a dirty fighter. Which, in reflection, meant he'd also helped her improve her fight skills, preparing her for the streets she'd be facing when she finally made it onto the New Orleans police force.

He'd also expanded the range of her taste buds. Since she'd been with him, they'd acquired an education comparable to what she'd get from an elite cooking school.

Everything he did intrigued her, but she took particular interest in how others reacted to him. Money always produced results, but the innate authority that made backs straighten and people snap to attention when he spoke to them was genuine, not just financially driven. He never talked down to anyone, even as he made it clear he expected their best efforts. He rewarded that effort with his genuine appreciation and respect, as well as his wallet.

She expected he'd probably learned that from Matt's example. So she wasn't at all surprised when she saw nodding heads. Within a few moments, someone had been summoned from the kitchen. Ben explained what he wanted, and then he was striding back to her, a man who could wear a suit or jeans with equal flair, and emanated an arresting, dangerous energy in either. "What?" he asked, seeing her smile.

She shook her head, rising from the sofa to lift onto her toes, brush a kiss to the corner of his firm mouth. "You're just...you."

He gave her an amused look, his arm cinching around her waist to lift her off her feet, deepening the kiss before easing her down, though he made sure they were right up against one another when he did it.

"Same goes, brat. They said there's a menu in the room and I can call down what I'm wanting directly to the chef. Preparation might take a while, but it'll be worth the wait. They'll bring it up when it's ready. Unless you'd prefer to come back down and eat in the dining room."

She enjoyed the ambience of the hotel restaurant, the jagged stripes of the French limestone floor and the intimate placement of the tables that gave the diners the sense of privacy to enjoy their meal. However, given everything else that had happened tonight, she wouldn't mind actual privacy. Plus...

"Will we order enough for the others?"

"Of course. It's being billed to their room, so we'll be particularly generous."

She chuckled and shook her head at him. Ben moved them toward the elevator, his hand coming to rest on the small of her back. Marcie liked the feel of that touch, his attentiveness, especially in public venues where female eyes, like those of the two desk clerks, would rest upon him with undisguised appreciation. She could handle that, because since they'd become a couple, well before they were married, the man's eyes had never wandered. Not once. And that kind of consistency? It could only be genuine.

Even when he studied a scene at their preferred BDSM club, he was gauging the responses and actions of the players as an experienced Dom did, with appreciation for what the other Dom was doing. He might be inspired enough by it to give whatever he planned for her an additional jolt, but his appraisal was never for the face or form of the females involved. Only for what was driving the scene itself.

When the elevator opened on the hallway of the top floor, the corridor had a hushed quiet. As Ben took the key from her and opened the door, Marcie immediately saw what Raina had described. The living areas of the two suites were joined by a connecting door. She didn't see Raina or Mikhael. Since the suite they'd entered felt empty, she expected they were in the other.

They hadn't said so directly, but since Ruby had "portaled home"— and didn't that just conjure so many thrilling ideas she'd always thought were only Hollywood fantasy—Marcie suspected Derek had done the same, which was why the additional suite had been offered to her and Ben.

The sitting and dining area, populated by antique-looking furniture, would be bathed in sunlight at certain times of the day, because one side was mostly windows. The heavy silver-grey window dressings were pulled back with tasseled cords. Through the sheers, she saw the panoramic view of the city and Mississippi River. The walls had pale yellow, broad-striped wallpaper, and delicate-fingered palm trees created separate spaces in the room. Gold-edged mirrors placed at key places gave the room an even larger sense of space.

The bedroom was accessible through a pair of open French doors. She saw the bed had a pillowy white comforter, piled with matching yellow and grey pillows. Flower arrangements that picked up the same colors were set around the room.

The room maintained the look of old New Orleans, the clean scent marked by the teasing hints of old wood and history, grandeur and style. She wouldn't have been surprised to see a woman sweep through in full nineteenth century clothing, a man adjusting his tie and picking up his hat before offering her his arm to escort her down to dinner. Or out for a stroll.

Ben's phone buzzed. He bit back a curse as he gave it a glance. "Since it looks like we might not be at work tomorrow, I better handle this." He nodded to the sidebar. "Menu's there if you want to give the desserts a look."

Her Master ordered her meal, but he always left the choice of desserts to her.

"You don't want me to order dinner for us?" she asked innocently. "Looks like they have chicken fingers on the kid's menu. Everyone loves chicken fingers. With ketchup."

He snorted. "I'll figure it out when I get off the phone."

He moved into the bedroom. When he dialed whoever had texted him, she picked up it was about legal paperwork related to bringing some of their foreign manufacturing operations back to the States, due to recent tariff changes. The attorney on the other end was over-seas, explaining the late hour call.

After she perused the dessert menu, she wandered through the lavish living area of their suite. She didn't intend to be nosy, but she paused as she reached the connecting door between the two suites, listening to determine if they were alone. She received a quick answer, registering the rumble of Mikhael's voice, the distracting chuckle of Raina's throaty reply.

Raina exuded the sex vibes, but Mikhael was no slouch in that department. He was fascinating, dangerous. Since Marcie had fallen head-over-heels for a fascinating, dangerous and dark man herself, she appreciated that in another male. In a purely objective way, of course.

She intended to move away. Even entertained thoughts of moving out onto the balcony of her and Ben's suite. Instead, she found herself standing in place. She closed her eyes, absorbing the vibra-tion of Raina and Mikhael's voices. Even if she couldn't hear the words, there was something about the cadence that held her attention, like a rising storm wind rippling across a woman's light summer dress.

She swayed with it, vaguely realized she'd moved a step toward that threshold. Then another. And another.

Their suite was done in bolder colors, a rich red and orange, with matching bouquets made up of blood-red roses and marmalade-colored lilies. There was a similar scattering of mirrors. She saw herself in them as she passed, a bemused looking woman moistening her lips, her hand rising to release her hair from its barrette, stroking through it as she shrugged her shoulders, freeing them from a sense of something... Maybe the world outside, which had boundaries that made little sense here.

The air was so close, she felt like it was carrying her. She was through the living area, past the dining room table. As she pivoted, she was facing the open French doors to the bedroom to the suite.

The knee jerk reaction to draw back, mutter an apology and flee, didn't come. Instead, that energy in the air circled and tugged her forward, closer to the threshold and what she glimpsed going on in there.

She had the presence of mind to curl her fingers over the doorway to keep her on the living room side of the threshold, but otherwise she couldn't compel herself to retreat.

Raina was up on her knees on the bed. Mikhael had one knee on it, but still stood on the floor. His hand was on her throat in a somewhat scary-looking way, holding Raina within inches of his gaze, but she had her hands on his face. Her jeans and panties were at her knees, her bra generously displaying her pale breasts. His shirt was open, his hair tousled. Though his slacks were not open, Marcie could scent the familiar musk of recent sex. Maybe no more than a handful of moments ago, he'd been inside Raina. Marcie's gaze tracked the moisture marking Raina's upper thighs and knew she was seeing Mikhael's seed and Raina's response there.

Sex done right joined things together in a way never meant to be put asunder. Maybe in some minds, what she was looking at would be considered a layout for a sleazy porno Internet site, but those judgments wouldn't be looking close enough.

They'd miss the lock of their gazes, the way Raina was touching his face, how their bodies still vibrated with the energy of being joined. They emanated that passion in such a way that it made everything around them disappear. They'd miss the beauty of those two bodies, Raina's curves and his hardness, the silk of her hair tumbling down her shoulders, the glow of his eyes as he beheld everything he wanted.

Mikhael didn't break that lock, though the flick of Raina's gaze toward her and then back to Mikhael told Marcie she was acknowledged...and welcome. Mikhael scooped Raina up in one arm, Raina's hands going to his shoulders, sliding over them. She buried her face briefly into his neck as he bent over, laid her out on the mattress.

Taking Raina's hand, he guided her, turning her onto her stomach. He unhooked her bra with deft fingers that caressed the valley of her spine, then removed her panties and jeans. He spoke, a murmur that only Raina could hear, an order from her Master, and she slipped the bra out from beneath her and spread out her limbs, her slim feet just over the end of the mattress. Now naked, she gripped the covers just above her, arms at shoulder height. Mikhael tunneled his fingers in her hair, let the ebony waterfall slide through them as he lifted it away from Raina. Marcie swallowed on a dry throat as the strands fell in a fan shape over the mattress and one silken shoulder.

Marcie could imagine him winding his hands in it, tying Raina to him, yanking on it as he thrust within her. Ben loved doing that with her thick tresses.

She could see Raina's breast pressed into the mattress, a tempting swell of pale flesh. Raina's buttocks were round and soft-looking, quivering with arousal. She had her exotic green-gold eyes lowered, her full lips parted. Mikhael still had his knee on the bed, now between her spread legs. He grasped one of her hands in his own, taking the arm down and turning her wrist so her knuckles pressed into the small of her back. He held her so their fingers twined together, except for his thumb. That nestled between her buttocks, rubbing in a way that had Raina making a soft noise of need, her thighs twitching, her upper body lifting in involuntary reaction and arousal.

Marcie enjoyed women, though her primary sexual preference was men, and Ben above all. But seeing Raina like this went past gender preference into a whole other realm. That energy she'd received in small waves from the woman was now a full, pulsing wash of heat, holding her in invisible bonds, as if coiling around her wrists, waist and thighs. As it inched up toward her throat, her chin lifted, but something in her soul protested, her heart tightening. Some things were one man's domain only. Only one...

A breath left her, relief and shuddering arousal, as Ben's hand closed over her there, over her collar, so the metal of the solid band pressed into her flesh. He tipped her head back against his shoulder. She could still see, but now her Master had her, his body against the back of hers, his arm strong around her waist. He molded his other palm over her hip bone as his long fingers stroked denim, over her mound and upper thigh. The contact, so close to her sex, had a moan slipping out between her lips.

"Getting into trouble, brat?" her Master said, a whisper against her ear.

CHAPTER SIX

"*A*lways," she managed breathlessly, and earned a dark chuckle, weighted with desire.

With his touch, Marcie realized something important. The magic Raina emitted was natural. It wasn't manipulating or coercing them. This was a familiar energy to her and Ben both. Every intense erotic encounter with him created this kind of energy. In the depths of her heart and soul, Marcie had even called it magic once or twice.

She'd meant it in the theoretical, symbolic or romantic sense. Now she knew it was real, a raw, wild and powerful force that Raina could weave and use to affect those around her. Marcie had no doubt she could compel with it. But this didn't feel like that.

Marcie's gaze slid to Mikhael. Here was proof, because this male emanated total authority over the situation. He was compelled by no one. Another type of energy she was quite familiar with.

The Dark Guardian had unbuttoned that exquisitely tailored dark shirt all the way and was shrugging out of it, revealing a powerful warrior's body, his chest covered with a gleaming layer of dark hair. He stripped the belt from his slacks so they rode low on his hips as he put a knee on the bed again. He had the belt doubled over in his hand and Marcie wet her lips, recognizing his intent.

She loved Ben in anything he wore or nothing, but he knew what his office power wear did to her. Especially his slim belt, the gleaming buckle, because she'd had that applied to her backside more times than she could count. He could cause unimaginable levels of pain with it, but she craved that pain, and he fed on her need, the two of them sometimes frighteningly insatiable.

But he protected her from the precipices that existed in that realm, because that was where he possessed breathtaking levels of control over her...and himself. He always called them back from that edge.

Outside those moments, she returned the favor, holding him back from his own destructive cliff edges. That was what Matt's last, lingering look had been about. He had no worries about Ben in a physical situation. It was the deeper, darker realms of the soul that Matt knew were Marcie's jurisdiction, when it came to Ben.

But right here and now? This was the moment she could relinquish everything to her Master, and she did, melting back into him as her attention clung to Mikhael. He bent over Raina, put his mouth between her shoulder blades and spoke in a low tone, but one Marcie could hear. "They take pleasure in pain, *malysh*," the Dark Guardian said. "And you have been teasing them all night. You took inordinate pleasure in it. You'll need to face the consequences for that."

"I take inordinate pleasure in everything," Raina managed. It wasn't a practiced, throaty purr, though. It was a raw admission. Especially her next words, uttered with her gaze fastened on Mikhael. "What I hunger for the most, only you provide."

He held his gaze on her face a long moment. "Good," he said. "So now I think you will make it up to them. You will keep everything below your waist absolutely still, unless I allow you movement."

He cupped the side of her face, and Raina nuzzled his palm, parting her lips to take his thumb as it pressed in past her teeth. She sucked on it with obvious implication, her tongue teasing along the knuckle. As she raised her lashes and pinned her jeweled gaze on Ben and Marcie, a full wave of that energy hit both of them.

Fuck. Marcie swayed in Ben's grip, her nipples hardening and sex convulsing. "Ben," she gasped.

"Hold steady, brat." His voice was rough, but his iron control didn't fail her. Even with that vibe pulsing manically through her, he held the line. Mikhael had lifted his attention to Ben and the two men were holding gazes. Two Doms working shit out, she thought desperately, just like the K&A guys did in moments like this, that intuition setting the boundaries, even as they mapped out the ways they intended to push their subs into crazy places. All without a word exchanged.

When Marcie brought her gaze back to Raina, she saw the vulnerable expression that said the witch was no longer in control either. She'd given it all to her Master, too.

"Ahh…" Marcie dropped her head back further as Ben's grip on her throat shifted. His long fingers spread out along her jaw, pressed so he tilted her head away from him. When he bit her neck, the clamp of his teeth was fierce enough she felt her carotid beating helplessly against it. She swayed as his other hand slipped the button of her jeans and he pushed his way in, the zipper giving way before his demand.

Crack!

Mikhael had brought the belt down, strap making contact with flesh. Marcie knew how that felt. Her buttocks flexed against Ben's erection, her nails digging into his forearms, seeking blood. When he bit her harder, as if seeking the same, she shuddered.

His hand moved against her, fingers tunneling in under the edge of her panties to find how wet she was. The thickness of those clever digits reminded her of other ways he could fill her.

Raina cried out, fingernails clawing at the covers. Mikhael's eyes flashed, and he gave her three more strikes as those pleading noises increased. Raina rubbed her face fractiously against the spread. Yet she obviously obeyed his command to keep her lower body still, even while the parts of her that were allowed movement showed the effort it was taking.

Whap! Whap! Marcie was whimpering in Ben's mouth, her body shuddering. Goddess, she could feel every blow, her mind whirling in the past, remembering her tears on her cheeks, Ben's lips pressing against them the times he punished her so brutally, then took her for a trip to the moon.

Mikhael laid the strap aside and knelt on the bed over Raina. Marcie's eyes came back to them as he leaned over the witch with a powerful curve of his upper body, a flex of his buttock against the strained fabric of his slacks. Slowly, he brought his mouth to her abused backside, even more slowly teased a cheek with lazy movements of teeth and tongue, making his chosen female whimper. Her fingernails were going to puncture those thick cotton sheets. As he bit down harder, her head came up, her hair tumbling down over her shoulder, back along the bed.

The movement sent another heady wave of energy through the suite. The lines of the furniture, the pictures on the wall, everything about their current reality, seemed to blur, darken, while all the shapes stayed in bold relief. Marcie's heart jumped, because dark wings expanded from Mikhael's back, ragged-edged, sinister looking things with talons at the joints, but also magnificent in their span, the texture like supple leather.

Ben's fingers thrust deep into Marcie, wresting a cry from her. Mikhael stopped, held. He didn't look toward her, but Raina did, green-gold eyes on Marcie's face, sweeping over her body, Ben's hold on her. Mikhael trailed his own fingers down his witch's back, slow, serpentine movements that had her licking her lips, her fingers convulsing on the covers.

All while Ben fucked Marcie in easy rhythmic circles that were anything but easy. The grip of his hand on her throat controlled the pace, keeping her still the way Mikhael was keeping Raina still. Ben's thumb stroked her pulse beneath the collar, moving the band so the reminder of his ownership rubbed provocatively against her sensitive flesh. Each pass along Marcie's sizzling nerve endings, every trail of fingertips down Raina's spine, wrested a plea from one of them.

Mikhael slid an arm beneath his witch. In a sinuous movement, she turned in the span of that muscular arm, her back arching over it as her hands latched onto his biceps, her legs rising to curl around his hips. Her expression was hungry. He buried his hand in her thick miles of hair as he lifted her head to take her mouth in a kiss.

Marcie moaned again, watching them, the way Mikhael swept Raina under with the demand that his mouth could bring to her. Ripples of response told her she might be in danger of releasing just from watching them kiss while her Master touched her, possessed her with his fingers. Ben knew her too well. He shook his head against her neck, a growl against her flesh a warning.

She didn't come without her Master's permission. She'd had that disposition from the first, but he'd taken it even further. He'd trained her so well, literally beaten it into her in ways she'd embraced. Every lesson had created the chain around her will. Even if the flames of

Raina's power were licking full force between Marcie's legs, she wouldn't release. Not without her Master's command.

Your climax, it's under my control, brat. Not yours. I let it go when I allow it. It's why you don't come until I say so. There is no other choice. It all belongs to me.

And he was right. Unless he deliberately made her fail for the pleasure that gave him, to reinforce the mandate once again, she could hold onto that edge as long as he demanded she do so. No matter if she lost pieces of her mind doing so.

Mikhael laid Raina back on the bed again, staring down at her as she let her hands drop over her head, the generous breasts and her throat offered to him, her wet lips parted.

Marcie swayed toward her and the woman's head tilted in her direction, gaze fastening upon her. Even in the middle of a haze of lust, Marcie did a double take, because those eyes were like a cat's now, the pupils a narrow slit in the midst of the brilliant color. The teeth that played over Mikhael's thumb and drew a drop of blood were needle sharp.

The energy likewise had changed, subtly, but her Master didn't miss it. Ben withdrew his hand from Marcie to hold her fast as his head came up, gauging what was happening.

Then that change became far less subtle, like a sudden wind change on a calm sea, a rising wind that heralded a swiftly approaching storm. Marcie felt the power of it building, expanding. It was all coming from Raina. Suddenly, Marcie knew the chilling truth; that the witch was a creature who could take their lives with the energy she had ribboning around and through them. The non-human eyes staring at them were avid...hungry.

Ben tensed. Marcie wondered if he was about to draw her behind him and back them out of the room. She couldn't blame him for his protectiveness, even though her mind was too fogged to want to do it herself. The fatal temptation of a succubus was now alive, present and pulsing in this hotel room.

There was a flicker in Raina's gaze, and Marcie was reminded of a wild creature trying to convey something without the benefit of speech. But she had someone to speak for her.

"She can unleash herself fully under my command and do no harm," Mikhael said. "For decades, she had to discipline herself, deny herself. Deny the very heart and soul of who she is to cause no harm. And she did so, all by herself, with no one to champion her. That will never be the case again. Do not fear her. She will call forth her energy, tangle it with yours, and take you places you've never been before."

Marcie met Raina's gaze. The words opened other things, other currents that fed that energy. Currents that came from the heart and soul of who Raina was. Marcie saw traces of vulnerability in the woman's gaze, in the way her fingers curved into Mikhael's shoulders as he bent in what was clearly a protective pose over her. Protecting her from the possibility they would withdraw, not certain of the witch.

Marcie imagined it, not being able to give herself fully to Ben, reach that soul-to-soul connection for fear that she would do him harm. He'd been worried about unleashing his own darkness with her for a strangely similar reason, but once he'd opened himself to her, trusted her, they'd indeed gone places neither one had thought possible.

She knew this decision was not hers, that Mikhael's words were for Ben, but she thought Ben had reached the same conclusion as she had. He had begun stroking her body again. Slowly, yes, as if he were thinking it through, but he wanted to hear her mind on it, because he spoke to her then.

"You want that, brat? Do you trust her?"

She moistened her lips. Held those amazing, otherworldly green-gold eyes, that nevertheless held things she understood, in any world or reality. She nodded.

Something in the woman's gaze reached out to her, beyond libido, directly to Marcie's heart. Gratitude. And with that, the sexual bond became something more.

The K&A men were possessive, monogamous in a narrow, highly defined exception clause kind of way. They might craft sexual experiences for their wives that involved others in their circle, but they rarely opened that option to those outside it.

This was one of those times.

She didn't see the exchange between Mikhael and Ben, but knew it was there, that Ben had the surety of her safety he required, because now he nudged her forward, though he came with her.

He guided her to the opposite side of the bed and let her put one knee up on it, lean forward, as his other arm circled her waist, holding her.

Raina stretched out her arms like a cat, and Marcie clasped her hands, leaning down further as the woman tugged her that way, toward her mouth. As they came close enough to sample breath, Marcie let out another little moan. As she'd bent over further, Ben had slid her jeans off her hips, his palm rubbing over her silk clad backside, grasping the crotch to tug, put pressure on her clit when she strained forward.

"What lies between our legs has its own heartbeat," Raina said softly. "Have you noticed?"

Marcie nodded. Raina's lips curved. "Let me make yours pound."

Then their mouths touched.

She'd kissed Dana, Peter's wife, before, the first woman she'd ever kissed in reality, not fantasy. Had she ever told Dana that? She should. When Dana kissed another woman, the alpha side of the former Army sergeant showed itself in a way that echoed the masculine power of kissing a Dominant male, though Dana was a hundred percent power submissive. And her lips were full, moist and playful, teasing arousal out of every erogenous zone of Marcie's body.

This was...different. Raina's mouth played upon hers, her tongue teasing. Ben could design the roller coaster of her arousal with his fingers, commanding every level of response from her he desired with that type of touch alone. Raina had a similar skill with her mouth. Marcie closed her eyes as Raina curled her fingers into Marcie's hair, her nape, and dug her nails into tender flesh, holding her.

Marcie swayed at the power of the magic that surrounded her, held her. Raina was...feeding, there was no other way to describe it. The witch was consuming the desire coming off her like waves, but she was giving something vital back, not draining vitality away.

Raina took her mouth away to move to Marcie's throat, tease the column with her tongue, work her way down. It caused Marcie to lift her face. When she raised her lashes, she found herself staring into Mikhael's dark eyes.

It was automatic, to look away, look down. Not merely because he was a Dominant like Ben, though that was reason enough. It was because of what he was, something in control of things way beyond her understanding. The need to respect that was as clear as a slap with a tawser, and too difficult to stare in the face.

But she realized in that brief look that Mikhael hadn't been looking at her. Though she had no doubt Mikhael was aware of every shift she and Ben made, every touch between Raina and Marcie, the Dark Guardian's gaze never left his mate. He'd opened up his slacks again, taken himself in hand, and Raina's body reacted as he thrust deep. Slow. As his wings arched back and spread.

Air from the wings' movement rippled over Marcie's forehead, her parted lips. She tipped her face up with a desire-suffused smile.

Her head in that position made it easy for her Master to coil his hands in her thick hair, add the pull to her scalp. The rush of sexual energy was indescribable. A river of heat flowed through her, the current getting stronger and wilder, even as their bodies were moving slow, savoring, absorbing all of it.

It might not make sense, but Marcie was seeing transparent colors swirling in the air around them, a mix of so many palettes, the reds rising and falling into the embrace of a vortex of blue, rushing along a current of greens, dark, light, and every shade in between.

Sex with Ben was always an over-the-top experience, narrowing the world down to just the two of them. In contrast, this was as if the world had widened. Everything she saw, felt, inhaled, heard, was saturated with sexual suggestion and promise, two sides of the perfect coin.

When Ben cupped his hand over her nape, brought her elbows back down to the bed, lifting her hips higher in the air, she pressed her mouth to Raina's again. Marcie made a noise in her throat as the power of Mikhael's thrusts translated through Raina's rhythmic movement against her. Then she bit back a soft cry as she felt Ben's bare flesh touch hers. The broad head of his cock rubbed against her sex, gauging the depth of her wetness. To take Ben, a woman had to be oiled up all the way to the womb, ready to baptize the head of his cock with a gush of juices. Fortunately, he was very good at finding that reservoir in her.

She widened her stance, lifted, and he slid in. Even drenched as she usually was when he took her, he was never an easy entry, because he was far bigger than the norm. Now, as he stretched her tissues and sank slow and deep, into the clasp of her body, she was gasping, pleading. Overwhelmed by…

Held in the grip of Raina's magic, every scrap of control she'd learned was lost. Things were getting crazy, overwhelming, a wall of fire swooping down on them. Ben grasped her jaw to turn her mouth to his, so he swallowed her rising cries.

Mikhael was thrusting into Raina, his speed picking up. Marcie wondered if his wings had ever lifted them as they were joined like this, if he'd ever taken her in the air.

"Hold onto her," Mikhael said shortly.

In some fixed point in the swirl of response, Marcie knew he was talking to Ben, and there were so many meanings to that, including the literal one.

She was very familiar with that moment of helpless, blissful terror when all control was going to be lost, when words like *please, help, no*, would break from the lips. All of them meant only one thing.

Hold onto me. Catch me. Go with me. Carry me through the storms, and ride the winds with me.

This was that, all of it, all at once. Ben had one thigh pressed to the outside of hers, muscle flexing against her hip as he pushed deep. When he was deep as he was going to go, he stopped and held, dropping to curl an arm around her chest. He gripped her shoulder, his forearm a solid bar before her, the roughness of his jaw against her cheek, his thick hair silk against her temple.

A world full of pure light and pleasure, all the questions and answers there together, darkness and light joining hands as they always had. The power of the magic wrapped around their souls, spun them.

Marcie could hear her heartbeat, her pulse pounding. The snow-white covers gleamed as if touched by starlight. The seascapes on the wall were so vivid she thought she could taste the salt on her lips. The room had tiny motes of gleaming gold and blue light dancing through the air, swirling.

The storm of magic rose, pulling their response higher with it. In some distant way she realized that she literally stood on a threshold between life and death. That was why she could hear the rapid beat of her heart, was so aware of the rasp of her breath, her gasps of arousal.

It was that, that impending mortality, that gave this climax its unforgettable, ephemeral edge. And it felt too damn good for her to care.

Raina's eyes were upon her. The witch was gripping Marcie's wrists where her palms were pressed into the mattress, restraining and supporting her at the same time. When her sharp nails pierced Marcie's flesh, she gave Marcie all the things she needed – restraint, support and just the right amount of pain.

Her breasts felt full and tight. Ben's hand closed over one, nipple stabbing into his palm, and Marcie threw her head to the side, turning her face toward his throat. She snapped at him savagely, like an animal. Her hips worked on him, her body taking his full length, deeper, faster.

He responded with a growl and pushed her down so her cheek was against the covers, in the soft fall of Raina's hair. It smelled like rain and roses. The wet sounds of her cunt sucking on his cock maddened her, made her lick her lips, cry out, snarl with a defiance he answered as she fully expected. He fucked her within an inch of her life as those waves of energy just kept coming.

"God... Ben... Master... Please..."

"Keep holding on, brat. This ride's not even half over."

Oh God. She really was going to die. She wanted him touching her everywhere. Her skin was on fire, especially where he was touching her. Did he feel it?

"You don't go anywhere without me," he said. "Nowhere I don't take you. Now, brat."

The climax was crashing over her, wave over wave, no time to breathe. She fought it as he expected her to do, even as the pleasure tumbled her over and over, leaving her no way to stop it taking over.

Wildly she bucked against him, cries becoming screams. He kept burying himself in her, hands pinching, squeezing, demanding, not giving her an inch of the virtual tether he always had on her, as if it were wrapped tight around his knuckles, making her feel the hold of her physical collar even more.

She knew the power her arousal gave him, the way it would push him to the edge. Now, deep as she was inside him, she felt it, the two of them going over together.

She gasped, her eyes widening as it felt like they literally joined hands and leaped, soaring on a pleasure with weight and substance, a river in truth.

Raina's eyes were black, teeth sharp and bared. She reared up and bit Mikhael high on his chest, much as Marcie had done, only Raina drew blood. Mikhael cupped her skull, holding her to him as he kept driving into her, taking her full climax before he let himself go. Every muscle in his upper body was taut. At the deciding moment, Marcie thought she saw markings appear on his body, etched in black fire, sweeping heat over all of them, here then gone. Raina licked the blood from his chest, bit him again, maddened.

She might have passed out. Or maybe the universe blinked. All Marcie knew was some time later, she was lying on her side on the covers, one hand loosely clasped in Raina's as the woman faced her in a mirror position, several feet between them. Ben was stretched out behind her, his mouth on Marcie's shoulder, nuzzling, nipping, as he stroked her from shoulder, to hip, around her backside and between her legs, which loosened automatically for him, always.

"Goddess," Marcie whispered. Maybe several times. But she literally couldn't move. So caught in a haze of aftermath, still so close to arousal, it didn't feel like they'd left.

At length, Ben turned her toward him, curled her into the shelter of his body. Marcie felt Raina shift closer, and murmured in pleased acceptance as the witch put her mouth to her ear, stroked Marcie's hair away from her damp neck to taste her there. Those long-nailed fingers drifted down over the soft skin between Marcie's shoulder blades, then stroked along Marcie's back, a continuous pattern.

Another movement of the mattress beneath them, and Marcie suspected wherever Mikhael had gone, he was back, and behind Raina. The witch's mouth went tight against her skin, an erotic response, and then she let out a breathy sigh that rippled over Marcie's flesh. The Dark Guardian had slid back into Raina. He began a slow thrusting while he fondled her breasts so that his knuckles brushed Marcie's spine as he did it.

Marcie wanted to turn over and watch them. She didn't have to say it. Ben knew, and would decide if she could do that, or if he preferred to tease her with the sounds, the hints of movement and touch.

When he used his arm around Marcie to shift them away, it was to give them enough space for Marcie to turn, spoon herself back into the curve of his body.

"Watch them, brat," her Master murmured against her ear. "You can touch only her hands, but you can watch all you wish."

Marcie extended her arm, laid her fingertips in Raina's palm, lying open on the bed covers. She traced the lines there as she watched the witch be pleasured.

Raina had a glow to her, a sated look that was more than just desire. There was a contentment to her that had been missing earlier, an easier sensuality. She had twisted her upper body to reach up and stroke Mikhael's face as he moved with such purpose inside her. Though he'd recently climaxed, he showed no signs of stopping, or needing all that much recuperation time. He kissed his witch's pulse, her forearm, all while holding her securely in one arm, keeping her safe and surrounded as he took her body.

Marcie understood. He'd channeled Raina's feeding so they could have the experience of a full surrender to a succubus's power, without risk of loss of life. And they had all fed her.

She also saw how very much Mikhael loved his witch, and how much Raina loved him. She thought of what Mikhael had said, about how Raina's life had been before. The witch had had the strength to persevere without aid, but no one's strength was limitless. Marcie wondered how close Raina had been to the end of that strength when Mikhael came into her life.

Whenever it had been, it was clear the witch had embraced her need for him, and Mikhael's intent to meet those needs appeared limitless, a hunger just as strong as Raina's succubus appetites.

Ben put his mouth to Marcie's shoulder, then he was moving down, leaving her with her cheek pillowed on her hands as he explored her back and the upper rise of her buttocks with his mouth. He gripped her thigh in mute command so she lifted it, bent her knee and braced the sole of her foot on the bed by the other knee, opening herself to him. Then he put his mouth between her legs, over her sensitive pussy, working his tongue in, sucking on her clit.

"Aah." She sucked in a breath, tipping her head back, though her half-lidded eyes still watched Raina, the way Raina watched her, a curve on her desire-taut mouth.

"Insatiable," she whispered. "The both of them."

Insatiable was the closest word for Ben's libido, and Marcie wasn't even sure if that captured it. Her man was capable of rousing again to full hardness in a matter of minutes and taking her again. Two, three, four times.

Since she was sure Mikhael had climaxed seconds before he put himself inside Raina again, it appeared he had a similar revival time. It was a vaguely alarming thought, that the two alpha males might get competitive, think they had to prove who could keep this going the longest, how many rounds they could take their women to that sharp edge, again and again.

Some men were drained by sex. Ben used it like nitrous in the performance machine that was his gorgeous, muscled body. Thankfully, his passion could fuel hers, always. Even if she had no energy to do anything but accept him in her body.

He proved it now, sliding back up behind her body and guiding himself into her once more. She opened to him with quivering thighs, and he held her, supported her through it.

"You'll let me fuck you to death, won't you, brat," Ben muttered.

In response, she locked onto him even tighter, earned a grunt and a dark chuckle. It was all his. Her life, her breath, her heartbeat. It had been, from the moment she first met him at sixteen years old, when he was nearly a decade older and so seemingly beyond her reach. Treating her like a little sister, when she knew she was meant to be his. She'd had to wait over seven years to prove it to him, but she'd refused to take no for an answer. She would have been his, or the most important part of herself would have died trying.

"You give them everything they demand, because there is nothing beyond that," Raina breathed, seeing the answer to Ben's question in Marcie's face. "Nothing that matters as much."

Their hands were tangled in a knot on the sheets. Marcie lifted her gaze enough to see Mikhael move Raina's thick hair, bare her throat and bend his head to taste her once more. Raina's eyes half closed, her hand tightening on Marcie's.

Even while fully tuned into their presence, wrapping them in Raina's energy to take them on that ride, the Dark Guardian still hadn't, not ever, not once, looked away from Raina. As if he couldn't get enough of absorbing her every reaction.

The power had been Raina, a star burning bright in the dark sky... and Mikhael was that dark sky.

Perhaps because they were creatures of another species, though still humanoid, the shape of Mikhael's Dominance and Raina's submission was different from hers and Ben's. Raina belonged to the Dark Guardian. No other defining parameters. The utter simplicity of that relationship underlined the incredible power that had surrounded all of it, clarified it.

Ben's tight glide to the root had Marcie shuddering around and over him. As she realized his attention was wholly upon her, because she was the center of his world as he was hers, she wondered if any differences were just window dressing.

What was between their two souls was no different than what lay between the otherworldly creatures who'd just shared a bed with them.

The knowledge was a reassurance, promise and comfort.

It was some time later when Ben slipped out of the bed, his hand resting on Marcie's shoulder so he didn't break the contact and wake her. It'd be too much to hope she'd sleep past them leaving for the cemetery, but he could at least make sure she was well-rested for the quagmire of what-ifs that was ahead. He'd have to wake her to feed her, but then he'd let her go back to sleep as long as they had.

She lay on her stomach, her head turned toward him but her eyes closed so her long lashes fanned her cheeks. Mikhael had shifted into a more comfortable spot on the bed for the sleeping Raina. The Dark Guardian didn't look tired at all. Maybe he didn't sleep. He had the sheet pulled up loosely over his hips. At the height of his climax, Ben remembered intricate symbols across the male's shoulders, around his arms, but his skin was clean now of everything but a couple interesting scars.

"What were those?" he asked, low.

At Mikhael's quizzical look, Ben nodded toward his chest. "The tattoos that appeared and then disappeared."

"They are magic-seared brands, declarations of my loyalty and service to Lucifer and the Underworld, for my immortal lifespan."

Mikhael tapped himself high on his chest. Ben remembered one tattoo that had been set apart from the others. It had looked like a star and a moon together. "That one is my oath to her."

Raina was sprawled over her Master, his arm around her as he watched her breathe. She had one arm folded up against her, the other low across his waist, so that her hand was beneath the sheet, resting on his upper thigh and hip bone, her fingers curled there. When she murmured in her sleep, Mikhael's attention returned fully to her, and that attention had many different levels, all of them familiar to Ben.

He bent and slid his arms around Marcie, lifted. She cuddled into him immediately, his brat. Like he was her teddy bear, one she could hold tightly through the night.

"I've got you, baby."

"I know," she murmured sleepily. "You take such good care of me, Master. I love you."

The simple sincerity was a miracle. Not just because she meant it, but because she'd made him believe it. He was her husband and Master, who owned every inch of her body. Who plundered it regularly, mercilessly. She was his. As much as he was hers.

Elagra couldn't touch that, and he would tear her apart if it even crossed the female's mind. He wouldn't waste a moment of guilt, self-reflection or doubt on the savage course of action.

The loving Master rode shotgun with the cold-blooded killer, and he had no problem with the wheel turning from one to the other whenever the need called for it. Marcie didn't understand that part of him, but had faced it, accepted it, soothed it.

Mikhael's gaze was upon him, giving Ben the unsettling notion that the Guardian was following the darker direction of his thoughts. Not one to be cowed, he met the male's gaze and gave him a short nod.

"There's some food coming up, if it's not already waiting for us outside the door. Help yourself when you're ready."

The Dark Guardian inclined his head, somehow remote yet connected in this moment, through the obvious bond they had with their women. Much as Ben liked calling Marcie his wife—to an absurd level he wouldn't ever admit—he liked what Mikhael had called Raina. His mate. Soul mate, mated for life, a perfect match.

Even if his bond with Marcie was beyond his understanding, Ben wouldn't question it. Not anymore. Too many questions might reveal it had been some kind of divine clerical error, so he wasn't going to keep pointing it out.

But even if it was, tough. He'd fought what he'd thought were his baser instincts to keep from holding onto her, but he'd lost that fight. The only fight he'd ever been glad to lose.

Now he'd fight all the forces of Heaven and Hell to keep her.

CHAPTER SEVEN

$\mathcal{W}$hen he, Marcie, Mikhael and Raina slipped into a side gate of the St. Louis cemetery, Ben reflected that he could count on one hand how many times he'd come to this place during daylight. Whereas as a kid and even later—hell, pretty much until Marcie—he'd been there after dark as often as the ghosts.

It looked different under a daylight sky, though it was a cloudy one. Despite the thirty-minute halt in the schedule, there were groups assembled out front, carriages waiting to take people to and from. Fortunately, the high walls around the place and the rabbit warren layout of the vaults meant once they were deeper in, they wouldn't be visible to the crowds. Mikhael wouldn't have to expend the energy to screen them from anyone but a wandering caretaker.

When they'd entered, Mikhael had spoken some incoherent words, moved his hand in a deliberate stroke through the air, as if sketching a symbol. Ben felt a light ripple of energy move over him, lift the hairs of his arms, then they settled. Mikhael gave him a slight nod, telling Ben the screen was in place.

"It works on sound, too," the Dark Guardian said. "So we may speak freely."

"Handy."

Ben took the lead, moving through the maze of vaults in myriad sizes, a garden of weathered gray and white stone. Their feet crunched in the gravel. He knew all the family names along this path, had spoken to them in the past like a guy might speak to the regulars at a bar he frequented. *Hey Harry, how's things with you and the family? Still dead, I see. Want some of this whiskey?* He'd pour some on the grave, because Harry was always a good listener.

He didn't take them to his intended destination right away. When they were near enough to it he could feel the back of his neck itching, he brought them to a halt, spoke low, no matter that Mikhael had said they could speak normally.

"Give me a minute."

He made a motion to Marcie, to get her to stay with the other two. Then he strode toward the Italian Society Vault, a cylindrical marble monolith, the tallest thing in the cemetery. His gaze lifted to the top, where the pensive statue of Charity stood, a female draped in soft robes, her hand lifted as she posed next to a cross. He'd sat up there with her a lot of times, his back propped on the cross. As he'd gazed at her face, he'd thought about the mother he'd never know.

He circled around to the opposite side of the vault, his fingertips gliding along the ornate curved drawers. Once out of view of the others, he put his back against the vault and drew a breath. Cursed softly but viciously to himself. But he knew what needed to be done, and was already reaching into the pocket of the open shirt he was wearing over dark T-shirt and jeans.

It had been awhile, maybe several months, but if any moment called for it, it was this one. He drew out the cigarette pack and the lighter.

No one snuck up on him, ever. But there were people so far in his trust zone, they could move into his personal space without raising the slightest alarm flags. It was a small group, but they were the people who mattered most to him.

Marcie's rich brown eyes captured the light even on this cloudy gray day. As she stood in front of him, between his braced feet, she gripped his hand, brought it down. Somehow the cigarette and lighter disappeared. Instead, his hands were filled with the sure grip of hers, and her, as she pressed closer.

"You don't need that," she said. "You're not alone. Not now, not ever again." Her palm was on his chest, the heat of it transmitting through the cotton. "I'm here."

"Yeah, you are." He stared down at her. And she shouldn't be. But she was, and he hadn't been able to say no to her. He pushed away from the vault. "Give me back the lighter, brat."

She produced it from God knew where. She gave him an impish look, and held it away from him, as if he didn't have a half foot of arm length and height on her. But she had a vicious stomach jab. "Marcie," he said, quieter. Even. "What you said, I heard it. But there's a reason for it. So give it back."

To be who he had to be in this moment, he had to cross a line in his head. From who he was, back to who he'd been. He knew one sure way to do that.

She was studying him in that penetrating way she did. But before he had to repeat himself, she'd put the lighter in his hand. When his fingers closed over it, she let it go. But she didn't give him the cigarettes. Instead, she fished one from the pack, brought it to his lips. Then she closed her hands over his holding the lighter, and positioned her thumb in front of his, flicking the flame to life, helping him light it.

As her hands slipped away, he took control of the cigarette, drawing on it as he put the lighter away. She stepped back, to the side. She slid her lovely denim-covered butt down the side of the stone to squat on her heels. At his side, but in his peripheral view, so he could get his head where it needed to be.

One draw, two... It took him back to dark, cold places, when the burn of the smoke in his lungs and throat told him he was a creature close to hellfire, but capable of staying one step ahead of it. The flames close enough to keep him warm, angry and driven to stay alive.

A dozen puffs and the stillness had settled over his shoulders. Every nerve ending on alert, while every muscle was deadly loose and ready.

He stepped away from the wall. He heard her rise, the whisper of her shirt, the light tread of her rubber-soled shoes. He could smell her hair, her female scent beneath it all, unique to woman, to her. In the shadows, one learned to assess everything in a blink about the unknowing marks who passed by. And determine which ones weren't marks, so as to stay out of the hands of the cops—and to stay alive.

To this day, he would never know what guardian angel had interfered with his judgment so badly when he'd attempted to pick Jonas

Kensington's pocket. Because the man was so obviously not a mark, a sign pasted on him couldn't have stated it any plainer.

No. That was the turning point in his life away from this. He needed to turn back. Not only face the darkness, but step into it.

He pivoted as she rose, and he moved, faster than she could anticipate. He swallowed her gasp as he pressed her against the unyielding surface of the vault. He closed his hand over her throat in a grip that was a little too tight, his other grasping her waist and hip as he took her mouth, diving deep, seeking and getting that tiny, maddeningly helpless whimper at the back of the throat. It brought forth a savagery in him he couldn't ever explain. That he didn't have to explain.

Not to her.

She was well-trained, his brat, her palms immediately pressing flat to the smooth marble on either side of her, fingers curling around the handles on the drawers. It gave him some pretty interesting fantasies of bringing her back out here one night and tying her to them.

When he lifted his head, he stared into her eyes. "You'll do as I tell you," he said. Not a question.

"Yes." That breath caught as he tightened his grip even more. "Sir," she added.

But her gaze stayed fastened on his face, her expression thoughtful. She didn't fear this part of him, and would never have the good sense to do so. But she knew when he wasn't fucking around.

He let her go, turned and walked. Two hundred steps. Then right. He could do it with his eyes closed, though he hadn't gone back there for years.

He'd left it to Marcie to signal the others that they were on the move, so when he came to a halt at their destination, he wasn't surprised to find Mikhael and Raina standing with Marcie, only a few steps behind him.

As Mikhael drew closer, Ben saw the Guardian's gaze had sharpened upon him. Mikhael had apparently felt the shift inside Ben. But he only made one comment about it.

"There is a time to switch gears, to call on the uglier parts of yourself to do what needs to be done. Just be mindful that you do not swing too far into darkness," he said. "It will give her an advantage you do not want her to have."

Ben might have told him to fuck off, but Mikhael wasn't taunting him or getting up in his business. Though Ben wasn't much on taking advice, the direction was valid.

Mikhael's attention turned to the crypt. It was one of the oldest here, the gray stone uneven and worn. The statue on the crest of the vault was recognizable, though the ears were tiny stumps and the face was a featureless oblong egg shape. A lamb.

"This is the crypt of a child," Mikhael said.

"Once. I relocated the remains a long time ago. He's in his father's vault now. Kid was a bastard who died when he was two. The guy's wife refused to let the baby be buried with them. But she's long dead, so I figured she's had time to get over it."

"Mmm." Mikhael placed a hand on the stone, his expression probing. Probably because magic was considered a miraculous thing to humans, his next move should have been punctuated by a dramatic soundtrack and a significant pause. Without that, there was merely a silent rearrangement of the air around him, then a slight grating noise, like Marcie scraping the sole of one of her mouthwatering stilettos against a cobblestone on Bourbon Street. Dust puffed out from the cracks of the vault, and Mikhael moved back. One hand lifted; he twitched two fingers right, providing directional guidance to the magic he'd summoned, and the door shifted accordingly.

"You weren't kidding when you said I didn't need to bring any tools," Ben said. He stared at that dark opening, felt the women drawing closer.

"No way I'm taking you down there. Fuck that."

Marcie slid her fingers in between his tense ones. "No way I'm letting you go without me," she said.

"If I can find her by following this passage, neither of you need to accompany us further," Mikhael interjected. "As non-magic-users, your presence might be more of a hindrance, regardless."

The male's voice was neutral, his expression bland. Son of a bitch. Mikhael could give Matt a run for his money in knowing the right strategy to get a person to do what needed to be done. From the tightening of Marcie's chin, the flash in her brown eyes, it appeared she felt the same way Ben did about it. His sweet, badass brat. Hell, they were doing this. Goddamn it.

"Much as I'd love to take that patronizing insult as a pass on this whole thing, there's a lot of ground to cover, and I'm not following a Point A to Point B map. Not a visual one."

Mikhael's gaze flickered. "You're linked to her."

Raina didn't say anything, but the Guardian's attention went to her. "You knew."

"I suspected. His story is his own to tell."

"Yeah," Ben said shortly. "And I sure as hell don't feel like telling it." For one thing, he couldn't explain it, and he didn't want the cosmic power guy probing and figuring it out for him. Ignorance wasn't bliss, but it sure as fuck wasn't as painful as the truth.

"Then I will not require that. Unless it becomes necessary," Mikhael added. "I will take the lead, and you will direct me."

The Dark Guardian's tone was a clear *you'll do what I tell you to do,* sure to raise Ben's hackles. "I don't need a shield."

"It's his job," Raina said, stepping to Mikhael's side and making a placating gesture. "Like a cop. And it will keep her safer. You can focus on her, while he focuses on all of us."

"Ben." Marcie rested her hand on his elbow. "If the big bad sorcerer wants to take the lead going down into the creepy tunnel, I don't think we should deny him the honor."

"Fine. He can clear out the spiders and rats waiting for us," Ben said.

Mikhael said nothing throughout the exchange. He merely appeared to be waiting, semi-patiently, for them to fall in line. It annoyed Ben, even as he knew he was going to let this one go.

"Spiders? I may go back to the hotel room after all." Marcie's lips twitched. "Order more beignets from the insanely expensive menu."

"Your husband wouldn't say no. Matt pays me more than enough to get you fat on pastries."

"I earn plenty from Savannah. I can pay for my own," she rejoined.

Ben looked toward the dark hole of the vault, felt the coldness in his vitals settle in. "Soon enough, you'll be earning a cop's laughable pay," he said absently. "Then you'll need my money for those pastries."

As he turned his gaze back to her, she flashed him a tight grin. But her eyes were serious as she checked the gun in the holster she wore over her form-fitting tank, under the loose drape of her open shirt. Mikhael's expression said it was time to stop shooting the shit and do this. Ben knew that. But sometimes one more minute was...one more minute.

"Stay close," he reminded her.

"I'll be right on your ass," she promised. "Every moment."

"Spoken like a true wife," he said.

Relief glimmered inside Marcie at the flash of humor in his gorgeous emerald eyes. Then it was gone in a blink and he showed Mikhael that grim face once more. "Let's go."

Ben went in first to remove the planks from the platform that would have held the body of the most recently dead. The area in back, where the bones of previous family members would have been swept while the latest one was decomposing, only had a thin layer of dirt, what time would have loosened from the surrounding walls.

The lamb was an indication that the vault had been sealed directly after the babe's death, the parents' grief such that they'd dedicated the crypt to a single soul. Marcie wondered about the baby's mother, the man's mistress. Had she come here, laid her hand upon the stone, marked it with her tears? Somehow, she knew she had, because there was some of that poignant energy still here. How had Ben found this entry point? More likely, it had been an exit. Had the bereft mother's surfeit of feeling drawn him, another lost child?

After the planks were removed, there was a door in the floor of the crypt, one that had been nailed shut. Ben backed out, giving Mikhael room to move in, drop to his heels and study the problem.

A squeaky sound, a little like mice, and Marcie saw the nails working their way out of the wood, carefully. They dropped away one by one, plinking against the stone sides of the platform before they dropped to the dirt floor. Mikhael just seemed to be sitting there on his heels, almost casually, but she was starting to recognize the signs when he was working magic. It was a shimmer in the air hard to describe, but upon contact with the skin it was somewhere between a vibration and a small electrical tingle. She'd felt it when he'd protected them from prying eyes, and it had stayed with them, a light veil dropping over them, moving where they moved. She was starting to feel like Harry in *Chamber of Secrets*, when he saw the Weasley house and proclaimed with wonder, "*I love magic.*"

Well, that kind of magic. When Mikhael moved out and Ben lifted the door, a palpable bad feeling wafted out of the empty hole. That energy was neither a protective veil nor a whimsical alternative to a claw hammer.

Ben retrieved a coil of rope from the back of the vault, checking its condition before he tied it off to a sturdy pipe driven into the concrete platform.

"It's not a long drop," he told Mikhael. "But the rope will be useful to climb back out. A thousand angels maybe can dance on the head of a pin, but down there, there's not room for even one birdman to spread his wings."

Mikhael gave him a bland look at the snark. He peered down before he squatted, took a grip on the rope and used it to swing himself into the opening, but then he let go. They heard the light thump of his landing.

Ben gestured at Marcie to come in and go next. Sitting shoulder to shoulder with him in the cramped space, Marcie peered over the edge. She saw Mikhael standing fifteen feet below, holding the rope steady. If not for the faint gray light coming in from the vault opening, she might not have seen him at all. It appeared to be pitch black below. Though she was sure Mikhael had some magical way of putting an illuminating glow around them, she wouldn't have minded the backup provided by Duracell.

Ben helped her over the edge and then she was lowering herself hand over hand, glad for all her upper body work. Mikhael's sure touch guided her to the ground. She stepped aside to make room for Raina.

The witch descended a couple feet, and then let go. Before Marcie could gasp, or even blink, Raina had dropped straight down into Mikhael's arms, who'd moved faster than Marcie could follow. Raina gave her mate her feline smile.

"You did promise to always catch me when I fell," she told him.

"I do not recall ever saying that," he said.

"It was implied," the witch responded.

He shook his head at her, but as he let her slide down his body to her feet, Marcie noticed his touch lingered at her waist, the curve of her hip, and he gave her a mild pinch of reproof, even if his face stayed locked in that total I'm-at-work mode.

Ben came down last. Marcie was amused to see Mikhael step back, following the unspoken guy code that men didn't want help unless directly asked. She also noticed she wasn't the only one appreciating Ben's flex of back muscles, tight ass and taut thighs, because Ben could wear the hell out of a pair of jeans. Marcie couldn't fault Raina for looking, especially when the witch rolled her eyes at her and showed her teeth in a mischievous smile.

"I have visually restored the opening," Mikhael said. "Though it remains open in reality, in the event a quick exit is needed."

Practical. She hadn't thought of that. Marcie looked around her. Her pulse jumped, seeing how pitch black closed in on the tunnel, immediately past where the light from the opening above could reach. It was a darkness so absolute there'd be no way through it except blind feel.

And then there was light. A dim yellow glow illuminated their way, like sensor lights in freezers at the grocery stores. Yet she saw no torches embedded in the walls, or old electric lights strung, running off noisy generators. The light turned everything the color of old dry newspaper, making all of them look like people in old photographs, so long gone there was no one still alive to remember them.

The tunnel was wide enough for two to walk abreast, but not quite tall enough for the men to straighten to their full height.

"The light is not from me," Mikhael said. The second the illumination had occurred, he'd gone on full alert. His words added to the chills spiking down her spine. "Someone knows you are here, Ben. Whoever takes the lead now makes no difference. We need to stay alert to front or rear attack."

The green of Ben's eyes was an almost colorless gray in the shadows. He nodded, his jaw set, and started down the tunnel, glancing back to ensure Marcie was close behind him. Despite the two of them being in the middle, Marcie noted neither she nor Raina dropped their own guard. Raina's radar was different though, seemingly attuned to something in the air itself, her gaze slightly unfocused as they moved forward. That worked. Marcie was good with having someone watching the paranormal attack points.

As they followed Ben, Marcie noticed the tunnel grew far wetter, the walls damp and the ground underfoot crunchy sludge. The smell soon surpassed Bourbon Street on its raunchiest night, that unforgettable aroma of human excess. Though the Monteleone food had been as good as advertised, Marcie was glad she'd eaten lightly.

She watched for alarm cues, not allowing herself to get fixed on any one point. But she did register that she was seeing a very different side of Raina now. No sultry flirtation vibes. She looked serious and dangerous. As she walked, she flicked the fingers of her right hand in a deliberate short movement, another indication she was using less obvious senses to probe their surroundings.

The tunnel opened up into a wider chamber. Marcie, already marveling at the idea she was walking through tunnels running beneath New Orleans, now understood why Ben had said Elagra used additional abilities to expand the underground system. The stone walls went straight up in a way that seemed higher than possible, because the ground had stayed level, going neither up nor down. As they fanned out, examining the new terrain, Raina came to a halt, facing a narrow tunnel that ran off to the right. Almost in the same instant, Mikhael and Ben turned in the same direction. Raina cocked her head, gaze fastened to that side tunnel. And waited.

A foot scuffed against stone. Marcie shifted to Ben's left, clearing her field as she drew the gun, held it muzzle up, her finger at ready on the guard.

When they saw the boy, she almost holstered it. Then she took a closer look at him, and kept it out.

Face of a boy, body skinny as a scarecrow's, eyes flat as a shark's. He wore only jeans, not a surprising choice in the cloying humidity. Marcie's shirt was already sticking to her. His upper body was covered in tattoos, all white against the dark skin. Bones. A skeleton tattooed to his outside, showing rib cage and limbs. The body art depicted more than bones, though. Fingers like claws curved over the rib bones, as if something was about to emerge from that cage. Or showing that there was something trapped within. She wondered what tattoo artist had come up with the design. Or had felt about being given the template, if it wasn't his or her original creation.

The boy wore the jeans a couple inches below his underwear. Sky blue boxers were an innocuous contrast to the rest of his macabre appearance, though they were dirty and worn.

"Boys come and go, but some, we know they come back. A dog chained to the yard still knows its yard, even when he thinks he breaks free."

The boy had a feminine, sibilant lisp. Marcie was almost certain he was a teenage prostitute, possessing a mesmerizing androgyny that allowed him to pass as either male or female. He also had a gift for theatrics, though the well-rehearsed line was obviously not his own.

"Follow me," the boy said, and turned toward the shadows.

CHAPTER EIGHT

$\mathcal{T}$he humans likely thought the boy was delivering a line, but Raina could feel the witch's magic gripping her puppet like barbed wire, controlling his vocal cords, his movements.

Such use of dark magic could take Raina to a bad place. Even as she shoved that away, hard, to focus on right now, she thought of how much she was going to enjoy taking this witch apart piece by piece, when and if the opportunity presented itself.

And she'd damn well make sure it did.

Then the singing started, before the boy could take them anywhere. It seemed to come from the walls of the tunnel above, below, in front of and behind them, which would be disturbing if the song itself wasn't alive with hope, joy and all the comforts of being held to a loving mother's breast.

Sleepsong. It was a lullaby. One that Gina, one of her succubi, would sometimes sing to the others to help them drift off to sleep, calm them after a busy night in the bordello. Sex demons had limitless sexual appetites, but that was how they were nourished. When it was not about sex, the younger ones, those under the age of thirty, were almost childlike and innocent in their yearning for simple pleasures. Like the comfort of a sung lullaby.

Raina remembered a night they'd decided to entrance their visitors by putting a provocatively dressed Gina in a human-sized bird cage, hung from a center beam of the choosing room. She'd sung to the guests as they milled, meeting the males and females who could be theirs for a price. Gina had won the top bid, a starry-eyed tech millionaire visiting the area on business from Houston. He'd wanted his own personal nightingale for the evening, cage and all. Gina said he was an amazingly inventive and generous lover. His sexual energy had sated her for several days afterwards. Since the young ones needed to feed almost every forty-eight hours, Raina had marked him down for special perks, to encourage his repeat business.

On other nights, the male sex demons sang. They particularly liked Barry Manilow songs, like "I Write The Songs." When the girls joined in for the chorus, their melodious voices were like a ribbon winding through every room that all could grasp, connect to the vibration.

There was no sense of connection to this version of "Sleepsong," but it was haunting. The poignancy of the notes awakened a strong wistfulness, the desire to believe, hope overriding skepticism, judgment.

Ben's shoulders had stiffened on the first note. He was affected by it, but his reaction proved he knew it was a trap. He'd obviously been caught in it before and remembered it vividly enough he could shrug off its effects, keep it from clouding his judgment without aid. Which was good, because buffering dark persuasion magic introduced a muffled effect to one's senses that neither she nor Mikhael could afford. So Raina nodded to her mate, letting him know Ben was okay. Marcie was the concern.

Or perhaps not.

The young woman threw her a glance, her lips twisting. "Good grief," she murmured. "Who told her she could sing? I'd drop a twenty in her hat just to shut her up."

"It's not pleasant to your ears?"

Marcie shot Raina an incredulous look. "Only if listening to a cat's tail being stepped on has suddenly become music."

Raina glanced at Mikhael, the realization in her mind.

A Pure Light.

They didn't say it out loud.

A Pure Light was a rare soul, one unaffected by dark magic, at least its webs and snares. Marcie would still be vulnerable to direct attacks, but her senses couldn't be fogged so that she couldn't see such an attack coming. It was a tremendous advantage, one that Raina wouldn't diminish by revealing it in a place where every word they spoke was likely being heard.

"Your caterwauling isn't impressing anyone," Ben said abruptly. "So shut the fuck up and stop playing games."

The boy turned his head toward them, his eyes widening. Then he stiffened, and cringed back against the wall. As he pressed himself into the shadows, he gestured, a nervous movement. "Go that way to her," he said. "Her mercy and wonder are forever."

Marcie shuddered at the flat lifelessness of the tone. Possession was now on the list of things she knew were real, that she wished she didn't. The vibration of pain from him made her want to reach out, touch, give him ease. As if sensing her unwise intention, Ben took her hand and drew her past the motionless boy. Her husband's gaze never left him, but the scarecrow was staring at the ground, making no eye contact.

Raina in contrast, moved a few feet into that narrow side tunnel. As the boy shrank up against the wall, she positioned herself square in front of him.

Marcie noticed the witch had taken off her shoes at some point. She must have left them behind, because she wasn't carrying them. Despite the rough, muckish substance beneath her soles, she didn't seem uncomfortable, her painted toes curled to grip, arches relaxed. Slowly, the witch extended her hand. There was a concentration to the movement, as if she was pushing through a wall of water. The boy stared at it. He shuddered abruptly and jerked, like a desperate fish, with a hook embedded in flesh. Raina took another step toward him. The temptress was gone. Her eyes were sharp as a warrior evaluating the battlefield before her.

Mikhael shifted closer to her, but whatever she was doing, he was apparently satisfied she had it under control, for he was continuing to sweep their surroundings with his alert glance, even as he'd put himself in a strategically better position to aid her if needed.

A wind cut through their tunnel, cold as winter. It whistled a mournful note that became sinister, like a growling cat.

Raina ignored it, though Ben's hand tightened on Marcie's.

The boy moved one step toward Raina. His expression creased, as if in pain, and his mouth opened on a soundless cry.

"Let...him...go," Raina said through her teeth. Marcie blinked, then jumped against Ben as a sharp crackle broke the tense silence. A wave of electricity jolted all of them, the boy most violently, knocking his young body against the rock like a rug being beaten free of dust. Marcie started forward, wanting to help, but Ben caught her and Raina's right hand lifted toward her, a warding off, though her gaze remained on her task.

The wave of electricity passed, bringing back the sticky close air. Ben's hands were on her damp shoulders, now steadying her. The boy's knees went out, but Raina caught him, in surprisingly strong arms. He clung to her, gasping, his dazed eyes darting about and eventually finding her face. She put her hand on his jaw, stroking his cheek, murmuring to him as he clung to her.

"*Fire and earth, wind and seas, restore the balance, drive out disease. Take your ease, child. Take your ease.*"

She did not have a perfect voice, a little off key, but it was female and warm, strong and sure. After she repeated the musical lines several times, the boy had stopped trembling, and his eyes had focused.

"Take the tunnel back the way we came," Raina said, touching his hair. It was dyed red with hints of orange, the colors of flame. "Go out of this place and never come near it again. Do you understand?"

She repeated it a couple times as well. Eventually, it seemed to penetrate. His wits returned, his awareness of where he was. As he made it all the way to his feet and looked warily around him, Raina brought his attention back to her with a hand to his face.

She touched the brace of earrings on his right ear and bent forward, taking a closer look. "A mouse. It's a little silver mouse, this middle one. Where'd you get that?"

"My...girlfriend. Then. Before. She liked mice."

"I like that. May I?"

He shrugged, fumbled to remove it, put it in her hand. The mundane task helped steady him further. When he straightened, he was taller than her by a few inches. He also had a vaguely sick look, as if nausea had come with the change in his circumstances. One more heartbeat, and Raina's admonition to get the hell out of here sank in fully.

He jolted into motion, skirting the wall past Mikhael. The Dark Guardian had stepped back to allow him passage, but Mikhael's formidable demeanor and penetrating gaze weren't exactly reassuring, so the boy quickened his pace to get clear of him. Yet after he'd moved a few steps beyond their position, he recalled himself enough to turn, look at all of them. "You shouldn't go in there," he said. He still had that feminine lisp, but a man's voice was starting to break into it, giving it a rasp.

"I know," Ben told him. "It's okay. I've been there. We know what we're doing."

The boy seemed unconvinced of that, but Raina spoke. "Go now," she reminded him with gentle firmness.

The boy turned and disappeared around a curve in the tunnel. As he did, Ben's hands tightened on Marcie, a fraction of an instant before another wave of energy shuddered through the open chamber, penetrating muscle and bone, gripping the heart and turning flipflops in the pit of the belly.

Anger, violence. Fear.

Turning to face it, Raina spread out her hands. As that disturbing wave reached her, she stood, absorbed it. In another blink an answering wave came from her, and it was all the opposite things. It was a day at the beach, in bright sunshine, with the warm surf rushing in against bare legs. Marcie was able to take a deep breath. Ben's tight grip became a caress of her upper arms.

Marcie noted that Mikhael didn't react to either energy wave. But his dark gaze was focused on the shadows ahead of them as if he was staring into the abyss, daring it to blink.

"Now, bitch," Raina said pleasantly. "As our friend said. Enough with the games. Show yourself."

~

"Pride goeth before a fall, sex witch." The voice that had sung the lullaby could purr like Raina's, but the notes had a different form of ensnaring enchantment, one that gave Marcie the heebie-jeebies. "Come forward. Into my abode, though it be too humble for a witch who has removed herself from the earth by planting her wide backside in a fancy house. One who chains herself to a man, rather than chaining him to her, as nature intended."

The satisfied look Raina threw Marcie reminded her of their exchange in the board room. This might just be a woman's fight, the men's presence notwithstanding. Raina stepped fully out of the side tunnel, coming to Marcie's side. She even gave Marcie's pony tail a light tug, a smile flirting over her features, but there was no humor in her vibrant eyes. "Trust your instincts down here," she murmured.

Marcie nodded, setting her jaw. Raina, satisfied, looked toward Ben. Ben considered them both, then pivoted. As he led them onward, the two women proceeded shoulder to shoulder behind him, Mikhael bringing up the rear.

Back out of one chamber, through a narrow tunnel, around a hairpin curve, and then they were in another chamber. One that made Marcie wonder if it was real or an illusion.

The damp, bad-smelling tunnel they'd traversed had been what Marcie would expect in a city at or below sea level. This room was another circular chamber, only much larger. Shelves were built into the walls, from floor to high ceiling. Those shelves were crammed with mismatched books, some spineless and others looking as if they'd been shredded by a cat's claws. Jars full of oddities had been placed onto the strips of shelf space in front of them. Some had been thrust between books, becoming book ends. Beer cans and bottles hung from the ceiling, around a light fixture made up of a strange mix of candles, lanterns and flashlights.

There were three tables in the middle, six-foot-long folding tables with thin wood veneers on top, like those from an office supply store, though these were likely salvaged from a dump, since the legs were repaired and the tops scuffed. What surfaces could be seen, that is, since there were books, rocks, shells, bundles of dried vegetation and more jars piled on them. There was also a cluster of scrolls, tied with multi-colored threads.

On the floor beneath the table was a basket, and several snakes were coiled there, winding over and under one another. Two white mice stood upon them, grooming or eating from a small bowl of food that had been left for them. Until they became food themselves.

Marcie glanced at Raina, noting that the mouse earring now

winked from a hole in her multi-pierced ears. From the tiny bit of blood around it, she realized Raina had self-pierced it in the time it had taken them to move from the tunnel into the chamber.

There was no sign of their adversary. There were several tunnels leading out of the chamber. Marcie fanned out with the others, the four of them scoping all approaches, including three-dimensional ones. Which was good, because suddenly, there she was. Standing between the opening of two of the tunnels, though Marcie hadn't seen from which one she'd come.

Having grown up in New Orleans, Marcie knew what the tourist-catering voodoo priestesses looked like. Elagra didn't disappoint, and managed to look pretty damn authentic. A colorful silk turban bound her dreadlocks, which fell all the way to her waist. Generous breasts and hips, small waist for the size of both. She was barefoot, and wore a yellow cotton dress. It was belted with a wide woven strap hung with what looked like animal parts and other talismans. She had on a necklace strung with various claws, mixed with feathers from different birds.

When she smiled, Marcie saw she'd filed her visible teeth to sharp points. All of them. Which was probably one of the creepiest things she'd ever seen. Especially when the woman smiled, because she jutted them out. The fingernails matched, a couple inches long, sharp points painted old bone yellow. She'd dyed her hands the same color, up to her bracelet-cuffed wrists. The dress had a low scoop neck, so her breasts were on tempting display. Marcie noticed her feet were coated with dust and mud, a glitter of sand.

As unsettling as the teeth were, the eyes were more so. With enormous, dark pupils, they were almost perfectly round and dominated her face. They also seemed tilted inward to align with the sharp, slim shape of brows, pointing toward the tiny mouth, slim nose. Tiny red mouth. It was a pixie, childlike face with the expression of someone far older, far less innocent. Her irises were pale gold with a darker gold ring around them.

That disturbing gaze passed over her and Raina, stopped on Ben. The priestess drew in a satisfied breath that made her breasts quiver and her body sway. "*Bebe*," she murmured.

Yeah, screw that. Marcie shifted, coming up on his right. She was sure Elagra was aware of her, but those strange eyes didn't leave Ben's face.

He was staring at her with a granite expression that told Marcie nothing of what was happening inside his head. Only that it couldn't be good. But like the kid, he likely just needed a moment to get his feet beneath him to figure out his direction. She'd never known him not to be fully capable of facing any challenge thrown his way.

"I know what you are thinking," the priestess said. "Yessss. You are thinking you are no longer a child, with a child's fears. Then, I could frighten you. But that wasss because you did everything with your mind. Too much thinking. Now you know the true strength issss in the heart. And if the heart is broken...well, we all know what happens to a broken vessel. It cannot hold onto anything."

The purr had disappeared. As she picked up a speech cadence obviously inspired by their own, the snakes became more agitated. But then her gaze softened in a way that turned Marcie's spine to ice.

"It is so glad I am to see you, *bebe*," Elagra whispered. "Never have I forgotten you. What you gave me...I hoped to have the chance to tell you one day. And here you are."

As she spoke, she'd sidled closer to Ben. He was still staring at her, his green eyes hard, his jaw rock. Marcie wondered if he was standing fast because he wouldn't give Elagra the victory of the slightest shift that could be interpreted as a flinch or retreat.

Mikhael and Raina had also moved. With Ben and Marcie between them, they now formed a semi-circle facing Elagra. No one in anyone else's line of fire, except Elagra. Marcie didn't know why they weren't asking her questions, distracting her, but perhaps this first moment belonged to Ben.

"I'm not here for you," Ben said at last.

Marcie remembered his sudden shift at the Italian vault, when he'd used the cigarette to flip some kind of switch inside of him. She heard that glacier coldness in his voice now. "They need information from you."

"Why would I give them that? What do they offer? Do you think they would meet my price? You did. You planted the seed, *bebe*." Elagra reached toward Ben.

Trust your instincts down here.

The woman froze. Ben had raised an arm to block Elagra's forward advance, but what had stopped the witch from touching him wasn't that. It was the barrel of the Glock that appeared two inches in front of her, held in a firm grip at the end of Marcie's steady arm, which she'd inserted beneath Ben's. The barrel was aimed directly at the bridge of the witch's perfect nose.

"You think a gun will kill me, foolish girl?" Elagra said, her eyes glittering. She didn't look away from Ben, which disturbed Marcie even more. She needed her to break that lock.

"Don't know. At this distance, it'll definitely mess up that creepy dental work." Marcie cocked her head. "Keep your hands to yourself. He may have trouble harming a woman, but I have zero issues causing you enormous amounts of pain."

That did the trick. The witch turned those soulless eyes to her. As their gazes clashed, Marcie felt it. The terror, the pain, something that made her heart speed up and her gut tighten unpleasantly. She was a masochist, enjoyed pain for pleasure, but she knew the dividing line. She'd found a Master who needed to give out pain, but part of the charge for him was breaking down all of a woman's preconceived notions of what she could handle. He'd take her to that terrifying edge and show her the kind of ecstasy in pain and service that made her beg for more.

Elagra didn't want that gift. She wanted fear. She wanted to break open what she hurt with the pain, so she could see the insides. She wanted to hear them beg for mercy and laugh, deny them until they stopped asking and accepted her Hell as their fate.

The witch's chuckle held the stuff of nightmares. Her gaze returned to Ben. He was still staring at her. Though she kept the gun where it was and her eyes on Elagra, Marcie laid her other hand on his back, a reminder of her presence.

She felt him twitch. In her peripheral vision, she saw him blink at last. She suspected he was back with them, but he didn't look toward her. She wasn't sure where he was in his head, so until she was sure, she would stay just as she was.

"He had something special, he did," Elagra said. "Could lift any prize or treasssssure for me, the dear child. At the end of the night, he had treasssssure to give then. Not willing, no. It's ssssweeter when it's unwilling. He knew that, walks that line himsssself, doesn't he?"

She arched a brow at Marcie, tossed her head in a dismissive way toward her. "I gave him that gift. You're sssso very welcome."

In the movies, they used a cocking sound to show the character's intent to blow away the bad guy. But in reality, the telling move was the one that Marcie did now. The gun was already cocked to fire, had been when she lifted it.

She moved her finger from the guard to the trigger.

It was the unbreakable rule of proper firearm use. *Don't put your finger on the trigger, ever, unless you're pointing at what you intend to shoot, and are ready to do so.*

She was ready.

But Ben, who was aware of everything when it came to her, noticed. And now he came fully back to her.

"Marcella." Her Master's voice was firm, quiet. He put his hand up, on her wrist, exerted pressure to get her to lower the weapon. "They need information from her," he repeated.

"Sssso they do." Elagra stepped back at last, turning her attention from Ben to Raina. Her demeanor became casual, the way a hunting snake was casual as it sidled up to prey. "A ssssister witch enters my world uninvited, insults my home. You are not welcome. Why would I give you anything you wissssh, let alone answerssss?"

"Because it gets us out of your dirt-infested, uncombed hair all the sooner," Raina responded pleasantly. "And you should see a speech doctor about that pretentious lisp. A beast stirs beneath the river. Our sources say you know of this being, know its nature. I assume you don't want your home flooded and destroyed any more than anyone else."

The gold left Elagra's eyes, turning them the color of black mud. Her lips stretched out into a clown's smile. Too wide, too bright.

"Chaos is creation, sister." Elagra moved toward her shelves. "Rebirth. Renewal." She passed her hand over a jar that looked like it held something's brain. Until she unscrewed the top, reached in and plucked out a piece of it, disturbing the rest inside so they bounced and jiggled in the brine. Pickled eggs.

Her eyes laughed at Marcie as she took a bite. Marcie noticed the thick lashes were the same bone-yellow color as the dye on her hand. Elagra tipped the jar her way. "Want one? I'm not happy you took Riot from my side. He brought me these from the gas station near the

Motorsports Park. That's where he begged from tourists wanting to drive shiny, fast cars."

Raina tipped her head toward the still silent Mikhael. "Focus. His patience is not limitless, and he is giving you more leash than you deserve."

"No male puts me on a leash," Elagra's expression turned ugly. She spat the words as she replaced the jar on the shelf. "Unlike you, a disgrace to the power of the Goddess. Subservient you are, a slave to his desires and pleasures."

Raina laughed, that silvery sound that could unbalance a mind. Marcie had holstered the gun, which was good, because she found both her hands gripping Ben's arm, his own on her forearm, clasping her firmly. Apparently Mikhael and Raina had decided to unleash her power on the room. Elagra swayed, her eyes glazing a bit. Then she jumped back, hitting her bookshelves. That crackle of energy was wilder this time, giving Marcie a nasty jolt of sensation. A metal lantern on the table showered sparks as it fell with a clatter to the ground, rolling to a stop against a repaired wooden leg.

Marcie saw Mikhael's hand lift, move in a sweeping motion. Whatever he did countered the effect of Elagra's reaction, protected them with a soft blue light that saturated the room, enfolded them.

"It is not I who do not serve the Goddess," Raina said. She stepped forward, squaring off with the witch. Marcie noted a slight tightening of Mikhael's jaw, as if he weren't pleased that Raina had now placed herself closest, and most central to the witch's attention, but he held his position. "Tell us what we need to know about this being."

Marcie put her hand back on the butt of the gun, but kept the other on Ben. He'd shifted himself so he was somewhat between her and Elagra, but not completely blocking her, so Marcie curved her fingers into the shirt fabric clinging to the middle of his back. She dug into the heat of the man beneath, a reminder of her presence. She also needed that connection. She didn't want to be in this terrible place anymore, and thinking of Ben as a child here…God.

"She will not ask again, witch." Mikhael spoke for the first time, drawing all eyes his way. "Nor will I tolerate one more insult toward her, so mind your tongue."

Until now, Elagra had not looked toward Mikhael, nor acknowledged the other male presence in the room. Interesting, because Marcie suspected the woman was the type of female who had a pathological need to be the center of all male attention, even as she scorned it.

Marcie wondered if Mikhael had been masking his true nature, making his presence seemed incidental until this key moment. Because when she looked at him for the first time, Elagra paused. It was a very brief moment, but there was a flicker in her gaze that Marcie was pretty sure she'd interpreted correctly, because fierce satisfaction surged through her gut when she saw it.

Fear.

Yet Elagra's tone stayed as patronizing as ever. "A Dark Guardian." She sketched a curtsy, a dip of her head. "You honor us with your presence, my lord."

"It depends on what you value," Mikhael said.

Elagra arched a brow. "My lord?"

"You asked if we could pay your price. That is my answer. It depends on what you value."

Marcie saw a slight flinch. Elagra somehow managed to give the impression of taking a sidestep away from the Dark Guardian even without moving. But she recovered her aplomb, too quickly. Her gaze returned to Ben.

"She's not a monster. She's a baby. She is wanting to be born, is all. Must be born. You understand, *bebe?* A baby, coming out of her mother, will twist and tear her, give her pain and upheaval. It is the way of birth, is all."

"A baby." Raina cocked her head, intrigue in her eyes. And measured calculation. "Whose magic created her? What spell can create such a thing?"

"Many spells, sister." Elagra chuckled, held up one sharp nail. "That all fed into one spell, one that took many years to come to fruition. Because what is a spell, after all? Just a single thought, a wish of the heart, rageful enough to stir things up. We think of dark and light, but there is nothing but chaos, destruction to creation, and back again. The cycle that keeps us all living. The world changing, the way it's meant to change. Humans, thinking they and their science are everything, when you and I, and him," she dipped her head toward Mikhael, "know it is nothing. They are nothing. The cosmos could wipe them out with little more than a deep breath. Chaos...it is truth, power. Something beautiful."

Her face changed, became sorrowful. "I wanted to make something beautiful. And I did. Chaos belongs to neither dark nor light, and I serve the Goddess. She is the epicenter of chaos."

Raina shook her head. "A true chaos witch wishes only good for the world. Her kind of chaos is like the disruption of the earth to plant a seed, to see something grow. Your intent is destruction of the worst kind."

"But a seed *was* planted, sister witch." Elagra spread her hands out wide, like a cormorant drying spiky dark wings on a cold rock, under a gray sky. "The seed had to be planted by a soul poised perfectly on the scale between dark and light." Her gaze turned to Ben.

Suddenly the knife edge of tension in the chamber had the power to cut, and cut deep. Elagra's voice dropped back to a quivering whisper. "I worked hard to get you there, feeding you a bit of one, then the other. This babe, she is a seed, planted from your darkness, and, even more powerful, your potential darkness. The darkness waiting when you shed the pretense of what you are not, to embrace who you are. The magnificent thing you could be. But even if you never do that, it is all fine, *bebe*. I let you go, because I had what I needed from you."

Marcie heard Raina swear under her breath, a startled hiss, but Elagra was on a roll, like a villainess monologue, only far less cheesy than it should have seemed, thanks to the tension and frigid blend of terrible feelings swirling in the room. Were the walls blurring, like they were truly spinning?

She shoved that away, locked her attention on Ben. He looked as if he were slowly turning into a statue.

Or a ticking time bomb.

"Like a garden, I tried to make it work with so many other seeds. To blend things, get that perfect mix. Many other boys. It took time, but everything worthwhile does. I knew, when I was finally successful, could finally plant that seed, it would take it decades for it to grow, be ready for this moment."

Elagra shook her head, pursed her lips. When she spoke again, it was as if she were discussing the matter with herself. "But I admit, when it finally worked, all the impatience and frustration about past failures I'd suppressed coalesced into this momentous surge of energy.

It is best you were not here that day. It burned every living thing in this chamber, scorched the walls." Her gaze slid around her, and Marcie saw it, the dark fingers that flame had left branded on the lighter colored rock, like jagged teeth. She also saw two small skeletons in a shadowed corner. Skeletons that clung to each other as they'd done in their last moments of death.

"Fucking Christ," she muttered, tears stinging her eyes.

"So sweet, aren't they?" the woman said, following her gaze. "Twins. It was not a bad fate, to die in one another's arms. They'd endured worse."

This time only Raina's hand curling around her wrist kept Marcie at Ben's side. The half-succubus flicked her a quick narrowed glance when Elagra turned away, toward her shelves. Marcie understood, though it was a bitter pill to swallow.

Let her talk.

She just hoped they had what they needed soon, because that voice was scraping the skin off her spine.

Elagra's voice returned to that seductive purr, her attention coming back to Ben. This time she acted and spoke as if no one else was in the room, though she stayed in front of one of her bookcases, her spine straight, chin up, eyes glittering. "Creation is based on possibilities, potential. It was what the magic required and you... there was no better source. This babe. It is your child, my child. When she comes forth, she will bring with her the need for destruction that rests in the darkest rooms of our soul. Like the God of the Old Testament, when we see our Creation, we will know how very good it is."

Elagra cocked her head. "Do you remember, *bebe?*" she crooned, sliding back toward Ben, making Marcie stiffen. "It was that night. You gave me seed and blood, a murderous rage. The life of an innocent. Everything I desired, you gave to me. Sweet, sweet Amy. You remember Amy, I know."

Any vestige of emotion left Ben's face, except for a burning fire in his eyes that told Marcie one thing without doubt.

He was going to kill Elagra, right here and now.

She moved a breath before he did. Not her smartest move, because it was going to be like stepping in front of an oncoming train. But though she was closer to him than anyone else in the room, somehow Mikhael beat her there. He planted himself directly in Ben's path.

In the same blink of time, a command flooded Marcie's mind. Mikhael's authoritative timbre, overriding every other thought she had. Talking in her head.

Guard our backs.

She drew and pivoted, facing off with Elagra. The witch had been on a beeline for Ben, but with Mikhael and now Marcie in her path, she pulled up short. Her eyes had that unfocused look Raina's had had when she was dealing with the kid. She opened her mouth, and what came out of it was a croak, a mix between a tortured beast and fingernails gouging furrows down a chalkboard.

"I mean him no harm, sweet girl. I cherish him. Move aside and let me help calm him..."

What was terrifying was how much she meant it. The look she shot toward Ben was filled with a terrible hunger, a longing.

Raina's harsh laugh fortunately interrupted that voice, and the horrible revelation. "Save your energy, *sister*," she said with mocking venom. She'd appeared at Marcie's side in the very second blink, the two of them a wall between Elagra and the two men behind them. Marcie didn't dare look, but she could feel the heat of Ben's temper, his rage. Mikhael had somehow moved him back to the wall by the farthest chamber entrance, the distance creating a buffer.

"Your tricks have no influence over her," Raina said. "She doesn't believe in you, because she doesn't have to. You can't touch her. And he's bound to her in ways beyond your comprehension. You can't touch him anymore."

Elagra's eyes narrowed. "No bond is unbreakable."

"Exactly," Marcie retorted. "He's no longer yours, and I doubt he ever was. You have power over desperate, frightened kids, here in your scary, dark hole. Back off and give it up. Nothing you do is going to work on us."

Elagra's lip curved back from those freaky sharp teeth. Marcie's finger did move back to the trigger, though it was a severe risk, the temptation of that slim curve of metal pressing into the crease of her bent finger. Her mind was full of thoughts of a young Ben, and Riot, and whoever this Amy was that apparently had also suffered at this woman's hands. Then there were the pair of fragile skeletons clinging to one another in the corner, reason enough to do what she most wanted.

"Give me a fucking excuse," Marcie said.

She wasn't a bloodthirsty sort, hated killing anything, but this woman's evil was something she wanted gone. The bad thing was she'd killed before, so she now knew just how damn easy it was. Yet she also knew the nightmares that came with the decision.

Raina touched the small of her back, a cue, and Marcie dared a quick glance. Ben once again stood at her side, just behind her right shoulder. The energy coming off him told her he was still on a dangerous edge, but he was in control of it. Marcie saw Elagra's gaze flicker in anger and frustration as she recognized it. That felt almost as good as putting holes in her. Maybe.

"Look at me, witch," Mikhael commanded. He was standing at Raina's other side.

Elagra's expression twisted, her lip curving high on her teeth, revealing pink gums. Her hands curved into claws, her gaze refusing to leave Ben.

The ground began to quiver. As Marcie's gaze darted up, rock came loose from the ceiling, a shower of pebbles.

"*Look at me.*"

A shudder went through the stone, this time bringing down more than a handful of debris. Everything went solid dark. She lowered and swiftly holstered her weapon to free up both hands, since she had no target. Instead, she had a whole lot of darkness, that total absence of light that had seemed so forbidding when she'd first dropped down into the tunnel.

There was no sense of orientation, no up or down, no forward or back. Those three words that Mikhael had spoken so sharply, *Look at me*, had set off an energy wave that took away courage, left only despair. That feeling wasn't dying away with the echoes, but building, as if doom had been unleashed in the chamber, stealing the light, leaving no escape. She was in darkness, in a hole, forgotten and trapped. Helpless.

Marcie backed into Ben, and his strong hands gripped her. Without that support, she might have curled up in a ball, arms wrapped over her head in a futile attempt to shut it all out.

A work colleague she'd met on her college internship in Milan had been an eyewitness to the terrible tsunami in Indonesia. She'd said, *"Power of that magnitude makes you rethink what you believe about...everything. There are no certainties anymore."*

Thank God and Goddess and everything in between, light flickered back into the chamber. Elagra was on the floor, on hands and knees, her body cringing as if she wanted to curl into that fetal ball Marcie had imagined. She was whimpering, her fingers digging into the ground. Mikhael hadn't moved. He still stood at Raina's side, hands loose at his sides, eyes pinned upon the cowering witch. Eyes so frightening in their endless darkness, some primitive instinct in Marcie told her not to look too closely at them.

"You dare test me," Mikhael said. A statement.

Holy shit. All that had come from him. Marcie could feel the pounding of Ben's heart against her back, and his body was rigid as stone.

Elagra's head came up millimeter by millimeter, pulled up by a force not her own. Her body was still immobilized in that half curl. Her eyes were full blind white. A terrified sound escaped her throat.

"I can leave you like this," Mikhael said. "Trapped in a box no bigger than yourself, forgotten by everyone. Or you can tell me what I need to know. When will this creation emerge?"

Elagra shuddered. Her sharp teeth had sliced into her bottom lip, so blood was wet on her chin. "She comes ssssooon. The emergence of the new moon. Do not...please..."

"Please." Mikhael dropped to his heels, a step closer to her. When she tried to draw back, she couldn't. "The children you've tormented said please," he said. "'Please do not hurt me.'"

His low voice conjured every nightmare Marcie had ever had and mercifully forgotten. Now they might be permanently branded on her frontal lobe, disturbing her waking moments as well as her slumbering ones.

"You had no trouble inflicting this kind of horror on them," Mikhael said. "Trapping them with your spells. I hear of it happening again, and I will be back. Your end will not be pleasant, but it will be a joy compared to the redemption that will meet you on the other side. Tell me what I need to know."

"I have...told you," Elagra whimpered. "She is chaos. I created a child...of chaos. Nothing can be predicted. Nothing can be foretold..."

She started keening, trying to thrash, but it was as if her limbs were locked against her. Even knowing she would have shot her with little more provocation, Marcie couldn't help a chill of sympathetic fear at the woman's plight.

Mikhael sat comfortably on his heels, his gaze probing as he stared at the witch. He looked bored, as the witch struggled against an exercise of his power that was reducing her to a terrified beast, caught in a trap.

Dark Guardian. The title was starting to make sense.

Raina stood at Mikhael's back, her own face expressionless, but Marcie had a feeling it wasn't easy for her to watch what was going on. She looked as if she knew how Elagra felt, though if she did, Marcie was certain it hadn't been at Mikhael's hands.

Suddenly, Elagra crumpled, body sprawling as if released from a net. The weight of fear and darkness lifted from the chamber. When Mikhael spoke, it was the voice he normally used.

"She's told us what she knows. Let's go."

CHAPTER NINE

*E*merging from that underground place, even into the morbid atmosphere of the St. Louis cemetery, had been like being given free tickets to Disneyland and a Fast Pass to go to the front of the line on every ride. Marcie couldn't stop drawing in deep breaths of the air.

However, when they first came out of the vault, she'd been startled at the passage of time. She was certain they'd spent no more than a couple hours below ground, but it was nighttime, and not early dark. It was past midnight.

"It was the magic Elagra used to create her little world down there," Raina explained. "When we crossed from the tunnels into her lair, it created a time lag. You wouldn't have been conscious of it. If I could have anticipated it, I would have told you to leave your phones at the hotel. They're likely fried now."

Marcie was more concerned about other things. While Raina was standing next to her, her mind seemed to be far away. After what she'd seen below, Marcie's natural inclination to reach out and touch was far more guarded, but she had to ask. "Are you okay?"

Raina blinked, focused on her. Her lips curved in a tight smile. "Yes. Thank you. Some of that, it brought up bad memories."

That was all she said, but she seemed a little easier, so Marcie was glad she'd asked. Mikhael was sealing up the vault as Ben moved to join the women.

"So," Ben said. "What's next on this scintillating adventure down memory lane? We could visit the alley where I spent the night holed up behind the body of a dead crack whore so no one would bother me. Best night's sleep I'd had in a month."

Marcie looked at him. Ben shook his head, swore softly. "Yeah, sorry. That was a stupid thing to say."

"No. No it wasn't." She would have reached out to take his hand, but his stiff body language told her she would likely be rebuffed right now. She pushed down the pang at that, and squared her shoulders. "Anybody would be messed up over what was happening down there. I don't like to think something like that is living beneath our city."

"It will not rank high on my list of favorite memories, either." Mikhael joined them. Raina's shoulders eased further as he pressed up behind her, wrapping a large hand over her hip bone. "We need a cleansing," he added. He looked toward Ben. "I have a thought on that. Let's go to the cars."

He took Raina's hand, led her away, giving Marcie and Ben time to make their decision to follow. The Dark Guardian and the witch walking away hand-in-hand, framed by the maze of silver-grey crypts and grave markers, made a Gothic-style romantic picture, but Marcie was still a little too caught up in things to appreciate it fully.

"She said the time difference fried our phones," she ventured, glancing at Ben's brooding features. "Good thing we backed ours up a few days ago, the way Lucas is always telling us to do."

"Yeah. Though that doesn't really seem all that important, does it?" He looked back at the now-sealed vault, his jaw tight.

Marcie finally laid her hand on his upper arm. She managed, barely, not to start. The man was built, so she was used to the feel of resilient muscle wherever she touched him. Right now it was so taut and cold, it was as if he were made out of some form of chilled iron.

"Ben..."

He jerked, then looked down at her as if seeing her for the first time. Fortunately, he dwelled there a long moment, giving her that look she knew he did when he was finding his center. At length, he touched her face. "It's all right, brat. Come here and warm me up."

Marcie slid her arms around him without having to be asked twice, gratified and relieved when he let out a sigh, and wrapped both his own arms around her. "Look at that," he said in a low voice. "So soft and alive. All the best things in life, right here in my grasp."

"You're just talking about my nine-millimeter."

"Yeah, forgot about that. Just thought you were happy to see me."

She snuffled a chuckle against him, held him tighter. She wanted to ask him a million things about what had happened below ground, but keeping his state of mind like this was more important to her. "Where do you think Mikhael is going to take us?" she asked instead.

"Hell if I know. But anywhere's better than here. Unless he is, in fact, taking us to Hell. Even then, I'm not sure if that wouldn't be preferable."

"Me, either."

He gave her a faint smile and drew back, offering her his hand, much as Mikhael had to Raina. In that way, they made their way out of the silent world of the dead. She trailed her fingers over several of the markers, husbands and wives who had spent their lives together, the journey she and Ben were just beginning. Those couples had moved on to the next journey together. That thought of the natural way of things helped ease the unnatural feel of what they'd left behind, so when they reached the side gate, she felt a little steadier. The reassuring grip of Ben's hand, the way he passed his thumb over her palm and wrist pulse in an unconsciously intimate gesture, also helped.

The neighborhood surrounding the cemetery was mostly quiet, though there was a current of noise on the wind coming from the nearby French Quarter. Not too raucous, but there was music. It was the time of night when the musicians weren't so much performing as jamming with their peers, while entertaining the final stragglers and staff doing clean up and shut down.

Mikhael and Raina were waiting at the side gate. From the way Raina leaned against Mikhael's side, his hand wrapped in her hair, fingers stroking her collarbone, Marcie thought maybe they'd been doing something not too different from her and Ben's embrace among the vaults. Touching base with love and the living.

But it was curious and unsettling to Marcie, seeing Mikhael so focused on steadying Raina, all while he could... It had been clear he could have ended Elagra at any moment. But he hadn't. And here he was, looking calm and unconcerned about Elagra's existence. The harm she had done. Why didn't he *do* something?

She bit back the question for another time. One thing she'd definitely understood from the display of his power was that one didn't really question him at the wrong time. Or possibly at all. She needed to think. And then maybe ask the far more approachable Raina first.

They proceeded away from the cemetery and up one of the neighborhood side streets. They weren't in a great area of town, but Ben knew a guy at one of the houses, a toothless black man named Short, and they'd left the car in front of his place. Raina and Mikhael had met them here, so Marcie wasn't sure how they'd arrived, though they seemed amenable to following them to their vehicle, rather than going a different way.

Short—who was so far over six feet tall Marcie figured he had to have been recruited by all the high school basketball teams when he was in his youth—was a forty-something black man with a cracked prosthetic leg wrapped with duct tape. He sat on his porch with a fifth of vodka sitting on a table next to him and a giant bag of animal crackers in his lap. Periodically, he tossed a couple to the pair of elderly pit bulls lying on the cracked boards in front of him. A white cat was perched on the railing behind him, studying the scenario with a typical air of feline disdain for the canine class.

As Ben stopped in front of the man's chain link gate, he glanced at Raina and Mikhael. The Dark Guardian leaned against a light post, his arm around Raina. She said something in a low tone, and he shook his head, stroking a piece of her dark hair out of her face. When his fingertips touched her lips, she attempted a smile. He murmured something, and she dipped her head into his hand, a short nod, before closing her eyes. Marcie saw Raina's hand tighten on his biceps. The Dark Guardian continued to hold her as he lifted his attention to Ben.

"Meet us outside town," he said. "The place where you liked to take your wife's car, when it was yours."

With that, he straightened and began walking away, taking Raina with him. Though her expression was almost as pensive as Ben's, Raina tossed Marcie a smile. "See you there," she said.

And then... Marcie blinked. They could have disappeared around the corner of the next intersecting street, hidden by a house, but she wondered if they'd literally disappeared just before that. Ben squeezed her hand, and went through the rusted gate to the porch. He said a quiet word to Short, handing some money to the man over the dogs' heads while he stroked them with his free set of fingers. There was the obligatory attempt by Short to refuse it, a shake of the head, but Ben insisted. Short had dogs to feed, after all.

Ben had already tried, more than once, to pay for a replacement prosthetic for him. Marcie remembered what he'd said Short's response was.

The duct tape works just fine, Mr. Fancy Suit. Things last a lot longer when we have faith in them, don't try to replace them when they get a ding or crack."

Short tipped his bill cap to her, and she smiled in response, though smiling felt hard. Everything she'd just seen, what they'd learned, and what needed to be discussed, were interfering with those muscles.

But Ben was here, with her, and she had faith in that. As he came to her and opened the McLaren's passenger door to help her inside, she gripped his hand an extra moment before letting him go. She usually teased him about taking the wheel of "her" car when they were together, but she didn't. Not right now.

When he got in and pulled away from the curb, she was glad that he reached out and reclaimed her hand briefly before having to turn his attention to the gear shifting. She laid her hand high on his thigh, ignoring the seatbelt in favor of scooting over and laying her head on his shoulder, her favorite position when he was driving, and particularly now. He pressed his cheek to hers, lips grazing her brow, before he accelerated, taking them out of the close, cross-hatched streets of historic New Orleans and moving to the outer areas.

She knew where Mikhael had meant, but she had no idea how he knew about it. But after him using that voice, and speaking in her head as he had, she wasn't surprised by a casual revelation about their lives.

Once out of the more congested city limits, there was plenty of open land and country roads. At this late hour, nothing stirred but them and the night wildlife. The car lights reflected off the shining eyes of raccoons, coyotes, a few deer. Plenty of other creatures were likely hidden in the long grasses, pine trees and thick foliage on the sides of the blissfully undeveloped roads.

Mikhael hadn't given them an exact address, but that wasn't a problem. They went around a curve, and there he was. Leaning against his Ferrari 458 Italia. With Mikhael's dark clothing and hair color, the car was a good match for its driver. Black, polished and mean-looking. Raina lay on her hip on the hood, her upper torso twisted on her back so she could gaze up at the stars. Her hand was stretched out so her fingertips grazed Mikhael's upper thigh.

"If we took a picture, I bet Ferrari would pay us a bundle to acquire it for their next advertising campaign," Marcie said.

"Yeah, but they'd probably have to visit Hell to get Mikhael to sign the paperwork."

She managed a tight chuckle. "I'm seeing a team of Ferrari lawyers in their nice suits, holding their briefcases, checking their Rolexes with that patented self-important impatience, waiting to get on the boat to cross the River Styx."

Ben snorted. "Patented self-importance? And I suppose the ferryman would take one look and say, 'Sorry, we've reached our quota of lawyers this month.'"

Marcie shot him a smile. "Glad you said it, so I didn't have to."

"When you're a lawyer, you have to stay ahead of the crowd when it comes to the jokes." Ben gave her a dry look as he decelerated and rolled up next to Mikhael and Raina. He eased his window down and swept his gaze over them.

"So, what next? Going to use the scary voice to drive crows out of the corn fields? The farmers would thank you."

Mikhael's expression didn't change. "It is time to prove your boast about your overpriced car."

Ben blinked. Then his lips curved in a feral smile, the hard light in the green eyes becoming something else. "Ready to get your ass kicked, are you?"

Mikhael's dark gaze flickered. "Actions speak louder than words, human."

"Yes, they do, Lord of the Underworld." Ben unbuckled the seat belt and lifted the door. But then he stopped.

Marcie gave him a curious look as he studied her. He raised his attention back to Mikhael. "It's her car."

Raina sat up, her braced arms holding her upright. Her dark hair fell forward over one shoulder and part of her eye. If Ferrari even hinted that each car purchased had been blessed by her body stretched out on the hood, they'd triple their sales. "You want shotgun?" Ben asked her. "Girls against boys?"

"Ben." Marcie reached out. "What are you doing?"

He leaned across the seat, cupped her jaw and gave her a firm kiss, one that turned deeper and had her stretching halfway over the steering wheel as he slid his other arm around her to hold her close, reach down and palm her buttock, squeeze. It was a kiss that promised serious, intense sex, possibly in the next few moments, so when he pulled back, she was breathless. A glance down showed her he was more than ready to deliver on the message. But he gave her another, unexpected one.

"I'm letting you kick his ass."

Mikhael was still studying him as if he'd done something unexpected, and he certainly had. When Marcie emerged from the passenger side and paused, hand on the car, she found Raina was totally on board. She slid off the hood of the Ferrari with a grin and passed Mikhael with a playful bump against him. She came to Marcie with a pendulum swing of her hips that couldn't help but keep both men's attention—and hell, Marcie's herself.

"Spoils go to the winners, boys," Raina purred. She seemed to have recovered her usual aplomb, which helped Marcie feel better. As did her playfulness when the witch hooked Marcie around the neck. Her fingers wrapped over her collarbone, nails caressing her, before she brushed Marcie's lips with hers. The light hand on Marcie's waist and hip lingered as Raina tossed the men a teasing look over her shoulder. "Whoever that winner is."

Ben shook his head at his wife as Marcie shot him a wicked grin and then circled around to take the driver's side. He gave Raina props for getting his brat to smile after that shit show they'd endured. For his own part, he sauntered over to Mikhael's side and joined him in watching the women take the front seat of the McLaren. Mikhael cocked his head at him. "I did not say you could ride with me."

"You didn't. But I'm not sucking your dick to get a ride, and she'll get mad if you leave me behind. I recommend you accept the new situation."

Mikhael's lips twisted. "Marcie will come back to get you."

"I didn't say it would be Marcie that would be mad. Your lady's got an appreciating eye for my ass."

"It will have a tire track down the middle of it if your own woman notices your attention to that fact. And I will draft in right behind her, breaking your spine like a dry twig."

"You're sounding more Moose and Squirrel by the moment. The Russian comes out when you're feeling all manly."

Mikhael shook his head and moved to the Ferrari driver's side. He folded himself into the car and started it up, the car making the anticipatory growl of a tiger ready to pounce. When Ben circled around, Mikhael had raised the upward winging passenger door, but as Ben started to get in, he had to hop nimbly as Mikhael edged the car forward a couple feet with a revving of the engine. Ben landed in the seat more heavily than intended, but squared himself there and gave the Guardian a look. "Really? We're going there?"

Mikhael made a noncommittal grunt that might pass for a chuckle in his world. The door folded down as Ben buckled in. He noticed Mikhael didn't. Being immortal had its perks.

"Why did you let her drive?" the Dark Guardian asked.

Ben lifted a shoulder. "To remind her that I love her more than anything. And because that car has a dick." He tipped a glinting look at Mikhael. "It gets along well enough with me, but it fucking loves her hands. Which makes her the better driver for it. I learned a long time ago that being on the top of the heap when you win isn't nearly as important as the win itself."

Mikhael studied him. Ben noticed he did a lot of that. Guy should have been a scientist with a microscope, but maybe what he did for a living was the magical warrior equivalent, determining how things were put together and anticipating their actions accordingly.

"You are a surprising individual, Ben O'Callahan. I would never let Raina drive my car." Mikhael grimaced. "Mostly because her energy does not mesh well with mechanical things."

"I get that. But if she really wanted to drive it, you'd let her. Because you love her more than anything, too. It has a look to it. Like recognizes like. But I gotta say, my hat's off to you. I thought my brat was a handful."

"Mmm. And yet you are purposefully letting them spend time together where she may give your 'brat' tips. You are a foolish man."

"That may be true." Ben paused. "Is she okay? Raina?"

Mikhael's brow creased, his dark eyes flickering, but he inclined his head. "Yes. She has demons in her past, much as you do. Your kindness is...appreciated."

Before Ben could respond to that, Marcie gunned the McLaren's engine. They'd lowered the top. The two women offered them smiles as she put the car in gear. With another challenging grin, Marcie peeled away from the roadside. The McLaren could make it from resting to eighty in a heartbeat.

Mikhael cracked his neck, glanced at Ben. "Enough of a head start?"

"Let's go get them."

Since Ben had been in plenty of high performance sportscars, he was already braced as Mikhael engaged, launching the Ferrari away from the turnout after their quarry.

The Dark Guardian might be centuries old, but Ben estimated he'd have only had a hundred years or so to learn how to drive. With the wings, there was no telling when he'd gotten into the car craze. Ben couldn't imagine he'd been all that hyped until the fifties, when the true ancestors of the cars they were driving had started to be engineered.

"Were you into horses before cars came around?" Ben raised his voice to be heard over the engine noise. The road was curvy but not too insane yet. The vehicles were settling into their paces, and he could almost feel Marcie's enjoyment of navigating the turns, letting the car respond to her touch.

Truth, the first time he'd let her drive out here, he'd been typically reluctant. Then he'd watched her ebullience build, her hair streaming, the sheer joy in her eyes. When they finally came to a stop, his cock had been like a baseball bat against the confines of his jeans. He'd taken her on the hood, stretching her out face down, her pert ass pulled up to slap against his pelvis with every thrust. That gorgeous hair had spilled over her shoulders, her pale skin shimmering in moonlight. Her fingers had caressed the hood of the car, as if the both of them, him and the vehicle, were having her.

"I preferred dragons," Mikhael responded. "Though I enjoy the challenge of riding waterhorses, when they give me the privilege."

Of course he preferred dragons. Who wouldn't, really? "You have to have a waterhorse's agreement to ride him?"

"Unless you wish to have every bone in your body crushed. Then be dragged a mile and held down in the closest body of water and drowned."

"Need your permission slip ready before hopping on a waterhorse. Check. J*esus*." The last syllable goosed up with some alarm, though it was followed by a whistle of pure appreciation as Marcie took the hairpin curve ahead on rails. She'd neither under nor oversteered, and had managed the speed so she accelerated out of it like a rocket launching. *But Christ, be careful, brat.*

He'd been on board with this idea, because it gave her something to think about other than that dark place below ground and the questions it had raised about him. He'd forgotten this side of her that could scare the shit out of him.

Mikhael followed on her heels, expertly enough he closed the distance, heel to toe working on the braking, gas and clutch as he managed the gear shifts seamlessly.

"Do you sleep with this thing?" Ben wanted to know.

"Up until Raina. Yes."

"Thanks for that disturbing, pre-Raina visual."

Marcie's blond locks whipped in the wind, alongside Raina's sable mane. Raina held a handful of strands close to her face as she called out something to Marcie. Marcie laughed, though she didn't take her eyes off the road. Ben just recognized from the movement of her shoulders she was laughing.

God, he loved her. It had been so easy to say it to Mikhael, because it was a simple fact at this point, nothing gushy or unmanly about it.

Another freaking crazy turn, then up a hill. And fuck, it was steep enough that the McLaren's wheels left the ground on the crest. Marcie wasn't as experienced with that maneuver. Ben tensed, leaning forward, breath caught in his throat, not even noticing as their own car took flight. He strained to keep his gaze on the McLaren. The car rocked precariously on the landing, fishtailing a little, then straightened. The Ferrari dropped more smoothly. Okay, maybe Mikhael *was* the better driver. But only because he had a few decades on her.

"When you are with her later, tell her not to do that again without a safer way to practice," the Guardian said. "I just balanced her. Else she would have spun out and flipped."

Ben's heart skipped another beat. "Don't tell her that. She'll think it's cheating, you giving her an advantage." But he glanced at him. "Thanks."

Mikhael nodded. "She is reckless. Like Raina. They are already fearless, and our love for them..."

"It makes them feel invincible. Whereas it reminds us just how fragile they can be. Yeah. I've had enough near-death experiences for the night. Take the lead. There's something up ahead we can show them."

Mikhael grimaced. "You are assuming I can take the lead. Without magical aid. Which, as you pointed out, would be cheating."

Ben grinned. "She's kicking your ass, isn't she? Making you work for it."

"If you tell her that, I will tell her you said she was the better driver of your car."

Ben scoffed. "It might almost be worth it. But we'll call it bro code. Okay, just turn off up at your next right. They'll see it and back-track to you. After they go joy riding another hundred miles or so. They look like they're having a ball up there. Total Thelma and Louise moment happening."

Raina had her hands up like she was on a roller coaster. From Marcie's posture, the tilt of her head and set of her shoulders, Ben could almost feel her absorption in the power of the car, the wildness of it, all at her fingertips. Never tamed, but responding to her in a way it responded to no other.

He wondered if she knew he felt like that when she was touching him, and suspected she did. Something else he wouldn't acknowledge, but it brought a fierce warmth when he was thinking about it. He wanted to give her that power, use it to pleasure her. Help her fly in other ways.

Mikhael turned where he'd indicated. As they bumped down the dirt road, the swimming hole appeared in their field of vision.

The little lake and dock belonged to a farmer nearby, but Ben knew he turned a blind eye to the teens and others who turned it into a romantic hotspot on weekend nights, as long as they respected the sign he'd put out here, painted in uneven red letters.

Two rules. Clean up your trash and don't hurt nothing. Including each other.

It was one of those maxims that probably had wider symbolic meaning, if Ben was one of those people who did a lot of pondering of that shit, like Jon did. Fortunately, he didn't. But he did have a niggling question.

"So, why are we doing this? Don't we have the city to save in a matter of hours?" He wasn't sure when the new moon was, not being up on lunar cycles, but Elagra had said "soon."

Mikhael made a noncommittal noise. "You and Raina have been in places where hope was not conceivable. At best, a mocking carrot dangled by capricious gods. Marcie has experienced some bad things in her life, but she has not come against something like Elagra. Taking a moment like this, when it can be taken, is as important as sharpening a sword before battle. The state of the mind is everything, particularly against a foe like this."

Ben considered that. "So this was all for Marcie?"

Mikhael turned his gaze to him. "If you did not have the darkness in you that you have, would you have been the right match for her? Would your souls be bound as tightly together as they are, ever more so every day? You might spend a tedious amount of time thinking you are not worthy of her, that something like you should not be touching her, but there is a reason you are such a formidable force together. And yet, if the mind is lost to darkness, darkness is all it can see, all it can imagine is possible. Then a soul can miss the lit path."

"So, this was for all of us."

Mikhael inclined his head. "There are different reasons we each needed this moment. We don't need to be female and analyze the why."

"Yeah. Hate to point out that's exactly what you just did before summing it all up." Ben chuckled. "It pisses me off that you're starting to grow on me."

"A feeling that is definitely not mutual."

But he saw a quirk to Mikhael's lips.

At that moment, they heard the purr of the McLaren. A blink

later, the silver car came bumping along the dirt side road. "Thank God," Ben said. "I thought we were going to have to sit on the hood like Sam and Dean and talk about our feelings."

The faintly puzzled look on the Dark Guardian's face gave Ben a small measure of satisfaction. The guy didn't know every damn thing. But he did pick up context pretty quickly.

"I would have driven the Ferrari into the lake to avoid that horror," Mikhael said dryly.

Raina sprang out of the car, doing a sexy little dance. Though the woman gave off fuck-me vibes with every breath that lifted her magnificent breasts, in this moment she looked almost girlish, a significant contrast to less than a half hour ago. When Ben noted how Mikhael's expression softened and warmed, he knew they had that in common, the overwhelming desire to see their women happy. Though he hated to admit it, it kind of made Ben like the guy even a little more. Mikhael was willing to say "Fuck Armageddon," long enough to make sure his woman was okay.

"Just had to give up, didn't you, boys?" Raina continued loftily. "Don't you dare say you let her win."

"Oh, he totally let her win," Ben said. Marcie shot him the bird. He tossed a grin to Raina before sauntering toward the McLaren.

Raina skipped—yes, skipped, which did very distracting things with those breasts—to Mikhael and did a hop that landed her in his arms, her legs curled around his hips. The male had been watching her approach with his poker face, but Ben had felt the energy from him. So he wasn't a bit surprised to see Mikhael grasp his witch around the waist and brace her against the driver's side as he put himself firmly between her legs. He took her mouth in a kiss that said he might just take her against the car, their company notwithstanding.

Ben was good with that plan, though he had his own take on it. As he reached the McLaren's open door, he offered Marcie a hand. "He didn't let me win," she said, her eyes smiling, but a quizzical note to the statement that said she wanted confirmation. She was a competitor, his brat. She didn't like to be given anything that wasn't earned.

He abandoned any attempt at banter. "Come here," he growled, gripping her hand and making it clear he wanted her out of the car. When she complied, he pulled her to him. He glimpsed a flash in her brown eyes, still lit with the excitement of the car race, and now infused with additional pleasure at whatever he might demand from her.

She liked attention, and that was fortunate, because he was the type of Master who liked to give his sub copious amounts of it, well past the point most women could handle.

But it was as Mikhael said. Something in her matched the limitless need in him.

He put her against the McLaren and kissed her with all the pumping demand he felt inside him, his hand grasping her hair and the delicate curve of her skull, his other arm wrapped around her waist. He felt heat everywhere her legs clutched him, from hip to ass to back of thigh. The more he kissed her, his tongue stroking and twisting, tasting, the more she clung to him, fingers curled into his hip and side through denim and his shirt. He tightened his grip on her face and throat, held her mouth to his as he dove and plundered. He ground his dick with rutting satisfaction between her thighs and she rubbed back, making a little moan.

Mikhael was right. No matter the fate of the world, they needed to have this. He'd torn open a part of his soul he preferred to keep walled off, and it probably wasn't going to be the last time before this was over. What had Mikhael called this? A cleansing. He knew of no better way to give his soul a bath than to immerse it in his brat's sweet body.

He backed off of her, his expression telling her what he wanted, and she damn well better not make him wait. He stripped off his shirt, tossed it in the car, and the avid look in her gaze as it coursed over his upper body, his chest, inflamed him further. When she licked her lips, he knew she wanted to taste, touch and bite. He was good with that, too.

"You can't outrun me," he said. A clear challenge. Her gaze flashed and she was off and running. Right for the lake and the dock.

Shit. In about ten seconds, he realized he'd better start joining her on her morning runs. Her police academy training was paying off. He had to push himself more than usual to gain on her. He had her on dodge and feint tactics, but she was getting better at that, too. Good. She'd need it against the lowlifes she'd encounter on the street.

His reaction to that thought was enough to give him another

burst, and he had her around the waist, lifting her off her feet as they hit the dock.

"We're going for a swim," he told her.

"Not with clothes on, I hope." She laughed breathlessly, and it was a sound that all by itself could get him hard. Hell, everything about her made him hard. Since he'd been running with half his blood supply below his waist, he should get extra points for catching her.

He set her down, stepped back, gave her a look that settled her, focused her on what he wanted. She pulled off her clingy shirt with a nice undulation of her upper body, revealing the lacy bra that held her gorgeous breasts just right, high and quivering. "Take it all off," he said.

She worked off socks and shoes, then straightened to unclip the bra, letting the lace fall away from tempting flesh. Unbuttoned and shimmied out of the jeans. Last came the panties, which matched the scanty pleasure of the bra. Even when going below ground to face down an evil witch, Marcie would make sure she was wearing nice underwear for her Master. It was one of many things he appreciated about her.

She was naked now, standing before him bathed in a flickering glow. A brief glance back showed him the firepit had been lit. Mikhael and Raina were silhouetted at the car, so if they'd lit it, they'd done it remotely, something he was mildly sorry he hadn't been able to see, but what he was seeing now took precedence.

As Marcie's gaze followed his, her eyes widened a bit. Mikhael was taking Raina against the side of the car, and they were well into the thrusting stage, Raina's head tipped back on the roof, her arms spread out to hold onto the frame of the car as her male worked himself inside her. No wings tonight, but the energy was there, waves of it, reaching the two of them. Marcie moistened her lips with the tip of her tongue, an unconscious sign of hunger, and her gaze came back to Ben. "Come here," he said, another order.

He called her brat, but she never bratted deliberately. However, she could be playful. As she was now, when she tossed him her 'come get me' look, turned and dove into the water.

It took him only a few extra seconds to strip, since he'd already removed his shoes and socks when she did. He dove in after her. She was halfway across the little lake, emerging and then diving beneath again, her silhouette like that of a mermaid. Then she doubled back and met him halfway. She came up right in front of him, her fingertips sliding along his thighs, her belly brushing his erection as his arms closed around her. She wound herself all around him, making a sexy sound of helpless yearning as he gripped her hair, sucked water off her throat. And bit.

She moved against him, a rhythmic rubbing, unplanned, simple need. He felt it, too, and stroked them back to where his feet could touch. He wanted all the physical leverage he could get to drive into her willing body.

He found her beneath the surface, his touch sliding along her labia, probing past the less lubricating lake water and into the slippery honey within her. He worked his fingers in there, opening her. He followed his touch with himself, lodging his cock in the opening of that channel. He did it while keeping his eyes on her face. Her eyes were half closed, lips parted, tongue touching her lips unconsciously. Her brown eyes glowed with the heat of her need.

Then he worked his fingers in her some more, around his cock. Nevertheless, when he removed his hand and thrust deeper, sliding into that hold before the water could follow and cause them a problem, he saw her catch her lip in her teeth at the brief discomfort of a quick entry. But she bore down, accepted, managed it. Embraced it. That spoke to the darkness in him, the way she took the pain he gave her and turned it into pleasure for both of them.

He returned his hand to her wet hair, firmly pulling against her scalp as he pushed her down on him, working her body against him. It was all him now, her holding on as he took her on the ride he wanted. Her lips were wet, her eyes shining and glazed, her body arched and pushed into his, offering, giving. Anything he wanted. He bent his head, nipped her breast, found her nipple, sucked hard, pinched it between his firm lips and heard her gasp, felt her shudder, the ripple of her cunt on him.

He adjusted his hold, taking a bruising grip on her buttocks, and found her rim, teasing, stroking. Before her, he'd been a total ass man, almost always taking his subs there. With his size, it was more comfortable for them and, admittedly, it was less intimate for him, presenting less emotional and physical risks both. His dick had had the welcoming heat and clasp of a willing pussy more in his relatively short time with Marcie than in most of his life. But fifty years from now, it still wouldn't be enough.

He still enjoyed plundering that sweet, willing ass, too, but even when he wasn't ass-fucking her, he liked the feel of slapping his body against her soft buttocks. So now he pulled out and, when she gave him a pouty look, hc took care of that, turning her around and shoving back into her before he could lose the sweet lubrication of her cunt. Another tough entry, and when she gasped at the effort anew, he banded his arm over her chest, between her lovely breasts, so he could grip her throat, hold her chin up. He dropped his other hand to play with her clit and around her stretched tissues, over his nice, big cock. "You going to fight me, brat? Give me attitude?"

She shook her head, but he felt her tremble. She knew he'd seen it, that brief protest and rebellion that could set him off, trigger that darkness in him. At one time, as Mikhael had said, he hadn't wanted Marcie anywhere near that part of him. But she'd refused to be deterred, had stepped into those dark rooms. And she wouldn't leave. By marrying him, she'd effectively locked herself in them and thrown away the key.

For better or worse—wow, did the thought bring those vows home —there was no going back now. He would never let her go. If she was determined to play in the darkness of his soul, he would make damn sure she'd find unforgettable pleasure within the pain he needed to inflict. He wanted her afraid to cross those lines, but wanting what he could give her too much to let the fear stop her.

He put his mouth to her shoulder and bit again as he tightened the grip on her throat, felt the frantic pounding of the pulse. He bit harder, teeth digging in with the desire to find blood. He'd made sure to latch onto the muscle, not the collarbone, and it twitched under his grip, responding to the clamp.

She was writhing on him, her buttocks rubbing against him as she struggled. She had both hands latched on his forearm, her fingers digging into him, too. He kept fucking her, deeper, harder. It felt like the water was heating up from the combustible energy coming off of both of them.

Her hair smelled wet, flowery, like when she came out of the shower, but it had the earthy, primal smells of the lake, too. He wanted to move to the bank, press her down to her elbows and knees, leave furrows in the mud from how roughly he took her. But he wasn't willing to move from here, to change a thing about how good she felt to him. He eased the clamp of his jaw enough to speak to her. Order her to do his bidding.

"Go up and over," he whispered. "Right now, or I will tear your ass up, little girl."

She tightened on him, lifted, struggled against him some more, and the climax took her, wresting strangled cries from her throat as his fingers worked her and he kept thrusting into her, feeling the bliss of her soft backside each time he shoved against it.

The water rippled around them as her release brought forth his own, and he spilled himself inside her. One of the things he liked about climaxing in her pussy was jetting that seed deep into her, knowing it would slip out of her, stain her panties, smell like him when she took them off later. He'd thought about that when he took her in the hotel room, before they came to see Elagra. He was a damn animal, wanting to mark her with his teeth, his seed, his scent, but he didn't have to apologize for that darkness. Not anymore.

She'd saved his soul. Not by pulling it out of that darkness, but by making sure he'd never be standing alone in it again. She was the single star in his night sky, but the one that guided him in all things. Mikhael was right about that.

Not that they had to be all female and analyze it or anything.

CHAPTER TEN

*W*hatever had possessed Mikhael to initiate that impromptu *Fast and Furious* moment, it had been a good decision. Because once back at the hotel suite, playtime was over. The urgency of their mission returned in full force. Though Mikhael didn't state their next step straight out, Ben knew what it was. He could feel the sense of expectation in the room. Waiting on him.

Raina was curled up on the couch. Mikhael sat at the dining room table, fingers templed before him, back straight, head up and eyes closed. It was a meditative look, but Ben had no doubt he was as cued into the energy of the room as any of them. All of them waiting.

Derek had rejoined them. Different set of jeans and shirt, same staff. He'd dropped his cowboy hat on the coffee table and sat on the couch where Raina was, his long arm along the back behind her, booted feet stretched out to the right of the table. Raina and Mikhael had caught him up on what had happened below ground, and the blue eyes had cooled at the mention of the new moon. They'd discussed when that would be.

Just past midnight, less than twenty-four hours from now.

Ben didn't sit down. He moved to the wet bar. He felt Marcie's brown eyes on him, and in his peripheral vision he saw her fingers tighten on the arm of the occasional chair where she sat. It was a small tell, but a significant one. He stared at the decanter of whiskey, but between taking a drink and ensuring Marcie didn't puncture the sofa with a death grip, there was no contest. He stepped back and away, moving to the high counter separating the small kitchenette from the living area.

As he leaned a hip against it, he saw there was a cheerful bowl of peanut M&Ms placed on the marbleized granite surface. They didn't look like a stock Hotel Monteleone amenity. Interesting, witches and sorcerers liking candy, but then, who didn't?

Marcie rose and met him there, moving to take a seat on the tall bar stool. Ben dropped his hand to Marcie's knee, a touchstone, fingers curling around the thin denim stretched over her thigh. His thumb moved idly up and down the inseam. He knew her body always heated at his touch, because even his most incidental contact had a tone of sexual command to it. But there was more to this moment than that.

His sweet sub scooped out a few M&Ms and spent a couple moments placing them on the granite counter. Some wanted to roll, but she steadied them, focusing on her task. He watched the smiley face take shape, and passed an affectionate hand over her back. She'd given the caricature one blue eye and one green.

"It is a hard memory," Raina said quietly.

Marcie lifted her head, turned the rotating seat of her stool to face the witch. Ben was facing her already, the counter guarding his back.

"I'm sorry, Ben," Raina added. "To understand what Elagra has done, we need you to fill in the blanks."

Ben nodded. He turned his head, looked down at the M&Ms. As he did, he picked up Marcie's hand, lifting it to his face. He cupped it against his jaw, holding tight to her wrist. Her expression held concern, but it was also open. Loving. He reached out with the free hand, caressed her face. Her lips parted at his touch on her mouth and she kissed his fingers, dipping her head to nuzzle him.

"They're just words," she said. "They're already in your head. It changes nothing to say them aloud."

She wasn't entirely right. Speaking words could give the emotions behind them, particularly rage, more fuel, like oxygen to fire.

His mind went back to the chamber, when everything had disappeared but the goddamn certainty it was long past time to snap the witch's neck, fucking end her.

Mikhael had stepped in front of him, the Dark Guardian filling up his vision, driving all of that back for a key moment. Ben had had to stop and recalculate the new variable, and Mikhael used it to hold his attention, help him rein it in.

"Be careful that your temper does not tip you back into darkness, because I will be there waiting for you," he said, low. In hindsight, Ben had realized it was a warning, not a threat, though at the time Ben had responded as if Mikhael had issued the latter.

"Bring it. That witch is scared of you, but I'm not."

"Only because you've learned fear is the true enemy and refuse to let it have you, no matter how foolish that is. Fear is often a wise guide. But I expect if you haven't learned that lesson by now, you never will." Mikhael lifted a hand before Ben could shove around him. Something in Mikhael's demeanor said Ben wasn't getting past him. Not without a hell of an ugly fight. Or the Guardian proving just how easy it would be for him to stop the advance of one mortal, no matter how pissed off.

"Darkness has lived within you," Mikhael said. "Almost claimed you. But it did not prevail. Do not let it prevail now. Your woman is here with you. Live up to her faith in you."

Which was exactly why he'd turned away from the call of that whiskey just now. The night he'd let his temper, that fear and darkness, take hold of him and he'd unleashed it on her, it had been helped by alcohol. He'd sworn that would never happen again. He'd gone a year without drinking to understand how not to use it as a dangerous crutch. He could drink now, and was glad for it, since he enjoyed the pastime, but he'd learned when he could. And when he couldn't.

Right now he couldn't.

Elagra's words had brought Amy back to him, and the girl had filled his vision, her cries hammering the inside of his brain. All those years ago, they hadn't registered, hadn't even penetrated his consciousness, until it was far too late.

He came back to the present, rubbed a hand over his face. "Sometimes it doesn't feel like there's anywhere you can go to escape it. The past. It's always tethered to you."

"Until you realize it's not a millstone," Raina said. "It is the classic story of the farmer and the mule."

She propped her head on her hand on the arm of the couch, her dark hair falling around the brace of her slim fingers. The sparkles on the rings she was wearing winked through the strands. The leg she had propped up on the couch put her foot close to Derek's thigh. Though Ben hadn't seen her clean them, the soles had no evidence of the different terrains they'd covered before coming back here, the painted nails still glossy and unchipped.

"Farmer and the mule?" Marcie ventured.

"The farmer gets so angry at his mule, he is going to bury him alive," Raina said. "So he puts him in a hole and starts throwing dirt into it. The mule starts stamping on the dirt, packing it down, and simply keeps stepping on top of it, until he is able to get out of the hole. At which point, I sincerely hope he kicked the farmer's brains out and went and found a kinder master."

Raina's green-gold eyes had settled into a burnished meld of both colors. "There is slavery in my past. Violation. A loss of every part of myself. I would not go through it again, not willingly, but I have used it to learn, and wield the power I have now. I have embraced love where love was offered and true." She glanced at Mikhael, a faint smile on her lips.

A touch of amused exasperation joined the expression, maybe because the Dark Guardian appeared to be taking no notice of them. His eyes were still closed, posture remaining straight and tall at the table. Both hands rested flat on the wood surface. "I found a better definition of myself, a stronger one," Raina said softly. She tilted her head back toward Ben. "As did you, though you still sometimes doubt it."

Derek reached down, gripped the witch's foot briefly, a squeeze, before returning his arm to the back of the couch. The gesture brought Raina's attention to him, and she inclined her head to the Light Guardian. "I forget you can sometimes be nice," she said.

Derek's blue eyes glinted. "Don't let it get around."

Marcie looked toward Mikhael. "What is he doing?" she ventured. "Some kind of meditation?"

Raina shook her head. "Checking in with his...boss. Telling him the status of things."

"Who's his boss? An angel, with wings like his?"

"An angel, yes. Lucifer. His wings are different. Black, but glossy and thick, with long, silky feathers."

"You've seen him? Lucifer? As in..." Marcie's eyes widened.

"Tail? Pitchfork? Horns?" Ben asked. "A trendy club in the heart of L.A.?"

"It is wise to show Lord Lucifer respect. He is not as kind and forgiving as I am. You will have to face him one day, Ben O'Callahan, and he forgets nothing."

Mikhael said all that without opening his eyes. But a moment later, he did, and there was a startling trace of crimson in the depths of his dark irises before it vanished. "It is time to tell us what the witch is talking about," the Dark Guardian said. "The night you gave her the key ingredients for whatever spell she's concocted."

It sucked to hear it put that way, to know that whatever Elagra had done that was now threatening New Orleans had involved him. But Ben wouldn't go down that road. She'd done it. Not him.

"Whatever happened with her, it made you who you are, to me and for me." Marcie took his hand. "Tell *me* what happened." A poignant smile played on her lips, though her eyes were suffering for him. "It's just us, in bed in the middle of the night."

The K&A men were a pretty insular group. Outside the guys, he didn't do a lot of sharing. But it was uncanny, how many times since Marcie had started sharing his bed, that he could speak to the darkness that cocooned them, say words against the curtain of her hair, inside the grip of her surprisingly strong arms, showing her more of himself than he had to anyone.

To the rest of "civilized" New Orleans, he was Ben O'Callahan, a kickass lawyer for Kensington & Associates, educated at some fancy college, yada yada yada. Not a kid Jonas Kensington had taken off the streets when Ben had made the best mistake of his life, trying to pick the man's pocket.

Fuck it. Time to just get it done.

He looked into her face, and shut the rest of his audience out. "Elagra gave me a place to sleep, food to eat when the gang was hunting me," he said. "She acted so kind at first."

His jaw flexed. "It's so fucking predictable, a kid hungry for a mom he never had. But she was no mom. And she didn't act like it for long. She had an eye for boys about my age then. She gave me food if I gave her what she wanted."

Marcie's gaze flickered, her jaw tightening.

He lifted a shoulder, stiff. "It wasn't a big deal. She never wanted sex for herself. Never wanted to be that vulnerable. She preferred to do stuff to me. Fuck with my head and body. Wasn't the worst thing that happened to me on the streets. But the way she did it... It lingered, in a way the other times didn't, perhaps because the others... it was just brutality and the streets, power, laws of survival. She was evil."

He said it flatly, no drama. When he glanced up, he saw Derek and Mikhael accepted the statement at face value. So did Raina, though her comprehension was obviously a little more personal. He saw it in the spark of fire in her gaze, the stab of her fingernails into the couch cushion. Or not exactly fingernails. Something that suggested claws. A blink, and the illusion was gone. Or maybe it was a reality she'd screened. Derek's expression was flat, but the set of his jaw said he had no tolerance for the likes of Elagra and a total, firsthand acceptance that evil existed, no shades of gray.

Marcie touched his hand, bringing him back to her before their close regard knocked him off track. "And Amy?"

He flinched, but that was where this needed to go. Marcie started to close her hand around his, but he couldn't do that, not and tell it straight. He slid his hand away, off the counter, but gave her leg a hard squeeze, softening the withdrawal, before he braced his other hand on the back of the adjacent bar stool. The cold metal cut into his palm, but that only made him want to tighten his grip, remind himself he was here. Not there.

"As you probably noticed, when all the lights are off down there, it's true dark. It's like a suffocating blanket, this claustrophobic weight that pushes in on all sides. One night she tied me to a chair and did that, took away all the lights. Don't know how she sees in that kind of dark, but she does. Normally."

He glanced toward Mikhael as Marcie swallowed. Raina offered a slight nod of acknowledgment, her glance going to her mate, who remained expressionless. Big surprise.

Ben looked down at Marcie's hand, still on the counter. Offered if he wanted, needed it. While his mind took him back to that night, the focus on it kept him in the here and now. Though he wasn't sure if that didn't make things a little worse, as he said the raw, vulgar words aloud.

"She made me jerk myself off while she screwed with my head, made me feel helpless, dished out pain until I was in a killing rage. One of the ropes she'd used to tie me up with snapped. So I thought."

He took a breath. He had to move away and did so, to an open spot between the living and dining areas. He had to stand alone, needing the space. The memories were too dense to allow anything close. He had to focus on keeping his head above the bog.

"Later, I realized she'd cut it. In that total dark, I jumped for her, grabbed her. I was totally out of my head. Hammered at her with my fists, with an old board on the floor. She was always collecting debris from the tunnels, bringing it into her living space, using it for different shit. The board had nails stuck all in it. Blood was on my face, my hands. Then she lit a candle."

He couldn't look at Marcie now. She would guess where this was leading. They all would. Instead, Ben found himself staring at Mikhael again. His face could have been carved of stone. It wasn't indifferent; he'd likely heard it all, seen it all. Whatever cosmic judgment was handed out for such a thing, he was just the guy carrying out the sentence, or the cop bringing the perp in, so saying it to him was like saying it to a priest, in an odd sort of way.

"You said I'd have to face your boss one day. Is that as reassuring as it sounds?" he asked. "A way to get clean, once and for all?"

What might have been a hint of surprise passed through his dark eyes, but Mikhael inclined his head.

"Okay then." Ben nodded, to himself. "Elagra had moved back, left Amy in her place. She'd hobbled her with rope so she couldn't get away, but her arms were free. I couldn't tell the person trying to protect herself from me wasn't Elagra. She'd taped Amy's mouth shut so she couldn't scream."

Amy had stopped being pretty long before Ben met her. Some guy had carved her up instead of paying her ten bucks for the blow job she'd offered him. So she'd learned to do other kinds of hustles. She also had a knack for talking restaurants into giving up their leftover food at night instead of tossing it into the trash. He remembered she'd scored him chocolate cake one night, the best piece of chocolate cake he'd ever had. She'd given it all to him, had only taken one bite. She said watching him savor every bit was better than eating it herself.

She'd been seventeen years old when she died.

"She had red hair. A brown eye. The other one was gone. And a laugh like a mule with laryngitis. But she could still laugh. Until that night."

Now everything had vanished except Amy, watching him eat cake. He was getting too deep. It was too fucking hard to dig this stuff up. He needed to skip ahead. He cleared his throat.

"So anyhow, it was as Elagra said, in that creepy way of hers. *'You gave me seed and blood, a murderous rage. The life of an innocent.'* I had hurt her badly...maybe, if I could have gotten her to a hospital, she would have made it. But Elagra wouldn't let me leave. Said I had to finish it, but she wouldn't push me."

Her voice had gotten that gentle note to it. The horrible thing was, even now, the memory of it brought back how badly he'd wanted that illusion of maternal love to be real.

You are a man, she'd said, her eyes fixed on him like a snake's. *You can decide when the suffering is enough.*

"Amy eventually begged me to kill her," Ben said. He knew his voice had grown as hollow as the dank and cheerless crypt they'd entered to seek out the witch. "Took me another half hour before I could. When I did it, Elagra called me a good boy."

His fists were clenched. The rage was there, boiling, festering. It was spreading out, wanting to take over. "I thought about going back down there, killing her," he said, his voice too flat, too emotionless. "So many times. Don't know why I didn't."

"Ben."

It was Derek who snapped him back into the room, with the one syllable spoken in a voice that was as calm and steady as the deepest part of the ocean. The Guardian had pulled in his feet, was leaning forward, his large hands braced on his knees as he regarded him with those ancient eyes.

"She is a powerful witch. Far more powerful than we anticipated. That power has increased over the years, but there is no doubt even then she was still far more than any mortal could have overcome. She tore up your soul, and some part of your subconscious knew how close she'd come to taking it altogether. If you had gone back as that child you were, you never would have left her again. The longer you're in the world she's created below ground, the more it holds you down.

She draws power from those who get trapped there. Staying away, you starve her."

"But someone always comes to feed her," Ben said. "Like that kid we saw tonight. She hunts us out. She's not trapped. She's got all her props and spooky magic show shit going on down there, but she goes above ground when she needs new meat, or has to do errands no one can do for her. She doesn't like to do it, since seeing her buying her own pickled eggs ruins the mystique, but sometimes she doesn't have a lackey to do that mundane shit. Hell...that's it. That's all of it. I need to leave for a bit. I'll be back in a few."

He moved abruptly toward the suite door. When Marcie started to rise, her brow creasing, he held up a hand. "No. Stay with them, brat. I'll be back."

Before Marcie could protest, he had his hand on the door latch, had turned, pulled it open and was through it.

Marcie would have chased him down, but Raina stopped her, rising from the couch and stepping in her path. Marcie shook her head. "I need to go after him."

"I think you need to hear what I have to say first," Raina said firmly. "And I think you already know he needs some space. You're just worried about him, but you know he'll be back. He said so. Let's go sit in the hotel bar and chat."

Marcie blinked at her, not sure how to change gears and be on board with that, but Raina forged on, her logic an irresistible force. "We'll regroup here when Ben comes back," she said smoothly. "Mikhael will let me know. That will give him and Derek time to go over some Guardian-level variables about all this, and for Ruby to get here. Even more importantly, Ramona will have opened up her store. We're going to need to talk to her, and it's easier to open a portal there, rather than at her home."

"Ramona?"

"A chaos witch," Raina said. "Elagra used chaos magic, tangled it with dark."

"Whatever is going to erupt out of the Mississippi will be enough to decimate the levies and flood out the entire city," Derek said. "Unchecked, it will be as bad or worse than Katrina. Especially if it disrupts the ley lines."

"Bourbon Street will smell better than it ever has," Raina noted. "Which might make it worth it. But regardless, this definitely calls for the insight of a chaos witch."

"Goddess help us all," Derek muttered.

"And the great Lord," Mikhael added. Then he closed his eyes and templed his fingers once more.

CHAPTER ELEVEN

*M*arcie knew Ben had killed before. He'd never spoken of the details, the who or how many, and she would never ask. Not because she couldn't handle it. She'd hear anything he ever needed to tell her, but that one fell in the same category combat situations did for Peter or Dana, who'd both done military tours in the Middle East. Some things a person didn't dredge back up unless there was an unavoidable reason to do so. And you didn't go there without their express invitation.

Like this. The things he'd done, that had been done to him, he kept buried deep, but never deep enough. He slept better now than before they were married, but more often than she liked she woke in the middle of the night, missing his warmth. She'd find him on the small balcony on the second level of their Garden District home, sitting silently in the night. Listening to voices of the past, centering himself with the peaceful stillness of the present.

Marcie shifted restlessly in the elevator, but when the doors opened and they stepped out, she hung back. "I really feel like I should check on him."

"You can of course do as you like," Raina replied. "But I think you should give him the space. Later he'll steep himself in you to handle the horrible things he just told us. But right now, he's collecting himself to deal with the tactical portion of our discussion."

"Like a boxer who's gone through a couple hard rounds, and is regrouping to come back into the fight."

"Yes."

Up in the suite, Raina had revealed, somewhat, how she had that insight, and Marcie knew enough about Ben to reluctantly acknowledge she was right. But it didn't make her struggle any less with it. Regardless, she followed Raina to the Carousel Bar. True to its glittering carnival appearance, the bar rotated, and so was always a popular spot, but they were in the small hours between midnight and dawn. She was surprised it was even open, but the one bartender and waiter were apparently doing some stocking and maintenance.

Raina didn't take them to the bar. She led Marcie into the lounge area, where intimately facing two-seat arrangements of deep wing-backed chairs were nestled up against the wide windows facing Royal Street. Raina slid into one and gestured Marcie into the other.

Even with Raina's energy buffered, Marcie wasn't surprised the waiter was almost on top of them before they settled into the chairs. He was a twenty-something with nose ring and a tattoo of a black dragon wrapped around his forearm. The design was revealed by the rolled-up sleeves of the dress shirt he wore under his hotel vest and with neatly pressed slacks. He had a bit of the computer geek look to him, with a husky build and intent, slightly squinted brown eyes behind wire-framed glasses. His nametag said *Simon*.

"A couple late night customers," he said. His voice had a youthful pitch, but was confident and affable. "Or early morning, depending on what you ladies are more comfortable calling it. Kitchen's closed for another couple hours, but I can scare you up some nibbles if you need them."

Raina didn't smile at him, but her gaze was warm. "Two Diablos, please." She looked toward Marcie. "In honor of the males we love."

"You got it. Two Diablos for the kind of women who could inspire a man to dance with the devil." He made a double thumbs up gesture at them and headed back to the bar.

Marcie lifted a brow, chuckling at Raina's pleased expression. "One of the many reasons I love New Orleans," the witch said. "Rich with colorful characters."

Present company included. Marcie realized Raina hadn't donned shoes, and no one in the lounge was saying anything to her about it.

Elagra's feet had been bare, too, neither witch obviously uncomfortable, despite the rough ground. As a result, Marcie would have expected Raina's feet to be callused. But, what seemed a lifetime ago, she remembered Raina on the bed, Mikhael lifting his mate's shapely leg to kiss her insole. Her feet had been soft and smooth, Mikhael's hands gentle and strong on them.

Like Ben's hands were when he touched her.

She wasn't surprised every thought was leading back to him. That was true on a normal day, but she particularly wanted to be with him right now. She hated for him to be alone with his demons, but Raina was right. Sometimes Ben needed his space. When it was time to share his pain, she'd be the one he'd come to for that. Literally. Giving herself a little breather made sense. Going right from one intense thing to another was a sure-fire way to lose perspective, miss details.

"Don't they hurt?" she asked the witch. "Your feet, like when you were walking in the tunnels?"

Raina shook her head. "Witches...certain types of witches, we pull a great deal of power from the earth, so it contours to us, so to speak. I don't get affected by gravel, sharp glass, that kind of thing, not as long as I'm connected to that energy. If my focus falters, well then, the relationship becomes less smooth. Like the relationship with many things."

Simon was back with their drinks. "Two Diablos," he said, putting them down with a gallant flourish. "The bartender put in a couple raspberries. Extra plump and juicy."

While instinctual and innocent, there was no way for a male to look Raina's way without his gaze touching on her generous breasts, the cleavage and appealing shape of them noticeable in the scoop-neckline of the cotton dress she wore. When he recognized how his glance and the comment might be put together, he colored up to his hair. "I mean...I..."

Raina chuckled and picked up the drink. "You intended no offense, young sir," she said, giving him a nod. "Don't distress yourself. You are a gentleman, through and through."

He recovered nicely, Marcie noted. Still flustered, but he sketched a credible bow. "My lady is very forgiving," he said with a courtly air. "My thanks."

There was a man who'd spent time at some fantasy cons for sure. And likely dressing up for them in some admirably detailed costumes.

The two women watched his hasty retreat and exchanged another amused look. It helped, Marcie realized. Doing this, taking her mind off things.

Raina lifted the glass to the light to study the red coloring and the several dark fruits floating in the top before she took a sip. "Oh, that's good. The blackberry and grapefruit work well together."

"And tequila always works," Marcie added, taking a healthy swallow. At Raina's raised brow, she shrugged. "Sorry, I needed a good shot there." Though she'd sip the rest, because when it came to drinking, she was a definite lightweight. However, the warmth it would spread inside her would help her loosen up further, let go of some of the darker things.

"Can I ask you about Mikhael?"

Raina had her lips wrapped around the slender black drink straw. The cocktail had given her mouth a distracting light gloss. "Depends on what you want to ask."

"Is he as scary as he seems?"

"He'd like to think so." Raina flipped her hair over one shoulder. Marcie could well imagine how the witch would use the move to goad Mikhael, their own provocative brand of foreplay. But then the witch's expression became more serious. "Yes. Scarier, if you're something he's hunting. Elagra knew that. Did you notice she wouldn't look at him? Part of that was her petulance, but the other part is in that environment, without any other reinforcements, she's outmatched by him, several times over. She won't get on his bad side unless absolutely necessary."

"That's reassuring." Marcie considered the enigma of the Dark Guardian. "He's so quiet. But not like shy quiet or even broody quiet. Or lake quiet. I can't put my finger on it."

"It's the silence of time," Raina said. "Time makes no noise. It just waits, watches. Marks the passage. There is nothing more powerful than time. It's unstoppable and eventually sees and knows everything. It predicts, it stores memory. It holds and captures the moment. Everything of importance relates to time."

Marcie digested that. "You're right. It's exactly that. How old is he? Late thirties, early forties?"

Raina shook her head. "You are an old soul in some ways. It makes it easy for me to forget you are mortal and not of our world, the paths we walk. Mikhael is over thirteen hundred years old."

Marcie nearly spit part of her drink back into the glass. "You're totally shitting me."

Raina chuckled. "Your old soul makes me forget just how very young you are. That brought it all back."

Marcie grimaced. "Now you sound like Ben. When he says that, I quid pro quo him. Tell him how often I forget just how immature he can be. Until he reminds me. Men can be such a pain in the ass. Thirteen hundred years old...wow."

She shook her head. "The quiet makes way more sense now. Scary, quiet, totally hot. That works."

"Yes, it certainly does." Raina reached out with her foot, past the small table, and tapped Marcie's sneaker braced by it. "He's a good male. Not kind, not of the Light, but his way is true, and I trust him with everything I am. He knows the line between Darkness and evil probably better than anyone but Lucifer, the Lord of Hell himself."

Marcie considered that. "So he can...I mean, something like Elagra. He could have ended her then and there. She certainly deserved it."

"She did, no doubt. But she may still be useful. Plus, while he has a certain latitude to be judge, jury and executioner, he exercises it carefully, and after some thought. Since it's impossible for most anything to hide from him for long, he has time to deliberate."

Thirteen hundred years old. That would give him a perspective far beyond hers, Marcie knew. Did that mostly answer her question? Or was it simply that the answer she really wanted was tied up with her fierce love for the man who'd been victimized as a child by Elagra, not a cosmic justice review? Even so, the question still felt unfinished. But she wasn't ready to ask the other part of it yet.

So she left it for now, in favor of lighter things. "Have you flown with him? Like Superman and Lois Lane?"

Raina laughed. "Yes. Once, when I was fighting an enemy and fell into a fiery abyss, he dove in, caught me before I could be swallowed by the flames."

"Righteous." Marcie imagined it, Raina tumbling through fire, Mikhael swooping in under her, an avenging angel, catching her and bearing her back up to safety. "But do you ever do it for fun? Like, 'hey, it's a beautiful day, let's go be birds'?"

Raina's laughter, while distracting, was genuine and female. "I need to talk to non-witches more often. Ruby and Ramona have little wonder about such things, as they are already part of that world. He has other ways of taking me off my feet," she allowed, "but if I wanted to do that, I'm sure he would take me for a flight."

She adjusted her chair so she could stretch out her legs, put her feet in Marcie's lap. Marcie comfortably laid her hand over her painted toes, studying them. "That's so weird. Your feet are so clean. Like you just stepped out of the shower."

"Also part of the magic. Though there are times when I want them coated by the elements for things to work properly, this is not one of them."

"Handy to protect your pedicure," Marcie noted.

"There is that."

Marcie leaned over to retrieve her drink from the table and used the straw to sip from it so she could leave one hand on Raina's feet. When the blonde tilted her head Raina's way, her brown eyes were thoughtful, and a little mischievous. There was no mystery to why Ben was so besotted with this one. Raina was ready to take her home and convince her to join the bordello. She'd fit right in with the playful sex demons, and would make Raina even more money, always an important consideration.

Regrettably, she suspected Ben would not be on board with the idea. The male would disembowel any customer unwise enough to touch her. An unfortunate stumbling block.

A smile touched her lips. Financially inconvenient, but not emotionally so. Since they'd been together, Mikhael had made it clear she would not intimately entertain any of her clients. Despite his advanced age, the Dark Guardian was emphatically monogamous. Something she'd come to appreciate more than she'd ever expected possible.

"So, is he a normal guy in some ways?" Marcie wanted to know. "Socks left out of the hamper, toilet seat left up?"

The question surprised another laugh out of Raina, and she didn't balance the surge of energy in time. Admittedly, it gave her a wicked spurt of pleasure when she heard a couple glasses get fumbled in the bar area. Mikhael was right. She did love to misbehave.

"He tells me I can choose. He can focus on getting socks in the hamper, or rescuing me from fiery abysses."

Marcie rolled her eyes. "Why does it have to be one or the other with guys? We manage to save their asses *and* keep toothpaste out of the sink."

"Hence the reason we are considered the superior gender. I think you and Ruby should spend more time together. You have her dry sense of humor. She also owns a gun store. She used to manage it, but she's turned the day-to-day operations over to John, one of her employees, to raise her son and help Derek. Regardless, firearms are a passion. From the comfortable way you handle yours, I suspect the two of you would have much to discuss in that area."

"Mmm." Marcie glanced toward the window. Her profile showed her expression had become pensive once more.

"Marcie." When the young woman looked toward her again, Raina met the gaze squarely. "As much as I'm enjoying our casual chatter about our men, I sense there's something deeper on your mind you're working toward. If I hadn't convinced you to take this time, it might not have sought the upper hand, but since it's just the two of us, it's starting to occupy your mind. So speak of it."

Marcie studied her. Between one blink and the next, Raina saw that her instincts were correct. When Marcie's gaze cooled, Raina saw what kind of police officer she would make. The young woman's back straightened, her hand tightening unconsciously on Raina's feet.

Raina didn't have the best relationship with law enforcement, whether they were from the mundane or magical realms. It had made her and Mikhael's initial relationship somewhat volatile. Yet over time she'd learned to be more appreciative—at least of his brand of authority.

She'd even learned to appreciate Derek more, for the most part. As a result, she didn't become immediately defensive as the girl spoke.

"When he didn't annihilate Elagra down there, I started thinking about it. And just now, you kind of confirmed it, the way you have to look at the big picture. I get that, but the big picture to people like you and Mikhael...it's a lot bigger than what we humans think about."

Marcie nodded to herself, as if approving her own choice of words, but then she lifted her gaze to meet Raina's again. "You're not human. Not fully. Not the biggest part of you. I know what you all told Matt, but he's as human as we are. Are Ben and I expendable?"

Raina blinked, startled. Marcie inclined her head stiffly, lifted a hand before Raina could say anything. "Ben has seen a lot of bad things in his life. Facing something like what we saw tonight, things come to the surface. Fatalistic things that scare me. He's tough, brave as hell, and will do everything to protect a woman or child, or one of the guys. Anyone who needs it. Or doing what he thinks is right. Whether he'll survive it..."

She shrugged, her own face getting more brittle. "That concern doesn't cross his mind. Deep inside, he never figured he'd survive to be where he is now, so every day since then has been borrowed time. He'll fight for me, for you, for whatever you're trying to accomplish, but I don't know if he'll fight for his own life."

She set her jaw, and now Raina drew her feet back as Marcie planted her own and leaned forward, those brown eyes sharp as drawn swords.

"So if your answer to my question suggests you aren't willing to fight just as hard for him as you would one of your own, I will do what's needed to get him to step back from this, and I'll fight as dirty as need be to make it happen. Because my life doesn't work without him in it. And yes, I will sacrifice New Orleans for it if I have to do so."

"I was wrong," Raina said after a moment. "I think you may be more like me than Ruby."

Before Marcie could get impatient and suggest she was dodging, Raina leaned forward, a mirror image to the young woman's resolve.

"I would burn the world down to protect what is mine. Mikhael. *Sweet Dreams*, and my family there. Ramona, Ruby. Cathair. And I do not bluff. I also will not lie to a woman who understands that feeling. Understand?"

Marcie nodded, a muscle flexing in her delicate jaw.

"Good. So listen and believe me. Mikhael and Derek are Guardians. One Dark, one Light, but they share a similar goal and mission. To protect the innocent. That includes those who are not-so-innocent, but who are fighting for the same purpose they are. Neither of you are expendable to us. That would be true even without us getting to know one another better, but," Raina let herself smile, though she knew her gaze remained hard and steady, "I am already very fond of you."

She sat back, her expression easing as she waggled a finger at Marcie. "And you should have figured that one out for yourself. Because even if none of that were true, Mikhael will not allow Ben to fall. It's a matter of male pride."

Marcie digested that. "Because Ben would be standing next to Death, talking trash like 'Yeah, the Dark Guardian acts like such a badass, but he couldn't keep me from getting dead.'"

"Exactly," Raina's smile deepened. Then she sobered. "We will work hard to keep you all safe, Marcie, as we would anyone else helping to protect others, as you are doing. You have my word. And Mikhael's."

"Okay." Marcie took a breath. "I needed to ask you that, because I expect Mikhael's not the kind to answer it straight out."

"Yes. Men over a thousand years old become even more monosyllabic than normal males. But be assured, it is felt to his very core. He is a cop, in your words, and Guardians are the purest, most uncorruptible face of that role. Sometimes both of them are so 'by the book' I want to hit them in the head with it."

Yet that quietness had a delicious side, Raina knew. As she'd said, it was the quiet of time, and the beat changed in the moment right before his lips were on hers. In that second, the universe experienced a dense, expectant pause. When Mikhael put his hands on her, he made her very aware of how powerful that one moment could be.

She'd once asked him how their relationship couldn't seem the same as any others he'd experienced over all those hundreds of years. The truth had unsettled her to the core. He hadn't had a significant relationship before her. Something about his one-quarter angel blood directing him to one lifetime mating, and one only.

Marcie sent her an impish look, back to that side of herself. "You're thinking about him. It's kind of comforting to know an all-powerful witch can get moony-looking over her guy, same as me."

"Yet I can still turn you into a frog for annoying me."

Marcie chuckled, ignored the threat. "I'll bet you can overlook that straight-laced behavior of his if it's balanced by other things. Thirteen hundred years of experience is a lot of time to get certain things right."

And then some. But Raina shrugged, studied her nails with a mock indifference that had Marcie grinning more widely. "That's what I tell him. He's far beyond having any valid excuses for ineptitude."

"What does he say to that?" Marcie asked, her expression one of female fascination.

"The challenge of learning all of a woman's needs, changing as constantly and unpredictably as they do, requires an immortal life span to conquer."

Mikhael had answered the question. Raina's mate was standing behind Marcie's chair. The young woman twisted around, startled. Mikhael looked down at her with an impassive expression that made Raina want to pinch him.

"But I do my utmost to keep up," Mikhael added gravely.

Her Guardian's wit was sometimes lost on the recipient, particularly when it made them think they had to run for their lives. Fortunately, Marcie was made of sterner stuff, and adept at picking up nuances.

"A humble man," she managed,

"He is many things," Raina said. "Humble is most definitely not one of them."

Mikhael's eyes glinted at her, but he nodded to their drinks. "Refill?"

"Absolutely. Don't make Simon piss himself. He's been kind to us, made us laugh."

"You are killing my joy." As Mikhael strolled toward the bar, Marcie stared after him.

"He has a sense of humor," she noted.

"Also something one needs to get through so many years. Or to deal with me. So he tells me."

Marcie sobered. 'I think it's pretty vital from the first moment of breathing, actually."

Raina noted Marcie joined her in visual appreciation. The two of them watched the tall male place the drink order and lean against the bar, exchange some conversation with the bartender and Simon. "Don't stare too hard," Raina said.

Marcie shot her a look. "You were outright ogling my man when he came down that rope. Quid pro quo."

Raina smiled, showing teeth. "Ribbit, ribbit."

Marcie grinned.

Though the conversation at the bar was casual, Raina noted a reserve to the men's responses to Mikhael that said they didn't feel the same relaxed rapport with him that they had with the two women. They might not know consciously what he was, but the deepest layers of the human psyche always knew.

She turned her attention back to Marcie when the girl spoke again, slowly. The question she had this time wasn't about life-and-death issues, but things far closer to the heart.

"When I first was with Ben...as much as I pursued him, when I got what I wanted, I worried if I'd be enough for him, for how much he needed and wanted, because of what he is."

The succubus side of Raina understood. Ben's appetites and needs were almost as deep as that abyss Raina had fallen into. The young woman had an overwhelming desire to please her Master, and he was not an easy one to please. His sexuality was shaped by his darkness, and it had the clear stamp of sadist on it.

Mikhael had no little amount of that himself, though the darkness was something with which he had a far more organic and balanced relationship than Ben did.

Marcie had a boundless sexual energy, with an intriguing mix of both dark and light to it. She was willing to stretch herself considerably, both physically and emotionally, to meet Ben's own astounding appetites.

"Were you worried that you might not be enough for him?" Marcie asked, looking toward Mikhael briefly. "I mean, he's a zillion years old. You won't...will you live as long as him?"

"No," Raina said softly. "I will live longer than a human, but not significantly so. He is immortal."

"That will matter not."

Mikhael had returned, the four words he uttered embossed with a heavier Russian accent. He put the drinks on the table but then closed his hand on hers, drawing Raina out of the chair. He took her place, bringing her back into his lap, nestling her down so she felt the promise of his always ready-to-be-called arousal against her backside.

She played it casual when she put one foot against the arm of Marcie's chair, the other back in Marcie's lap, under her ready hand, but her toes curled under Marcie's touch when Mikhael did what he did next.

Dipping his finger in the drink, he painted the liquid in a light reddish line along Raina's throat, trailing sensation there. She tipped her head away from him, lips parting as he sucked the fluid off of her flesh. Her eyes half closed. Though she'd tried to look at Marcie as he did it, offer the girl some pleasurable provocation, there were times the way he touched her took her deep into her head, into a world of heat, crimson swirls, honey sweet dampness.

When he lifted his head, he showed a hint of teeth and touched her chin to guide her face back to him. He caressed her lips with possessive pleasure.

"When you travel behind the Veil, *vedma*," he said, "I will find you. The afterlife is no barrier to me. You will never escape me."

"I'll hold you to that," she said, somewhat unsteadily. She couldn't think about being without him. She pushed that worry away and instead gave him a look every bit as uncompromising on the point as his was. He brushed her chin with firm fingers, but then he turned his attention to Marcie. Raina could tell it surprised the girl, that Mikhael would answer her question directly.

"The vastness of time doesn't matter, not when it comes to love. It happens when it happens, and there is never enough time to explore it the way the heart wishes."

Desperate need, insatiable hunger, and a fierce, overwhelming love were things he always gave her, making her believe he would always demonstrate them, in all he did for her.

His gaze came back to her. He'd heard the essence of that thought, because he answered her as well. "You will be the center of my universe, *koldunya*. My enchantress. In every moment we are given."

Raina's heart twisted. She curled her fingers against his nape, caressing his thick hair. They knew so much about one another, and yet there was still so much to explore. She'd never tire of it, and he wouldn't either. If he did, she'd turn *him* into a frog. She'd warned him of that, more than once.

His lips curved, and he brushed them over her mouth. He rose and turned, settling her gently back into the chair. He caressed her face before he straightened.

"Derek and Ruby are here. You have a few more moments, but come join us when you're done with your drinks."

He held Raina's gaze an additional moment and then left them, striding from the bar with a glance toward Simon and the bartender. He injected the look with a clear message. While Raina and Marcie were in their domain, he expected the men would watch over them. It made both of them snap to attention as if they'd been given an order by a commanding general.

And that was likely quite accurate.

"Wow," Marcie said, her eyes wide and mouth soft. "The vastness of time."

"Well, that's his take on it. I'm just using him for sex until I'm tired of him. But he's really, really, *really* good at it, so I think that will take a while."

Fire flitted across Raina's fingertips, a quick burn that threatened her manicure. It made her swallow a yelp and douse her fingers in the drink before it was ruined. She shot a narrow glance along the path he'd taken.

Marcie chuckled. "He also has really good hearing."

"Far too good." But then she yielded, giving in to her feelings for one precious moment. "There's no need to question it or doubt yourself, Marcie. If every time he touches you, it feels like the very first time, then you know. He touches you like that because he feels the same way."

CHAPTER TWELVE

When they returned to the room, Derek and Ruby were there, in deep discussion with Mikhael at the dining room table. Raina moved to join them but gestured to the balcony, drawing Marcie's attention to Ben's presence there.

Taking the cue, Marcie left their new friends to their planning.

Ben was on his feet, in front of the railing but not leaning on it. He had his hands in the back pockets of his jeans. One hip was cocked, along with the angle of his broad shoulders, and he seemed to be studying the city, which was outlined by a rose and gold sky limned with blue. Dawn had arrived. Maybe Raina had some kind of spell that would give Marcie an extra day's worth of energy, because she had a feeling the day ahead was going to be busy.

New Orleans was one of those cities that woke up at night and went to sleep in the morning. Maybe it was all the talk about magical energies that made Marcie notice it more than usual. The sense of vibration and electricity that had flavored the New Orleans night had faded away, replaced by a lazy hum, like bees going to roost in their hive. Bees probably didn't roost, but it worked in her head.

Ben turned at her approach. His smile didn't quite reach his emerald green eyes, but it came closer as she slid her arms under his, around his taut body, and pressed her cheek to his chest. He took his hands out of his pockets and folded his arms around her. In that one movement, he gave her his heat and strength, his clean male smell, the faint scents of aftershave and soap she knew. He'd showered, eradicating the smell of Elagra's world.

He put his lips to the top of her head, then tipped up her chin to settle his mouth on hers. The curve of his lips deepened.

"Diablo," he said. "Appropriate."

He had a drink sitting on the railing. When she reached for it, still standing in the span of his arms, and took a sip, she found it was a Jack and Coke. Mostly Coke, with just a splash of Jack, for flavor.

She put it down, rested her head on his chest again. "You know how you can do an Irish accent, or a Cajun one?" And when he spoke with either, it made her toes curl.

"Aye, lass."

She smiled. "I think you need to cultivate a Russian one, too."

He snorted. "I think you need to spend less time around bad influences."

She tightened her arms around him. She didn't say anything else for a little while. They just held one another and looked out at the city. Though, after a while, she did lift his left hand, tangled the fingers of it with her own. He had a big, strong hand, with fingers he called thick, but she thought of them simply as powerful, gentle or ruthless by turns. As their fingers locked, the morning sun flashed off her wedding rings. They were still a new enough accessory to catch her up, dazzle her in a silly way that would make him chuckle at her. It would also make something soften in his eyes, a confirmation that he felt it, too, in a male though equally wondrous way.

His fingers lapped over hers, tightened, as his arm shifted around her back. He slid a palm down into her jeans pocket so he could grip her buttock, hold her even closer.

She wouldn't hover. But he would know she was here, always, in whatever way he needed her. She was getting better and better at telling him that without words, the way he best heard it.

I love you so much. There is nothing I will not do for you. Nothing. As long as it's the best thing for you.

With Ben, she always had to add that caveat. It was the line in the sand she'd drawn. He'd learned, no matter how indomitable a Master he was, she'd never turn from it. Love trumped even Master, though it took that strongest force in the universe to stand against him when he had his mind set on something. The submissive nature that formed her center wanted nothing more than to please him in every way.

"Ben, Marcie?" Ruby was at the doorway. She was in an outfit similar to what she'd worn yesterday, jeans and a tank, only this shirt was burgundy with a slim strip of matching lace embellishing the edges. Her thick brown hair was pulled back in the same functional tail, but she wore a silver triquetra around her neck and ear cuffs etched with the same design. Her hazel eyes were tired, but sharp. "Think we're about ready to lay this out, if you guys are ready to jump in on it. But we had The Ruby Slipper deliver an early breakfast so we could all eat something first."

If Marcie wondered why they hadn't asked their breakfast preferences ahead of time, the question was answered, pretty quickly. When she stepped back into the room, Ben's hand at the small of her back to courteously guide her in ahead of him, she saw no less than seven bulging bags of takeout from the restaurant. It appeared they'd ordered some of everything, explaining why the Slipper, who normally didn't offer delivery, had done so.

They spread it out on the high kitchen counter as a buffet, and then everyone grabbed a plate. Amazed, Marcie watched as Derek piled his as high as possible without toppling it. He sat down at one of the stools on the opposite side of the counter to dig in. Mikhael's appetite was similar, though he appeared to prefer to fill his plate less ponderously and come back for more.

She, Raina and Ruby went for the more normal portions, and then took a seat around the dining room table. Ruby shot an amused look at Derek. "He'll likely get a second plate just like that. It's a good thing he has good table manners, else that would have been a relationship deal-breaker."

Marcie eyed Derek's muscular form. If he had a soft spot, she couldn't find it. And she was really looking because, well, she couldn't help that the room was full of men nice to look at. Three different, fascinating types.

Derek had taken off his hat inside the room, emphasizing those manners Ruby had mentioned. He had one of his boots propped on the base of Mikhael's stool, a comfortable camaraderie, and an interesting contrast, the alligator-type skin footwear propped so close to Mikhael's shiny Gucci loafer.

"Give me a reason not to hate them deeply," Marcie said. "Tell me they have to work out like fiends."

"They do have to stay in fighting shape, and that burns off a lot, but it's the use of magical energy, how Guardians use it," Ruby explained. "They can run through thousands of calories in one fight, but more than that, their connection to a lot of things, the way they monitor the energies around them, and in places far beyond what we see, requires an energy outlay as well."

"Okay, just as long as they're breaking a sweat. Even if it's not detectible to the human eye. And what kind of boots are those?"

"Dragonskin," Raina said, without missing a beat. "Normally he gets along with their species, but not that time."

Derek grunted in agreement, and continued eating.

Marcie gave Ben a wide-eyed look as he circled around the table. He shook his head.

"I don't think I'm even surprised," he said, and dropped buttered toast onto her plate. "You need more carbs for today. The bread is good. It's fresh."

She transferred some of her fruit to his plate. "The pineapple is, too. And seasoned with grated coconut. You'll like it."

He'd kept an apartment above The Ruby Slipper before they were married. She wondered if their new companions had known that, known how particular Ben was about his food. Though Monteleone had a good restaurant and chef for lunch and dinner hour room service, if they'd sent up the usual hotel room service breakfast fare of powdered eggs and dethawed fruit, he would have opted to starve.

Ben took the chair closest to the island. Despite their proximity to one another, there wasn't a whole lot of conversation between the men for the next little bit. At their end of the table, the women chatted comfortably, as women would. Marcie clued Raina in on good places to shop for clothes and shoes—after they saved the city, of course. She and Ruby discussed the best firing ranges, particularly the ones that allowed reloads and unjacketed rounds.

"I want an assault rifle like Dana's," Marcie said, shooting a petulant look toward Ben. "He refuses to find me a loophole on the permitting."

"Damn straight," Ben grunted. "I can beat you in hand to hand—"

"Barely," she said under her breath to Ruby and blinked innocently as he gave her a narrow look.

"—but give you an assault rifle? I won't have a chance next time I piss you off."

"It's a fair point," Ruby agreed, with a smile. "I tried to shoot Derek once. He turned the bullet into a flower. But that was because he saw it coming. It might do more damage if I have the element of surprise."

"She's given thought to this," Mikhael said to Derek. "Take that as a warning.'"

"At least she hasn't tried to turn me into a bug for her raven familiar to eat," Derek said between mouthfuls.

"That was merely a threat. She didn't mean it."

"Yes, I did," Raina said sweetly. She turned her attention back to Marcie and Ruby, and their conversation about shopping. "Ruby may act like all she cares about are her guns, but get her into a shoe store, and she loves her stilettos. Probably because of how much he likes them."

Raina tossed a glance at Derek as he handed over the salt to Mikhael, a wordless communication.

"She buys them for him," Mikhael said. "They make his ankles look so slim."

Derek grunted, ignored them all. "He takes his eating pretty seriously," Ruby explained. "We'll get down to business when he's done. The only thing that can distract him from a meal is Jeremiah, our son."

"Well, not the only thing. You in stilettos...and nothing else," Raina interjected slyly. Ruby nudged her with an elbow and rolled her eyes.

"Do you have pictures? Of your son?" Marcie added hastily as all three men looked up in unison. Raina burst out laughing, and earned a faint grin from Ben, a scowl from Derek.

"I do," Ruby said, biting back a smile. A small, handheld photo album appeared on the table before them, making Marcie jump back. She recovered with admirable aplomb, in her opinion. "Okay. No need to carry a purse if you're a witch."

"Nope. Unless you're in a public place. Kind of hard for people to miss you pulling things out of thin air."

"Which gives you an excuse to go purse shopping," Raina said. She drew the album closer to her and Marcie, and opened it up to the first page.

"Oh, look at him." Marcie studied a solemn-eyed baby, who gazed at the camera with unsettling forthrightness. "He's amazing. His expression...it's like he's saying..."

"Whose ass do I have to kick today?" Raina put in. "He is both his mother and father's child."

"Jackson Jeremiah Stormwind," Ruby said fondly. "We call him Jem. Sometimes Jeremy or Jeremiah. We're not sure which he likes best yet."

"Jeremy is a nice name, but I like Jem, too," Marcie said after a moment. Ben reached out and gripped her hand briefly. Marcie gave him a look that told him she was okay, and then offered another question, not wanting to draw attention to the emotional hitch the name had given her.

"Does he have magical abilities, being the child of a witch and a Light Guardian?"

"I'm all human," Ruby said. "My abilities were taught, though there was some natural talent there."

"Some," Raina mimicked. Derek shot Ruby a look that said she'd tossed out a serious understatement. Ruby lifted a shoulder.

"Okay, more than some. But my point is that the talent had to be learned, practiced. That said, magical ability at its most basic level is within most people's grasp, if they're willing to study and practice. And open themselves to what lies deep inside all of us. But Derek, he's not human, so it's expected his son will have some abilities that aren't exactly in the usual human gene pool. We don't know what they are yet."

"He never cries," Raina said. "That's already an improvement."

"Yes and no." Ruby looked at the picture of her son, her thumb moving over his serious face. A shadow crossed her expression. "I wish he would. He hasn't laughed, either. Sometimes he almost smiles. He watches, and listens."

She shook her head, trying to pass it off with a shrug, but Raina put her hand on hers. "Ruby, he's fine."

Ruby nodded, but her eyes stayed fastened on Jeremiah's image.

"It's as if he's waiting to see if we're going to do something awful to him. Or if we're really going to love him."

"Well, we aren't, and we do." Derek turned from the counter. "We love him more than I thought it was possible to love anyone, and that's saying something, since I love you with everything I am. He's good, baby."

The firm declaration, coupled with the endearment, was unexpected from the reserved Guardian. However, the combination of tenderness and ferocity revealed the truth of his words, how deeply his love for his wife and child ran. Though Ruby didn't move from the table, when her gaze met her husband's, Marcie saw her very soul gravitate to the shelter of that reassurance. Even a badass witch had vulnerabilities that needed protecting.

"He's come a long way, a hard road in his past life, to be in your arms," Derek told his wife. "When you wake from a lifelong nightmare, it takes time to believe you're no longer in it."

His gaze shifted to Marcie. "Though his soul did carry the same name in that past life, he is not your brother, Marcie."

Jeremy had died not too long after she and Ben had started dating, and his memory still brought bittersweet feelings. Like Ben said, she guessed she should stop being surprised at the things the group they were with knew or had experienced. But then she realized...

Ben's hand had stayed on hers, tightened, as her gaze shifted to Mikhael. Her heart pounded up in her throat. She couldn't ask. She wouldn't. Jeremy had been an addict, had wasted most of his life, but at the end, he found peace. Surely...

"Marcella," Ben said quietly. "Don't. Just don't. Don't do that to yourself."

Mikhael's profile was to her. She was certain he was hearing the conversation. He'd stopped eating, had the tines of his fork resting in the food, his gaze upon it. She didn't know what was going on in his mind, but he did not look toward her, his stillness a wordless reinforcement of what Ben was telling her.

There were things one didn't ask a Dark Guardian. But how could she not? How...

She closed her eyes. Thought of Jeremy the last time she'd seen him, the peace in the gaunt face. She thought of how Mikhael had spoken to Raina. The center of his universe. He was a male who served Lucifer. He also believed utterly in love, and the power it had.

That was her answer. She summoned the will to believe that with all her heart, and posed a different question.

"Who's with your son right now?" she asked Ruby.

Ben's firm grip on her hand tightened, and she saw a flash of deep approval in his gaze, fortifying her. She also saw Mikhael and Derek exchange a look, Mikhael making a slight nod, before he resumed eating. And Raina giving her a nod that told her she'd just made an impression. A good one.

"Ramona is with him," Ruby said, and some of her own shadows dissipated into a smile. "Which some might consider entirely irresponsible parenting, handing your baby over to a chaos witch, but there's no one we'd trust more."

"Except me," Raina said.

Derek scoffed. Raina narrowed her eyes at him. "It was not my fault that he liked the waterproof vibrator," she said haughtily. "It hadn't been used, after all. It had just been delivered and was sitting on the top of the open box. Gina turned it on. It sparkles, and there are these little balls inside that rotate. He was teething, and it's a good quality rubber for that, so she gave it to him."

"Which is why the vision of my infant son chewing on an eight-inch phallus is permanently seared in my brain." Derek sighed.

"Such a drama queen. Are you sure you want to keep him?" she asked Ruby. "He's so...old."

"Mikhael is older," Ruby pointed out.

"You didn't seem to mind that at one time."

"Whoa, hold the phones," Marcie said, her eyes widening. "Ruby and Mikhael—"

What she was going to say wisely got caught in her throat and stayed there as Derek proved there was another thing that could turn his attention from his food. The look he shot Raina could have left scorch marks on ice. Ruby gave her friend an exasperated look.

"Always poking the bear," she muttered.

Raina tossed her hair, but had the grace to wave her hand at Derek, a pacifying gesture that might have been equally inspired by the look Mikhael shot her, an unmistakable warning *and* admonishment.

The witch cupped a hand on the side of her mouth and spoke in an exaggerated stage whisper to Marcie. "Too soon."

"Which will be true for the next century," Ruby said under her breath.

It was a story Marcie would have been happy to hear regardless, but Ben pressed his foot on hers under the table. A different kind of warning this time, but a warning all the same. He'd partially finished his meal and had his other foot propped on the edge of the chair next to him. As he continued to eat from his plate, he scrolled through his new phone with the other hand. He'd ported in his email, so was tapping out messages.

Marcie noted he was close enough to the men at the bar to indicate he had no issues with them, but he'd distanced himself from the corner around which she, Ruby and Raina sat. That buffer distance that men seemed to like, being on the periphery of female chatter without being required to directly participate in it.

She assumed he was likely checking his work emails, a mundane but important thing. While New Orleans stood on the brink of annihilation, it was important not to get behind on the things the office needed. Because, well, if the world didn't end, work would go on.

Since Ruby hadn't asked anything about the things they'd discussed earlier, Marcie assumed Derek and Mikhael had brought her up to speed. She was glad, so Ben didn't have to rehash even the highlights.

"Matt said if he doesn't get a useful update soon, he's bringing the whole team in," Ben said, pausing on one note.

Mikhael pushed his now empty plate away, wiping his mouth with his napkin. "He should have one shortly. We may also need his assistance with some mundane logistics, if he is willing and able."

"Able, for certain. I don't think any of us really want to do what we're about to do. It just has to be done." Ben clicked off his phone, and tapped it on the table, a suddenly thoughtful expression gripping his features.

"Born," he said slowly. "She said born."

They looked his way as he squared himself with the table so everyone was in his view. "It won't erupt. It will be born. That's what she said."

"To a creature like Elagra, birth and utter destruction could mean the same thing," Derek pointed out.

"No." Ben shook his head. "She's completely nuts, but she's very precise, when it comes to certain things. She means what she says. It feels relevant."

"Then it likely is," Mikhael said. "Time to get our chaos witch on the line. I'll open a communication portal to Ramona."

"Maybe let Derek do it," Raina suggested. "Probably better to have her energy scrambling a Light Guardian's magic than a Dark One's. Since her chaos doesn't change the emotional nature of the magic. Just plays havoc with it."

"Good point," Derek agreed. Mikhael shrugged, conceding the issue.

Derek slid off the bar stool. He crossed the suite, taking a central position in the living room. As he faced the open balcony doors, he didn't reach for his staff, which stood in the corner. Instead, he slid his hands in his back pockets as he faced the New Orleans view, a seemingly relaxed pose that was likely anything but. It reminded Marcie of Ben's posture when she'd come back to the suite. The Light Guardian tilted his head a little to the left, as if considering a painting on an invisible wall in front of him.

Raina and Ruby stood and joined him, standing a few feet back in a loose semi-circle with Mikhael. Glancing at Ben, Marcie rose and followed, adding to the formation. Ben flanked her on her left. That was when she noticed the air movement in the room stilled. Energy pressed in against them, like when New Orleans had a humid summer day unrelieved by any breeze, everyone's least favorite weather in the city. One of the few things she wasn't going to enjoy about the job was having to be a beat cop in pounds of gear on those hot days.

That humid feeling began to lighten. At first, she didn't trust her eyes, but she knew she wasn't imagining it. It was like watching an actual painting being created in the air, an invisible artist brushing a clear canvas with swirls of translucent color. Blues in a variety of shades, a shot of fiery gold, a hint of red...

They began to swirl in a cohesive way, and a center opened in the middle. Rather than seeing the balcony and city view beyond, now she saw a place that wasn't *here*. It took her mind time to make sense of the input without context, but when she did, she was seeing what looked like the inside of an eclectic junk shop, filled with colors and textures, and a cozy sort of clutter.

Then she let out a shriek, as something hurtled through the opening, straight at her.

CHAPTER THIRTEEN

*E*arly on, she'd learned that Ben had an almost superhuman hypervigilance when it came to her well-being. As fast as the object was moving, his hand, his arm and part of his torso were in front of her before it made contact.

Which was why he was the one who caught the lop-eared, wriggling rabbit against him.

As he shifted with a surprised curse, Marcie caught the next one that came somersaulting through, end over end. Black and white speckled, with enormous back feet.

Apparently, it was raining rabbits. A quick glance around the room showed at least a dozen, scattered on the floor, the coffee table, the couch.

She would have expected the one she was holding to scratch the daylights out of her, but the female seemed nearly as perplexed as Marcie. The speckled creature gazed up at her with wide eyes, her nose twitching at high speed. Ben's was gray with white feet. It was currently trying to work his way up his chest and sniff at his neck, making him squirm in a way that Marcie had to admit was more than a little adorable.

Raina had two in her arms. The witch appeared remarkably calm about being pelted with small mammals. She adjusted and cradled the two bunnies like newborn twins against her ample bosom and stepped closer to the opening to another world, time, dimension. Marcie wasn't going to limit the possibilities.

"Ramona, what are you doing?" the witch asked. "Where are you?"

"And where is our son?" Ruby added. Derek had a baby rabbit sitting on the toe of his boot. It was sitting up on small haunches to wash its furry face. Ruby stood at her husband's side, her hand on his arm.

"Raina? Ruby?" the voice came from a muffled distance, and then a woman with long, straight red hair appeared in the opening, blinking at them with lavender grey eyes. She'd emerged from behind a stack of old books, topped with what looked like an unstable miniature tree made of peacock feathers.

"Oh, there you are. I couldn't figure out how I was hearing your voices, but the rabbits kind of interfered with the portal hail. 'Hail' as in greeting, not balls of ice. Hellfire...hold on a sec. Silas, can you...he's headed for the...oh, okay, he's got him."

"Who is headed where?" Derek asked tersely.

"The rabbits," Ramona assured him. "One of them was headed for the door of the shop, and I had it propped open, though with a baby gate up, don't worry." Reaching down, she lifted Jeremiah into view, which relaxed the line of Ruby and Derek's shoulders almost simultaneously.

The child curled his hand in her crimson hair and chewed on it thoughtfully, reaching out his other hand toward the portal. Ruby lifted her hand, and Marcie saw a tendril of that colorful energy reach through, touch him, since apparently they couldn't physically reach through, rabbits notwithstanding.

While she'd said the baby didn't laugh and rarely smiled, there was no doubt how he reacted to his mother and father. That touch of familiar energy gave him an instant ease of expression that conveyed pleasure. A tentative happiness.

"He's been helping me with the inventory, haven't you, Jem?" Ramona said.

"Why all the bunnies?" Ruby asked. "And why is your hair red?"

"It's normally gold," Raina murmured to Marcie.

"Oh, you know how it goes. I just wanted a change. On the hair, that is. As far as the rabbits, I'm doing a top hat display, each top hat decorated a different way, and I started thinking you know, to connect to the magic shop side of things, I'd put stuffed bunnies around the display. So I'd ordered this box of them in different sizes and colors, and Jem was so taken with them. I thought about how much he'd like it if I could turn just one of them into a real bunny for a few moments. Oh crap, sorry..."

This time Derek intercepted, neatly catching the next pair that jumped through. The baby bunny on his boot had hopped off to places unknown. Mikhael studied two more at his feet, one nibbling at the cuff of his tailored slacks.

"Communication portals aren't supposed to allow corporeal passage, just sound and image," he said.

"I know that," Derek told him, with a touch of annoyance. "You think I'm capable of upending the laws of portal protocols that have been set in magical stone for millennia? Only a chaos witch can do it."

"Inert," Mikhael said. Suddenly, all of the rabbits in the room were stuffed animals again. However, since he'd issued the command while the one at his feet was in mid-nibble, it was now fixed to the cuff of his pants like it had been sewn there.

Raina hid a smile behind her hand when he raised a baleful gaze to her. "Serves you right," she said. "Marcie was enjoying cuddling hers."

"And getting way too attached," Ben said. "I'm grateful."

"Rabbits can be litter trained you know," Marcie said, waving the floppy ears of her now stuffed black and white rabbit at him.

The mysterious Silas came on screen, so to speak, though Marcie wasn't sure that was the best description. It felt like they were only a few feet away, where she could reach through the opening and put the rabbit down on the worn-to-silk wood counter of the shop's checkout area. She could even smell the mixture of scents from the place. Paper, silk flowers, velvets and candy. Except for candy, she'd never noticed the aroma of such things, or realized she'd recognize them when they touched her nostrils. And of course, she smelled rabbits. The warm body in her hands had had such a rapid heartbeat

Silas was a tall man, his height emphasized by his leanness, but Marcie wouldn't consider him slight. He stood straight and had a dense strength to him, like a gray tree in a forest, a conifer of some type, maybe a fir, whose needles made a rushing whispering noise when the wind blew through them. His eyes matched that same silver-grey-green color that would have tinges of blue-green in the right light.

When those eyes turned their way, he paused over each one of them. Marcie swayed, for it felt as if the universe took a breath when his attention was on her. Something in him reached out, touched, held and examined her, before easing back. But not before giving her a reassuring push of warmth to let her know the probe had not been done with any harmful intent.

His gaze passed over Ben, but Ben's hand rose, a warning, and his expression hardened.

Silas's brow raised, but he inclined his head. He brought his attention back to Ramona, where his gaze dwelled with a different type of focus. His regard was no less distracting to the subject. When Ramona looked at him, the woman seemed to lose her train of thought and forget they were there at all.

Marcie noticed Raina and Ruby exchange a significant look. Raina's full lips pursed, and the concern in her expression matched Ruby's. The two witches obviously had some sisterly trepidation about the woman's relationship with Silas.

But since now clearly was not the time to address it, Raina brought them back to the matter at hand. "Ramona. We need your help."

"Yes. Of course. Anything." Ramona pulled out of her absorption with Silas. Giving Jeremiah an extra squeeze, she put him back down on the floor, pausing a moment to ensure whatever he was doing would keep him properly occupied. Then she squared off with the portal, a smile crossing her face that lacked self-consciousness of any kind.

"Sorry. Silas has the oddest look sometimes. Like a puzzle he's trying to solve, and it's me. Not really sure if he's looking for a response. I don't want to be difficult for him, but I don't think he's going to figure it out from looking at me, you know."

"Have sex with him. Then he won't care if he can't figure you out," Raina said dryly. "In the meantime, New Orleans is having a bit of a crisis."

Ramona's gaze widened, then sparked with female annoyance at the other witch. Silas coughed and turned slightly away. Marcie was pretty sure he was hiding a smile. But from the way he'd gazed upon

Ramona, she didn't think he'd oppose Raina's plan. At least the first part. He looked like a man who enjoyed figuring things out.

"Someone here who calls herself a chaos witch is in the middle of it," Ruby said in her no-nonsense way. "The bad thing under the river is the work of a creation spell she rendered."

Instantly, Ramona's demeanor changed, her expression hardening. "Tell me what she said. Exactly."

Raina spent a couple minutes relaying the Elagra meeting details, throwing in some terminology Marcie expected meant something to the Guardians and witches, since they seemed to be following the conversation without questions. She got the gist of it, though.

A movement in her arms drew her attention. Her bunny was once again alive. Ruby cut her gaze toward Marcie and gave her a quick wink before tuning back into the discussion with Ramona.

Ben was close enough her elbow brushed his upper abdomen. Marcie looked up into his face to find he was gazing thoughtfully down at her and the bunny.

"We already have three feral cats, who are about as feral as goldfish in a bowl, thanks to you feeding them, getting them fixed and vaccinated," he reminded her in a low voice. "I left my office window open the other day, on the second floor I might add, and came back to find the black and white one curled up in my chair. He hissed at me. In my own home."

She smiled, looking down at the rabbit, smoothing back the floppy ears. She felt Ben's hand do something similar to the hair along her temple. "Tired, brat?" he murmured.

"Yeah. But like a kid at a macabre kind of Disneyland. Too much to see to go to sleep, but I think I'm going to have to crash for a few hours before we keep at it, unless they have some hocus pocus way of removing the human need to rest."

"Hmm." His arm settled around her shoulders, encouraging her to lean.

During the briefing, Ramona took a seat on a stool by her cash register, crossing her ankles and folding her hands in her lap. Her lavender eyes were still, her attention on them now unwavering. Silas had moved behind the counter and leaned on it, his elbows on the wood and interlaced fingers in a loose knot. When Ramona took a hand out of her lap and rested it on the same surface, they were almost close enough to touch. Marcie could see the thread of energy connecting them. Either they were already involved, or it was going to happen a lot sooner than later.

When Raina was done, Ramona closed her eyes. She didn't say anything for a few moments. Because it was obvious that she was turning over some pretty weighty thoughts, no one else said anything, either. Until she did.

"He's right," Ramona said. She pointed at Ben to indicate who she meant. "Absurdly handsome man with dangerous eyes. She meant born. It is a child, of sorts. It's best to relate to her as a child."

"How do you know it will be a girl?" Mikhael asked.

"Because Elagra has no respect for males. She has a deep loathing and fear of them. It matches her equal hatred of women. She's an island, isolated by her evil, evil simply being a word that means cutting yourself off from all good, so you have no empathy, no connection to balance."

"But she's a chaos witch, like you?" Marcie asked. "She seemed to refer to herself like that."

Ramona cocked her head, taking her in at a glance. "Hello there. Yes and no. She's a witch, but Elagra is an agent of destructive chaos. I'm creation chaos. We're two sides of the coin, somewhat like Derek and Mikhael, only an agent of destructive chaos is typically only dedicated to the destruction, if they let themselves forget the balance. They're the child that forever tears down the building blocks of another child to see the reaction, the tumult. She particularly exults in her victims who fall so deep into her darkness they lose their own way to the light."

"Sounds like her," Ben commented in a flat voice.

"An agent of destructive chaos feeds on the pain and despair of others and takes no pleasure in the ability of the spirit to overcome and rebuild," Ramona agreed. "She seeks the silence of the void, not the stillness of peace."

Her tone took on an urgent note. "But defeating Elagra isn't the focus here. She's a distraction. She's evil, but what she created isn't. It doesn't have a malicious intent to destroy the city. The egg just got too big, was nurtured too close to a populated area."

Derek glanced at Mikhael. "That explains why we didn't detect it, even though it's been growing all this time. A natural event like child-birth wouldn't register as a problem."

"So that means whatever Elagra is doing to prepare for the 'birth' is what set off our radar," Mikhael agreed. "She'll want to make sure the event is a violent one, capable of disrupting the ley lines and creating the destruction she craves."

Ruby frowned, thinking. "So if what was created could be contained..."

"Not in the prison sort of way. And calmed, not contained." Ramona waved a hand and then blinked as she found herself twirling a pair of handcuffs. She laid them down on the counter without missing a beat.

"I'm thinking we should consider a way to cocoon her, so she can be transported to a dimension and place where she has room to grow and be. In order for that to work, we need to figure out how to make her birth a calm, happy experience."

Ramona's eyes turned to Ben. "Getting her attention when she first emerges is key."

Ben glanced at Mikhael. "Why is she looking at me when she says that?"

"Because you have the only direct link to her," Mikhael said. "She will recognize the connection, much as Jem does with his parents."

Ramona's attention shifted. "You're worried about nothing, Ruby. Jem's okay when I tell him you're coming back soon, but he wants me to remind him that's the case about every other hour."

"He's talking?" Ruby said, startled.

"No, of course not. But ninety percent of language is nonverbal. For babies like him, ninety-nine percent." She hopped off the stool, circled around behind the counter, to a wall of cabinets. "Okay, what's the perfect book...the perfect book..."

"Wait," Ben said. "Elagra's assertion that I helped create this isn't the same as saying I'm the giant monster's dad."

"Yes, it actually is," Ramona said. "But fortunately for all of us, Elagra is definitely not her mother."

Silas obligingly moved over as she bent to rummage in the cabinets directly behind him. Her voice was muffled, but they could understand her. Ben had tensed, his eyes fastened on the portal opening.

"It was your seed that fertilized the egg," Ramona continued. "Elagra created the egg out of dark magic, but she couldn't give it the life spark without actual life. Creation magic that draws from the natural way of things. You can only leave nature and balance out of the equation to a certain point. It's why everything seemingly evil has a backdoor, a way in, to call it back to balance."

As she began to drop handfuls of various things on top of the counter, Silas's quick reflexes kept them from rolling off. She sent him a distracted smile, put down a fistful of neon-colored plastic spiders. They instantly became animated, scuttling off in every direction.

Marcie stepped back. "If those come through, I'm not catching one. I don't do spiders. How on earth does she pass as normal when she gets customers?"

She directed all that to Ruby, keeping her voice low, since she didn't want Ramona to think she was being rude. The chaos witch seemed absorbed in her hunt beneath the counter, however.

"It's partly a magic shop." Ruby smiled. "The customers think it's parlor tricks and sleight of hand when things like that happen. But it's more than a magic shop, too. There's a little bit of everything in it. If you need a picture to make your living room feel cozier, you'll find just the right thing there. It will project a welcoming energy to those who come into your house. It will never hang straight, and may occasionally seem to rearrange itself, the picture that is, though you can't clearly remember the original arrangement, so you doubt not only your eyes, but your mind."

"Of course." Ramona was back with them. She had a small book cradled in her hands. "People think chaos is random, but it never is. It just gets to where it's going in an unpredictable way. Ha! I knew it wasn't only about the top hats. The rabbit thing, that is."

She lifted the book, which had two rabbits on the front, a bigger one bent attentively to a smaller one, suggesting parent and child.

"It's a children's book, somewhat your typical bedtime story, talking about how much the parent loves the child, but it's uniquely charming and rhythmically repetitious. It's the perfect structure for the spell craft. I can use the physical book as the focus. See? It's one of those hard page ones, and shiny, so it will be resilient to water. Until it gets really doused."

An amused smile crossed Derek's handsome mouth, but his gaze was thoughtful as he considered it. "An attraction spell. It activates and gets the beast's attention with the first line. As each subsequent stanza is called out, the power builds, layer upon layer."

"Exactly. We won't use the actual words, only the spirit of them, since we have to use words that align with the essence of the one executing it. As that power builds, it also builds the chaos spawn's sense of security, so that as we wrap her up to move her, it will feel like we're wrapping her in a blanket, not binding her in ropes. It's no different from you and Jem."

Ramona's gaze slid to Ruby. "There's an instinct for that connection with our parents. A parent can destroy that connection, as your mother did with you, but the initial bond was strong enough that you stayed with her, long after you should have, right?"

"Without a doubt," Derek said. Ruby shot him a glance, her mouth tightening.

Ramona waved a hand, avoiding the obvious old argument. "That's how strong that connection is. But in those very first few moments, there is no questioning it. That's our window of opportunity. We just need to keep her attention on Ben, and he can reassure her that what we're doing is okay, while we swaddle her up in a warm blanket of magic to transport her."

Marcie saw everyone was nodding. Well, everyone who understood what Ramona was talking about. Her husband, however, was scowling. His expression had morphed from confusion to annoyance, to a few emotions that obviously fell in the not-pleased category.

"You want me to read her a bedtime story," Ben said. "I'm re-thinking the first thought I had on the parking deck."

"What was that?" Ruby asked.

"You're a bunch of nuts from a Cosplay con."

"Oh, I love going to those." Ramona beamed widely. "You can dress up as whatever you want." Her gaze slid over him. "For what you're about to do, you'll be fine wearing what you're wearing. But you may want foul weather gear, rain boots, because you're going to get soaked, no matter what."

Ben rubbed a hand over his face. Temper was about to go from simmer to boil in his eyes. Thankfully, Raina stepped in to expand on Ramona's plan of action.

"The root of good magic is in focus," she said. "When she

emerges, she will be quite...large. Getting her attention in a positive way is a challenge. Ramona will put a focus spell on this book, so that when triggered, it will initially project itself like a tap on her shoulder, a tug of her ear. As you continue to call out the words that match the spirit of the book, but come from your heart, your experiences, the spell will unfold, wrap around her, calm her. That will give us the moment we need to create the cocoon around her she describes."

Ben stared at her. Shaking his head, a sharp movement, he went to the couch, propped his hips on the back of it, stretched out his legs before him. As he crossed his arms over his chest, he looked toward the ceiling. "We're dealing with something big enough to disrupt the floor of the Mississippi, cause an earthquake that will swallow New Orleans. To avoid that, we have to convince her to tiptoe out of her egg, pod, whatever. And our great idea for that is reading her an improv bedtime story."

"Exactly," Ramona confirmed. "What's more soothing than a parent reading a child a bedtime story?"

"What's the rest of the world going to be doing?" Marcie interjected hastily, as Ben's fiery green gaze snapped down from the ceiling. "I mean, how are we going to have the time and space to do this with every law enforcement agency in the state descending on us, along with the news media and any idiot who wants to record it on a cell phone?

"Ruby and Derek will craft and hold a shield on the river to screen our activities from viewers," Raina said.

"Along the whole river?" Marcie asked incredulously.

"No. We have a pretty good idea where she is emerging," Ruby said. "We've been studying the ley line patterns for several weeks. It will happen in front of the Aquarium and mall."

"Of course. The most popular section of riverfront in New Orleans, aside from Jackson Square." Ben shook his head. "Any way to keep her asleep?"

"Keeping her dormant is like trying to keep a baby from being born," Derek responded seriously.

"The only way to do that is kill her in the womb," Mikhael said. "It was an option. Still is."

Ramona's gaze went him, her hands falling to the counter to grip the edge. "She's an innocent."

"Many innocents get sacrificed in the turn of the wheel. Regrettable as that may be, it often keeps the wheel moving the way it is intended," he said. "Those rabbits feed many wolves."

A chill ran up Marcie's spine. He was serious. His eyes went peculiarly flat and dark as he spoke.

Derek didn't disagree with the Dark Guardian, but there was a tightness to his expression that said it wasn't his normal *modus operandi*.

"Marcie." Ruby spoke, drawing her attention from the unsettling male. "Protecting the world isn't nearly as glorious and clean as people imagine it might be. Hard choices often must be made."

"But in this case, sacrificing the rabbit is our last resort," Ramona said sharply, her lavender gaze suddenly sword sharp and directed at Mikhael. "Right?"

"Of course," he said mildly. "But we also need to be alert to threats far less innocent in nature." His mouth tightened as his gaze swept the others. "Elagra will want to witness her triumph. She will come ready to fight. We have inadvertently let her know there will be active opposition to her plan."

Ben straightened from the couch. "Assuming Elagra's right about the *when* being the new moon, we're at less than a day and counting. And we're still standing here."

"We have time to get what is needed in place," Derek said. "As we said at the beginning, this is often our usual lead time for such things."

"Glad it's a routine day at the office for you guys. But I'm not feeling hugely reassured to hear that." Ben drew out his cell phone. When all eyes turned to him, he hit a button and lifted the phone to his ear. "Out of every insane thing I've heard here, there's one I can address in a practical way."

He turned his attention to the phone. "Hey, Matt. Yeah, I'll catch you up in a minute, but we need to pull in favors from our utility contacts, and probably throw in some serious bribery. We need to shut down the Aquarium section of riverfront before midnight tonight."

Ben glanced toward Mikhael. "No way to do a C-section of sorts, do it on our timetable?"

"Her birth must happen naturally; else it would be even more frightening and alarming to her."

"Just like a female. The rest of us have to stand around, waiting on her to get ready." Ben sighed and moved away to the balcony, continuing to work out logistics with Matt. Marcie expected there was going to be some creative cursing on both sides. Ben was also going to have his work cut out for him, convincing Matt and the others to stay clear of this. She understood his urgency. While she didn't understand everything that the Guardians and witches were planning, there'd need to be a lot of oversight happening on the "mundane" side of things, to keep people safe. Matt and his team would excel at that, even though they would hate letting Ben and Marcie stand on the front line alone.

She looked at their four companions, and remembered what Raina had said down in the bar. Ben just had to convince Matt that they wouldn't be alone.

"Crazy as it sounds, I sort of understand what his job will be," Marcie said to Raina. "What will mine be?"

"You and I will have Elagra. You'll be my backup when she shows up to cause trouble. If she interferes, we will take her down with the level of violence necessary, magical or physical."

Marcie's lips curved in a feral smile. "How broad is your definition of necessary? Because when it comes to her, mine is as wide as the fucking ocean."

"Oh, I like her," Ramona said.

CHAPTER FOURTEEN

*C*onvincing Matt and the others not to get involved had been the hardest task so far, enough that Derek had murmured something to Ruby about a spell to take away memory. But Ben didn't want them fucking with his boss's head, or any of his brothers, so he used every argument in his persuasive lawyer arsenal. Including the less fair ones.

"You have a daughter," he told Matt on their final phone call about it. Final, because in about an hour they'd be on their way to the waterfront. He had to make sure Matt and the others weren't there. "Get her the hell out of New Orleans in case the worst happens. Or at least to a higher elevation. Get all of our family somewhere safe, so I'm not worrying about them. These guys...they know what they're doing."

He knew shit about magic, but his experience with Elagra had told him it could be powerful in the wrong hands, or the right ones. Despite his admitted incredulity over the plan they were contemplating, his brief experience with Mikhael, Raina, Ruby and Derek told his gut they were the right hands. They were every bit as accomplished as they believed they were. A person skilled in their chosen field projected a certain kind of confidence, and they all had it.

"You know when we have the right number of people on the job, and any more are just going to create fuck-ups?" he told Matt. "This is that point. I'm not bullshitting you." And he wasn't. For one thing, there were three people in his life he couldn't bullshit. The first had been Jonas Kensington. His son had that same superhuman radar for a lie.

Marcie had become the third. She might not question or call him on it the way Matt would, but those big brown eyes would tell him she knew exactly what kind of line he was feeding her...or himself.

"I know you guys would stand with me until the end," he said gruffly to Matt. "This isn't about that, or me being noble. If we fail, or even if we don't, you guys will be needed to help with recovery, same as with Katrina."

Matt paused a long moment, during which Ben could feel him struggling with it. It was hell and gone from his nature to stand back while any of those he saw as his family stood in the path of danger. When Peter had been in Afghanistan, it had sucked for all of them. The anxious gnawing in the gut never went away. Half of them tried to tune out news reports, while the other half tracked them like hawks.

"Fine," his boss said at last. "But only because Marcie is going to be watching your ass."

Ben snorted. "If I could tie her hand and foot and dump her on your doorstep, I would."

"Yeah, I'd like to see that."

"You don't think I could take her?"

"I think we could lay bets on how many broken bones you'd have before it was done, but yeah, you could. The problem is you could never untie her, because when you did, she'd shoot you in the balls. And then beat you to a bloody pulp with those tiny, lethal fists of hers."

Ben's gut eased at the low-level teasing. Matt was going to trust him on this one. But Ben knew what that could cost his boss. His friend and brother. "You've been busting your asses to get the water-front evacuated while we've basically been living it up in this hotel suite, napping and watching the clock. You've done enough, I prom-ise. I'll keep you posted, but Matt, whatever happens, you're making the right decision. I promise you that."

"Survive this, both of you, so I'll be sure of it."

"Do our best."

When he clicked off, he went to the bedroom. Mikhael and Raina were in their suite. Marcie had wanted a shower before they got ready to go. He'd joined her for that, but had left her to her post-shower prep to make those last couple calls, tie up some loose ends.

As he came into the still steamy bathroom, he discovered her standing in front of the large mirror over the sink. She was wearing her panties and bra, and she was still and quiet, her head dipped down.

"Marcie?"

She had her fingers on the solid silver band that rested just above her collar bones. The circlet of stainless steel had a key pin locking mechanism in back and an etching of forget-me-nots on the front. She liked calling them forget-me-knots, with a k.

Her collar. She rarely took it off, the symbol of his ownership even more a part of her than her cherished wedding set. He met her gaze in the mirror. Holding it, he fished the tiny wrench out of the watch pocket of his jeans. Her lips trembled slightly as he pushed out the pin. Before he could remove it, her hand shifted, closed over the collar fully, tightening.

"I can't wear it during a fight," she said. He knew that. Working for Savannah, she'd been able to wear it pretty regularly. As a cop, she wouldn't be able to wear it on the job, couldn't wear it to her current academy training classes. She knew he knew that, but he realized she was telling herself that, warring with herself over it.

Gently but firmly, he took the collar off her, his fingers caressing the bones at the base of her delicate throat. He fitted the pin back into it, laid it on the counter.

"Look at me," he commanded.

"I never stop," she said.

Curving his hand over her throat, he lowered his other hand out of view of the mirror, passing over her firm buttock. He traced the seam of her ass with his thumb as he found his way lower, and under. She adjusted for him, opening her stance, and bit her lip as he found her, rubbed against the already slightly damp fabric. He tightened his grip on her throat.

"The collar's always there," he said. "Right?"

She nodded. Dropping his grip from her throat, he hooked his thumb in the lace connector between the bra cups, tugged and twisted. He pulled them up so the underwiring pressed against the tops of her breasts, revealing her generous curves to him, quivering with her quick breaths, her nipples tight. She was a gorgeous woman physically, from head to toe. But her *beauty*, a word that had so much meaning that it could hit him in the chest and take his breath, had very little to do with her outside appearance.

He nudged her head to the side to dip his own down, touch her mouth with his lips, take a bite of her full bottom one.

"You forget how to address me, brat?"

"Yes, Master," she corrected herself, her pupils dilating and that breathiness increasing. "The collar is always there."

He hadn't donned a shirt, and had only threaded the belt into his jeans, hadn't buttoned or buckled them yet, so it was easy to push down the zipper one handed, moves slow and deliberate as he watched her in the mirror. Her eyes were fastened on him, her lips parted, breath shallow.

He put a hand against her nape, palm sliding down to spread over her back, between her shoulder blades, push her forward so she braced herself on the counter. He pulled down her underwear and pushed her forward onto her toes.

She moaned as he went into her. He didn't hurt her, but he didn't take his time either, letting her feel every inch of his substantial length. She was as wet inside as she always was for him. He settled himself to the root.

"Always, Marcella," he said, his eyes boring into hers. "The collar is just a symbol. The damn thing is branded onto you, so even when you're not wearing it, I see it. And you feel it, don't you?"

"To the soul, Master." That last syllable went up as he thrust in harder. Her lips parted, her tongue touching one in a way that made him wish there was time to put her on her knees, make her go down on him after this, but they were on the clock.

He'd make this count, and damn well make up the difference later. "You'll come while I look at your face and think how goddamn lucky I am."

She tried to look at him, too, as he built her up higher and higher, as her cries grew thin and pleading, as she went over, grabbing hold of his arm for support as she writhed and bucked against his grip. And then he held her tight, as he took his own pleasure, let his release build and build, and then jet into her, bathing her with his heat inside as he pressed against her shoulders to thigh, giving her the same warmth on the outside.

As they came down, breathing and heart rate settling, he had his arm wrapped around her, holding her up on shaky legs. "If I fucked you into near collapse, you wouldn't be strong enough to go with us," he said, a low growl against her temple.

"I'd find the strength," she whispered, but she had her eyes closed and she pressed her face to his shoulder. He dipped his head over hers, brushed his lips over her forehead, her temple, stroked her there with his fingers.

He was far too tempted to do what he'd told Matt he would, so he turned his attention to more immediate, practical concerns, though equally pleasurable. He kept her leaning forward like that, his hand light but firm on her nape. One-handed, he pulled down a washcloth, ran it under the warm water tap, and then used it to run it over her still slick cunt, her inner thighs where his seed was trickling, marking her.

"Ben," she murmured, her eyes large and deep. "Master."

He tossed the cloth to the side after he used it on himself. "What are you going to wear?"

She gestured to a pile of neatly folded clothes on the side counter. Jeans, tank, functional fight clothes.

"If I'd known action hero was on our list of to-dos this week, I would have ordered that latex *Underworld* outfit for you," he said, though his voice was rough, his delivery of the joke flat. Nothing better damn well happen to her, or someone would die.

He helped her dress, and she didn't question why, merely stood docile as he had her step into the jeans, brought them up over her long thighs and toned ass. Lifted her arms when he threaded the tank over them and her head. He tucked it in, slipped the slim belt she was wearing through the loops, gave it an extra tight pull, making her breath skip a beat as the rough motion pulled her to him. Then he eased it out, put it at the normal hole.

He brushed her hair, having her face the mirror. Her fingers rested on the counter, her lips pressing together nervously as she looked at him. When it was silk on her shoulder blades, he picked up the band and wrapped it around the thick tail.

Done. Even without the Kate outfit, she looked better than any woman he'd ever seen. She wore no jewelry except her wedding set. She was worrying it with her thumb, those platinum bands, the marquis diamond in the center.

"It's not the outfit, but the woman in it," he said. "Though I'm still getting you some latex when this is over."

A tentative playfulness crossed her features when her gaze coursed over his bare chest and jeans.

"You really need a duster so I can bring my Karl Urban dreams to life," she said.

"You just made sure I'll never own a duster," he said, making her giggle, as if nothing more was happening than her going off to work. She'd plan it that way to keep his head in the game. She was a nurturer, his brat. Good thing she had him to watch over her, too.

So here they were, an hour before midnight, standing on the roof of the Aquarium, surveying something rarely seen—a deserted New Orleans waterfront. The only other time Ben had seen it was right before Katrina, when he and the other guys had helped with final sweeps to evacuate any homeless people, misguided stragglers or pets left behind.

Ben looked toward the not-so-distant French Quarter, the buildings on Canal Street. He remembered standing in hip deep water on that main thoroughfare after Katrina had passed. While the I-10 overpass had loomed in the background, on the street itself only the windows and roofs of the cars had been visible over the water. Businesses had been swamped, debris floating everywhere. Despite the inadvisability of it, a handful of people had been making their way through the water on foot, or in boats, with the same stunned looks on their faces. All while the sun beamed down cheerily as if nothing had happened. The air had been so temporarily clean and soft, the way it was right after a catastrophic storm. Right before humidity and bugs set in with a vengeance.

Well, if he didn't survive this, he wouldn't have to deal with that. The real upside was he wouldn't have to endure Peter and Lucas's ribbing for the rest of his life. Which was exactly what would happen if they heard he'd stood on top of the Aquarium and used a kid's bedtime story to placate something spawned from his seed and an evil witch's doom fantasy.

The others might be convinced not to talk about it, but Marcie would tell. Corporate secrets couldn't be tortured out of her, but the Doms in their unique family circle could get her to spill in a heartbeat. His beloved sub, who trusted them the way she trusted him.

Because they deserved that trust, and he was fucking glad they weren't going to be in the middle of this. Truth, he'd be glad to tell them all about it when this was over and done. And it was going to be done. The bad guys, or gal, in this case, wasn't winning. Elagra's winning days were over tonight, one way or another.

He knew the main objective, but taking Elagra out the way he should have done years ago was going to be right on the heels of it in priority order. He just wanted it to be before Marcie had to engage her.

Across from him, Mikhael, Derek and Ruby had point on the long, flat expanse that paralleled the railway side of the Aquarium. It provided them a closer than bird's-eye view of the water and docks.

Marcie was on the riverside roof, the smaller section adjacent to the Aquarium's impressive cylindrical roof feature. The insulating concrete structure of glass had been installed during the post-Katrina re-roofing. The slanted glass top faced the water. The position put her and Raina, standing a few feet away from her, in the best position to view the cluster of mall and Warehouse District buildings. That was the direction from which they had determined Elagra would most likely come, if she made her presence known.

He knew what their job was, and he didn't like it. As he'd said from the beginning, he didn't want Marcie anywhere near Elagra.

At least Matt and the guys had done their job. Ben didn't see any cluelessly curious random New Orleans natives or tourists wandering the docks. But as he looked at the vastness of the Mississippi, he wished there'd been some way in hell to evacuate the whole waterfront along the train tracks. Ley lines, plate movement and storm surge—it could all go very bad. The witches and Guardians might know more about this, but Ben was feeling the burden of protecting the people of his city. It mattered to the Guardians, no doubt, but it couldn't be as personal for them.

But he couldn't fault their diligence. They'd been up here for about an hour, waiting, watching, and their alertness had never flagged. He was just about to wander over to Mikhael and see what he was thinking about the current status of things, when that status changed.

He saw it in the sudden stiffening of both Guardians, like Rottweilers suddenly scenting danger. Ruby, too, had become tight as a drawn bow. She turned her attention skyward.

Normal nighttime darkness on the New Orleans waterfront was punctuated by the radiance of city and dock lights. As he followed her gaze heavenward, he saw the clouds moving in. The stars were disappearing in that cover, like when a storm was looming, but that darkness was closing in faster than seemed natural. And it wasn't staying up in the sky.

The streetlights and building lights dimmed as if there were fog, but there wasn't. Then they started to wink out. Several near the train tracks popped, with an explosion of sparks that was swallowed by the dark like fireflies by a bat.

Glancing over his shoulder, he saw...nothing. No colorful entrance signs to Harrah's. No city lights. The thickening air had a heaviness to it that made drawing a breath an effort.

He might have wondered if the smoke-and-mirrors magic Ruby and Derek were casting and the evacuation would be enough to keep every straggler off their periphery. But with that odd blanket of darkness, and the feel of an impending storm in the air, he suspected any sane person was going to head for shelter. And he had a strong feeling that even wilder weather was coming.

A flicker, and a dim, silvery light coated the roof at their feet, throwing up enough illumination to make out the silhouettes of the others, their intent faces. Derek's doing, apparently, as he lifted back to his shoulder the staff he'd stretched out and swept over the area.

Raina and Marcie were standing shoulder to shoulder over on the other portion of the roof. Raina was saying something to his brat, gesturing down toward the warehouses.

As Derek and Mikhael drew closer to him, he assumed to confer about the latest development, Ben shook his head. "Tell me again how this thing about to be born isn't a bad guy?"

A few feet away, Ruby had her hands on her hips, her head tipped back, eyes half closed. Unexpectedly, her lips curved, though her expression remained intent, on guard.

"Birth is a very focused business, Ben," she said. "During labor, everything else disappears. It's a communication, between the mother, her body, and the child. Wondrous, violent, but ultimately natural."

He raised his brows. "You think that's what this is?"

"Somewhat. It feels like it." She nodded to Derek and Mikhael, both watching her closely. But then her attention snapped back up to the sky, as did theirs.

Even Ben felt it, a sharp change in the nature of the energy. Ruby's lips tightened, her hazel eyes flashing. "Then there are those who are determined to disrupt what is natural," she said.

Ben sucked in a startled breath as a cold wind cut through the normal humidity. The thick cloud cover far above was breaking into pieces against a grey sky. And it wasn't behaving like clouds. It split as precisely as a coke addict creating lines on a table. Those lines morphed, grew wings and shapes that were way too humanoid.

Mikhael's eyes narrowed. Derek shifted his staff to his other hand. "Servants of an Underworld demon," he growled. "Elagra is strong, but she does not have this kind of power."

"No," Mikhael answered. "She bartered for the aid of something far more powerful than herself. She'll likely pay for that mistake with her soul."

Derek grunted. "They're not corporeal yet. Whatever's controlling them likely won't let them fully materialize and unleash them until the birth. This is going to be a harder fight than we anticipated."

That didn't sound good. But since Ben was getting antsy, standing around with nothing to fight, he figured the impending action would fix that.

Mikhael's gaze flickered over the set of Ben's shoulders, the curl of his fingers into near fists. The Dark Guardian pointed to the river. "That is your job. This will be ours."

"Fuck that. I'm not standing around waiting with my hands in my pockets while you guys fight...whatever that is."

Derek braced himself on his staff. "Exactly. How would you fight the mist, the magic in the air? It was as you told Matt. Everyone in your business dealings has a role, correct? If one man tried to do another's job, your own job would not get done."

"That was a private conversation," Ben said, since it was the only thing he could say to what he knew was annoyingly correct.

"Sue me, lawyer," Derek said, curling his lip.

"I was wondering how long before the lawyer trashing would start," Ben retorted.

Ruby touched his shoulder. He saw Raina and Marcie had joined them as well, the new developments in the sky apparently requiring a full group review.

Ruby nodded to the river. "It's never easy to stand by while others fight, but handling that will save New Orleans. You're the one who can connect with her."

"At least, that is our hope," Mikhael put in. Just to add a seed of doubt and another boatload of pressure on what Ben was already feeling.

"If you can't connect with her, it's unlikely anyone else can," Ruby added, giving him an even look. He hadn't accepted that bullshit father stuff Ramona had talked about, but Ruby was a practical woman, so no matter how grudgingly, he had to give her opinion more credit.

Ben's attention went to Marcie. She had that look on her face she got when she was thinking thoughts that shoveled way beneath everything else and found the root of it. Usually something revelationary. And yes, he meant it that way, though revolutionary sometimes applied, too.

But she didn't necessarily feel comfortable sharing it with everyone else. As she stepped closer to him and glanced toward Raina, the message was received. Raina withdrew to a discreet distance, and continued to watch the warehouse side. Mikhael and Derek moved back across the roof with Ruby.

Ben held out a hand to his wife. "What is it, brat?"

She came, lacing her fingers in his. As she did, she tilted her head up in that way she did that made him feel tall and strong and the center of her universe, capable of handling anything. He'd take an immeasurable amount of pain and aggravation to live up to it.

She bit her lip, worrying it as her shrewd eyes assessed the sky. "Raina told me that when energies like this are swirling around, you follow what your gut tells you, even if there's no context for it." Her eyes lowered to meet his. "My gut wanted to tell you something, though it's going to sound kind of weird and disjointed."

"Well, the rest of this has made so much sense. Let's live on the wild side."

She smiled faintly, though her gaze remained serious, and boring into his with an exceptional intensity. He tightened his fingers on hers. "Tell me."

"When you're being really tough and strict with me...that's when I feel safest. And I think Bonnie is a really pretty name for a girl. The Scottish word for pretty. It tells her that she's wanted."

"Marcie, I'm not really buying into the whole parent-kid thing. If she'd snatched a lock of my hair, or used a scrap of my clothing, no one would have come up with that crazy thought. I was just an ingredient."

"I don't think you really believe that. But even if you do, I think there's a reason they're putting you at the center of this, to reach out to her. You know what it's like."

"What what's like?"

She took a breath. "The hardest part about what my parents were and weren't. So caught up in the disaster of their own lives, it wouldn't have mattered to them if we were there or not. We were just debris, orbiting around them. Don't underestimate how important it is, letting someone know you see them, that they matter. That they're more than some crazy bitch's plan to ruin everyone else's day."

She gazed up at him with her deep earth-colored eyes and soft mouth, her hair wisping around her face from the wind, pieces blown free from her functional ponytail. He tucked a strand back behind her ear. "Got it."

Then his gaze moved behind her, and coldness cut through him again, but this time it wasn't from a wind.

He'd seen her even before his companions, probably because he had a connection to her as well. A detestable one.

There were a few lights still illuminating the docks. He could see Elagra, standing on a warehouse rooftop a few buildings away. She no longer wore the cotton dress she'd worn below ground. She wore a thin shift, and that bone yellow paint covered her face, her torso and limbs, marked with symbols and splashes of what looked like mud, or dried blood. She had a thick necklace of what he expected were feathers and animal parts around her neck. Her dreadlocks were down, heavy ropes against her painted flesh.

As she stared across the expanse between them with her dead large eyes, that wind started to move and swirl, picking up a low moan. It reminded him of things that had happened below ground too goddamn long ago to affect him now, but it still did, bringing the fear back, the confusing mix of what love was, and what it sure the fuck wasn't.

Like Marcie had just said.

Even at this distance, he knew Elagra's gaze was challenging, malevolent, with that empty darkness he knew far too well. Whatever she was here to do, it was not going to help the situation. But when she only stood there, watching them, Ben figured it out pretty quick. What was holding her back was what they were all waiting for.

As Derek had said about those things in the sky, until the creature, monster, force of nature, whatever it was, started to be born, no one could execute their plan of action. If Elagra attacked them now, tried to get them out of the way, and it turned bloody and violent, her creation might get spooked, caught in the crossfire, what have you. They were like two opposing squadrons posted outside a labor delivery room.

Marcie glanced over her shoulder, followed the direction of his gaze. Her hand landed on his forearm, gripped. "She's not as smart as she thinks she is. She should have waited until things got started to reveal herself."

"But she knows her presence is a disrupting effect," Raina said, drawing closer to them again. She nodded to Marcie. "Time for us to go."

He didn't think, just reacted. He clamped his hand around Marcie's wrist, holding her in place.

Yeah, they'd talked about this. He'd said no then. He wanted Marcie at his side. No, correct that. Where he wanted her was not here at all, but since he couldn't have that, he wanted her close.

"Ben," Marcie said softly, resting her hand on his chest.

"No," he said.

Raina was giving him the fisheye. She could kiss his ass. Ruby, apparently reading the sudden tension, had approached. Raina tossed her that annoyed look. "If his attention is going to be split if she is in danger, then it's best for her to stay with him."

Damn straight. Fine by him.

"That's not true, and he knows it." Instead of arguing with him, Marcie lifted up on her toes, brushed her lips over his set jaw. She pulled back, only a couple inches, her fingers curling into his shirt, her body leaning into his. "You know what's funny? You've always made me feel safe. Always. Even when I'm away from you."

She tightened her grip on his shirt, tattooed her fists lightly against him, once, then twice. "I've got this, Master."

When he put his forehead to hers, she shifted her grip to his face, her slim fingers in his hair. "It's no easier for me not to be the one watching your back," she said. "But I'm pretty sure these guys have fought a lot worse things. I think we need to trust that they've given us the right roles to play in this."

He could point out that Mikhael and Derek had just said this fight might get a lot uglier than anticipated. He could make a lot of arguments. Instead, he sighed, slid his arm around her. He cupped her skull, digging his fingers into her hair. "You will be in one piece when you return to me," he said darkly. "And you will pay for every bruise and scratch you put on my property."

He meant it, with every savage cell that made up the fucked-up, twisted darkness of the heart which was all hers.

"Deal," she whispered, and met his mouth with eager lips. She was usually gentle, his demands being the initiating force that drove her into mindless passion. But this time she kissed him with the wildness of the wind building around them, the simmering violence that waited for them all, and the fierce love she'd believed in so much she'd gone after his heart with the single-minded purpose of a rabid terrier.

She had soft lips, a giving mouth and tongue that could stroke, plunge and tease him in ways that had him growling into her mouth. He wanted to take over, thrust deep as he held her so close he felt her from breast to hip, his cock pressed into the heated cradle between her thighs.

Even in a moment like this, she'd be wet for her Master. He could take her right here, and she could handle every inch of him, with writhing moans and the bite of her nails into his flesh, if he didn't tie her hands. It was always a tough decision. He loved bearing those marks as much as he loved to make her helpless.

She drew away far too soon. He still held her hand and brought it to his lips, brushing a kiss to her palm and then biting the heel of it, sharply enough she drew in a breath. "You remember your promise to me."

"Always, Master." Her eyes were alight with love and desire, and a focused purpose that made her basically the hottest woman he'd ever seen.

She turned to Raina. Raina gave them both a studied look, but nodded. Then the two women were on the move. The way Marcie drew her gun and checked it told him she knew her job, and he was going to have to trust Raina to watch out for her. Which he still fucking hated.

As they reached the stairwell, he made himself turn away, but only after the door closed behind them. With an act of will, he tuned back into what Derek, Ruby and Mikhael were doing. They were still watching the sky, which had filled up with even more clumps of those shadow creatures. It was starting to look like an alarmingly much bigger army.

The only good thing about Marcie leaving was it made his erection deflate some, though maybe whipping out his monster-sized dick would scare away those demonic-looking clouds. Game over, and they could all go home. If the guys had been here, he fully expected Peter would have made that suggestion.

Ben drew closer to join in on the conversation. Derek had pushed back the brim of his hat and now tossed comment at Mikhael. "If you can take the six on the left, I'll take the three hundred on the right."

The dry humor was unexpected from the Light Guardian, especially to Ben. However, Mikhael flashed his teeth, suggesting it was not an unusual side of Derek, right before a fight. "I was going suggest you could go have yourself a snack while I took care of all of them."

"Like him." Ben nodded down toward the wide concrete dock in front of the Aquarium.

On his earlier review of the emptiness of the waterfront, he hadn't counted the one freaking tourist still there. Or rather, a guy acting like one.

Silas was sitting on one of the benches. He appeared unconcerned by the odd cloud behavior, the rising wind or building sea level, already creating cat paws across the choppy river. He was eating beignets out of a bag, likely getting the powdered sugar on the long lanky legs of his jeans.

"Remind me again what he's supposed to do here?" Ben asked.

"Nothing," Derek said. "He does not get involved in such matters. It is forbidden because of what he is, his power over life and death, and how that can disrupt the determinations of Fate."

"And he is...what?" Ben prompted. When Mikhael and Derek exchanged a look, including Ruby in the sweep, Ben raised a brow. "Really? After all this other stuff, you can't tell me that it's a secret."

"He's a Grim Reaper," Ruby said. "He collects the souls of the dead, but that's only one responsibility he has related to the threshold between life and death."

"Yet that responsibility is the one that makes a Grim Reaper's life a very isolated one," Derek added.

Ben took a second look at the male calmly indulging in baked goods. Definitely not what he'd expected *the* Grim Reaper to look like. "Though I can probably guess, why does that make his life isolated?"

"When a Grim Reaper looks at you," Derek said, "he knows the moment of your death, and how it's going to happen."

Ramona was down there as well. She'd periodically appeared and disappeared among the various buildings, wandering with what Ben was sure was a misleading aimlessness. Each time she appeared, Silas's attention immediately moved from contemplation of his surroundings to her.

"So what is it about her that's holding his attention?" Ben asked. His gut tightened the moment he spoke the question. Shit. He didn't want to see the benevolent witch in harm's way.

"She is what Grim Reapers call a blind spot," Mikhael said. "He doesn't know her fate. Grim Reapers meet only one blind spot in their immortal lives. The person destined to be his soulmate, if she or he will have him."

"So if the individual in question doesn't want to be with him, he's lost his one and only shot at finding his better half."

"Yes. The irony, at least in this case, is that Grim Reapers are known to be incredibly organized," Derek said. "They always have a plan."

"So Silas has fallen for a chaos witch, who may or may not want him." Ben shook his head. "The universe has a messed-up sense of humor. Somebody should smack the crap out of it sometime."

"True, but a topic for another time," Mikhael said. "Returning to the original question, I suspect he has two purposes for being here. One, to collect the souls we are about to kill."

Ramona had reappeared by a giant whale statue, on loan from another museum, some place out in California, if Ben remembered correctly. She appeared enchanted by it, putting both palms on the broad base and leaning in. Her mouth was moving as if talking to it.

The chaos witch had decided on an entirely different look from the rest of the women. Ruby had worn another version of what Marcie had. Even Raina had paired her jeans with a short-sleeved black cotton shirt with a triquetra painted on the front in a slash of bold red color. Her long hair had been braided into a thick tail down her back. Marcie had told Ben why Raina didn't wear shoes that often, but it had still been startling, to see the witch walk across the rough, uneven rooftop with no apparent discomfort, her toes pressing firmly into the surface.

In contrast, Ramona looked as if she'd fit right into a misty-looking romantic medieval painting. Her glossy red hair was streaming back, loose. Her close-fitting, long-sleeved black dress, which seemed to have a lot of lacy bits on the hem line with sparkles that danced in the wind, emphasized the thinness of her torso. The woman needed a sandwich.

She turned and looked at Silas with an indulgent smile, coming toward him to take his outstretched hand. He pulled her gently to him, offered a beignet. When she took it from his fingers, closing her own over his wrist, what was in his eyes became a lot less gentle. Ben knew that look pretty well.

"Two," Mikhael said. "To watch after her. I expect if anything tries to hurt her, he'll be in the middle of it. No matter who he pisses off with it."

"Which would go a long way toward putting him on our approved suitor list for Ramona," added Ruby.

"Let's make sure we don't give him a third task." Derek said. "To escort our souls off to the afterlife."

Suddenly, the dense feeling that Ruby had earlier described as the focus of childbirth became so thick, it felt as if Ben were in an illegal backroom poker game, closed up in a humid space with no windows and way too little air. His gaze snapped back up toward the heavens. That army of sinister psychotherapy inkblots was starting to churn like a whirlwind about to cut loose.

"The birth has begun," Ruby said.

CHAPTER FIFTEEN

*T*he river bucked, heaved. Ben had seen pictures of the Katrina storm surge, but he hadn't been in its path. Now he saw the water starting to rise in a very non-river-like way, and recalled those pictures. As the clouds descended like an endless rolling surf, he wondered if the clouds and the water would slam together somewhere in the middle, forming a complete line of advancing elements to overtake New Orleans. He really wasn't liking the look of those clouds, the way the winged shapes separated like bees in a hive, then came back together.

"I'll be with Ramona, wherever it's best for us to be," Ruby said to Derek. "We'll be ready."

The Light Guardian bent and brushed his mouth over hers, touching her face. "I'll be close."

"Close as here," she said with a soft smile, placing his hand briefly on her heart before she gripped it, dipped her head to kiss his knuckles. Then she glanced toward Ben, and her voice took on a snap of urgency.

"When things start breaking loose, make sure you're over on that roof edge," she said, nodding to it. "You need to be in the right place at the right moment."

Bossy woman. She reminded him of Marcie's sister, Cass. A woman he was exceedingly fond of. "Got it, General."

Ruby grimaced at him and headed for the stairs at a trot, the alert set of her toned, athletic body looking ready for whatever was coming.

Derek obviously had confidence in that, but Ben saw the same brief flash in his gaze that he harbored in his own heart whenever Marcie left his side. You couldn't give into it, because you'd end up chaining your woman to a pole in your basement and becoming an episode of a crime show. It was tough as hell sometimes, letting them be as fucking amazing as they were.

As she passed Mikhael, she touched his arm, said something to him. When she disappeared down the stairs, Derek tossed Mikhael an arch look. "She asked you to watch after me?"

"Of course. Just as I assume Raina asked you."

Even as they spoke, the men were starting to fan out. Ben took comfort in the easy exchange, evidence that they'd faced stuff like this before. But then, men in combat bantered, too, and still got blown away seconds later.

"Good fortune to you, Ben," Derek told him. "We'll keep this force occupied so you can get the job done."

"Just see that you do. Else the customer satisfaction rating I turn into Guardian headquarters will be zero stars."

Derek flashed him an unexpected grin. It made him look more like a guy in his forties, instead of a centuries-old wizard. That is, if Ben didn't focus on his eerie-ass ancient eyes.

He moved back to his corner. Since it was practically on the opposite end of the roof from them, he figured not only was it the best vantage point for the birth, it would keep him out of the line of the fire they'd purposefully be drawing toward them.

Though he knew Mikhael was correct, that he didn't have the magic arsenal to face their kind of threat, Ben still wished he had a task as straightforward as theirs. A vs B, A's purpose to kick B's ass.

He knew how to fight, lethally enough to have a better than average chance of walking away the winner, no matter the odds. He could walk through the darkest alleys of New Orleans, even in his most expensive suit and shoes, because the predators smart enough to meet his gaze would recognize he wasn't a mark. He'd put a lot of polish on it and grown into more, and knew that. But there was a place inside of him that was still one of them, and he'd call it up when needed.

He also knew how to combat an opponent in more civilized ways, with his sharp mind and even sharper tongue. He knew how to bring business rivals and allies alike to the decision Matt wanted from them.

He wasn't sure where on the spectrum of his dual arsenal this task would fall. They'd given him an important job, but they couldn't tell him how to do it. Every bit of information they'd deduced could be somewhere between an educated hypothesis and a wild-ass guess.

He just hoped it happened soon, because if the battle engaged the others first, it was going to be hard as hell to sit here and twiddle his thumbs, waiting to do his thing. He also didn't see Marcie and Raina, or Elagra, which bugged the shit out of him. Had they disappeared into the warehouse area? Were they already engaged with her? It was too damn dark down there.

Mikhael lifted both hands, speaking in a sonorous voice. Ben didn't catch the words, but felt the shimmer of power. Whatever Mikhael did slowed the descending things, like they were plowing through snow or molasses. Derek was watching, but on alert, probably waiting to jump into the fray as soon as the first one broke through.

Hell, Ben guessed he could always go sit with Silas and eat beignets until his number was called. A glance down below showed the guy had finished his snack, tidily handled the trash somehow. Ramona had disappeared, likely joining Ruby wherever they were setting up.

He envied Silas his calm, but he wondered if it was a front. It was unsettling, how still the guy was sitting, his arm stretched out along the back of the bench, his ankle balanced on his knee. The rising wind that was whipping flags against flag poles with a rhythmic clang didn't seem to be doing more than rippling his hair lightly across his forehead. Just a guy enjoying the waterfront in the deadass of night, as the denizens from hell came screaming from the sky.

He didn't want to play poker with this guy, ever.

Ben thought of the more challenging projects Matt had thrown his way with little guidance. Yeah, it might seem stupid to compare what happened in the venues of courtroom or board room to this, but he expected some of the principles were the same. He could also go back even further, to situations on the street that would seem fucking unimaginable, to put it mildly. But he had figured it out. Mostly it had been base survival strategies, a lot of luck, and more than a little violence. Everything riding close to that edge.

In his gut, he knew this was going to be way different. What the hell was he doing?

He started. "Jesus."

Ramona was at his side, as if she'd materialized from thin air.

"It would be easier to fight," she said. "It's always easier to fight. But this is a situation where you listen. Think of it like the way you are with her. How you use all your senses to detect the things she needs. There's a place you go inside you, isn't there? A state of being, where everything becomes that one focus?"

Yeah, there was. Reluctantly, he stopped looking for Marcie and made himself listen to what she was saying to him.

"And yet," she continued, "You're hyper-alert to all external stimuli as well, to everything that comes your way, to make the outcome what's best for her. It's very much the same in this situation, Ben."

He hadn't thought of going there. Maybe because they kept referring to whatever was going to erupt out of the river as a baby, he hadn't automatically gravitated toward a solution he usually associated with sex and his deepest cravings to dominate the woman he loved.

"You are the oddest mix," he commented.

"I am chaos," she said. "Chaos is never one thing. I am the mother, the maiden and the crone, and the spaces in between, the shadows."

"I bet you had it tough as a kid. Nothing predictable."

Her attention was back on the sky, the water, Silas. Never stopping, no pattern to it, and then it rolled back to him, her gaze stopping and holding. "As you well know, there is no better sculptor for a child than the sharp knife of their reality," she said. "Instead of watching Derek, Mikhael or Marcie, and I know that last is the hardest, you need to watch the water. Close your eyes to watch it, listen to it, feel it. Feel the energies that are going to unfold there. Whether you believe it or not, you have a connection to what's going to come out of there. You will feel it, but she will feel it, too, the female that will come forth. Birth is a terrifying and wondrous process."

She touched his arm. "I mean it. Close your eyes. That way you won't be distracted by what the others are doing. Raina will protect Marcie. I swear it to you. Be open and still. The time is close."

Ben sighed. Maybe it was good he didn't see Marcie or Elagra now, because no way he could close his eyes if they were about to engage.

Double fuck. He was going to have to trust. Not the easiest thing for him, even under the best of circumstances.

He closed his eyes.

"Good." Ramona's voice seemed to come from inside his mind, a quiet sound. "What is coming forth, she is your child."

He automatically recoiled from the thought, dismissed it as persuasive psychobabble to get his head right, but then her tone became more pointed. "You need to say it to yourself, understand the full weight of what it means. You're her father, the closest thing she has to one. Before you dismiss that, the alternative is Elagra as her mother. It doesn't have to make sense. Nothing in the world that matters does. The most important thing in the world to any of us quite often doesn't make sense. Love. That's why it only makes sense in the way we feel it, not in the way we think about it."

Ramona's voice had fallen to little more than a murmur, as natural as the wind, not even really all that human. The words surrounded him, holding him in a non-binding manner. More like a support, like when he leaned against a tree.

"Think of those moments when you and your soulmate are perfectly in sync. No words are needed. It is all energy, and that energy is in the stillness. Reach for that stillness, Ben. Focus on nothing, know that it contains your objective."

Fuck, he actually understood that. What Ramona was talking about was being guided by your gut, and he had a pretty lucky gut.

Unconsciously, because he'd done it so often he didn't have to think about it, he let himself level out, his breathing, his center, his focus. Probably what Jon would consider the Zen state during his yoga. Ben had always found it when Mastering a sub, sometimes even when doing nothing more than planning out a session. As much as he ever planned it. He was just guided by what he knew he wanted, what she wanted...what the energy said was needed to make all of it work.

Ramona had fallen silent, but the words lingered, drifting in the quiet, surrounding him. At first, there was nothing. Just sounds, scents, everything he expected. Then that icy wind came back, started to swirl. It also started to heat.

With a start, he realized he wasn't really standing on the roof of the Aquarium anymore. His body was, but his mind, his consciousness, wasn't. It was on the move.

Before that could startle him into a full-scale slam back into his physical body, an incorporeal hand tightened on his incorporeal shoulder. He told himself he had to be imagining that to give himself some context. Or Ramona was helping him make this first vital step, the push-off at the starting line.

The rest disappeared. If the fight with the clouds had started, he didn't know it. He dropped, descending, into the Mississippi River, drifting down, down, down. There was darkness, but that darkness felt full of life, so it wasn't claustrophobic. He could move his arms and legs. What was above, below and to the sides was so vast, a deep well.

Creation magic, they'd called it. Something about to be born, so it was all concentrated here, getting ready for it. Because suddenly...

Christ on a biscuit. Holy fucking hell. He felt it.

He felt *her*.

He reached with an arm that wasn't an arm, reached out toward the center, and felt the shape of it.

It closed around him.

He almost pulled back, because something he couldn't see had latched onto him. But somehow he overrode the involuntary reaction and made himself wait, see what was happening.

It was like...something had coiled around his mental idea of his arm, was checking him out. He put his other hand out to it. It twitched, not sure, but when he laid his hand there, it didn't withdraw. There was darkness, water, energy, and now this. It felt like skin, warm skin. That first mutual contact told him he'd found what they were seeking. The tendrils wrapping around his virtual self, for lack of a better term, were living. As they coiled, he was given a far more intimate feel for that energy.

Though it was holding him, when he put his palms in that current, he was reaching out, holding her.

He'd freaking connected, just as they'd said he would. It was so unexpected and overwhelming, that for a blink he almost forgot the import of what he was there to do. He was like a fucking idiot, marveling at a field of flowers.

He always gave Jon such a hard time about the crunchy granola shit because, as he'd told Raina, his exposure to magic had only been to the horrible side of it, easily attached to the evil of human nature, which was more real to him. He didn't really believe in all that good energy stuff, but in this case, he couldn't deny he actually *felt* the being.

And yes, she was a child. A motherfucking Godzilla-times-ten sized tot, but a child all the same.

The first time he'd touched Angelica, Matt and Savannah's daughter, she'd done the expected thing, latched onto one of his fingers with a tiny fist. Apparently, every baby had their version of that, because that was what the coil of energy felt like. A child wrapping around his offer of touch.

She might be big and strong enough to destroy the entire city, but she was a baby, being born. Whatever cocoon Ruby and Raina could put her in to get her to a safer spot for all of them, that was good. A world with more room for her, they had said. Where she could spread her wings and fly...

They had assured him that they would be doing that. Now Ben wanted to revisit that and be absolutely sure.

She is my daughter.

She is my *daughter.*

Perhaps Raina and Ruby had known this moment would come. He remembered Ruby placing a hand on his on the table, meeting his gaze and saying, "Unless she leaves us no other choice, we will get her somewhere where she can live how she was intended to live, in an environment that is welcoming."

They hadn't said she could fly. He had said that, thought that, just now. He knew she could fly. That was part of what she was.

Marcie's words came to him now, the ones that she hadn't been sure made any sense. He smiled, because they couldn't be more perfect for this moment. He couldn't wait to tell her.

"Hello, Bonnie," he murmured. You could speak when you were a spirit, even if you were underwater, and not get your lungs full. Who knew? "Hello, baby girl."

You must come back to your body now. She will look for you when she emerges. I am bringing you back. Do not be alarmed. Much is going on right now. Hold fast.

A sudden shudder went through those energy tendrils, and he was jolted back into his body on the roof. As his eyes opened, he realized why Ramona had shot him the warning.

Holy fuck. A solid front line of winged creatures with empty eyes, rotting mouths and clawed hands were swooping toward the rooftop, less than a hundred feet away and closing. He was directly in their path.

They looked like creatures put together in the wrong way, with the maximum capacity for violence. Huge talons, long teeth, broad, muscular arms and upper torsos. Gorillas crossed with werewolves crossed with every nightmare a kid could have.

Hold fast.

Ramona wasn't standing by him anymore, and it wasn't her voice in his head. It was Derek's, the sharp tone of a battle commander.

Only the fighting experience of a lifetime, which had taught Ben to keep a portion of his mind calm even in the most terrifying situations, kept him there. Though self-preservation had him bracing and wondering if he should have brought a weapon with him. Derek and Mikhael had advised against it and he'd listened. What an idiot he was.

Derek brought up his staff at the same moment Mikhael lifted his right hand. The first line of flying death was a pebble's toss from the roof. Ben was breathing fast, fists clenched. "Shit, shit, *shit*."

He had those fists up and ready when the creatures slammed into an invisible wall only a few feet in front of him, just beyond the roof's edge. The ones behind crashed into their brethren, unable to pull up in time. Derek spun that staff in a wide arc, and blue lightning illuminated the cluster of their attackers. As the electricity jolted through them, screams and burning flesh filled the air. Mikhael snared most of the rest in a rope of flame that expanded and engulfed them in the blink of an eye. The flame became ash, whipped away by the wind.

Ben had to admit; it was freaking awesome. He looked for Marcie. And now at last, he found her.

She and Raina had gotten past the mall and were headed purposefully down the docks. He thought of the two of them in the car, racing the wind. They'd established a rapport from the first moment, and he told himself that would help. They already had trust, the best advantage for anyone working with a partner in a tricky situation.

They'd come to a halt when Mikhael and Derek started their light show. He suspected Raina's heart had accelerated like a freight train, seeing all that coming at her mate. Marcie had probably been the same.

Yet his brat, always on the same wavelength as him in moments like this, turned her face toward his. She'd seen what the Guardians had done, and he couldn't help the grin her mouthed words gave him.

Holy fuck.

The two Guardians didn't have the luxury of marveling at the results of their work. They were already engaging again, Derek with his staff and Mikhael with an honest-to-God sword charged with light. No longer in an expensive suit, he wore some kind of battle gear, a short half tunic, his bare chest crossed with a harness for daggers, his dark wings fully out. It was like seeing one of the computer games that Nate, Cass's little brother, played, now come to life in full vivid color.

But some things were horribly different.

Ben started forward with a shout as a trio of those things broke through. They were on Mikhael in a heartbeat, taking him down to the rooftop so hard they practically bounced together, a tangle of arms, legs, wings. Then the whole slashing, snarling cluster of them were in the air. A second later, they came back down on the slanted glass roof. A trio of panels, built to withstand 130mph high winds and random projectiles that could be carried by them, shattered as the combatants crashed through.

"Hell..."

Derek was on it. He made a sharp movement with the white wood staff. A wall of shimmering silver energy hit the next line of attackers, held them. Once again, electricity crackled, making them scream and filling the air with a foul stench. His expression concentrated, grim, he extended his other hand toward the jagged hole where Mikhael had disappeared and made a fist. Derek shouted a harsh command, and the crackling blue-white energy that appeared in his grasp shot from it, gaining size and velocity as it headed toward its target. By the time it reached the opening of broken glass, it was the size of a Humvee.

Which was the same moment that Mikhael came up out of that hole, propelling the creatures before him in a tangled mass of claws and teeth and rage. Mikhael thrust them into the ball of crackling light with a snarl. They shrieked and shuddered, and tumbled down along the slanted face of the cylinder, landing heavily on the flat part of the roof. One struggled away from the pack, the others inert. Mikhael landed on the moving one, slamming him back down, and thrust his sword through the shoulder blades, giving the pommel a decisive twist. Then he was back up again, but Ben noticed he had blood running down his neck and chest.

Ben jumped as electricity zapped his flank. He spun toward the direction from which it had come, sure that one of those demon-minion things had circled behind him. Instead, over on the mall rooftop, Ruby gestured to the water with fierce purpose. The gun store witch had zapped him in the fucking ass. He scowled at her, but guessed it was better than Ramona slinging an arrow of chaotic magic at him that might have done far worse, like turning him into a rabbit. Or a stuffed rabbit.

Ramona was waving her arms for extra emphasis. *Focus there. Now.*

While he'd been distracted by the light show, he'd missed his cue. The heaving and bucking Mississippi erupted. In the time it took to draw a breath, a wave came up and over the dock. It slapped down onto the concrete, rapidly flowing over the area. Nearby day-cruise boats slammed against the bulkheads, pitching the craft against the pilings. The hull of the Algiers ferry had a sizeable dent in it, fiber-glass falling away. One or two hits more, and it would be on the bottom.

More waves were coming up behind the first one, getting bigger. Something was pushing the water up. He remembered what the witches had warned. If that ley line got disrupted too badly, New Orleans could literally crack down the middle, fall into the sea.

He didn't dare look for Marcie now, because if she was in trouble, he wouldn't be able to focus. Everything depended on him doing this right. How had he, the least heroic member of this cast, gotten the hero's gig? Christ.

Taking a breath, he closed his eyes again, opened his mind. Shut everything out. The next ticking seconds were the longest moments of his life, getting to that still place without Ramona's help, but she'd been right. He knew how to do it. When he locked into it, there was that thread of energy, just waiting for him once more.

He grasped it, hauled himself to it, and it to him, hand over fist, mentally, bringing it up taut, but not too taut. Like fishing. *Easy. Easy. It's all right.*

Make it a calm birth. That's what they said they needed. But even calm, what was about to rise out of the Mississippi was going to cause a hell of a storm surge. He'd been right to tell Matt to get everyone ready and out of harm's way.

He let her feel him, feel his presence the way he'd felt hers, below water. *There you are. Come on, baby.*

Water was dripping off his brow. It brought back to him the drip, drip, drip of Elagra's lair, how nothing good ever came out of that place. The color of blood in the pipes. The rotting smell of it all.

He shut that out, cursing as the pressure on the energy line increased and he had to let it out some, start over from a lower point.

It's okay. It's okay, little one. Calm.

On Disney flicks, they waved their wand and the pumpkin turned into a coach, the fairy godmother not even breaking a sweat. Mikhael was bleeding, and at last glimpse Derek had the look on his face of a guy being pushed hard, carrying a lot of weight. Now Ben knew why they ate thousands of calories at one sitting.

He got it. He'd done two-hundred-pound presses with Peter in the gym that were featherlike in comparison to the mental and physical energy this was taking.

There, she'd eased off, was coming back to him again. He reeled in the slack, putting everything reassuring in that contact he could.

Complete focus. Nothing but her, but keeping her safe, watching and feeling her every reaction. Just like Marcie, under his control.

You're good. Come on. You can do this. Up. Slow and easy.

The building shuddered. Waves smacked against the side of it like a gunshot, the spray hitting him in the face. He thought of all the sea creatures inside the Aquarium, imagined a shark or manatee, a giant loggerhead, swimming in a baffled sort of way down Canal Street. Not happening. Not going to happen.

A long, low wail vibrated through the soles of his feet and up through every nerve ending of his body. Like a whale call. No, more like a freighter foghorn, with a much wider vocal range. More water showered down on him, and the significance of that hit him. He was on top of the Aquarium. Something was dropping water down upon him.

Opening his eyes, he lifted his face to what loomed over him.

He'd gone over all sorts of visual scenarios for this, and had come up with an amalgamation of all the monster movies he'd ever seen. He'd thought maybe she'd be like a mythical beast of old. A dragon would be pretty damn cool.

It was all of that and none of it. What it was left him astounded, unnerved. And catapulted into the past.

~

He sat on Elagra's floor, in her main underground chamber. She didn't need anything from him right now, but she'd said he could stay while she worked with her potion stuff. It was quiet down here, safe for the moment. Without much to do, Ben had found himself a section of the tunnels where the floor had broken and left dirt. A trickling line of water coming from somewhere above was mixed with the clay. He used it, sticks, random rocks, and some approved leavings from Elagra's stores, to create a mud monster.

After a time, Elagra came to see what he was doing. As she squatted by him, she ran her fingers over it. The mud dried, hardened beneath her touch. When she lifted it by the midsection, it had become a finished figurine instead a blob of sand and clay. He liked it. Elagra smiled at him. But the way she studied it, so hard, was as if it was giving her an idea. An idea he wasn't sure he liked. He wondered if the discarded leavings she'd given him permission to use had really been discards at all.

"Can I keep this?" she asked him, in that warm honeyed voice she used to make a kid think she cared. That if he'd do enough for her, she'd love him. So he said yes, just like any of them would.

Until they knew better. But by then, it was usually too late.

~

Elagra had put it on one of her shelves. For a really brief time Ben had liked that, thinking it was like a mom putting up her kid's picture on her fridge.

This being, the one before him now, had drawn on the riverbed, all the debris beneath that, and turned into the creature he'd made all that time ago. Long before the terrible night with Amy.

Ben lifted his gaze, slowly. And kept lifting it as what his seed and Elagra's twisted magic had created tilted its head, a new shower of river water sluicing off its appendages.

He'd seen pictures of magical creatures. He'd watched a few sci-fi/fantasy movies when he was younger. He actually kind of liked that Harry Potter offshoot movie, the one featuring the guy with all the creatures. What he was looking at reminded him of the teapot thing that got way big in a bigger space. Only it was mixed up with a dragon, because it had wings that he suspected would almost span the river if stretched out.

The teeth were about fifteen feet long. There was a smattering of bat in there. As well as cat, snake, and medieval church gargoyle. The creature looked as big as several city blocks, so in comparison, he was...an ant. There was no way an ant could catch a human's attention. But an ant wasn't carrying what he was. A freaking magic-charged storybook with bunnies on the front.

"So...not so little, you."

The curved skull was crowned with more horns than he could count, and they were squiggly, like a bovine who'd butted heads with Medusa and gotten the snakes stuck and petrified on its skull. The head was also as wide as a trolley car squared. The neck wasn't excessively long, but it set upon wide, powerful shoulders. The clawed hands could rip open the front of the Aquarium like a Tupperware lid. If he could see the creature all the way out of the water, he knew it would look a lot like a T-Rex who could sit back on its haunches, because like all kids he'd liked dinosaurs.

There were fifteen eyes. The fifteen he'd put on the mud-and-stick creature had come from the rhinestones of a beaded purse he'd snatched. Which meant the beast that had risen out of the river before him, whose body had a mix of slick brown and dark black coloring, also had eyes in various sparkling shades of royal purple, emerald green and sapphire blue.

He was supposed to be doing something. Maybe he'd forgotten because, in the face of something this size, the idea seemed even more outlandish than it had when it was first proposed in the hotel room. But since he didn't have anything better in mind, he yanked the book out of the back waistband of his jeans, where it had been resting in the small of his back.

"Hold out both of your hands," Ramona had said. "Palms up." When she'd laid the small book in them, she'd placed hers over it, on the edges, so her fingers overlapped his and tightened. She'd lifted her head, and her lavender-grey eyes had fastened upon his. As if she'd found something in his gaze she'd hoped to find, a light smile had crossed her face. "When the time comes, you will hold it up above you, in both hands like this. Like a knight holding up a sword to swear an oath to the heavens."

Now that that moment had come, he felt foolish, a fly trying to catch the attention of a 747. But he did it. Lifting the book in both hands, the cover facing toward the creature, he raised it to the full reach of his arms. He tilted his head back to ensure that he had it angled in the right direction for the creature to see it, if it deigned to notice him.

He understood in a blink why Ramona had wanted him in that pose. His body was an arrow, stretched upward, a straight conduit for the rush of energy that came through him and made the book feel as if it had become a living thing in his hands. In the next blink, energy hit it from a different direction, illuminating it in fire in his hands, a fire that didn't burn but flashed like a lighthouse beacon.

A quick glance to the nearby roof showed Ruby and Ramona had been ready, sending that ray of attention-getting magic to the icon, as Ramona had called it. They were an unlikely pair, the tough-looking, gun store owning witch shoulder-to-shoulder with the ethereal, flowing dress, long hair streaming Ramona. But the integrated power of what they were channeling toward him told him why they treated one another like sisters, even without the tie of familial blood.

He brought his attention back to the creature. And in that moment, it turned its focus to him.

"A key moment," Ramona had said. "Start calling out what we've talked about in that second, because it will take no longer than that to lose the baby's attention."

She'd told him what the book was about, two rabbits, presumably parent and child, coming up with whimsical measurements of their love for one another. She'd let him read it, but emphasized the words had to come from him.

The structure of it is important, both for the rhythm of it and the underlying power of parental love that drives the story. But because you are the one executing it, the words must be yours.

"How much can I love you?" he shouted. He stumbled over the words, not entirely sure of himself, but as soon as they left his lips, he knew that was what he'd intended to say. They didn't know one another. So the world of possibilities was open to them.

The beast's head drew back, like a snake thinking about striking, going higher, up and up and up. He probably looked like a morsel of food.

He knew he was forgetting something important. Something he'd known a few moments ago, before it had emerged from the water and that memory with Elagra had disrupted things. But he kept going, because the only way through this was forward.

That massive skull reversed direction, drew closer, the big shoulders bunching as it crouched to come down closer to him. As he shouted out more words, "As wide as my arms can reach, as tall as ten Mt. Everests stacked on top of one another," he got the distinct impression it was less than impressed. Maybe they should have used the actual words, which were far more poetic.

That was when he remembered what he'd forgotten, because only a female could pull off that 'you're not all that' vibe with just a crease of her brow, the purse of her mouth. The flash of her eyes, all seven and half pairs of them.

She wasn't an it. Bonnie. She was Bonnie.

He couldn't say he blamed her for her lackluster opinion of him. But as he chose the most central of the eyes to stare into, he was hit by another wave of energy.

This energy wasn't summoned or concocted magic like Ruby and Ramona had used to charge the book. Or what Elagra devised in her dark lair. This was deeper, innate. A magic created by things far beyond human abilities, but which touched the deepest part of human understanding.

He looked into her eyes and saw...himself. He saw the darkness Elagra had talked about. She'd reminded him of all the things he'd done with it to survive, no noble purpose. What she had commanded from him the night he killed Amy was the violence, the visceral, primal things in the darkest corners of himself.

But as he stared into Bonnie's face, he knew that darkness wasn't evil. It was simply part of who he was. In its pure, original form, it was part of the natural order. He could use it for evil, or to defend or fight for his family, for himself, the kid he'd been.

"I love you across the river and over the hills," he said. He was soaked, just as Ramona had warned. And the water kept coming as Bonnie hovered over him. The book was getting wet.

She made that noise which reminded him of a mix of whales and thunder. Then she reached out to him, with a clawed hand bigger than a dump truck.

She could easily kill him if she grabbed him too enthusiastically, but recoil was the wrong idea. He looked down at the rabbits and remembered. Rabbits hop. His best tactic was going to be to jump when the claw drew close enough, land in the cup of the leathery palm.

Fuck it. He stuffed the book back in his waistband and got ready to jump.

Instead, he was forced to duck.

The air exploded with fire and heat, perilously close to Bonnie's head. The concussion took it further, slamming against her skull, tearing into sleek brown flesh and taking out one of the emerald green eyes.

Blood the color of gunmetal showered down on him, mixed with the water. Bonnie screeched in pain.

And then all hell broke loose.

As she cried out in pain, his sea creature threw herself backward, her mass hitting the river with maximum force. He saw her tail for the first time, a brief glimpse of the scaled length. It was thick as a redwood.

The Aquarium shuddered, like a table rattling from a slammed door. But it didn't stop. An ominous growl, the rumble of the earth, joined the sounds of wind and battle, and started to overtake both.

Shit.

He'd done what he was told, shut everything else out, but now everyone else's reality hit him from all directions.

He'd been in alley fights, but he'd never been in combat, not in firefights like Peter or Dana. But their descriptions leaped to mind. Dark, swirling shadows, explosions of fire, flashes of light. Mikhael and Derek were right in the heart of it, fighting with sword and staff, in the air, on the roof, turning, twisting, sometimes buried in the swarm for a harrowing moment before fire and electricity incinerated or threw their attackers back. The sky had become something right out of an Armageddon scenario.

They were hellishly good fighters, but no way they were able to keep all of that off of him. A glance right showed him he had Ruby and Ramona to thank for the shielding. The women were twenty feet apart on the mall roof, planted like willow trees with arms lifted. Their bodies vibrated, swayed, mouths moving, whatever was needed to keep a net of silver energy domed over him. The threads glimmered like a spider web.

But with Bonnie's violent reaction, the ground shifted in a way that had him stumbling. That net wavered, broke free like the snapped lines holding a ship to the dock. The sound of glass shattering told him they'd lost more windows in the Aquarium's cylinder roof feature, but he didn't turn to look. What was in front of him captured his attention and wouldn't let go.

Bonnie had disappeared from view. Not because she'd ducked back under the water. It had swallowed her. He was staring at an absolute darkness that wasn't darkness at all. It was a wall of water, rearing up from the river, building high enough to reach the roof of the Aquarium where he stood.

He understood violent situations, having been in more than he cared to remember. He knew how fast and how slow things happened. The reality was so incredibly fast, while the things you tried to stop from happening seemed to take forever.

He dove for the rooftop utilities and wrapped his arms around a pipe. If there'd been time, he would have pulled his belt loose and wrapped it around the fixed structure, adding to the reinforcement. As Marcie could attest, he knew how to do that pretty damn quick. But the water was quicker.

The force of the impact, if it didn't land on him with the power to crush him into a bag of bone shards, would probably yank him loose, send him spinning. He'd be pitched off the roof, dashed into something unyielding, and end up a crumpled heap anyway.

But that wasn't his primary concern. He was on a tall building with a slim chance of avoiding that fate. Marcie was on the docks with none.

He had time to do one more thing. Maybe it was a prayer, maybe a demand. *Let Marcie be safe. Fuck, let her be safe.*

Even though it was the one thing his brat never was. She had the courage of an army. Braver than anyone he knew, really. And considering the company he kept, that was saying something.

CHAPTER SIXTEEN

*W*hen they'd left the men on the roof, they took the stairs down to a side exit which put them close to the street side. Marcie didn't know who had given them access to the empty building, but Matt had connections all through the city. If they didn't have bigger priorities, she would have been tempted to dash through to see the penguins, her favorite part of the Aquarium. Another day. She hoped.

"Stay watchful," Raina said. "And always stay behind me or to the side, but don't cut in front of me."

"Same goes," Marcie answered.

Raina shot her an amused look. "You really are like Ruby."

As they emerged from the shadow of the Aquarium and headed down the dock, they saw Ramona. The chaos witch was *on* the waterfront railing, and she was dancing. Turning, twisting, her arms out and head tipped back. She pranced and dipped like a ballerina, seemingly oblivious to all of them. She never looked down, and yet she never misstepped.

"Don't try to talk to her right now," Raina said. "She's getting a feel for the different energies, what's gathering. Dancing helps her get in tune with those rhythms. Once she knows what she needs to know, she'll go up on the rooftop there." She nodded to a section of the shopping center, the corner closest to the Aquarium. "With Ruby, so they can be in the best position to help Ben."

They passed not far from a bench where Silas sat, eating beignets. Marcie felt strangely loathe to meet his glance, remembering that odd, probing feel when he'd first looked at her, but she chided herself for that. He seemed okay, even if his appraisal had made her feel uncomfortable. So she made herself look directly his way.

A flicker passed through his gaze, as if her regard surprised him, but he nodded politely. Then lifted the bag, a wordless offer.

Hanging around these guys was a surreal experience. Sure, why not have a beignet before fighting a crazy battle against paranormal forces to save New Orleans? She imagined him waiting in line at Café du Monde, taking out his wallet to pay. Freaky.

She shook her head. "No, but thank you."

He nodded with a faint smile, and went back to watching Ramona.

"She couldn't pick a shopkeeper," Raina muttered. "Or an accountant. *That's* what she really needs."

"Well, he's a little odd, but he seems...nice," Marcie ventured. "He's not human, is he?"

"No, he's not." Raina didn't elaborate, passing between Silas and Ramona, giving Silas only a quick nod of acknowledgement before she continued onward.

Up on the Aquarium roof, they'd been able to see Elagra, but on the ground, the warehouse where she'd appeared was around a curve, not visible to them at this angle. Marcie didn't expect she'd remained in that spot, anyway. She wondered that Ramona didn't seem as concerned as they were about immediate threats, but then she thought again about Silas. As relaxed as he had looked, his eyes hadn't been. They'd been moving pretty constantly. Which explained maybe why Raina also didn't appear worried about Ramona's possible proximity to the dark witch.

What was he? Marcie hoped there'd be time to ask at some point.

Down on the ground, there was no chill wind like that strange one they'd felt on the roof. But the sky was still unnaturally dark. The energy in the air was likewise getting denser, making it harder to breathe. It had a quality that raised the hair on the back of Marcie's neck and made her once again search the rooftop, reassure herself that Ben was still standing there. Though he was way too uncomfortably close to those menacing winged shapes.

"Marcie."

Marcie snapped her attention back down at Raina's sharp tone. There. Elagra stood between two buildings. She'd even stepped up on a cluster of crates, the better to be noticed. It made Marcie even more wary, and she saw Raina was the same, sweeping her glance around them, looking for traps. As they drew closer, Elagra's focus remained on the darkened sky and the suddenly much choppier river. Even now the cat's paws slapped against the bulkheads, sending up spray behind them.

Marcie wasn't fooled by Elagra's apparent lack of attention. The witch was every bit as aware of them as they were of her. She proved it a heartbeat later, when she spoke.

"I am here to make sure what should be born will be born," she said. "Without interference from you who do not understand."

Her voice, pitched above the rising wind, was flat, no inflection. It crawled over Marcie's skin, but Raina shot her a look Marcie read easily enough.

Steady. She's going to fuck with your head.

Well, she'd been mindfucked by the best, for far better reasons. She could hold her own when it was for worse ones.

"We understand just fine," Raina said. "You want to kill everybody. It gets you off in a way sex never has. But your twisted fuckery affects more than you. An' it harm none, do as you will. So this shit isn't happening."

Elagra's gaze turned to them. It took an act of will for Marcie to hold her ground, not start back. Her eyes were red. Like blood-red marbles, unnaturally glossy. Disturbingly enough, it reminded Marcie of the nail polish commercials where they coated a ball with one of their cheerful colors, just to prove how resistant the polish was to chipping. Elagra's lips peeled back from those eerie sharp teeth.

"You don't know me, witch," she rasped.

Raina pulled the band loose from her thick hair so it tumbled free, whipping out around her like a glossy cloak. A shimmer of wind currents around her, and she changed. She still had her lush human body, but now there was that otherness to it. Her fingers had transformed into wicked talons, and when she bared her teeth, the canines were sharp, curved. The real thing, not filed like Elagra's. Raina's eyes had also morphed, the exotic gold and green expanding, the pupils narrowed to slits like a serpent's.

A mist swirled around the half-succubus, reminding Marcie of the powder thrown out at the Holi Festival of Color in India. This was a pale crimson color. The wind picked it up and twisted it outward. Some of it touched Marcie, a sex demon's ensnaring power.

She remembered that from the bedroom, only this time it was fully unleashed, summoning one horrible reaction. Helpless terror. Because with this intent behind it, Raina's sexual compulsion wouldn't be resisted. It had one end goal. Death. A pleasurable death, but death all the same.

It was the most disturbing duality she'd ever felt, and fortunately only for a heartbeat. It rushed toward Marcie, looped around her in a whirl and then left her, headed for its true target. Trembling in the aftermath, she wondered if Elagra could see it. The witch didn't seem to be mounting any defense, though her appearance was scary enough, hinting at a weapon cocked and ready to be fired.

Raina stepped forward. Her voice had changed as well, deepened, yet was as female as the Earth itself. "Destruction won't fill your emptiness, Elagra. You have too many holes in your soul. I'm here to put you out of your misery."

The power wound around Elagra, and with one flick of Raina's fingers, cinched tight. The other witch stiffened and howled, and flung her hands out, unleashing a disruptive energy of her own. The explosion of power held the reds of flame and blood, and the smell of death.

Marcie drew her gun, aimed and fired. Elagra was gone in a flash. Marcie felt the rush of air, heard the shout of warning from Raina that saved her life. She took the knife blade on a defensive raised arm and kicked out, using nothing but instinct, but she connected.

Elagra dropped out of the air and rolled, and Marcie was on her. She landed one solid punch in the witch's face, across the sculpted cheekbone. Then Marcie screamed, choking on the sound as electricity rocketed through her. The witch broke free and whipped around. Marcie had no control of her muscles, no control of anything. Her vocal cords were seized by the same power, unable to give voice to the intense pain.

Then it let go, leaving Marcie gasping in relief. Elagra had been knocked backward, ass over end. Hit by nothing more than a solid fist of air. Raina stood over Marcie. Marcie still held the gun in her nerveless fingers, and she staggered up from the ground to stand at Raina's side.

Elagra spread her hands out to either side, the curved nails rippling in a calculated wave of sinister movement. She was in a half crouch, the posture and her painted body enhancing the impression of a deadly, primitive force of nature.

"You wish to play, sisters," she hissed. "Then we will play. It has started. Your actions will stop nothing."

"Except you talking," Marcie retorted. Her voice wasn't steady, but that was physical. Her mind was as fixed on her goal as a sniper on her target. "That's a win in my book."

The witch's attention slid past them. Raina and Marcie braced together, Marcie ready to back up Raina's play. But Elagra's next strike wasn't aimed at them.

Raina snarled a curse, her body whipping forward to follow the lunge of Elagra's as the dark witch fired an arrow of jagged silver lightning past them. Raina intercepted it with a stream of fire and a mass of energy that seemed to bend the air, but the arrow cut through it, flew true.

Marcie spun with the half-succubus and saw what Elagra had seen. Ramona.

The chaos witch was no longer on the rail. She was wandering aimlessly along the docks, picking up random shell shards, left there by seagulls dropping and cracking open the shellfish they'd fished out of the river.

Despite Ramona's unassuming presence, Elagra had reacted to it with an immediate, scorched earth attack. Elagra's crackling electrical current was headed toward the chaos witch like a locked-on missile.

"*Ramona.*" Raina's shout echoed over the docks.

Ramona picked up another shell piece and straightened. She examined it as if she were on an isolated beach somewhere, her skirt fluttering around her bare calves. That was when that bolt of magical energy reached her.

Or would have. Silas stepped in front of it. Jagged white-blue fire turned to fluttering ash, whirled away on the wind.

Silas didn't look like Silas anymore. His grey eyes had become the color of lightning, with the vibrant light of the same behind them. Instead of jeans and crisp, ironed shirt, he wore a gray robe that billowed around him, the hood up. In his hands, held up before him, was what had stopped the projectile. A scythe, just like the stereotype, only the reality was something far different. The curved blade gleamed with blue and orange flame, the fires of Heaven and Hell together. The shaft was threaded with a red color that moved, like running blood.

There was a blurriness to the edges of him, as if he was something not defined by matter. When Elagra saw what had stopped her attack, she went noticeably pale, even under her dark-skinned coloring. But Marcie couldn't fault her courage—or maybe it was stupidity—because she confronted Silas, though her voice had the sense to shake.

"You cannot interfere with how things unfold, Grim Reaper. You overstep yourself."

"You do not know enough of my role to instruct me, witch," Silas said. His voice reminded Marcie of the granite of an old cemetery's wall, worn smooth by decades of elements. "I see two paths to your death," he said. "One later. One now. You try a direct strike against the chaos witch again, and you will make that choice. Do we have an understanding?"

His voice changed when he posed the question. The expression "cold as a grave" came to mind. It crept into Marcie's subconscious like skeletal fingers and incited a hard shiver, bone and muscle deep. Marcie could taste the dirt of her own grave.

"Silas." Ramona had extended her hand. "Look. It's a pearl. One of the gulls must have dropped a mollusk."

Elagra's lip curled, but she didn't move as Silas dipped his head briefly, looked at what Ramona had in her open hand. He lifted the knuckles of his free hand, sketching a brief caress along the curve of her face. "It is lovely," he said. His voice was back to that cultured, smooth tone. Warmly courteous to Ramona, as if she hadn't just stepped into the middle of a potentially deadly fight. Marcie kept her attention jumping between all the players, watching for cues.

Ramona nodded, then glanced at Marcie and Raina, as if seeing them for the first time. She gave them an absent smile, and then her lavender eyes went to Elagra. "Do you know how pearls are formed?" the chaos witch asked. She turned to face Elagra fully, began to move toward her. It said a lot about what Silas was that Elagra didn't attempt another attack, even with such a clear shot presented to her.

Or maybe, like all of them, Elagra was caught up in Ramona's incomprehensible detachment from the volatile atmosphere.

Ramona didn't wait for an answer. "They're a defense mechanism. Something attacks the mollusk inside the shell. A parasite, or just something that irritates it. Or maybe something tries to pry it open and injures it. The mollusk creates the pearl around that spot to seal off the irritation. It overwhelms the wound, the parasite, and becomes something beautiful."

She swept her gaze over Elagra, head to toe. "Aren't you cold, in that thin dress? Don't you want to come inside?"

Ramona flung the pearl up into the air. It erupted into a white fog that billowed outward, swirled, hissed like scalding steam. Raina grabbed Marcie's arm, yanked her right. She felt the heated grasp of the energy that whipped past. A howl, and when it cleared, Elagra wasn't there. Ramona was frowning.

"I guess she wasn't cold enough yet," she said.

The wind rose again, only this time there was a different tone to it, one that pivoted them all swiftly toward the water. Silas was back in street clothes, no evidence of his scythe, but Marcie wasn't forgetting it anytime soon. *Grim Reaper?* Now she knew why she hadn't wanted to look at him. Could this day get any weirder?

Her heart caught in her throat. On the roof of the Aquarium, Ben had moved to the very edge, so she could see the tips of his shoes over it. If she was still up there, she would have reached up, gripped the back of his belt, because he didn't seem to be aware of anything but what was happening in front of him. His gaze was trained on the water. No. She squinted to see better. His eyes were closed, though she sensed his attention was on the water, something below it.

Then it broke that surface, slowly emerging.

"Beautiful," Elagra cried. Marcie and Raina spun back together. The witch stood against the dock rail. There was a shimmer around her that Marcie suspected was some kind of shield, because Raina wasn't immediately resuming the attack. Instead she was focused on that shimmer, a concentrated look on her brow.

The witch didn't seem to notice them. She was riveted on what came out of the Mississippi.

Elagra had called her beautiful, and Marcie couldn't disagree. It was like a dragon and a gargoyle rolled into one, with sleek, dark wet skin, a lot of curved horns and claws. There was an exceptional grace to its movements, despite its gargantuan size. Its eyes seemed to have so many darkly rich colors that sparkled when an explosion of fire bloomed high in the sky. She saw the silhouette of a winged Mikhael diving into the center of that fire, a giant swirl of darkness with moving parts converging around him.

Marcie saw Raina's gaze cut over to that fire and darkness, her throat work, as her green-gold eyes returned to full human and witch. *Mikhael.* Her lips moved over the word noiselessly.

A shot of blue fire crackled across the firmament, but seemed to originate from the roof, drawing Marcie's attention back to Ben. He was talking to the large creature.

To Bonnie. Marcie remembered what she'd told him, and a brief warmth cut the cold fear. The name fit her. Bonnie, who'd just been born, who was emerging into the world. Ben had that little book in his grasp, lifted toward her, holding her attention with that idea Marcie knew he'd thought was bat-shit crazy. But he'd do it anyway, her man. Marcie's heart pounded a little harder as the creature's head began to descend closer to him, bringing all those teeth and horns with her.

He wasn't afraid. She could tell. He was the bravest man she knew. Reckless as hell, but in this case, she felt what he likely did, what Ramona had tried to tell them. Bonnie didn't intend harm.

Any more than a human intended to step on an ant. Though that didn't change the outcome for the ant. So she held her breath as Bonnie's head lowered. But she had obviously connected with Ben, just as they'd suggested, and it was a miracle to watch. Maybe—

White fire shot across the water. It had a tail of blue electricity following it, and it moved too fast. It exploded next to Bonnie's head like a cannon blast, tearing flesh, striking far too near her eyes. The creature recoiled with a piteous, enraged howl.

Marcie cried out, even as she cursed herself for her stupidity. She suspected Raina was doing the same, but as she turned to re-engage with the witch, she saw Elagra had bolted, was running away from the docks with surprising swiftness, since Ramona's spell hadn't been a complete miss. One part of the woman's leg looked encased in a grooved substance like a mollusk's shell. The witch's dreadlocks whipped around her as she threw a wide-eyed look over her shoulder Marcie realized wasn't for her or Raina.

The ground was shaking, and a swelling roar that seemed to be all around them was coming from one specific direction. The river.

Raina dragged Marcie into a retreat, but not before she saw the wall of water rising up from the Mississippi. In the darkness, with just the dock lamps, it gave the eerie impression of meeting the starless sky, creating an abyss of blackness bearing down on them.

Raina was calling out something, some kind of spell Marcie was sure, her voice breathless, urgent. Worried. Whatever she was doing, she wasn't sure she'd be in time. She kept them running away from the docks, even as she spoke the words harshly. Marcie noticed Elagra wasn't attempting any spell craft. Which suggested the amount of water about to hit them was something nothing could stop. It was reaching out like the hand of a giant, coming down to splat a bug.

And they were the bug.

CHAPTER SEVENTEEN

*R*aina spun the cushion around Marcie as fast as she could think the spell. It almost fell short, but she saw it enclose Marcie in its bubble right before Raina had to turn her attention to her own survival.

Too late.

The water slammed into her, picking her up and tossing her forward, then catching up to swallow her, tumble her over and over. She hit something that felt like it jammed her shoulder into her chest cavity. Her arms were flailing, so she couldn't get them wrapped around her head to protect it. When her forehead bounced off something, she blacked out, but she was jumpstarted by sheer panicked survival instinct.

She wasn't a fan of being out of control anywhere but in Mikhael's arms, but she'd been there often enough to get her panic under control. She oriented herself enough to cast a shaky levitation spell. It had enough strength to bring her back to the surface, though not smoothly. She bounced off the side of the blue, usually-sparkling globe crowning the Harrah Casino's entryway. A cut in her shoulder immediately burned from the saltwater, but pain had always been a good focus for her. She scrambled to the top of the globe, breathing hard, and clung to it as the water washed past.

Marcie. Where was Marcie? And Elagra.

Raina.

The urgency of his voice in her mind was a blessing, but she didn't want Mikhael worrying about her when he had an army to fight. Her heart had stopped, seeing him dive into that nest of winged death.

No time to talk. Busy handling an ass-whooping over here.

His affectionate scoff in her mind was just the shot of adrenaline she needed, laced as it was with concern and deeper things. *Watch* your *ass,* vedma. *It is mine, after all.*

Yes, it was. As his very muscular one was hers. She held that thought for the moment, steadying herself, then got her head back into the game. Just in time to see Ben dealing with a very fractious sea monster and a second wall of water coming in behind the first.

"Hell," she muttered, and braced herself, but this time the water washing in wasn't as high. After it roared past the Aquarium, it hit Harrah's and doused Raina with a heavy sheet of spray, but that was all. When the water tumbled onward, she was able to swipe her wet hair out of her eyes and look for Marcie.

There. Raina felt the tight fist of fear around her heart ease. The bubble had protected the girl from both waves, thank the Goddess. A floating dock, torn loose and thrown between two pilings, had firmly lodged there at a lopsided angle. Marcie's bubble had bumped against it and held. After her initial start at realizing there was nothing but empty air beneath her, the girl had put her foot out, found her way to the knee-deep water on the sloped dock. She had the presence of mind to hold onto a coil of rope twined around the piling. She looked as if she was doing what Raina was doing, taking current stock of the situation around them.

A boat had been torn loose from the dock. It was in the middle of the street on its side, swaying in the water. Based on its position, Raina guessed it had crashed into the tiki-style bar and restaurant in front of the mall on the dockside and then rolled from there to the street. The bar was little more than a hollowed-out structure of broken timbers and crumpled tin from the roof demolition, visible just above the churning water.

But nature was the least of their problems. The whipping wind, the unnatural darkness in the sky, took her attention back over toward the Aquarium. Fire and lightning still streaked the firmament. Against it, she caught a glimpse of Mikhael's silhouette, a winged humanoid figure in among a heart-stopping number of winged not-human ones.

She saw the unique blue-gold light of Derek's magic illuminating the sky with those explosive flashes, and knew he was still right there in it with Mikhael.

They'd been fighting at a low enough elevation, the army would have had to scatter to avoid the wave. They'd obviously rallied, but if they'd broken formation, even momentarily, that meant...

Raina dropped and rolled behind the globe as a rush of dark energy passed over her. The extended talons came so close they snagged her shirt, ripped it across her back, taking flesh with it.

Damn it, but also good. She had a blink to think *oh shit* as she saw two pass over Marcie's position, but they paid no attention to her. Whatever blood-and-soul price she'd paid for them, Elagra had obviously contracted them to occupy the magic muscle interfering with her plans. She didn't see the mortals as a threat. Yet.

Raina scrambled back to her feet, putting the globe at her back, and crouched. The trio of demonic minions that had tried to snatch her up arced above her and then turned, a pelican style plunge back toward her position.

Though hand motions, staffs, wands and words made excellent focus channels, she didn't need them. She'd been a witch from the moment she'd been born. A practitioner for whom magic had long ago stopped being practice. Instead, it was the air she breathed, the blood rushing through her veins.

As the enemy dove for her, thought and intent came together into projectiles of fire and ice, and a wave of disorientation that snared them like a net. Two crashed into one another and spun away, while the third made it through and cloaked himself in smoke, but not before she saw the gleam of the blade. She dodged right as the sulfur-smelling fog engulfed her. The blade shrieked across the metal of the globe, and she flung herself at the attacker. Slime and muscle. Goddess, she hated demon minions. Like malevolent, squirming, deadly worms.

She'd already yanked her knife from the ankle holster Ruby had given her as a gift last Yule, bless her violent soul. She used it now, jamming it into some soft tissue.

The beast howled. A claw swiped her face, but she jerked back fast enough it was superficial, though she tasted her own blood in the corner of her mouth. She shoved into close quarters again, and was yanked up, then thudded back down in a tangle, her foe unable to get himself turned around into a launch. They rolled along the Harrah's rooftop, but she got the upper hand, jamming the knife into her enemy in three rapid stabs, stabbing deep. Then twisting.

"You're done," she snarled. Though it was her least favorite kind of magic, she pulled the heart energy of the thing into her as she took its life. She needed the fuel and the strength. She'd do a deep cleansing later. Along with a deep tissue massage. Li, her eldest incubus, had great hands.

As she kicked free of her now lifeless opponent, a quick look said that was the last of them. But she had another problem. Fucking hell.

Her slim hope that the dark witch had been pushed to the bottom of the river and was drowning there under a big rock was dashed. Fifty feet down the docks from Marcie, Elagra had resurfaced. As she stood on top of a warehouse whose roof was half torn off, her target was obvious.

Ben was full of surprises. The cynical, wise-assed human had reconnected with the injured sea monster, was calming her down. Ruby—Raina recognized her energy signature—had levitated Ben so he could better communicate with the "baby," and he was still there, now, eye to multi-eyes with it. He had his hands on her, a remarkable sight. Raina wished she could see her fellow witches, but if Ruby had done that, then she and Ramona would be busy getting the cocooning energy ready to wrap around her, so they could transport her out of there.

They were doing their job and she needed to do hers, keeping Elagra out of the mix. As the witch stood on the warehouse overhang, her hands were moving in a fast, graceful motion, her mouth moving just as quickly. Raina could feel the malevolent energy vibrating off her, even from here. And damn it all, the witch was smart enough to still be shielded, so that she couldn't be struck down unawares by another witch.

Raina knew what was turning the wheels in the dark witch's head. She'd tried hurting the newborn to get her to accomplish Elagra's destructive goals, but that hadn't succeeded. Ben had established a bond. So Elagra had to get rid of Ben, a far more vulnerable target than the creature she'd wanted to see born. It was unexpected that she hadn't tried that angle first, but then, just like the minions' dismissal of Marcie, it was clear Elagra hadn't anticipated the humans being such a threat.

Raina wasn't the only one who'd noticed what was happening on the top of the warehouse. She also wasn't the only one who considered neutralizing Elagra her mission.

Marcie had gotten off the piling, likely stroked through the now waist deep water to the warehouse. Raina expected she'd hauled herself up to the roof using the drainpipe. The girl was now on the roof, running flat out across it toward the edge where the witch had stationed herself.

Screened by the wind, thunder and firefight, Marcie was banking on Elagra not detecting her approach. The girl had noticed the shielding on Elagra, same as Raina had, but Raina realized Marcie was taking the chance that Elagra's shield was only to deflect magical threat.

And hell, she was right. Thank Goddess for Elagra's tunnel vision. The magical force field didn't stop Marcie. She went through it as if it wasn't there, and plowed into the witch like a battering ram.

They rolled across the flat expanse. Elagra snarled and struck at Marcie's face, raking her with the lethal nails. As they hit the raised lip of the roof edge, Elagra brought her legs up like a lithe cat to shove at Marcie's midriff. Marcie blocked and countered with a punch to the face. This one made direct contact with the bridge of Elagra's nose.

Marcie had the advantage in hand-to-hand. But Raina knew all Elagra needed was enough of an opening, enough space. She'd blast Marcie with a fatal dose of magic as soon as she could be sure the recoil wouldn't take her out with it.

It would only take Elagra a few moments to recognize that as her best option. Whereas Marcie might not realize it was the only kind of opening Elagra needed to win the fight. Or maybe she did, because it was next to a miracle that the fight hadn't broken apart enough, even for a moment, to give Elagra the chance to do it.

Raina had to get over there before it was too late.

Marcie had expected to be dead, or washed halfway into the Business District when that wall of water hit. Instead, as she was tumbled around, she realized the water wasn't touching her. She was in some kind of cushioned hamster ball, where she could look up and all around and see things, all while remaining dry. Except she was being tumbled too fast to look at anything. However, since she was also not drowning or being impaled on storm debris, she wasn't going to complain.

When her protective shield landed her on a twisted floating dock lodged between two pilings, she was bruised and had a heart rate somewhere in the three thousand beats per minute range, but she was alive and pretty much unscathed. She was certain she had Raina to thank for that, though she was worried because she didn't see the witch.

She did see Elagra, and the sight of her fired her blood, gave her a needed shot of rage-induced adrenaline. She was running across the flooded docks, bounding like some strange frog along the water's surface until she reached the top of a warehouse. Then she was on solid ground, but she was doing freaky things with her hands, her mouth moving even faster, and her attention was on something up ahead of her, in the sky.

When Marcie followed that line, her heart triple hammered again. Ben, suspended in the air, was back with Bonnie.

The vision of the witch striking and hurting the creature, the blast coming narrowly close to taking Ben with it, was still technicolor clear in Marcie's brain.

"Oh no, you don't," she said, scrambling to her feet and taking off after the dark witch. Thank Goddess the hamster ball let her go. She plunged into the water, stroked toward the warehouse as fast as she could. The drainpipe was the quickest access. She hauled herself hand over hand onto the roof. Once there, she broke into a run. Though Elagra was her primary focus, she had to let herself look toward Ben for just a moment. Standing on air, saying something to the baby, throwing his arms out, laughing, talking, doing a variety of things to get her attention.

She also noticed Elagra wasn't looking at the sea monster. She was looking at Ben as she made her crazy hand gestures and mutterings. Oh, Goddess. Elagra had realized removing Ben from the equation was the better way to secure her victory.

You touch him, you'll be too dead to savor anything but your own grave.

Every workout, everything she'd done to prepare herself to run down perps, she put into this. She would catch the witch. She would get there in time.

She wasn't going to get there in time. The witch was lifting her hands, drawing back.

A fireworks explosion of movement snapped Elagra's attention to the top of the mall. Even Marcie glanced that way, briefly distracted by the odd sight.

Ruby seemed to be containing some more water Bonnie had churned up, while Ramona was keeping a half dozen winged demon things off of them. At least Marcie thought that was what she was doing.

The chaos witch turned her back on the creatures and lobbed a ball of crackling energy in the opposite direction, almost as if she was encouraging them to chase it like a pack of dogs. The sparks sizzling off it were what had caught Elagra's attention. The projectile arced up, then came down. Looped around, bounced off two building surfaces, came back, all in half-a-blink of time. The creatures were almost upon Ruby when Ramona's weapon hit them. It shot through their sides, leaving fire-blasted, fist-sized holes. All of them dropped into the water on the dock like bricks.

Marcie was becoming a real fan of the kind of chaos that could turn stuffed bunnies into real ones, and take out bad guys using the same approach as a pinball machine. The demonic things hadn't anticipated the lethal blow, or the direction from which it had come.

Something Elagra was about to experience.

If Elagra saw her a split second before Marcie reached her, things might get really ugly. But Marcie didn't give her that chance. She didn't stop at the roof edge, didn't consciously calculate anything. She threw herself out into the air. When she landed, she took Elagra down with a bone-jarring thud and metallic vibration, onto the unforgiving tin roof.

Raina was not telling Ben O'Callahan his wife had died at the hands of the witch he hadn't killed years ago, the way he so adamantly felt he should have. It would break him. She knew men enough to know that.

She also knew about the kind of love that was so strong its loss could break a soul.

She used a solidifying spell to jump down on top of the water, race across it like a brick path, toward the warehouse roof. Marcie bounced back on the balls of her feet, shot a sharp kick at Elagra's knee that almost took it out, if Elagra hadn't twisted away at the last moment.

Raina sent a concentrated stream of fire into that opening, whipping Elagra around, distracting her, but it wasn't powerful enough to take her down. Marcie closed in again.

Goddess, the young woman was a good fighter, a natural. Mikhael himself had said she was going to be a formidable warrior, already well on her way to it. But that was about to end unless Raina did something that might not be advisable, but was likely Marcie's only chance to survive this.

What she sent this time had to be strong enough to ensure Elagra didn't get back up.

And the time was now. Raina had reached the roof, but Elagra had broken free once more, was throwing a taunt Marcie's way. It was a distraction, something to give the girl pause, line her up for Elagra like a target. But it made Elagra a target as well.

Raina launched the spell she knew she needed to use, hoping it had the momentum it needed to get there, even though it wouldn't have the finesse she desired. She projected her voice, sending the command booming across the expanse between them.

"Marcie. Get clear."

Marcie glanced toward her, but Raina's magic traveled faster than her words. As energy crackled from Elagra, exploding toward Marcie, Raina's spell struck the dark witch.

CHAPTER EIGHTEEN

*B*en knew the power of water. He lived in a river town, after all, not far from an ocean. He'd stood in the surf like any other kid and nearly had his feet knocked out from beneath him by water no higher than his knees. Storm surge was the one force in the world not to be fucked with.

As that wall of water advanced, now a good ten feet higher than the building, he realized if he tried to hold onto the utility pipe, his arms would be ripped out of their sockets. He'd lost sight of Derek and Mikhael.

Letting go of the pipe, he ran toward the water. He had a plan, based on wild luck and his estimate of the angle of that water, all being made in near darkness. And he'd gotten the idea from a freaking kid's book.

He put it in verse, shouting it out in case the spell was still active, and Bonnie was listening. And to give him something to occupy his mind, other than being dead in the next second with the possibility of never seeing Marcie again.

"How much can I love you? As high as I can jump," he bellowed.

As the water began to crest, he was twenty feet from the edge of the building. With a burst of energy, he closed that distance, leaped onto the lip of the building and flung himself as high as he could.

The velocity of the water caught him in midair, swallowed him up. He heard the shriek of the building as the water hit it, but then that was cut off abruptly. He wasn't knocked brainless by the battering ram of the crest, fortunately, but there was no controlling anything once the water had him. The likelihood he'd be dashed up against something that harpooned him like a hapless fish or took off a full layer of skin to the bone was pretty high. But he kept his arms wrapped around his head, tried to pull up his knees and roll in the water like a ball, the way he'd learned to fall early on in his street life.

He let out an oath and swallowed sea water as he crashed into a solid surface with a thud. His teeth snapped together on the curse, the impact jarring every bone he had. He rolled, things jabbing and scraping him, tearing at his shirt and jeans. He knew what being stabbed felt like, and his lower belly clutched as he felt that familiar slice and burn in his side, his back, his shoulder.

Then the water was washing past. Fucking Christ, bless the holy Virgin and amen. He'd landed where he'd intended.

He wasn't one to thank the gods, but he'd have to give them their due, because no way that should have worked out the way he'd hoped. As the water poured off the building in every direction, he was skidding along the slanted surface of the circular glass roof of the Aquarium. And sending an additional thank you Jesus to the architects who'd come up with that useful design, that had acted like a catcher's mitt.

The weight of the water had broken through a dozen places, pouring into the building like water through a sieve. It created the danger of jagged glass, but also provided a useful network of crossed beams. As the water spun him around, he risked grabbing onto one of them. It cut the shit out of his hands, but he held on.

He had to fight the pull of the water, snarling to give himself extra strength. But then, between one breath and the next, the worst had passed. He could shift until he was sitting on the support, his feet braced against a cross piece as he took his bearings.

He looked for Marcie first, but all the magical light the Guardians had generated was gone. He couldn't see shit along the waterfront. The only living soul he found right away filled up his vision and made him start, because Bonnie was a rock's throw from him. She'd moved onto the docks, was probably sitting in twenty feet of water, which for her would be a shallow pond. He'd been right about her back legs. She was like a T-Rex at rest, though her upper arms were far more powerful and wide-reaching. Her shoulders and the length of her torso said she could go to all fours and run down anything.

Yet right now she was touching her face with a clawed hand, tentative. As she found the head wound, the punctured eye, she made a whimpering crooning noise that startled him, the way it twisted his heart. It was the sound a child made when she was hurt. Not understanding what had hurt her.

A familiar feeling filled him, one he'd felt way too often around Elagra. Helpless rage when she harmed something or someone he cared about, just to make him more isolated. Or just because she didn't give a shit and wanted to hurt someone.

It didn't take much to put together what had happened. He'd been making progress in the way they desired, and in the way Elagra definitely didn't. She'd struck out at her creation to summon the destructive chaos and rage she wanted.

Damn it, where was Marcie? Where were the others? His heart hammered against the inside of his chest as if it was going to explode. Had he been the only one to make it? He couldn't see much, but from Bonnie's position, he knew the whole waterfront had to be covered in water.

Where was she? He scanned every rooftop, hoping to see a human silhouette, some kind of movement, despite the blackness everywhere. There was no fire in the sky, no lightning. Where were Derek and Mikhael? Had the storm surge driven back the army, even if temporarily?

A thunderous voice yelled out something in a language he didn't know. Light flooded the area, like a lighthouse with a rotating beam.

Derek was above him, on the top crest of the Aquarium roof. His hat was gone, his shirt was torn and bloody, much like Ben's. He'd set his staff along that upper frame and anchored it. The top part of the staff was emitting the light, angled down to sweep the area several buildings out on either side.

Mikhael was flying fast, left, right. He appeared to be doing what he could to reinforce the building so it didn't topple off its foundations. Right before he shot back up into the sky, because that army had regrouped and were swooping down once more, a nightmarish flock of darkness and death.

Ben couldn't help with that, which pissed him off. But what pissed him off more was not seeing Marcie. That feeling tripled when he saw the one he least cared about seeing. Elagra. She was on the roof of a warehouse nearby. Had she hurt his brat? If she had, he was going to kill her slow.

"Ben." Derek was calling to him. "We have to finish it."

He snapped his gaze up to the Light Guardian's grim face. Marcie might be hurt, or worse. He had to deal with that, find her, fuck anybody else's priority. But then Bonnie made that pained whimper, and her multi-colored eyes rotated, as if looking for someone to make sense of things for her. She'd just been born, for Christ's sake.

Hurting him was one thing. Hurting an innocent, or his family? That required one simple response, no need to analyze or question it. Then there was the other side of it. If she flipped out again, they'd lose the waterfront and most of New Orleans. Or Derek and Mikhael would be forced to kill her to prevent that.

Over his dead body.

He didn't have to analyze the unexpected strength of that conviction, because his heart leapt out of his feet and straight up into his throat. He saw Marcie.

She was swiftly closing ground on the same warehouse rooftop Elagra was on, but with the sound of the water, and the wind still a rushing roar, the witch likely hadn't heard her yet. She had a calculated look on her face. She was twisting her hands together, and Ben could see her lips moving. Ben would lay money she was going to hurt Bonnie again, to get her even more riled up.

Marcie was wet to the skin, and she was bleeding. He saw the stain on her jeans and shirt, which gave him a what-the-fuck moment, but she was moving fast. Even fueled by adrenaline, she wouldn't move that fast if she was truly hurt. That's what he told himself.

Elagra never heard her. Marcie landed on her like a ton of bricks, no fear of falling. And somehow Raina was in that mix, too, because when the two broke apart, Elagra was momentarily thrown back by a projectile of swirling color and sparks. When it hit, it was like Elagra was seized by invisible hands, lifted up and slammed down against the rooftop A/C unit so hard her already disheveled up-do came falling all the way down.

He bit back another curse as he saw Marcie take advantage of the moment, duck under Raina's fire and be there to meet Elagra when she scrambled up, staggering. His brat hit her mid-body with a length of timber that had probably been thrown on the concrete landing by the monster's thrashing tail.

He couldn't deny it. He was freaking proud of her. And he realized Derek was right. He had to get back to his job. Elagra was theirs. They were going to take care of it, the succubus witch and his wife.

"That's my brat," he murmured. "Put that bitch down."

"Ben." Derek wasn't messing around. He injected triple urgency in the one syllable, and he didn't take further time to expand on it. At the same moment, he disappeared from the top edge of the circular slanted roof and rematerialized on the flat roof where they'd started, only now he stood in calf-deep water in those dragonskin boots of his. Mikhael landed back at his side.

Derek had left his staff where it was, lighting up the area to give Ben visibility, but he obviously didn't need it. As he landed, an explosion of fire as wide as the building rooftop launched from the impact, meeting the next line of attackers. Mikhael charged in behind it, cutting through the flames, his sword flashing.

Ben's attention was yanked away from them as Bonnie reached down, plucked up the giant whale statue in front of the Aquarium. It was sitting in the water, gently rocking like a rubber duck in a kid's bath. With a snarl, she flung it down the docks, the thing bouncing across the water like a skipped rock. It hit one of the warehouses with a resounding boom of metal and crashed through.

Bonnie had decided, as babies did, that if something had hurt her, the best reaction was to get pissed. Her talons curled into fists and she slammed them into the side of the bulkhead. Through it, under. She cracked the concrete like she was taking the top off an Oreo and had gotten too enthusiastic, breaking it in half. As the Aquarium shuddered once again, Ben hoped Mikhael had added some pretty hefty magical super glue to keep it standing.

She was writhing, thrashing as she howled and beat at the docks. Another wave of water was rising.

That was when Ben was grabbed.

At first, he thought Elagra was doing some weird shit to him, but Ben was leaving the rooftop of broken glass, carried seemingly on a platform of air. Then he realized Ruby and Ramona had reappeared on the shopping center roof.

They must have dodged into the building right before the wave hit, because they were still mostly dry. Ruby had her hand lifted, pointed in Ben's direction. Her other hand was up and extended, fingers spread, palm flat as she made a spiraling motion with it that matched the rhythm of what he felt beneath him. Energy, coiling around him, below him, taking him up and up. Ben could see nothing but open air under his shoes. He wouldn't be looking down again.

Ruby's eyes were flat steel, jaw hard as granite in concentration. The wave of water coming this time was somewhat smaller, but still deadly. The difference between having a three-story building fall on top of you and a one-story one.

Ramona stepped forward. She began to turn like a pinwheel, her arms straight out from her body. As she did, the water began to turn on itself, like it was becoming a giant waterspout, going up and up. She called out something to Ruby, and Ruby jerked her head, a bare nod of acknowledgement. The hand she had spiraling lifted, like a traffic cop bringing everything to a halt. The water shimmered, one side of the spiral flattening as gravity tried to move it forward and couldn't. At the flat part it looked like smooth glass, the water dark blue and churning in the night, glittering from Derek's light.

Ruby was weaving another spell. He could see the laser intensity of her gaze, the sparks of power coming off her skin, her body like a lean cord drawn taut. The air around her was blurred, as if she was calling in every element above, below and around her to her aid. Now he understood why Derek and Raina had scoffed at her understated reference to her magical skills.

The building wasn't going to hold through a second impact, because otherwise Ruby and Ramona wouldn't seem so hell-bent to keep that water from breaking over the docks this time. But doing their damnedest to get him closer to Bonnie while at the same time holding the water back was coming at a cost. Blood had started to seep from Ruby's nose, dripping onto her shirt. Ramona had planted her feet, arms still raised, but her body was twitching in its rigorous stance. As Ben watched, she fell to one knee, looking as if a weight was coming down on her, trying to crush her beneath it on the rooftop.

He didn't tolerate a woman suffering on his account. He had lost the book and Bonnie was still fussy and pissed, her eyes on everything but him, but it didn't matter. He would bring her gaze back to him, even if it was like drawing the attention of a bird way up in the sky. He gave himself a moment to think, closed his eyes again as Ramona had showed him. Though it should have seemed impossible with all the pandemonium going on, he was going to do this, damn it.

He recalled Ruby's words in the hotel room. *Magical ability at some level is within most people's grasp, if they're willing to open themselves to what lies deep inside all of us.*

He thought about the feeling, the connection he'd felt at the beginning. When he reached for that inside him, he found it, waiting, like a rope tied to his objective, guiding him to it. He remembered the simple, strong words of the book, the things Ramona had told him, the way she'd gripped his hand. She'd acted as if doing this, knowing it in his heart, was the easiest thing in the world—once he got out of his own way.

Well, that applied to a lot of things in life.

"How much can I love you? I can love you this much." Ben bellowed it out. If he hadn't been as focused as he was, the thunderous sound of his own voice would have startled him. He flung his arms out wide, a swift, exaggerated movement.

Two eyes swiveled his way, one green, one purple.

"'How much can I love you? More than the whole world and the universe and everything."

Everything in the whole universe, the vastness of it, narrowed down to one thing, one important thing. Now he understood what it meant, a million angels dancing on the head of a pin. That was what love was. So much in such a small space, one heart, reaching out to another, connecting.

Water churned around Bonnie's haunches as she shifted, six more eyes looking toward him.

"I can love you all the way to the farthest meadow. To the last moment in time."

He'd said he was no poet, but now the words came just like the energy, a rush of fire through his lungs, his arms, his head. And he knew the source of that magic.

Marcella Ann Moira. Had he not had Marcie in his life, he wouldn't have found those words now, because he wouldn't *know*.

They were her. Everything he felt for her, everything he was willing to do for her.

Now he realized what Derek had been trying to tell him, why Ben hadn't gone back down to kill Elagra when he had the chance.

There would always be Elagras. Loves like his and Marcie's, they were the fabric that held the line against the Elagras of the world. Crushed them like that wall of water, absorbed the pieces that remained. When he reached the end of this life, he wouldn't be thinking of what the witch had twisted in him, how she'd hurt him. He'd be thinking of Marcie, the softness of her hair, her smile, her sweet, sweet submission. She was the true miracle, the rare thing in the world.

He thought of all of them. Matt, his chosen brothers and their wives. Even Raina and Mikhael, Derek and Ruby. Jem, their new son. It was all there, all fucking there. Bigger than Elagra, bigger than anything, and he could gather it in to him, pull his daughter's attention to him, and hold it with that tether. It was the strongest magic of all, the member of the team that never flagged, the weapon that never dulled, as long as you knew how to keep it sharp.

A grin wreathed his wet face as another shower of water landed on him, but this wasn't from the surf. This was from a large head, poised just over him, the water dripping off her nose and chin.

He turned his face up to her. It was the first really close look he'd had, and he saw the beauty of the sparkling eyes, the layered silver and bronze scales on the neck, the dark, dark eyes with absurdly thick lashes.

There was uncertainty in those eyes, hope, a little bit of fear, a lot of intelligence and worry. He knew those emotions, that mix. He knew what was needed when they came together like that, and now a very smart woman's voice was in his head.

"When you're being really tough and strict with me...that's when I feel safest."

"Enough of this, little girl," he said, in the most uncompromising Master's voice he'd ever used. It had a different note to it, but the underlying no-nonsense, *I am going to take care of you, no arguments* tone was there. "You have to trust me. We're going to get you somewhere better than this."

He took a step forward, then another, and extended an arm out to her, palm up, fingers splayed wide. He waited with bated breath to see if she would figure it out, if it would work so he could give Ruby and Ramona some help. When Bonnie dipped her head further, he thought he might have to go with Plan B, which was making an awkward jump to her head and grabbing one of her horns, which likely wouldn't go over as well. But then, slowly, she lifted her clawed hand. Emulating his gesture, she extended one questing claw, all six of her talons opening to reveal a creased, leathery palm.

"Smartest kid in the whole damn class," he said.

He tried not to think of Matt and Savannah's toddler, Angelica. Specifically, the way her fist closed around a toy, right before she shook it until its innards rattled. He stepped onto the broad palm, wrapping his hands around one of the curved talons to steady himself. It was the color of rough ivory.

He was lifted off Ruby's bed of air, and up closer to Bonnie's face, way above the water and the buildings.

The snap of retreating energy that hit his back heel as he took that step told him just how close Ruby had been to the limits of her strength, holding him and the wall at the same time. He risked a glance and saw the reassuring sight of her making an impatient swipe at her bloody nose before she threw her focus behind Ramona's, toward the wall of water the two women were holding off the docks.

She called out guttural words, made a sharp movement forward. Ramona advanced with her. However, Ben noticed that Bonnie's attention had also been caught by what they were doing. With a tilt of her head and wide eyes, she studied the water they were holding back.

"Oh, hell. Maybe not the best—"

She leaned forward, her head breaking through the wall of water, horns dripping as she blinked down at the two women. Her other claw lifted, cut through the flow. At first Ben's gut tightened, thinking she was reaching for one of them, but she just moved that talon back and forth, like a person checking out the flow from a spigot.

Despite everything else, he couldn't help the warmth that spread through him. Damn. Curiosity. They'd distracted her from her pain, like using a shiny bauble to draw a crying kid's attention.

Ramona beamed up at Bonnie with all the warmth of a sun. She included Ben in that, her gaze sliding over him, standing so comfortably in the grasp of their sea monster, leaning against the fence of her talons, holding onto one for balance.

Then the chaos witch called out something and Ruby nodded. The two witches channeled the water left and right, coordinating. The water flowed off Bonnie's talons, the wave dissipating back into the river, until that invisible shield that had held it back could be dissolved as well.

Ruby caught Ben's eye, made a gesture. Yeah, they weren't done. It was time to start the next part, where they'd need the greatest distraction level of all. The cocoon.

He gripped the taloned finger harder, stroked it, a caress that drew Bonnie's attention to him again, though reluctantly, since she was still intrigued by what Ruby and Ramona were doing. He wondered if they made ADHD drugs in dosages that would have to be transported in a tanker truck.

"How much can I love you?" Ben continued. "Enough to take you to a fast food restaurant when you want to eat pre-packaged food. My love is wider and longer than this river. Than your memory, or mine, or the memory of everyone who's ever lived."

A rainbow of thread drifted over Bonnie's head. At least that was what it looked like. He could imagine Ramona casting it from one side, Ruby reeling it in from the other, then he saw more strands drifting over Bonnie. The blanket analogy hadn't been as far off base as he'd initially thought. Those strands were being woven above, below and beside the gigantic creature, as they slowly brought it down, like a blanket over a baby in her crib.

He saw Ruby make another gesture toward him and interpreted it easily enough. He needed to start moving back, out of range, so he wasn't caught in the same net. He was pretty sure that meant she'd re-cast his platform so he wouldn't back off into space and smack down into the water about two hundred feet below, but there was only way to find out.

Even so, he was reluctant to leave Bonnie, no matter that they were doing everything possible to keep her safe. But he began to retreat, moving between the claws, Fortunately, he discovered the salt spray from the water sluicing off Bonnie had left a kind of fuzzy limning on the re-cast platform, showing him the outline.

But the second he stepped onto it, Bonnie's demeanor changed.

Her back straightened, the giant head came up on the thick stalk of her neck, and the teeth bared. Ben dropped to his stomach as she tossed her head around, nearly whacking him off into the water like a T-ball. She wasn't attacking him. She was snapping at the tendrils of energy.

Ramona shouted something to Ruby and the threads lifted high in the air, like a magic carpet fluttering on the wind, taking it a safe distance away. The force and speed at which they did it knocked Ruby back as if she'd been picked up and thrown by an explosion, but she knew how to land, too, tucking herself into a ball. Even so, Ben winced as she slammed into the wall of the rooftop entrance to the shopping center.

Before Ramona could go to her, Ruby was on her feet, obviously cursing a blue streak. She met Ben's eyes, and mouthed the word he fully expected to hear.

"Again."

They tried twice more, Ruby bringing the platform so close to Bonnie he could put his hand on her, calm her down. They'd bring the colorful blanket near, slowly drawing him back out of range.

Each time it was the same. Except with each attempt she was starting to get more pissed, so that Ruby and Ramona had to divide their attention between that and the rising water level again.

The passage of time was bringing back his own frustrations and worry, even though he knew that wasn't helping things. But since Raina hadn't shown up to reinforce Ruby and Ramona, that meant the fight with Elagra was still happening or...something he wasn't going to fucking think about.

He had to believe the former, which meant that them getting Bonnie out of here was the key to all of it. But the plan as originally formulated wasn't going to work.

They needed to—

Shit.

He hadn't ducked fast enough this time. Bonnie, still aggravated by the latest attempt, had shifted unexpectedly. Her shoulder shoved through the energy creating the platform and slammed into Ben. He tumbled off, fell about ten feet and landed against her side. The only thing that kept him from falling further was grabbing onto a protrusion of bone shaped like a shark's fin.

Crazily, he remembered the mud creature he'd created, the stick he'd stuck in just that spot. He'd imagined his monster having protrusions of bone like spiked weapons, probably inspired by that bony, round-backed dinosaur whose name he couldn't begin to remember.

Bonnie's head swung around to him, all fifteen eyes lighting on him. For a second, he was face to flaring nostril. Her fang pressed against his flailing feet, giving him a purchase point. Or a starting point for her to draw him into her maw like a spaghetti noodle.

No, she wasn't harming him. If he hadn't lost his mind to false hope, it appeared she'd gone still, specifically to give him a second to steady himself.

He put his hand beside the nostril, observing his entire head could probably fit in there. It was uncanny, how much she felt like the earth and stick creature he'd made so long ago. It had come to life, just as he'd hoped for it to do. Becoming something he never could have imagined.

Deep in that dark and hopeless place, he'd created a ray of light, with a spark of child's imagination and a sliver of hope and perseverance. A belief that something different lay ahead.

"I have to go with her," he shouted. The sound didn't seem to bother her, but again, with her size, he probably sounded like *Horton Hears a Who*, the little "We are here's." When the hell had he read that book? Maybe he'd seen it on TV at some point.

He managed to look over his shoulder, shout it a couple times until the two witches got the gist of it. Bonnie opened her mouth, wide, and a long, low note came from it. She was tired of this. She was hungry. She was scared. She didn't want to be here anymore.

"I know, baby," he said, stroking her nose, as wide a sweep as he could manage. "Daddy's going to take care of it, right damn now."

Ruby and Ramona were looking at one another, saying something, but there was no time for debate. Two swipes of her tail had swamped the riverfront all the way past the casino. If she kept stomping around, that fault line, ley line, whatever they hell they called it, could set off a full earthquake.

"Fuck it," he muttered. "I need to go with her. We'll figure out the rest. Let me go with her."

He pointed upward, in the general direction of the blanket of energy, and made a sharp, insistent movement. *Put it over us and let's get it done.*

The mental struggle he saw between the two women told him his return trip, wherever they were taking her, wasn't guaranteed, best case scenario. Worst case, they weren't sure he would survive the trip. Maybe the magic was only configured for her.

If there was one thing he had learned growing up on the streets, second guessing and "what-if-ing" yourself was the one sure way to die. He powered through on guts and a lot of street smarts, and hoped for the best. Or he didn't hope at all. He just saw where he wanted to go and how best to get there, and then fired the starting gun. If he'd ever found himself on the other side of the dirt when all was said and done, it would have been what it was. Glory hallelujah and let's all raise a drink in memory of the daft bastard.

Ultimately, this choice was him, or a lot of people here getting hurt. Including Bonnie. It was the only choice they had that made any sense.

Apparently Ruby and Ramona had come to the same conclusion, because he saw Ruby nod, meet his gaze. Then her attention lifted and she and Ramona started chanting.

"Okay, Bonnie," he said. "Okay, let's do this together. Hey."

He hoisted himself up another spike, so he could lay both hands on her snout. She tilted her head this way and that, considering him from different angles. He rubbed both his hands around her nostril, then up higher, inching his way up, stroking. Marcie said he had strong hands, hands that always made her feel safe, cherished when he caressed her, stroked her. The first time she'd said it, inside he'd reacted like a school kid, as if he'd received the best compliment anyone had ever received. The thing was, he still felt that way.

I love you, brat. If this doesn't work out, well...you know that.

As he told Bonnie how he'd climb the tallest tree to show her how much she was loved, or jump the widest river, or swim down to the deepest part of the ocean...all the superlatives, he wasn't talking just to her. And even though they'd just met, it didn't feel that way. That connection between them was over thirty years old, wasn't it? Hell, for all he knew, he'd stayed in New Orleans because she'd been sleeping and growing beneath the Mississippi. He'd had plenty of chances to leave, find other streets to scour for marks.

He'd never admitted it to anyone, but when Jonas Kensington sent him to college up in New England, gave him that law education, Ben had been so antsy to return to NOLA that he came back anytime he could, even if he could only make the long drive for a weekend.

"You're fine. We're okay. Just going on a little trip. Getting away from this place. It's a little crazy here right now. Be much better where you can spread your wings without knocking everything over." She hadn't unfurled them yet, but there they were, tight against her body. He'd love to see her fly.

"A bull really doesn't want to be in china shop."

Bonnie had quieted and kept blinking at him, so he took that as a good sign. He had both hands on the section of her nose just beneath the eyes. He noted she didn't blink them all in sync, but seemed to blink in threes.

He felt the warmth as the blanket descended. The colors, streaming like an aurora, filled the night sky right around them. "Wow," he breathed. He gestured, drawing her gaze to it. "Look at that. Feel how warm that is." The blanket settled onto her shoulders and back, started to draw forward. She twitched, glanced at it, but now that it had made contact, Ben knew she had to feel the same infusion of calming energy in it he did. Motherly.

Every kid gravitated toward that feeling, whether real or feigned— Elagra was proof of that. But even if they never found it outside the womb as a kid, the desire for it stayed there, planted deep. When they felt the real deal as he felt it now, inside them, all around them, it awoke the soul-deep memory anew.

It was the first kind of love anyone experienced.

He suspected Ruby's bond with her infant son helped give the magic that extra wattage. If her love for Jem contained even a tenth of what Ben was feeling from this magic, he knew she didn't have anything to worry about. That kid would eventually laugh for her, smile for her. Because if Ben had had a mother who loved him like that, he would have gone around with a stupid-assed grin on his face his whole damn life.

He also felt Ramona's contribution to it. She was like a whole chaotic mess of motherly, sisterly, nurturing earth energy. If Jon and Rachel had her over for dinner, the concentration of crunchy granola feel-good would sprout a new Garden of Eden around the house.

He could hear the sound of the water, Bonnie's breathing, the wind. Other sounds, distant booms, disturbing cries cut short, a rushing sound like gouts of flames. If anyone on the periphery stumbled on a hole in that illusion shielding that Ruby and Derek had put in place, able to see not just the effects of wind and water, but the magic going on, he could only imagine what they'd think about the current scene on the New Orleans waterfront.

He wanted to find Marcie one last time, see her, but he knew he couldn't look away, couldn't chance losing that connection with Bonnie. But it was okay. Marcie had broken open that locked place inside him that he'd built to keep himself safe from Elagra and a bunch of other nightmares. Marcie knew everything that was there and still knew she could need him, rely on him. He was her Master, would always be her Master. She also knew he needed her in a way so desperate and deep, no way he wouldn't find her again, no matter how far he was taken from her side.

"Let's do this," he told Bonnie, as the waterfront disappeared and the world became just a rainbow of colors around them. They were rising, as if they were in a hot air balloon. He shifted to sit on a protrusion of horn, gripping the one just above it with both hands. He patted her side as she made a questioning croon. "Yeah, we're okay. Just a roller coaster ride, little girl. You're going to love it, I promise. At the end of this rainbow ride, there's a much better world. All for you."

CHAPTER NINETEEN

*A*s Marcie well knew from her police training, when her life was on the line, she wasn't supposed to mess around with trying to shoot someone in the leg, a much more difficult and unpredictable outcome that could get innocent bystanders killed. She was trained to go for center mass, the kill shot.

She suspected that was what Raina had done. In a nuclear explosion kind of way, not having the handy and neater use of a firearm.

Out of the corner of her eye, she'd seen Raina reach the opposite end of the warehouse, brace herself, shout the command to Marcie. Right after she'd let loose whatever she was hurling this way.

It all happened in a matter of seconds. The spell struck Elagra, caught the magic she'd been trying to toss at Marcie, and locked up with it. Marcie could see the two forces pitted against one another, but in the end, Raina's was stronger.

Elagra shimmered. Marcie had a weird thought about holograms and wondered if Elagra was really there. But she was. Her existence wavered, and then it was as if it started to come apart. A brief indrawn breath where her eyes went wide, almost like a frightened child's, her breath choking in her throat. Her hand reached out, helpless, flailing. Marcie, instinctively reacting to anything in distress, almost reached for it.

But the hand snapped away and things started cracking, the

integrity of the internal body somehow breached, while the skin outside stayed eerily unmarred.

Then the explosion happened.

A flash, and a concussion that took away thought and time for an indeterminate period. When she was able to recapture awareness, Marcie felt like she was covered in painfully itchy fiberglass and viscous brain matter, and something else she couldn't define, until it unraveled in her mind.

Visions of other people's lives. Their feelings and emotions. To a level that was... Oh God. To move was painful. To breathe was painful. Something was really, really wrong. She turned her head to her true north, and saw Ben. He was standing on Bonnie's shoulder, his hand on her, and he was talking to her. Marcie wanted to smile, to cry, because she knew how soothing that voice could be when a female was on the edge of shattering. If he was the one causing the shattering, he could hold her there on that edge with his voice. If he wasn't the cause, he could draw her back, away from that pain.

There was a transparent rainbow of color enclosing them, like one of those long, wavering bubbles kids could make in their backyards. A vortex was opening in the air above them, him and Bonnie rising toward it. It was going to swallow them, and he didn't seem to notice. She felt worse than she'd ever felt in her life, but her fear for him drove those feelings back, all those visions and voices. She tried to struggle weakly toward him, drag herself across the rough gravel roof top. *Ben.*

She had to warn him, protect him. Nothing else seemed to matter, and she wasn't even sure why that mattered, but her will knew why, and it made her body move.

"No, love, here. Stop..." Raina was with her, trying to hold her. "He's okay, I promise. He has to go with her. It's the only way. He'll come back. Ruby and Ramona will do everything they can to bring him back."

She was past listening. All she could see was Ben disappearing, and the things that felt so awful, so wrong, became exponentially worse. She was lost, just so lost...

Oh God, he was gone. One minute he was there, and then, not. No, no, *no*...

"Marcie. *Marcie.*" The sharp physical blow, a slap, startled her, jolted her attention to Raina. The witch was holding her, halfway across her lap. Marcie had been digging her fingers into her arms, trying to claw away from her, her body arched up over her knees as she'd tried to twist around, see Ben.

"We have to make sure you're here when he comes back," Raina said urgently. "We don't want to lose you, too. All right?"

She was already lost. Marcie had never felt anything like this. She thought she knew hopelessness. She'd experienced it more than a few times growing up, and then later, when she'd thought Ben would forever be beyond her grasp. That paled in comparison to this, because then she'd still had her family, herself, her work. This was loss of hope for anything good in life. *Anything.* It brought indescribable pain that twisted the heart, lungs and stomach, coupled with the knowledge that she was far beyond the point where anything would ever get better. Ever.

This was what Hell meant.

Everything that gave her strength disappeared. Her family, her friends, her pride in herself and her own accomplishments, and worst of all, her love for Ben. All of it sucked away through a hole inside her soul, vanishing before she could even grab onto it. Life contained no more value. Only never-ending despair.

It was a knowledge she'd never wanted to have. That no one wanted to have, because once it possessed the mind, it connected to everyone else in the history of everything who'd ever felt it. It compounded the feeling, over and over again. Every creature in the world forced to suffer, suffer, and suffer some more.

Much as Ben had been sucked away from her, it was all gone, there was nothing left. She wanted to die and let go. If she could just figure out how to get there... Ben wasn't coming back. She had a vague knowledge of people who cared about her, but they were so distant, so irrelevant and beyond her grasp. Life would move on without her. That grey world beckoned, and now she knew why that was the color of aged tombstone, the color of peaceful nothingness.

"Marcie. Damn it. Marcie..." Raina squeezed her hands so hard Marcie was aware of pain. She handled plenty of pain. Broken bones were nothing next to a broken spirit.

"Your Master will not be pleased with you."

A cry broke from her lips, because a ripple tripped her up, brought

232

her up short on that threshold to the tempting place of grey nothingness. Cold fingers slid along her skin, her soul, gripped hard, dug in. Those words meant something to her. They were uttered by one who was a Master himself, who knew how a Master thought, what he expected. A male who, no matter what the world said was proper or right, followed a very different, blood and bone level code about what was his.

It was a code that she knew, that she'd always known. It applied to her, defined who she was in a way nothing else did. When nothing else could stop her forward motion, that could.

A Master's word was everything, and above God, hell and demons and whatever else, would be obeyed. He didn't care what kind of pain she was in, or that all hope was lost. Service to him was everything.

"He expects to find you here for him when he returns," the Master said. "If you are not, you have failed him. Fight for him. Tell me you understand."

That nod was the hardest thing she'd ever done in her life. She did it, even though another cry of pain tore from her when she managed the movement. But she would fight for Ben. She would. Even if she lost, she would fight until the last breath. Which would be soon, because that despair whispered to her. Twisted those words.

You have *failed him. You are not stronger than death. Your love, your bond, it is not stronger than death and this kind of evil. It will take him away from you and you from him. You won't remember what it felt like, except for the sharpness of a loss beyond bearing. You won't know what it means, which will make it even worse.*

"Ben..." The whisper would have been a wail if she'd had the strength. Then his name was lost to her, like everything else.

～

Elagra had been a damned repository of souls, the energies of all those she'd snared in her power. Keeping that energy inside her, she'd used it to galvanize her magic, maintain her allure. What Marcie was feeling was the despair that those boys had felt when they knew, without a doubt or shred of hope for something different, that their souls had been lost to her forever.

Once the souls realized they'd been freed, Raina knew they would see the light outside their jail cells, and that feeling would become something else. However, though it only took a moment for a bullet to pass through a body, the damage it left could still be fatal.

She sent a prayer to the Goddess, even as she kept talking to Marcie. It wasn't the words that were important, except as a focus for her to channel as much healing energy into her as she could. Healing wasn't Raina's forte, but she knew how to do the basics. "Hang in there with me. There you are, hold on..."

This was beyond bad. However, one good thing had happened. Neutralizing Elagra had broken the contract with the entity who'd sent his minions to serve her purpose. They'd disappeared into the night sky as if they'd never been, so Raina could once again see stars above, even a sliver of moonlight.

Mikhael. Help.

He was there no more than half a dozen heart beats later. She assumed he'd left Derek to handle mop-up. As he landed, Raina's concern for the girl was momentary eclipsed by the blood she saw on him, the numerous cuts, a severe burn wound on his abdomen. As he dropped to his heels, the stiffness to his movements suggested his ribs were in less than stellar condition.

She rarely saw him right after a fight, she realized. The last time had been when he was crushed under a pile of stone and she was sure he was dead. Even knowing now just how resilient he was, her heart turned over to see the wounds. She reached out to touch his shoulder, reassure herself that he was okay.

He met her gaze, drew her to him with a quick, strong hand behind her nape to brush his lips over hers. He smelled of smoke, blood and raw power, but he was still Mikhael. He squeezed her neck, hard, nodded. "I'm good, *malysh*," he said.

Baby, she remembered. The endearment he called her in some of their most intimate moments. It told her he was glad to see she was in one piece as well, and was likely cataloging every scrape and bruise she bore in the same way.

But there was someone in far more dire straits. She drew his attention to her, but he was already there, evaluating Marcie's condition in a blink. Curling his arms around her shuddering form, his broad blood-stained shoulder brushing Raina's breast, he drew the girl from her lap into his own.

He cradled Marcie's face, bringing her wide, pupil-dominated eyes closer to his, holding her to this plane with his sheer force of will, and his words.

"Your Master will not be pleased with you."

Raina knew Marcie had struggled, as even Derek still did, with the nature of the Dark that Mikhael served. But as a succubus, she understood it. Mikhael called on it now, his pure Darkness standing against the evil of Elagra's.

There was no sympathy or compassion in Mikhael's words, his touch or gaze. Only sheer, ruthless command, his tone and energy promising far worse to Marcie if she didn't obey, dig deep and find the will to hold on.

One didn't disappoint the Master. There was no forgiveness for failure there.

Raina fucking hated the kind of Dark Soul Magic Elagra had tapped. It was the most twisted, detestable form of magic, and whoever used it deserved to have it turned on themselves. So Raina had once thought, until she discovered Ruby had resorted to it in a moment of utter despair. And Mikhael had used his Darkness in a way uncomfortably close to this to hold Ruby back from the fiery edge of eternal damnation.

Well, all things happened for a reason, right? As she watched Mikhael hold Marcie here by that tentative thread, a flicker of his gaze, a tightening of his jaw, told her it wasn't enough. They needed something else.

Might as well pile one inadvisable thing on top of another, make a damn wedding cake out of it. Raina left them to run to the edge of the roof. She drew Ruby's attention with an arrow of mental intent, but underscored it with urgent body language, waving her arms at her sister witch, in an unmistakable "get your ass down here now" kind of way.

Though the demon's army was gone, Raina knew Ruby and Ramona still had their own struggle going on. They were twisting the threads of magic that had followed Ben and the sea creature through the portal. They'd intended to let that line go when the monster was all the way through. But now that line was the only tether they had to bring Ben back. And since the plan hadn't been for Ben to accompany her, those threads were far too tenuous.

But that was the good thing about having magic users powerful enough to tag team one another. Those bonded the way Ruby and Derek were meant one could pick up the magic of the other without a catastrophic disruption. Especially if one of them was a Light Guardian.

Derek appeared next to Ramona. There was a melding of energies, Ruby's unique aura color wrapping around his, and then his taking over, fusing to Ramona's. Derek shifted over as Ruby backed out of the mix, so he and Ramona were shoulder to shoulder.

As smooth as that appeared, Raina knew it was a risk. Even a momentary transition could lose Ben to the alternate world forever. But it was a judgment call. While they might have a slim-as-hell chance of pulling Ben back into this reality after sending him off with a one-way spell to another world, she had zero chance of saving Marcie without Ruby.

And, truth? If they lost Marcie, it was better for Ben to be stuck in another world, thinking she was still alive.

Ruby thankfully chose to utilize the transport magic Derek had been teaching her. She still wasn't entirely sure of it, but this time, probably because she wasn't overthinking it, she managed the quick, shimmering transition from one roof to another without a hitch, avoiding the delays of getting here on foot.

"What? *Raina*, what—"

The exclamation came as Raina dragged Ruby down to her knees next to Marcie. She didn't take time to explain, just put Ruby's hand on the girl's leg.

Ruby was one of the best intuitive magic users in existence. It had taken her most of her life to understand that about herself. One of the ways she'd come to that knowledge was a path no witch with any sense walked. She'd worked with Dark Soul magic, and nearly lost herself to it. Though Mikhael had held her from the edge, it had been Derek's love and the strength of their combined magic that had brought her back. It left Ruby with a knowledge of both sides of the broom most witches didn't have.

Now, her brow furrowed. The look she shot to Raina was not the one she wanted to see.

"No," Raina said decisively. "There's a way to fix it. Here."

She grabbed Ruby's other hand, and muttered the spell that would show her what she had in mind.

In surgery operating rooms, they used blacklights to see if they'd cleaned up all the blood. This was like that, only what Raina was illuminating was far more disturbing.

Those souls that had infected Marcie should be letting her go, taking flight as they discovered they were free. But the damage to them had been too all-encompassing. They were spun into knots, tangled with her essence, down so deep in a well of despair they had no idea they'd been liberated. They had to be shown the way.

But several had a different structure to them. They were the very small percentage of Elagra's victims who'd escaped her still alive.

A soul was strong and fragile both. Pieces could be broken off and lost, sacrificed so the rest of the soul survived, though it weakened the overall spiritual matter. It made the person who carried that broken soul more susceptible to the call of darkness throughout his or her life. However, the very fact the person had found the strength to break away suggested a will stronger than average. Particularly those souls who'd escaped Elagra with their earthly form still breathing.

Marcie was a Pure Light. If one of those pieces could be burrowed into Marcie, where her core of light and hope still existed, even beyond where she could feel it now, it would recognize the call of the Light, and have the strength to reach through the Dark for it. It would spread that energy to the others, a connected network. It would become the key that turned in the lock, opening the door to let the others go.

The downside of that was they'd have to integrate that piece of soul with Marcie's, and removal after embedment was a complicated issue. The upside was there was one soul fragment in particular that had the very best chance of doing what Raina hoped would work.

Ruby's gaze shot to Raina. "We have no right to do that," she said. "You know what that could do. Will do."

"Then we let her die, and these souls are lost in the ether, where their energy fuels monsters like what Derek and Mikhael just fought." Raina set her jaw. "I don't really give a damn about the rules."

Her gaze shifted to Mikhael. He still held Marcie, who was muttering incoherently, rocking in his grasp like a mental patient.

Tears were on her face, and her curled fingers jerked against his forearms, her nails creating bloody furrows in his flesh.

He didn't seem to notice it. He and Derek weighed right and wrong on a daily basis, made decisions and passed judgment on others. In the short timespan when this decision needed to be made, she fully expected he'd weigh hundreds if not thousands of potential variables.

Someone else had joined them on the roof. Knowing who it was, Raina shifted to block Marcie from him, her hand out in a menacing gesture of warding. He wasn't taking her.

"Raina," Mikhael said. He lifted a hand from Marcie, closed it on her wrist. He was probably the only one other than Ruby who'd dare such a maneuver when she was coiled to strike. Her fingers had already lengthened into claws, and she was reaching for that power within her that could lay most entities low, take life when she chose. Not that it would have any impact on a Grim Reaper, but she'd die making her point.

"No," she said. "No, we're not there."

With the dense energy of intent around him, Silas drew close, dropped to his heels a step away from Marcie's twitching feet. After he pushed the hood of his cowled cloak to his shoulders, he didn't touch her, his attention on her face. Her eyes opened briefly, but she didn't see him. Her staring eyes said she saw only the horrors written in her mind, unleashed from Elagra's consciousness.

"It is written that her soul should be taken now," Silas said.

Like hell, Raina was going to say, but Mikhael tightened his grip, giving Silas a chance to continue.

"However, these are unusual circumstances. There is time for...a pause. For things to change."

Giving Raina an even look that said *Be still*, Mikhael leaned over Marcie's twitching body, laid his hand on her brow.

"Marcie," Mikhael said. "Can you see them? The souls?"

"Yes," she moaned. "Oh, God. Help them. Please...help them. They're so lost."

"There is your answer," Mikhael said, looking at Silas. "You take her now, more than one soul is lost. How much time does that give us?"

Silas studied the restless form in Mikhael's grasp again. While his eyes held a timeless, chilling wisdom, they also showed compassion. "A few moments," he said. "No more."

Ruby's jaw firmed. "Move back," she said to Raina, and then surprisingly, also to Mikhael and Silas. "All of you."

They complied immediately. However, the terrified whimper Marcie made, as if she were buried alive and they were abandoning her to her fate, nearly tore Raina's heart in two. Mikhael drew her back, holding her by the shoulders, standing behind her. Seeing Marcie left there alone, the way she curled into a ball, that keening, terrible noise coming from her, made Raina doubt herself. Mikhael's grip tightened once more.

"Even when you're wrong, you are willing to be wrong at full, breathtaking power, my witch," he murmured. "Don't doubt the effectiveness of that."

Raina knew how powerful each of her sisters were, and she herself was. Yet her own magic was something she felt in her gut, much as Mikhael had just implied. She had formidable, learned skills, but nothing like Ruby. Ruby had a grasp of the tenets of magic Raina would never have.

Even knowing that, watching Ruby do the complicated work with such incredible skill and swiftness that it seemed deceptively effortless, was awe-inspiring.

Raina closed her eyes so she could see more clearly what was happening on another plane. Marcie's life force was fading so frighteningly fast, perhaps seconds left to go. Silas hadn't been exaggerating. The broken souls were like razor blades, shredding her life energy. Ruby's magic, a strong, clear magenta light, moved over them with purpose, found the piece that was important, touched it. Raina heard her murmuring the words, her voice growing in strength. Then her gut feeling told her it was time to lend Ruby additional reinforcement.

She joined in, echoing the words, adding to the magical layering. Mikhael followed, his deep timbre vibrating through her where their bodies touched.

Something had happened with Ben. Hopefully something good. Because now Derek joined them. Male and female voices blended, overlapped, rose and fell.

Derek knelt behind his wife, his large frame sheltering her, hands landing on her shoulders like Mikhael's on Raina's, gripping. Raina tensed, worried he might tear her away, interrupt her. Derek's sense of right and wrong had the most indelible lines in the sand, on the Light side of things.

She needn't have worried. Love was a force that existed on both sides of the line, so that often the lines didn't matter. Only the love did. He wrapped his arms around Ruby. Though this magic work had to have Ruby's sole signature, he could give her strength to do it. Raina saw his Light energy pour into Ruby. It had been a long night. Her voice, which had been faltering under the strain, strengthened once more.

Raina turned all her senses toward Marcie, except her eyes. She closed them again, so she could better see what was happening with the girl, find that flickering flame that was her struggling life force.

The hold of those despairing souls was loosening. Whereas the one Ruby was focusing upon grew tendrils that burrowed into Marcie. They went into her blood stream, into the beat of her heart, the breath in her lungs. Into every organ and system. A small cry wrested from her throat, and her arms came up, but not to push Ruby away. Marcie cradled her own body in her arms, but it wasn't her body she was holding. It was the pain and essence of one young boy, one who'd become the remarkable, dangerous man she loved beyond all others.

As she accepted it, that fading light flickered...and went out.

CHAPTER TWENTY

"Marcie. *Marcella*. Brat, if you do not answer me, you will wish you were dead. If you think I won't come drag you out of Heaven by your hair, you are seriously mistaken. Talk to me."

She was so exhausted, she had no strength. There were nights Ben had taken all the strength from her, with orgasms and pain, and more pain and orgasms, until she couldn't walk. He'd carry her to their gigantic garden tub, and they'd lie there in the heated water. His breath would be on her brow, her lips, and he'd slowly bring her back to life and strength again. He took it away, he gave it back. It was what her Master did, because he owned her, everything she was.

Which meant, no matter how exhausted she was, she needed to obey.

The effort of that small movement was like the agony of one more stomach crunch when she'd pushed her workout well beyond the level of insanity. Or Crossfit. Which were two words that meant the same thing, according to Ben. She couldn't do it. But she was trying, enough that he apparently noticed a flutter of her lashes, the grimace of effort on her face.

"There you are. You damn well better answer me."

"Y-yes...sir." Her voice didn't sound like her. It was small, weak. But it was enough.

She was lifted like a balloon and then lowered again. It took her a minute to realize the movement had been caused by the giant inhalation of breath Ben had drawn into his lungs. She was in his arms, his lap, her upper body lying against him the way she lay against him in their big tub. He'd known. He'd known the best way to bring her back to the familiar, the comforting. He knew all her triggers, and how to ground her after pressing them.

They weren't in their tub at home, though they were sitting in water, a shallow, mucky amount of it. The smell of the river and wet roofing material was in her nose. As her eyelids cracked at last, she saw the sky, with silver gray and smoke colored tracks against it. It was dawn.

There were people around them. It took her a moment to place them. Raina...Mikhael. Her gaze lingered on the Dark Guardian as she remembered. He'd called to her, the way a Master would, commanding her to hold on. Derek, another Master, had the kind of stern but compassionate look that Jon sometimes did. He was looking at Ruby. *Ruby*.

She tried to struggle up, and was rewarded with another shriek of agony from every muscle fiber. The witch was the color of gray paste, and appeared to be unconscious in Derek's arms. "What...she needs help..."

"She's fine," Derek said. His brusque tone matched the tight concern on his face, though the way he stroked his wife's hair with his large, capable fingers showed only comfort, reassurance. No urgency. "She's well. It took a lot out of her to bring you back. It will take her some time to recharge. Just as it will for you." His gaze turned to Mikhael. "We need to go back to the hotel before we're noticed here."

It told her she'd regained consciousness in the immediate aftermath of everything that had happened. Details were a little cloudy, but since she was soaked, and her backside was still immersed in water, that came back first. The storm surge.

Her gaze shifted outward, over the roof's edge of the warehouse where they were assembled. Her grip tightened on Ben's forearm, banded strong beneath her breasts. "Oh shit."

For once, Ben didn't get after her for cursing. Never mind the man would curse like a sailor with the least amount of prompting, though he tried not to do it front of her, or any woman. Still, Ben was honest about it when it happened. The swear jar they kept at the house was full enough to pay for a year of college tuition.

Or to make a sizeable donation for storm cleanup.

Riverfront windows were shattered, buildings were caved in. The concession stands on the docks near the shopping mall were piles of kindling or gone entirely. There was a trolley car lying in the street on its side, companionably bumping against one of the ferry boats that normally took NOLA tourists and residents across the river to Algiers Point.

The river had receded within normal boundaries—on the extreme high tide full moon side—but there was standing water everywhere, including on this rooftop. Her gaze slid to the Aquarium and held. The picturesque glass cylinder on top possessed a grid of jagged toothed openings.

"A lot of physical damage," Raina said. "But nothing that can't be rebuilt. Just a sudden storm surge that will cause some excitement on the news, create a lot of clean-up, and be forgotten in a few months. The ley line was only mildly disrupted, so we avoided the catastrophe an earthquake would have caused. Though it was a near thing."

Her exotic green and gold eyes had a fierce light to them, like a tigress who'd just had a particularly nasty encounter with another tigress and was checking the status of one of her cubs. Which brought back another thought.

"Elagra..."

"Barely alive, but nothing but an empty shell."

Mikhael's mouth tightened fractionally, and Raina shook her head. "If I pay for it, I pay for it. You know nothing else would have assured Marcie's survival and freed those souls."

Derek's expression was equally grave, but he put a hand on Mikhael's shoulder, an unexpected reassurance. "We deal with it later," the Light Guardian said.

Anger flashed through Raina's gaze, increasing that fierce tigress look. Yet when she began to speak, obviously to lash out, Mikhael's sharp look made her hold her tongue, barely. Marcie expected Mikhael was one of the few who could accomplish that miracle, but she knew that look herself, pretty well.

She wasn't sure what the issue was, but she wanted to defuse the tension. Because well, this was a victory, right? Her man was holding her, and they were all alive. "They're just mad because we took her out." Her voice was still pathetically weak, but gained a hair's width more strength as she used it, looking at Raina. "All we needed was girl power. Right?"

Raina summoned a smile, as Marcie had hoped. The witch's hand, curled into a fist on Marcie's leg, loosened, her fingers stroking. "You can fight at my side any day."

"Not during my lifetime," Ben said.

At last Marcie found the strength to drop her head back so she could see him. His hair and the rest of him were as wet as she was. He was dirty and bloody, his shirt gone. Though he held her firmly, she noticed that beneath the determination was an exhaustion likely as deep as her own.

Bonnie. He had taken Bonnie to another place, and Marcie had thought she'd lost him. "How did you get back?" she managed. Despite the lack of strength in her arms, she managed to reach up and touch his mouth, his hard jaw.

"Ramona and Derek. Ruby. They drew me back, like a hot air balloon ride out of Oz. I'd have been here sooner, but Ramona kept me lying down for a few minutes. Something about all my molecules flying apart if I moved too soon."

He was here. They'd figured out how to bring him back. She would love all of them forever for that.

She always felt closer to him than any other human being in the world, but maybe because of the aftermath of her near-death experience, she felt even closer, in a way hard to describe. It was as if she truly could feel his heart beat in her chest, his air in her lungs.

"Where did you go?" she whispered.

"To a good place." His vivid green gaze rested on her face. She saw the lines of concern in his, as deep as those on Derek's face. Her hand was shaking. He closed his hand around hers, steadied them both. "But not good enough to keep me there. That's only where you are. But she's safe. Bonnie's safe. The place where she is...it has every magical creature you ever read about as a kid. And she flew, brat. I got to see her fly for the first time. She flew away, over miles and miles of purple ocean."

"Who wouldn't want to live near a purple ocean?" Ramona said wistfully. For the first time, Marcie noticed her there, and wondered if she'd been elsewhere. Or if her brain was just now filling in some of the empty holes in the scenery around them.

"Indeed." Silas stood behind her, his hand resting at her waist. He gazed around them with that look that said he was taking in a bunch of things they couldn't see, but his tone, the glance he gave Ramona, said he was also very much in the here and now.

"If I remember the place correctly," the chaos witch said, "there are caves on that beach. A couple giants already live there. They'll love her, think she's amazing. Probably try to talk her into letting them ride her."

"And get themselves eaten for their trouble," Silas said dryly.

Marcie tried to chuckle, and shivered instead.

"You're right. It's time to get out of here," Ben said to Mikhael and Derek. "She needs a hot bath, dry clothes."

"We both do. One of our baths," she sighed in agreement. "In that giant, amazing tub."

A smile crossed Ben's face when she tipped hers up to him again. "Home it is, brat."

He gathered her up, lifted her as he rose. Though she couldn't imagine the effort it must have taken him, he lifted her as he always did, as if he could carry her for miles without tiring. Derek likewise had scooped up Ruby. Marcie wished she would wake. Even though the behavior of the others said she'd be okay, Marcie still wanted to see evidence of the woman's sharp hazel eyes, her serious smile, her compact, lean energy that emanated a full yard all around her.

Marcie wondered if it would all come back to her, everything that had happened in those minutes she seemed unable to find. She felt a million crazy things, a jumble she couldn't parse into memories, thoughts. They were so close, though. She expected as she put some time and space between her and the trauma, it would come back. What she did remember was a strong mix of energies, and knew without asking that everyone on this rooftop had played some part in her and Ben still being alive.

Raina had delivered on the promise she'd made. For that and a lot of other reasons, Marcie would forever count her among her small but extraordinary group of female friends she trusted without question.

"I understand the desire to go home," Mikhael said. "But it is best for us to stay together for a short time period."

Marcie noticed Raina touching Mikhael's arm, giving him a significant look. The Dark Guardian nodded imperceptibly as he continued.

"Magic use like Marcie just experienced can have some unexpected aftermath effects. It is best that she be where we can monitor her. At least for a day."

Ben's expression tightened, but Marcie squeezed his arm again. "The hotel has a giant tub, too," she said.

He glanced down at her, and his gaze softened slightly. "I wasn't going to disagree, brat," he said. "Much as I want to be home, too, making sure you're okay is more important."

She wanted to say she was fine, but she really wasn't sure she could. She was alive, and very sore, she knew that. But there was something else...it was as if her brain had been dismantled and put back together in a slightly wonky way, and her body likewise felt like it did when standing in the ocean all day, as if it was moving to a different rhythm, where she wouldn't be entirely steady on land. There was a tingling everywhere, inside. Like a jar of bees had been let loose. They weren't mad, angrily buzzing. It was more like when they came out in droves during the blooming season and were busy drifting from flower to flower.

In short, there was a lot happening in her head and with the rest of her. She wasn't going to argue with Mikhael and Derek's logic either, as much as she would like nothing better than a soak in their tub and a month-long nap in Ben's arms in their king-sized bed. Their bedroom was done in lots of soft whites with slashes of black, and reminded her of being in a cloud.

"Silas and I have one issue to address," Ramona said. "And then we'll portal back to my home. But we'll be close if you need us."

The chaos witch's expression was abruptly far less dreamy and amicable. Following her gaze, Marcie stiffened in Ben's arms. She suddenly understood the import of Raina's words.

Barely alive. But alive.

Elagra lay on the flat expanse of a utility box at the far end of the roof. Marcie expected they'd brought her there to keep an eye on her while assessing her own condition.

Raina had said she was a husk. While Marcie wasn't sure what that meant, it likely had something to do with how the woman looked almost boneless, limbs slack, body at a twisted angle. She looked like a doll that had been dropped from the sky and had no animation to move herself into a more natural-looking position.

But she *was* still animated. As Marcie looked her way, she heard a low moan, saw the body twitch, turn over, slowly. Marcie didn't want to see that face, not ever again, but when Elagra's staring eyes rolled in their direction, Marcie felt a chill deep inside.

Empty husk was the right word for it. The golden hue of the eyes had turned dark, the unnaturally round eyes focused like a living corpse. The woman was still in there somewhere, hating, destructive, deep, deep inside, likely screaming to get out. But something else was holding her imprisoned in her subconscious. A determination to live, to spite all her enemies, to spit on those who would try to control her.

Her body was twitching now, a repetitive thing as she tried to push herself up. Blood was on her lips, and she licked it off.

"She's rotten to the core, but hell and damnation, she has a powerful will," Raina said. "No one else would have lived through that."

"I'll take care of her," Ramona said. "There's a place to put her where she'll do no more harm. She'll get what she deserves in time."

Her gaze met Mikhael's. The Dark Guardian's fathomless eyes flickered. Marcie expected that he already knew which room in hell Elagra would be assigned when she finally faced that final justice. It might be wrong of her, but she hoped it was the darkest, deepest hole they had available. Yet she couldn't deny a twinge of compassion as she looked at the woman, and saw the soul trapped deep within her, desperate, driven by hate and a hunger for violence that would never be assuaged.

But then Marcie's attention was caught by Silas. He wasn't a chatterbox by any means, but now there was a palpable weight to his stillness, an expectant energy she didn't understand until she lifted her gaze to Ben's face.

"Will you take her?" he said to Mikhael. "I'll catch up."

"No." Marcie tried to hold onto him, but she was too weak. Ben shifted her into Mikhael's arms. He did lift one of her hands, kissed it, but before she could try to latch on, say the words trying to free themselves from her locked-up throat, he was already striding away. She struggled, but Raina's hand was on her, stilling her. She noticed

Derek and Mikhael had exchanged a look, and had matching impassive expressions.

She couldn't control a lot of things, but she could control one, damn it.

"We wait for him," Marcie said. She aimed that at Raina, and though she wanted to be fierce about it, the best she could manage in her current state was pleading, a desperate, adamant need for Raina to understand.

Raina met her gaze, nodded. She looked up at Mikhael. "We need to wait," she said quietly.

Ramona had stepped close to Silas's side, but this time she didn't touch him. She merely stood there, silent, watching with the rest of them, as Silas drew his hood up, shadowing his face. The first flash of sunrise glimmered along the blade of his scythe, gripped in his long-fingered hand.

Ben had reached the utility box. As he'd walked toward the witch, Marcie thought their eyes had locked, his and Elagra's. When he got close, her lips peeled back. A couple of those sharpened teeth had broken off and there was blood on the others, her lips cracked. The look in her eyes when she gazed upon Ben made Marcie feel a little sick. Even now, the woman had a way of making the skin crawl, her dark energy reaching out like spiders coming down a wet rock wall, out of the darkness.

Ben dropped to his heels beside her. His voice, though low, carried.

"You said you could turn and twist a man's heart, anyway you wish. Make him abandon his soul, so he could never find it again. You were wrong. I found my heart and soul. But you gave me something, too."

He reached out. Put his hands around her throat. Marcie knew the strength of those hands, and swallowed as he obviously tightened his grip.

"Don't watch, Marcie," Raina said.

But she couldn't look away. She would never look away, because she knew just how important it was for her to never turn away from any part of Ben, light or dark. She made an alarmed noise, gripped Raina's arm, as magic sparked off Elagra's skin.

Marcie felt the shudder of that energy reach their group. It was as if Elagra had found some last vestige of power within her, something to try and throw him off, knock him back.

Raina had said she had a powerful will. But so did the man who held her life in his hands.

His expression didn't change, a thing as chilling as Elagra herself. Marcie remembered when Matt had told her that she and all of them —the men of their inner circle, the wives—were Ben's moral compass. But that if anyone threatened that family, he would annihilate the threat without thought or remorse.

Elagra's magic couldn't touch him. Those sparks flickered out, and her base human survival instinct kicked in. She scratched at his hands, her feet weakly kicked, but he never let go. Just kept staring into her eyes until he apparently saw the life go out of them, and she was limp in his hands. Then he let her drop. As he began to straighten, he noticed that the hem of her thin shift was rucked up high on her thighs. Though the water that had drenched all of them had revealed early on Elagra wore nothing under it but the now streaked paint, he adjusted the skirt so it modestly covered her. Then he folded her hands on her breast. Her empty eyes stared skyward.

He nodded, and said something else. Marcie felt the impact of those words in her heart.

"It's done."

Silas lifted the scythe and moved forward. Marcie didn't know what would come next, but all of it, everything that had happened, took her past what her body could handle. She struggled against losing consciousness, reaching out with one trembling arm. Ben was walking toward her. His gaze was on her face.

He wasn't the only one with a strong will. Though the pain grew in waves, she wouldn't let it have her, not until his hand closed on hers, until he took her back in his arms. "She can't have you," she whispered. "It can't take you from me. None of it."

"I know, brat." His voice was rough, harsh. It reminded her of what Raina had said about Mikhael.

Not kind, not of the Light, but his way is true, and I trust him with everything I am.

Not kind, but the love was there. It didn't have to be pretty, as long as it was strong enough to survive storm surge and shadows.

"Everything I am—it all belongs to you. God help you."

CHAPTER TWENTY-ONE

"You're giving me crap for breaking some stupid law that would have let Marcie die? While feeling lost like that? You know she wouldn't have been able to figure out where the afterlife was. Even with a damn Grim Reaper guiding her, she would have become a lost spirit. Eventually a demon's pawn, like those dark things you were fighting, someone else's minion. Want to explain that to Ben O'Callahan? Or lie to him, feed him bullshit about her going to a happy place?"

Raina wasn't going to point out that Ben had killed Elagra's body. She'd destroyed Elagra's soul, ripped it up, pinned down what was left of it in the rubble of her broken body. No getting away from that. Derek stood at the mantle in their hotel suite, his arms crossed, thumbs under his arm pits, feet braced. His steely blue gaze was hooded. Mikhael was at the bar. When he looked toward the Light Guardian and their gazes locked, Raina's temper broke its already strained leash.

"Oh no, you don't." She stepped in between them. "You're not doing the 'menfolk are having a silent conversation about the decisions the womenfolk made.' Fuck that, and fuck the both of you."

"Raina," Mikhael said, his tone exceptionally even. Usually when she got mouthy, he'd get all cold and snarly. "It has nothing to do with that. We are conversing with...someone else."

"Oh." Realizing the implications, Raina blinked. She might have unwisely fired off something snarky to the Lord of the Underworld, but fortunately Ruby, sitting on the couch, reached over the back to grab her hand. She yanked Raina halfway over the edge, bringing her around it to join her on the cushions. "Do not make me lose a sister today," Ruby hissed. "You made a decision. Let them figure it out."

Raina would have snapped at her, too, but Ruby was still looking at half strength. Plus, there was a relaxed though exasperated look to Ruby's features that told Raina she likely didn't have to be concerned about the conversation happening between the Guardians and Lucifer.

It still rankled. For form's sake, she glowered at them, but she settled on the cushion, pulled her knees up to her chest. She put her hand on Ruby's bare foot, stretched out on the couch, and squeezed reassuringly. Derek's wife shook her head at her, but dropped her cheek to the couch's back cushion again, eyelids going to half-mast.

"You look like you did right after you had Jem," Raina observed.

"I feel like I had ten of him in a row. But it's all good." Ruby reached out and Raina obligingly lifted her own hand so they could clasp. "We did it. Saved the day and all that. Kept everyone from dying. Until next time."

"Maybe you'll have time to do a few baby yoga classes and limber back up before the next catastrophe hits," Raina said lightly, keeping her sister witch's worries at bay. But platitudes didn't cut it, not in their world. She squeezed Ruby's hand. "You two are always going to be busy, because the world can be a dangerous place. But that means we make the best of the in-between time. Right? July 4th is coming up. We're hosting that big picnic on the lawn at *Sweet Dreams*, and you promised to bring your kickass potato salad that my boys especially love. You forget to do that, and you'll long for a save-the-world raincheck. Nothing more annoying than a bunch of pouting incubi."

Ruby attempted a half-smile. Raina knew some of those shadows in her eyes had to do with other things, things going on in the adjoining hotel suite, so she caressed her fingers, tugged, to draw Ruby away from those concerns.

"We'll talk about it with her together. Right now, let's just be glad we ended up where we ended up. We'll figure out the rest. That is, if I'm not moldering in some Underworld redemption chamber for saving a Pure Light's soul. All because of some stupid, goddamned technicality in the Underworld's 'how to kick evil's ass in a politically correct way' battle manual."

"Sshh," Ruby admonished, pinching Raina's arm with pincer-like fingers.

"Ow."

Fortunately, Derek and Mikhael's expressions cleared, suggesting they were done with their otherworld meeting. Confirming it, Derek shot Raina his patented stern cop face that always made her want to yank his chain. Or choke him with it.

"You've not broken the laws of either Light or Dark," Derek said. "The destruction of Elagra's soul was her own doing. Her punishment at your hands made you the instrument of her deserved fate."

He looked toward Ruby, his expression softening, then came back to Raina. This time, the look didn't change, reminding Raina that the Light Guardian cared for his wife's best friend, and would have her back, always.

No matter how uncomfortable it made both of them.

Even so, it still always surprised her whenever Derek went out of his way to be kind to her, but maybe because it had taken so long for her to see him as a friend.

"You did the only thing you could," he said. "Believe that as truth and don't doubt yourself as time passes. You saved Marcie's life."

"It's not the end of it, though," Ruby said, saving Raina from the embarrassing desire to give him a hug. All eyes turned to her. "There's the rest of it."

"Later," Derek told her, reinforcing what Raina had. "We rest, and celebrate first."

"Come." Mikhael held out a hand to Raina. "Derek and Ruby are going to portal to Jeremiah. You and I will stay here and watch over Ben and Marcie. But there is room in that for us to take our ease. We'll regroup on what remains to be done later."

Raina nodded. She moved across the couch first, though. She saw the surprised flash in her friend's eyes when she gave *her* a strong hug, holding her lean body close. "You are the most amazing witch I've ever seen," Raina whispered. "Take the same advice your semi-tolerable mate just gave me. Whatever paths you walked to get here, saved her life today. A lot of lives. You can't live backwards, only forwards."

When she rose, Ruby's eyes were suspiciously wet. Raina was glad

Derek was there to take her place. He lifted Ruby and put her back in his lap, cradling her, stroking her hair, holding her tight. In a few minutes, when she was more composed, Raina was sure they'd portal to *Sweet Dreams*, where Jem was being spoiled beyond repair by all her doting sex demons.

And didn't that just sound a little weird when one said it aloud?

It was possible Ramona had already retrieved him, and Derek and Ruby would go to her shop to see him, take him home.

After Marcie had mercifully lost consciousness, Silas had sent all of them off. When last they saw him, he'd been standing by Elagra's inert body, his head bowed as if praying over her. Raina suspected he'd been doing whatever a Grim Reaper did to prepare a soul for being pulled from its body and taken to where it was going to go.

She had visualized Elagra's soul being torn from her flesh and blood, her incorporeal wrist locked in Silas's unrelenting grip as he dragged her, screaming, struggling, into a place as dark as the life she'd lived. Because of her malevolence, she'd face a redemption sentence that was three times the suffering she'd inflicted on others.

Though she accepted it was justice, Raina didn't feel any satisfaction at the thought. Truth, as most things of this nature, it hit a little close to home. She remembered the flash of pity that had crossed Marcie's face, looking at the broken witch. A Pure Light had empathy that surpassed that of an angel's. Raina was nowhere near that generous of heart.

Ramona had portaled straight back to her shop, saying some crazy thing like she had to get the rest of her stock unpacked. She'd just left it lying around in open boxes. But she'd considered leaving it that way, letting people rummage through it.

"They like finding treasure in disorder," she'd said, with a tight smile. Her gaze had slid to Silas for a brief moment, but then, in a blink, she'd been gone. Well, in a swirl of energy that Derek and Mikhael together had fortunately contained, so it didn't spin all the buildings around backwards or turn them upside down on their roofs.

Mikhael's hand closed on Raina's, bringing her back to the present. He took her to the door of their room. Thresholds were significant to witches, to cross over into different ways of thinking. The closing of the door decidedly behind them, his palm pressing against it, added to the potency of the moment. But that image of Elagra she'd planted in her own head remained.

The depletion of her body had given Marcie the blissful escape, even if temporary, from this. The aftermath of a fight that, while a victory, was also a reminder of how much evil existed in the corners of the world. Voices crying out for help that didn't come, voices that had been silenced forever.

She closed her eyes. Then Mikhael's hands were on her shoulders, her upper arms, bringing her back against his solid body. His mouth was at her ear.

"Whatever darker sins you have committed, witch, you have more than paid for them. And if you have redemption coming in your after-life, I will petition Lucifer for the right to handle it personally."

She wanted to smile, but instead she pulled his arms closer around her, and he understood, holding her with undeniable strength. "It disturbs me, down deep in my soul," she whispered. "And it makes me so very afraid. Reminds me of when that was my whole life. Fear and hatred. Pain."

He made a quiet noise, dropped his head to kiss her collar bone. "Hear me well, *vedma*. Should you be required to pay any price in redemption that I deem too painful, I will take it upon myself. You will never suffer like that again. Not as long as I am alive to prevent it."

"Oh, Mikhael..."

When she squeezed her eyes shut tight, there was a hard ache in her chest and throat. She was a tearless witch, physically unable to cry in the mortal world, but it didn't mean she didn't feel the need some-times. Fortunately, he had other ways of bringing her catharsis.

His head pressed against her throat, so she heard the vibration of his words inside her. "There was a moment, when we first saw Elagra, when I could tell Marcie wanted to ask the question all humans want to ask. Why evil like Elagra committed happens. The answer is far too complicated for human understanding. But I would have told her this."

Mikhael's hands tangled with Raina's fingers, gripped. "The several of her victims who escaped her; a couple brought things to the world it needed. They could not have done that without the harsh sculpting of their souls her abuse inflicted. The ones who didn't...their souls weren't strong enough, not this lifetime. But in another, future path, that former life experience will bear fruit. It is the way of things. Not a comment on how it should be, but it is how the world turns. No memory or thought or experience is ever wasted. Elagra served her purpose. It always serves a purpose."

"So why did you come to Ben instead of to one of them?" she murmured.

"He was the only one still in New Orleans. It was a geography matter. You and I...our paths converged because of geography."

"Also because of darkness."

"Yes." His arms shifted, one wrapped securely around her waist, the other above her breasts, his hand firmly cupped over her shoulder. She made a soft noise and he tightened his grip again. Sometimes she thought it could never be tight enough, but it always was. Enough to steady her world, help her find her feet again.

He ran his touch along her arms, her waist, to her hips. Then he was lifting up her skirt in the back, so he could put heated palms on her hips and buttocks beneath it. She'd changed into the loose-fitting cotton dress when they came to the room, something dry, but she hadn't put anything on under it.

"Maybe something before we take a more thorough bath," he said against her ear.

She nodded. But he didn't initiate the rough and urgent sex she expected. Instead, he turned and lifted her, so her legs wrapped around his hips. He pressed her head down to his shoulder, let her fold her arms around the broad expanse of both of them.

He moved to the bed, putting her down on her feet beside it. With his powerful fingers, he traced the cut on her forehead, his dark gaze getting even darker. "When did this happen?"

"I lost track. Probably when I was hurled onto the Harrah's entranceway."

"You did not shield yourself quickly enough, in order to protect Marcie." He kissed the cut. "You may not be a Pure Light, but your heart is true. Even as you make mine stop far too often with your reckless courage. *Moya edinstvennaya.*"

My one and only. Turning her away from him, he nudged her with his thigh. "Lift your arms. I want this dress off."

She complied. He dropped the dress to the side, dipped down to kiss another cut on her back. She turned her head to her shoulder, odd feelings swirling in her chest.

"Mikhael," she breathed.

"*Ty moya edinstvennaya lyubov*," he murmured. "You are my only love."

He knew her heart, and what to say. Just as he knew how to do this to her, open her up down to her soul. Help her let the nightmares go, the lingering, wrong kind of darkness. He worked his way down, caressing or kissing every bruise, cut or scrape. There were quite a few. When he was done, he'd dropped to one knee behind her, was holding her hips. She was trembling. Not a single one of them had been quick, perfunctory kisses. He'd lingered over each, pressing his mouth over them, tracing them with his tongue, suckling gently to give her a brief increase in the pain, followed by a fizzing of nerve endings as he soothed them.

Distantly, she was aware of the regular rise and fall of sirens through the French doors. First responders, still handling the variety of aftermath crises the storm surge had created. The number of wounded would be low, thanks in large part to the near-miracle Matt and his team had pulled off, getting the affected waterfront evacuated.

Since the reason had been cited as a potentially very dangerous gas line leak, she supposed they'd offer some additional convoluted and very improbable justification, like it had caused an underground explosion that created the storm surge. People filled in the blanks on the things that seemed incomprehensible. It wasn't her issue to worry about.

When her Dark Guardian straightened to stand behind her, he cupped his hand over her throat, tipped her head back to his shoulder. "Mine," he murmured. Her eyes were closed, so the word vibrated through her, over every wound, the current and past ones, soothing all of them. And keeping every nerve ending aroused to his desires.

She almost believed him, that when her time in this body came to an end, he would personally supervise whatever time she had to spend in Hell. And come up with his own form of punishments.

But she'd never let him bear the weight of her pain for her. As much as he loved her, that was a two-way street. She'd endure every moment of what punishments she'd earned, holding tight to the idea that, when it was over, just like this day, she'd end up in some quiet, lovely bed with him, cool sheets tangled around them as they rested in one another's arms.

Somewhere along the journey her life had taken, that had become the best version of the afterlife she could imagine. Or want.

He removed his own clothes, and then bent and lifted her onto this bed, lying her back. Her eyes coursed over him. As he'd noted, they'd all cleaned up some when they first arrived back in the suite, removing the blood and dirt. He healed quickly, her Guardian, but she could see faint tracings of his wounds. She wanted to do what he'd done for her. Put her lips on every place that had been hurt. Maybe he would let her soon.

He could take her in a variety of creative ways, but that wasn't his mood right now, and she knew why. In this simple, emotional position, their gazes upon one another, faces inches apart, there was nowhere to hide.

"You did well," he said.

"So did you," she whispered.

He shrugged, dismissing the praise in typical warrior fashion. His eyes were full of her, his only focus. "I look forward to getting you back to your sex demons and your bordello," he said. "I much prefer to have you there, reasonably safe, rather than out here with me."

"I'd much prefer to have you there, with me, rather than out here, not reasonably safe at all," she returned.

His lips curved, though his eyes remained serious. "You will never be rid of me, witch. I am not that easy to shake. Or defeat."

She hoped so. She prayed for him every day, more so when he wasn't with her. She didn't know if anyone listened to a succubus witch who had a serious problem with authority, including the divine kind, but if They did, she wanted to make sure the ticket was in Their queue often enough to be noticed.

As he came down upon her, she slid her arms around his back, palms over his shoulder blades. He didn't let his wings come forth. Not yet. He could choose or not choose to do so, and perhaps liked the feel of her hands where they were now. She tipped her head back as his mouth found her throat, nipped and suckled, teased with kisses that she felt all the way through her breasts, cunt, toes, and back up to her accelerating heart.

"Please," she murmured.

"Please...this?" He lodged the head of his substantial erection at her opening. A fight always drove up libido, as the fierce need to live, to love, surfaced more strongly than ever. "Beg, sweet witch. You know I love to hear you beg for my cock."

"Please...Master. Be inside me. I miss you so much."

She wasn't often tender, so when she said the words in her heart, his eyes darkened, and he demanded nothing further of her, beyond the willingness of her body. He slid inside her to the root, making her draw in a deep, shuddering breath at the size and thickness of him. Her tissues spasmed around him, already preparing for climax.

She had innumerable sexual skills, but with him, her natural sensuality came forth, making every movement a willing and eager offering of pleasure.

"We will take this journey together," he said. And he meant it. Sliding into her, retreating, slow, deep penetrations that had her writhing in the iron band of his arms. His eyes became living flame as her desire built. And his stillness, his absolute attention, absorbed her every reaction, taking her even higher.

When she was so close she was begging again, he gave her what she wished, launching them off that peak together, making her cry out as his thrusts became demanding. He laid his hand on the side of her face, the other at her hip, and possessed her in all ways. He left no part of her alone or bereft. Together, they soared.

As she'd told Marcie, Mikhael took her flying quite regularly.

CHAPTER TWENTY-TWO

*M*ost humans might not possess the kind of magic that could levitate them or zap evil witches a hundred feet away, but Marcie would argue a whirlpool tub filled with hot, soapy water ranked right up there with the best that the paranormal world could offer.

Especially lying in one, in Ben's arms, after a day like today. Or night, rather, since most of the excitement had been done by dawn. Ben had spent a short amount of time on the phone with Matt, giving him an update, but the benefit of their long friendship was that a lot of words didn't need to be exchanged. He basically said what he needed to say, put in "Marcie needs me now," and that had ended the conversation.

She drifted some. It was hard to know how to feel, so she didn't direct her feelings much. She just rolled slowly over the whole terrain. Things were coming back she didn't want to remember. The cries of despairing souls, prisoners of Elagra for so long. Their voices could still make her shudder, burrow deeper into Ben's embrace to try and not remember. But then she'd remembered that lightness of feeling, the spreading of heat energy. The souls torn loose, the removal of the nails pinning them to their despair. Somehow, they'd been directed where they needed to go, free to find the peace they sorely needed.

She'd watched *The Little Mermaid* with her younger sister Cherry. She remembered the scene when all the prisoners were freed from

Ursula the sea witch. She also recalled the scene from *Indiana Jones and the Temple of Doom*, when all the kids came home, running joyously up the hill.

Those had been moments of celebration. This was, but it wasn't, as well.

It didn't erase the horror they'd had to experience for so long, but it did ease her heart to know that suffering was at an end. She wasn't sure if she could have lived knowing it was otherwise, which made her want to be absolutely sure, ask Raina and Ruby later if those souls would now, truly, be okay.

Another part of her was afraid to ask, since there might be nothing she could do if they'd simply engineered a spell to protect her from the truth.

The whole amazing sequence replayed in her mind like a movie, the things she'd only briefly seen coming in flashes. Mikhael and Derek, fighting the demon's minions in the sky. Ruby and Ramona, wrapping up Bonnie, taking her out of harm's way. Ben up there soothing her, helping her stay calm.

Then there'd been Raina and her, fighting Elagra. That huge wall of water, coming down. Or that explosion, when Raina's magic hit Elagra. Marcie remembered realizing, in an oddly detached way, that this could be it. The end.

The death of those she loved; that was something she worried about. Her dying? She worried about the impact on those she loved, especially Ben. But for herself...she didn't know why, but the death part itself, she didn't really think about, especially when she was in the middle of something like that, where she had an objective. The objective became the important thing.

Which was probably good, because without an objective, situations like that could be downright terrifying.

"What was it like?" she murmured. "Going where they took her. Passing into a different world, a different place."

"It was..." Ben paused, as if gathering his thoughts. His hands slid over her soapy curves, caressing idly, a Master enjoying his sub as he wished, touching her whenever he desired. Her nipples hardened against his palms, responding to it. Though she expected he would be exceptionally gentle about it, he would have her before long. Unless he was dead, Ben was pretty much a daily sex kind of guy, even in exhausting circumstances like these. On the less tiring days, well...she stocked up on energy drinks. But right now, he just ran his hands over her, and appeared to be thinking about her question.

"The trip there was like going down a slide," he said. "The last part of it. I think Ramona engineered it that way, to make it whimsical. First, we went through these different tunnels, but they were open, so you could see things on either side. Like how the gondolas were in Venice, going under the bridges at night."

She nodded, remembering their honeymoon. All the lights along either side of the canals, the canopied restaurants, the clink of glassware and soft music as people drank wine, ate and talked. The colorful facades of the buildings facing the canals, there for so many centuries. She'd thought of them like the spirits of indulgent ancestors, still solid and there, the reassuring power of the past mixed with the vitality of the present.

They'd spent some of their honeymoon days tangled in the sheets of their suite, the double doors open to the scents and sounds of the ancient city, but the nights were spent in those gondolas. When he'd realized her favorite part of the many wonderful memories of the trip were those nighttime rides, her leaning up against him as they were poled along the waterways, he'd dedicated one night to it. The gondolier had taken them up and down the waterways at a dreamy, leisurely pace for hours.

"Then it opened up, and we slid down into this grassy field," he continued. "Softest grass I've ever felt. It reminded me of your hair, when it blew against me, while we were sitting in the gondola together."

"That's nice," she said softly, thinking he might be saying it to make her feel included in a moment she hadn't been able to share directly with him.

"It's truth," he said, and his hand tightened on her breast, so that she tipped her head to look into his face. He stared hard into it, studying every feature. "Everything connects to you, brat. Everything. I'm sorry for that."

She swallowed and turned toward him, rising up in the water to straddle him. He let her, arms curling around her hips, palms sliding up the center of her back, molding to the contours beneath her shoulder blades. She cupped his face, her wet hair falling forward and brushing his jaw as she brought trembling lips to his.

"The only sorry you *ever* have to say to me, Ben O'Callahan," she said, "is for believing, even for a second, that you had to live without me."

His lips curved, his green eyes warming as he coiled his hand in her hair, drew her an inch from him, teasing her with the proximity of his mouth. "We took care of that in the wedding vows. I promised to be a selfish bastard, refusing to give you up ever. Or something like that. They figured out a nicer way to word it."

She coiled her arms around his head as he lifted her, put his mouth on her breast. She dropped her head back with a shuddering sigh as he suckled the nipple. Slow and easy, taking his time. He could be cruel and demanding, but not when her body was weak. He was in no rush and, just as she expected, he would be gentle with her. He would still demand everything from her, but in this loving, inexorable way that took her over just the same.

He rubbed his face against her, tightened his arms over her back. "I wanted to be with you, but the time with her, it still seemed too short. I climbed down, dropped into that grass. When I did, she had her head lifted, was looking around. She made this curious sound, a questioning noise. I didn't know if it was for me or everything around her, so I just said what came into my head. 'This is home. This is where you're supposed to be. It's going to be okay.' She gave me this look. She had fifteen eyes, did you notice?"

She'd noticed multiple eyes, but not how many, so she shook her head. She threaded her fingers into his thick, wet hair, her jaw resting on top of his skull, elbows pressed into his broad shoulders. "I caught a couple glimpses of her, but she was so large, and so much was happening..."

"Damn, should have taken a picture. I had my phone. Well, had. Somewhere in the river now. Two gone in two days."

She smiled, but something tight in his voice kept her quiet. After a moment, he spoke against her flesh again.

"She was...she looked like this mud creature I made when I was in Elagra's tunnels, when I was a kid. I used rhinestones from a stolen purse to make those eyes."

She closed her eyes, held him closer. He was here. A man grown, and she reminded him of it, of his victory over that dark time, with her touch on his broad back, tracing the tense lines of muscle there, though she kept her touch light over some of that terrain. He'd claimed to be fine, but he was as much a mess of cuts and bruises as any of them.

He'd undressed her to put her in the tub, which meant she'd had the chance to watch him remove his own clothes. A couple of the deeper slices on his abdomen and side had given her a bad moment, but nothing was bleeding anymore, and he'd reiterated that all he needed was to soak with her.

Since he was moving okay, she'd accepted that, but it still made her want to hold him even tighter, thinking how much worse it could have gone for all of them.

"I'm glad you took her home," she said softly. "I'm glad they brought you back to me. One day, I bet we'll see her again. At this point, it's hard for me to say we'll never travel to a different world, since we have new friends who can do that. And who run a bordello of sex demons."

He chuckled. "Don't forget the gun shop. I know you're already plotting how to get that assault rifle from Ruby."

"I admit nothing, counselor," she said. "I have it on good authority the best thing to do under oath is keep it to short, one-word answers."

She drew back as his arms loosened. He brought her down more firmly on his lap, his hands lifting to frame her face, run wet thumbs over her lips. "That mouth," he murmured. "I'm fucking hungry for it."

She caught her breath as he dropped a hand beneath the water to find her, rub his knowledgeable fingertips between her labia, finding the lubrication he needed to guide his cock there, ease his penetration past the less slippery bath water. The powers-that-be really should have thought about making water a better lubricant, but Ben O'Callahan would let nothing deter him when he had his mind—and his cock—set on a goal. He'd already added bath beads to the water that made it soft and slippery to the skin, with oils that would also soothe sore muscles. He coiled his hand back in her hair, his other hand on her buttock as he adjusted his hips and started to bring her down on him.

When she bit her bottom lip, focused on the effort of coming together, his gaze latched onto it. "There's my brat," he said huskily. "Take every inch."

"Take me the way you want to do it," she said, a plea in her voice. "Don't be careful. I need to feel how much you need me. We came so close..."

Maybe because of what their coming together always unlocked within her, the most terrifying parts of it all flooded her now. She had been fading, going away, buried under those desolate souls, far beyond where she could even feel him, the fierce love he had for her.

She tightened her muscles, never mind the pain that shot through every bone as she pushed herself down on him. She took every glorious inch in one fast slide, filling herself with him. Her hands, gripping his shoulders, turned into claws, digging in, telling him what she needed.

His expression changed, the green eyes glittering, his jaw setting, but her Master chose to be demanding in his own way. He gripped her hip, held her in place, with him deep inside her.

"I'm right here, brat. Always." His gaze flickered, that penetrating look that devoured every feature, every inch of her. "Always yours. No matter what would have happened, I would have found you, brought you back. Or gone to where you were."

"I was so lost," she said. "It was...oh God, Ben, it was so awful, feeling all of them, all those souls she hurt. And knowing you went through that..."

He shook his head, captured her lips, the kiss taking away everything but what he wanted from her, right now, in this moment. He lifted and lowered her, drove in deeper, swallowed her cries. "I'm here with you now," he muttered. "Show me how much you want to please your Master. That's all that matters right now."

She could do that. Or she thought she could. Her energy failed her, quickly. At one time she would have worried about that, worried that she couldn't keep up with how insatiable her husband was, but he'd cured her of that fear. Everything he felt for her was in his eyes, and it wasn't just desire. If possible, that might have been the least of it. The love was everything.

He slowed her down, the hands that had taken the life from Elagra, that had held Marcie with such ruthless power a blink ago now gentle once more. He made her go slow, easy, taking all control from her, so she simply followed his movements. She met his mouth, again and again, endless kisses until she was crying and smiling, holding his face to her throat as he found his climax and took her into a shimmering glide right with him.

∼

It was rare that Ben slept so deeply that she could slip from the bed without waking him, but the underlying exhaustion she'd detected in him had finally caught up. Her own body was still gripped by the lassitude that came in the aftermath of a night like they'd had, but her mind was oddly awake. So, after she went to the bathroom, Marcie put on her robe and went into the main room of the suite.

She didn't see Mikhael or Derek, but she found Raina, Ramona and Ruby sitting out on the spacious balcony. Ruby turned around almost as soon as she emerged, and then the other two looked. Marcie had an unsettling feeling that they'd been waiting for her. Had they woken her specifically to come to them at this moment? Or made Ben sleep more heavily, in order to talk to her alone?

Probably not. Though they hadn't said it outright, they seemed reluctant to do things that interfered with people's will, unless it was absolutely necessary.

Even so, as she stepped out onto the balcony, she felt a frisson of nervousness, studying the serious faces. "If you tell me that New Orleans is facing another crisis, I'm going to suggest we head for the Bahamas and let someone else handle it."

A ghost of a smile flitted around Ruby's mouth, helping Marcie feel better. However, her hazel eyes stayed serious. "We need to tell you the full story of what happened on the docks."

"Well, you saved my life. And Ben's. It'd be hard for me to object to the method. Unless you slaughtered a litter of puppies to make it happen."

Ramona blanched. "Oh Goddess, no. We'd never do that. Even if the universe depended upon it. It wouldn't be worth saving if that was what was required."

"I'd agree with that." Marcie came around the end of the wicker sofa where Raina was sitting. When the witch held out her hand to her, she took it, let herself be drawn down into a sitting position near her.

The sounds of the city seemed strangely muted, probably because the event had driven most tourists home, and most locals had the day off in the aftermath of the "storm phenomenon." She realized she would be hungry soon, and found herself anticipating the meal with the people they'd met only a couple days ago. Casual conversation only, no need for grand strategies to save anything.

At least she hoped that could happen. Looking at their faces one by one, she drew her knees up, feet curled over the sofa edge. Smoothed the long robe over her shins. "You're scaring me a little bit. Is Ben okay? He didn't sell his soul or something while I was out, trading his life for mine. If he did, I'm going to kill him."

She said it lightly, though the moment she uttered the words, fear tightened things inside her. Because he would do something just like that, damn it all. If he did, there was going to be some way she could fix it. They now had friends who could do...magical things, involving life, death and the afterlife. They could help them reverse fate.

"No," Raina said. "He didn't. Rest easy on that." She looked toward Ruby. Whatever she saw in her face apparently told Raina that Ruby wanted her to take the lead on the explanation. Marcie's fingers tightened on the soft terrycloth.

"Please just tell me. I can't do anything to help or fix it until I know what we're dealing with."

Raina put her hand out again. Bemused, Marcie took it. It did help, having the witch touch her, letting that energy she carried wash over her. Raina must be modulating it, because though it was definitely sensual in nature, it had a more relaxing component to it.

"Are you doing some kind of magical Prozac on me?" she asked.

"She isn't, but there is a version of that I use in my shop," Ramona said. "If someone comes in feeling tense and unhappy, it helps. It's not to manipulate or talk them into a sale. Just to help them leave the shop feeling better than they came in, no matter if they buy anything or not."

"Which is entirely impractical," Raina said. "No harm in earning a few dollars while providing a service they're glad to have."

"Raina," Ruby reminded her.

"I know," Raina responded, an edge to her voice that sent a

ripple through that energy. But then she sighed, squeezed Marcie's hand, let go, though she kept the hand on the sofa close to her. "When I struck Elagra with the magic I used to make her...shatter, for lack of a better word, it dislodged all those souls from her. You felt them."

"Yes." Even now the thought made Marcie grip the collar of her robe in nervous fingers. All that pain and despair. Ben had helped loosen the grip of those memories, but she'd never be able to forget that a soul could exist with the weight of all that hopelessness upon it, a never-ending torment and nightmare.

"I redirected them, released them," Ruby said. "If it was a piece of soul with a still-living host, it returned to them, restored their soul to wholeness. That's the ideal outcome. For the souls belonging to the dead, they might drift for a time, but they will drift with purpose. They will find their way home."

"This is all sounding really good," Marcie said slowly. "So where's the 'but'?"

"We made a decision," Raina said. "Mostly me, and I bullied Ruby into it."

"No, you didn't." Ruby tossed her a look. "For one thing, you can't bully me into anything. For another...I made the choice."

She looked toward Marcie again. "There was one piece...we realized we had to embed it in you so you could channel your particular energy through it, let the souls understand they were free. What helped was that particular piece wanted to stay with you, as if it knew you already were bonded with the original soul."

The import of it took a moment to sink in. "Elagra had a piece of Ben's soul?"

Ruby nodded. Marcie felt a mixed wave of emotions. Fury at a witch who was now dead. A renewed grief that Ben had literally lost some of his soul to a childhood nightmare. And wonder, that it was within her now. Marcie's hand crept into her robe, pressing against her beating heart.

"So you're saying a piece of Ben's soul is now part of mine," she said slowly. "I like that idea."

"Yes...but it connects to what else we need to tell you. Soul magic is the ultimate concentrated life energy. Because of the way I had to craft it to save your life, at the time I embedded it, it overrode

anything that blocked life energy. And its effect would have been...
retroactive, for lack of a better word."

When Marcie gave her a puzzled look, Raina tapped the top of her
hand. "She's saying if you've had your man inside you in the few days
leading up to our fight on the docks, any type of birth control would
have been completely useless. Except abstinence." Raina's gaze flashed
with humor. "Though honestly, I think that male could make you
pregnant, just from the way he looks at you."

"This isn't a laughing matter, Raina," Ruby said tersely.

"But it's not necessarily a tragic one." Raina tilted her head toward
Marcie. "Is it?"

Marcie's mind couldn't hold onto it. It was too much. "Are you...is
this a 'maybe this is going to happen' thing or...are you sure? Has it
happened?"

"I can find out, if you'll allow me. May I?" Ramona rose, stood
before her.

Her heart was thudding in her ears. Marcie started to get up,
thinking she had to stand, too, and her knees went out. Raina was
there, steadying her, pressing her back down on the couch.

"Easy. Put your head between your knees a second. You went white
as a sheet."

"No. I'm good. How silly; I'm being silly." She bent her head down
a moment, though, taking breaths. The sounds of the city had briefly
disappeared behind a hum of white noise in her head. Raina was gripping her hand again, and Marcie put her other one on top of it until
that noise stilled.

"We should talk about this later," Ruby said stiffly.

"No. Oh hell no." Marcie let out a laugh that she knew sounded a
bit hysterical. "I mean, there's no way you can come back to that kind
of subject, right?"

Raina's fingers touched her chin, and Marcie looked up at her. The
witch's eyes were warm, a smile on her lips. "Okay now?" she said.

"Yes and no."

"You don't have to get up," Ramona told her. She'd circled to the
other side of the couch and now dropped to one knee. "Is it okay, if I
open your robe?"

Marcie nodded. The chaos witch tugged the tie of the robe loose.
She didn't open it so much as slipped her hand inside, resting her palm

over Marcie's womb, her other over her heart. She closed her lavender-grey eyes. In this position, Marcie was looking past Ramona's shoulder, into Ruby's face. The woman looked concerned, tense, obviously not sure how Marcie was going to feel about...

It was a thrum, like a vibration. Marcie let out a little gasp and started back. She stared at Ramona, and realized she'd wrapped her arms around her middle. "I can feel it."

Which seemed a ridiculous thing to say, because right now it was just a tiny egg and sperm, less than a couple days' old.

But Ramona smiled, and nodded.

She was carrying Ben's child. Their child. Oh God.

Her eyes went to Ruby, who was looking at her, oddly expressionless. "You can terminate the pregnancy in the normal way, of course," she said. "If you do, it will send the piece of Ben's soul back to the Hall of Souls, which will eliminate the issue of your mortality being linked. It will be safe there until Ben's death, whenever that happens, at which time it will rejoin his soul, make it whole again. It's sensible. An option you understandably would want to consider." She took a breath. "But...I can't...I can't do that part for you. I'm sorry. I know how to do it, terminate a pregnancy, but I can't. Raina, or Ramona..."

"Never. No." Marcie wrapped her arms more tightly around her middle, as if afraid just the suggestion would take what was growing in her, right then and there.

The relief on Ruby's face was palpable. It also made Marcie realize what the witch must be thinking about her shocked reaction, up until this moment.

"I need to..." She didn't finish it, just got to her feet. Ramona rose, moving out of her way, but she and Raina were both there to steady her as Marcie moved around the coffee table between her and Ruby, then sank down at her feet. Her hips were pressed against Raina's legs behind her, suggesting she'd shifted closer to sandwich Marcie in between them, a show of support to both women. Ramona had likewise moved to flank Ruby on the other side. Protective. Family.

Marcie gripped Ruby's hands, both of them. "You saved my life. You protected that lost piece of Ben's soul. You did the absolute right thing. Thank you. And I would never, ever...it's him and me. Our love created it, as much as soul magic. Right?"

Ruby nodded, her gaze locked on Marcie's face. Ruby was a beautiful woman, but not one with much spare flesh, and when she was worried, the angles of her face were sharply sculpted and tight. "I will do anything to protect this baby," Marcie told her, squeezing her hands hard. "Because that's what being a mother's all about, right?"

Tears abruptly flooded Ruby's eyes. But Ramona bent down, the hand she had on Ruby's shoulder now coming around the other witch to hold her. Glancing up at Raina, Marcie saw a similar look of love on her face for her friend. Regardless of what those words meant to Ruby, Marcie knew they'd been the exact right ones to say.

Problem was, they were as much a reassurance to herself as to Ruby. A declaration of determination. Because she knew the decision didn't belong to her alone. And as her mind turned to that, she felt a clutch of total trepidation in her lower abdomen that dropped her stomach to her feet.

Oh God. He could not want it. The idea of being a father terrified him deeply, because of the darkness within him. He became quiet, or tense, if he even thought she was going to bring up the idea of kids. So she hadn't yet. That had been fine. They were still just newlyweds, after all.

Having pulled herself together, Ruby drew Marcie out of her head with further explanation. "Thank you for that, Marcie. But you need to understand, because of how the babe was created, we're not sure what kind of child it will be. He or she has as much chance of being healthy as any baby; it's not that. It's just...when magic is involved in a pregnancy, the child could be...different."

"Whoever he or she will be, will be perfect," Marcie said softly. "Because it was meant to be."

She looked down, then pressed her forehead abruptly to Ruby's hands. "But I am... God, I have no idea how best to tell him. He is going to majorly freak out. He freaked out about marrying me, because he was terrified he was going to ruin my life. He's going to panic over the idea of being a father."

"Maybe not as much as he would before this," Ramona said, making Marcie lift her head, look toward her. "It's funny how chaos can reveal truths about yourself you didn't expect."

"This might delay your career with the police department," Raina said practically.

That one was a blow, no denying it, but life could change in an instant. She knew that. Marcie managed a wan smile. When she lifted her chin, she didn't know she showed them the determined face she'd showed Ben when she'd declared her love for him, a defiant shot across his bow that had ultimately won her the war for his love.

"I had to wait seven years for the dream I most wanted to come true," she said. "I know how to be patient."

But first things first. She needed her cell phone. Fortunately, unlike Ben, she'd left the new one in the hotel room, and it still sat on the wide square coffee table in the living room.

When she left the balcony to retrieve it, she was surprised to see Mikhael sitting on the couch in front of it. He appeared to be doing that meditative thing, and she didn't want to disturb a conversation in process, so she hesitated, unsure about scooting in between his legs and the table to get it. The coffee table was too wide to reach across.

However, before she could debate it, he lifted his head, and fixed his dark eyes on her. He knew, she realized, and not just because he might have been sitting there long enough to overhear the conversation.

"Um, I'm just getting my phone," she said.

He stretched forward and picked it up, offering it to her. When she took it, he held onto it an extra moment, rising so he stood before her. He was imposing even sitting down, so the unexpected gentle note to his voice caught her attention.

"You like to tame the lion in him. You do it not with force, but with your submission. The depths of the darkness within him needs your light, to reach all the way down to what he thought was a fathomless bottom. He asks much of you, more than most are willing to give, but in return, you have compelled him to give all of himself to you, so the balance is there. The two of you are proof that the universe sometimes knows what it is doing."

His fingers tightened on hers. "Don't forget that."

He left her then, disappearing back into the room he shared with Raina, making Marcie wonder if he'd emerged specifically to give her that message. He and Derek both had a way of talking like this, as if they dug wisdom out of the depths of places she'd never be old enough to know, and she guessed they did.

She also noticed, maybe not for the first time, he smelled like smoke and fire. The good kind of aromas associated with those elements. A bonfire on the beach, the heat of the sun, a hearth fire on a cruel winter night.

Peculiar.

Holding the phone, she wandered out to the balcony again. So deep in thought, she barely acknowledged the three women, though she wasn't deliberately being rude as she moved away from them to the railing, the view of the city.

Their presence gave her a privacy buffer. When Raina made the suggestion they could go inside, Marcie shook her head. It was okay for them to be nearby. They'd warn her if Ben came out of the room.

The sun was warm, but the air was soft. In the aftermath of the storm, there was even a cool breeze, like sometimes happened after a hurricane blew through. The city had that expectant, things-aren't-the-norm feeling that also came in the aftermath of a storm, though this time they had far more to celebrate than they'd had after Katrina. As Raina had said, some clean-up of the waterfront, and things would be okay again. They'd made sure of it.

If things could be okay after a very large Loch Ness type creature had emerged from the Mississippi, this was manageable, right?

Marcie leaned against the rail for a long series of moments, pressing the phone to her forehead. She should be able to put the phone down, go and handle this directly with Ben. But she couldn't. She just couldn't.

She hit the preset number. Matt was down in Texas with Savannah and Angelica. She almost never called him. She always called Savannah. She didn't know if it was a sub thing or what, but in this case, she knew she needed to talk to him directly.

"Marcella."

Ben must have given Matt both their new numbers, such that Matt had answered, knowing who it was. His authoritative voice made her smile a little, even as it choked her up. It was the kind of voice that immediately told everyone in the room, "Whatever is wrong, I will fix it."

Good luck, Angelica, finding a guy out there more awesome than your own father.

Though he might not appreciate hearing it, Marcie was glad to be able to turn to him in this moment like she might have turned to her own father, if she'd had one who was a tenth of the man Matt Kensington was.

"Um…Matt. I'm pregnant."

Another thing about him. He understood what she needed, without another word said. "How do you want to handle telling him?" he asked quietly.

"I don't know if I can." It was hard for her to admit that. She'd fought Ben over things where no one else could and prevailed, but this… "I'm brave about a lot when it comes to him, but if he reacted really badly to this, Matt, it would just crush me."

Most of the times she'd stood toe-to-toe with him, it had been because she was convincing him they were meant to be together. At that point, he hadn't accepted it yet, accepted that she was his submissive, his and his alone. Because of that, she'd had some level of shielding, flimsy though it was, protecting her in case she failed.

When he'd accepted what she had always known in her heart, that he was her Master, the submissive in her had dropped all those shields, so she could give herself to him fully, unconditionally. Which meant that line past which she could push, had pushed before, would tear her soul up to do it now. He could destroy her heart and soul, because she trusted him utterly not to do so.

There were some things that needed time to build a foundation in a relationship. This was going to drop them both into the deep end of a pool they hadn't expected to experience for some time.

Love healed a lot of things, but maybe because of recent events, her soul was a little more fragile than usual. She didn't mind calling on the strength of four other Masters to come to her aid.

"Can you…"

"We'll take care of it. We're coming home tonight. Timing is important. We'll meet with him…"

As they worked out the details, the band of worry around her gut loosened.

A bit.

CHAPTER TWENTY-THREE

$\mathcal{T}$he next couple days were non-stop activity, the entire K&A team and their wives joining in local relief efforts to clean up the waterfront. Knowing Marcie wouldn't be able to hide something this momentous from Ben if they were alone together for more than ten minutes, Matt had miraculously engineered their respective schedules so that didn't happen. When she was with Ben, she was with the group, and it helped to distract her as much as him.

At night, Matt volunteered the men to help with the citizen patrols to prevent looting, and she and the other women went to give relief to the homeless shelter volunteers.

Initially, when Matt told her on the phone they'd sit down with Ben in three days, Marcie thought he'd lost his mind.

"I want you to have time to digest this," he told her firmly. "A decision this big, it's important you know your own mind on it before you share it with a personality as strong as Ben's."

Though she missed Ben intensely in those nighttime hours, she found, as usual, Matt was right. The separation time gave her space to think, come to grips with everything herself. As much as she could when one half of the equation wasn't yet in the loop.

His baby. Their baby. When she was alone in the shelter shower, to clean up and put on a fresh set of clothes before helping with dinner, she'd leaned against the wall, clasped her arms around herself again.

She'd helped raise her siblings, so she knew she had a leg up on a lot of women in terms of the day-to-day, with kids needing lunches packed, homework done, temperatures taken, a few firm words when they needed them.

But this part of things, this was new. A person was growing inside her. She would harbor that soul for nine months, and bring her or him into the world. She would hold this baby in her arms, and from the first second it breathed air on its own, it would know who she was. Who she would always be.

Mother.

It scared the absolute shit out of her, even as she felt something she couldn't describe when she thought about it. She guessed the best description would be kind of a quiet awe, as if some part of her was standing perfectly still, marveling at a wonder beyond her comprehension. She felt so grateful to be given the chance to look at it, be a part of it.

Ruby had told her dryly to keep that in mind when morning sickness had her throwing up her intestines. But she'd said it with humor, and a softness that told Marcie even in those moments, that feeling had been there for Ruby, too.

Matt had also told her he wouldn't share her news with anyone until they met with Ben, with the exception of Savannah.

She felt kind of guilty, not telling Cassandra, her own sister, but Ben was the baby's father. Getting Matt's help in knowing how best to tell Ben was different from sharing the news that she was pregnant. When it was time to share and celebrate it with her family, she wanted Ben to be part of that.

She desperately hoped he would be.

As she worked the breakfast line at the shelter on the second day, the thoughts of what might happen were starting to crowd in on her, way too fast and heavy. That was when she felt an arm slip around her, and looked into Savannah's reserved blue eyes. Matt's wife brushed her cool lips against Marcie's creased forehead.

"Breathe," she said softly. "And think about who's breathing with you. It helps calm you. I promise."

She didn't say anything else, just started dishing out pancakes again, but Marcie tried it. One breath in slow, out slow. Again, and again, as she imagined her heartbeat synchronizing with that pulse of tiny life inside her. It did help. Things settled.

God, she missed her Master so much. She had gotten used to being open with him, to him, about everything. She was glad she was at least getting to be near him, because she really needed that. She needed that on any day of the week, but feeling like something major was about to change, and not knowing how it would work out, made it all the more vital to be around Ben, yet without the pressure of facing the question to come.

Working side by side to help clean out the flooded homes and businesses of their neighbors gave her that space. They piled up the resulting debris to be carted off, convinced homeless people who considered the flooded area their home turf to go to shelters or relocate to safer, drier areas for the time being.

Yesterday, when they'd taken time for lunch on a corner of Canal street, eating box lunches donated by local restaurants, Ben had sat her on his knee, since they were short of folding stadium chairs. While she'd crooked her arm around his neck and grinned, he'd talked trash to a group of hookers mercilessly teasing him right back, making her laugh out loud. When she hopped up to help a homeless man open his boxed lunch, since he only had two fingers on one hand, the old man gave her a wink.

"That's a lucky fellow, there. Hope he knows it."

She glanced up to find Ben's eyes upon her. "I'm lucky too," she murmured. "We both are."

It was going to be all right. It had to be.

Their magical guests departed on Day Two. As they gathered in front of the hotel, Marcie wondered what it would be like to see them again. Would she and Ben invite Derek to have dinner with them next time he was in town, saving the world? How did it work with beings like this?

It was ironic that Ramona, the chaos witch, would make order of that confusion.

"If you ever get to North Carolina, come see me at my shop. We'll get the whole gang together for dinner," she said. "You can meet Jem, who I know will love you. You and Ruby can go to the gun range and shoot inanimate bad guy targets. Ooh, and we'll visit Raina's place.

You haven't lived until you spent an evening with her sex demons. They're like a bunch of really sweet hormonal teenagers."

Ben's hand brushed her back, and Marcie looked up at him, but he was talking to Derek and Mikhael. They had already exchanged the typical minimalist conversation men did, but one part of it caught her attention, made her smile.

"Thanks for helping to get me back here," Ben told Derek. The Light Guardian lifted a shoulder.

"It was entirely self-serving. God only knows what introducing a lawyer into another plane of existence might do to the order of the cosmos."

"And we're back to lawyer bashing." Ben sighed. "That's okay. I know how it works. I'll be the first guy you call if you get arrested at the airport for carrying a weapon of mass destruction." He nodded to the staff, then looked at Mikhael. He tipped his head toward the curb, where the Ferrari was waiting for him and Raina to take the front seat. Mikhael had said he was in the mood for a drive back to North Carolina.

"You should leave that here," Ben said. "I could loan you my smooth-riding minivan to get you home."

Mikhael lifted a brow. "Then where would you have your clients sit that you've stolen from ambulances?"

Ramona clasped Marcie's hand, drawing her away from the male banter. She was smiling at their teasing just as Marcie was, but when Marcie faced her, looked into the woman's eyes, her heart tightened in a way that she would feel if saying good-bye to friends she'd known much longer than a few days.

She wasn't one to question her feelings, though. Or not say the words in her heart.

"We didn't get much time to know one another, but I really like you," Marcie said. She shifted her attention to Raina and Ruby, standing in the same half-circle. "All of you. And thank you really, for everything. For doing what you do to take care of us."

"You were a vital part of it." Ramona hugged her, so naturally affectionate Marcie couldn't help holding on extra tight. "Remember, chaos isn't random," Ramona whispered in her ear. "It simply doesn't take the route you expect. But it's amazing how often you end up in the right place with it."

While she was still holding Marcie, Ruby and Raina drew closer, put their arms around all of them. Within their circle, Marcie was reminded of everything she'd seen them do, and what she'd done with them.

"You have a little bit of witch in you, Marcie," Raina said. "We all do." She brushed her lips over Marcie's, touching her chin, her throat, with lingering fingers, that sensual promise she did so well. When she drew back, Marcie swayed toward her before she could stop herself.

"Come to see me," the half-succubus said with a wink, a wicked gleam in her eye. "And bring your Master, his brothers and their wives with you. We'll take good care of you at *Sweet Dreams*. Oh, plus there's an unforgettable ice cream shop in town."

"Don't forget the shoe store," Ruby put in, elbowing Raina. She rolled her eyes at Marcie. "She just can't help herself. Has to turn on the sex."

"Turning it off is so rarely worth the effort," Raina retorted.

Ruby shook her head at her, but then she sobered. Her voice lowered as she tightened her grip on Marcie's shoulders.

"As strong as you are, you think there are some things you're not strong enough to handle. But believe me, you're about to discover a new level of strength. You have the power of two souls now. Or three." A light smile touched her serious mouth. "It will help you handle anything to come."

Day Three. Matt had told her to be out in front of the K&A building by ten in the morning. So here she was, sitting on a stone bench in the graceful front courtyard. The circle of white concrete benches surrounded a natural area. It contained a bronze sculpture of two cranes, along with lots of pretty trees and landscaping, everything she'd expect a guy with mega-millions and Matt's sense of style to have embellishing the front of his building.

It was a peaceful place, classy and clean, overseen by watchful security just inside the doors. As a result, it was a popular lunch locale for people who didn't even work here. They'd come and eat their meal on pretty days, certain they wouldn't be harassed by panhandlers.

Though street performers were always welcome, as the guy nearby playing an upbeat tune on metal buckets proved.

Marcie's fingers twitched, playing over the satiny steel of her collar, now securely on her throat once more. What was happening up in that board room? Was she ridiculous for not insisting on being there, hearing what was said?

No. For the past couple days, even as she'd hauled trash and done a bunch of stuff that pushed her body to the limits, another part of her had felt so fragile, breakable. More than once, she'd thought of Bonnie. The expression of the newborn creature when Elagra had struck her, the puzzlement, had made Marcie's heart hurt.

You will *be loved. You will. He will love you. He can't reject you. He just can't.*

She curled her arms over her stomach, a gesture that had become her most frequent way of comforting herself when she was alone. She was holding something within her that felt like...Ben. Maybe it was crazy, but she could feel the life there, even though it was only three days old. Maybe the strength of that soul piece made it more evident to her. Or maybe it was the power of suggestion. It didn't matter. The soul didn't have a trimester schedule. The soul was what it was, immutable, and Ben's piece of soul had brought forth that new life, a combination of their DNA. She would talk to it when it was micro-scopic as much as she would when it was making her waddle like a duck.

She was in a precarious place, she knew it. She'd told the women it needed to be his decision, that it was his child, too. But she already knew if he said he didn't want it, there was no way in hell she was killing this child in the womb. Or giving her or him up to be adopted to strangers.

The only option open to her under that scenario was having the child adopted by another member of their devoted extended family. And that would happen. She'd bet Rachel and Jon would be the first ones to step forward, but they'd relinquish the honor to Peter and Dana, who'd be a close second, no matter Dana was still freaked out about the idea of having kids because of her blindness.

But God, the pain of that. She couldn't. She would, if she had to, if the choice was being with Ben or not. But in the dread that gripped her, she knew how that would tear into them both, create a rift that would be hard to bridge. Could she bear being with him, knowing that wound was there, festering? She didn't have a choice. She would always be with him. But the happiness she'd embraced as his wife would have a permanent blight going forward.

It would be an unbearable situation she would bear, and they would both suffer from the decision. But the alternative? Raising the child on her own? Would he really withdraw from her, force her to do that?

She'd wanted to wear a badge, be a cop. She still could be, but she had wanted to be one *now*. Since she'd first made that decision, then finally won Ben's support, the idea had grown in strength every single day. It had given her a sense of purpose that she had known would become her defining core, the career that would shape her life as much as her love for Ben did.

But whether deferred or not, that core was there, no matter what. Being a cop wasn't about a badge or a gun, or a certificate from an academy. It was a state of mind, wanting to serve and protect others, wanting to take that path to change things for people, one person at a time. She'd just helped save a big chunk of New Orleans. That should cover her for a while, right?

She'd also dreamed of having Ben's child, of being parents together. It had been a dream tucked down deeper, maybe for a lot of the reasons she was apprehensive about now, but it was there. If being with Ben had taught her anything, it was that there was room and time for more than one dream to come true.

She was going to lose her mind if he didn't come down soon, even as she dreaded it...

Her heart leaped into her throat. There he was. In the spacious K&A lobby, he'd stopped at the reception desk to say something to the security guys. Since it was through the tinted glass, she couldn't tell if it was banter or just some mundane whatever. Then he was out the door.

He had an uncanny sense of her proximity, such that he didn't look around for her like a normal person. His gaze went straight to her, held.

She couldn't move. She just couldn't. She couldn't tell a thing from his face. It was wary, guarded. Wasn't it?

There were people moving around her, talking. The sun was shining. A bird that had landed in a nearby crepe myrtle tree was chirping. None of them knew how close they'd come to annihilation. But he did know, and she did, too. Yet it was not the uppermost thing in her mind at this moment.

His face was too locked down, she realized. *No, no, no...please.*

The past few days, while helping with clean up and relief efforts, he'd been wearing frayed jeans and worn, soft T-shirts that molded his body in ways that gave women of all ages a lot of fantasies, herself included. Today wasn't a workday, but when they came into the office even on an off day, all the K&A men tended to be a little more formal. As a result, Ben wore a dress shirt with rolled-up sleeves, untucked over a pair of dark blue jeans and loafers.

His dark hair feathered over his brow with the breeze, and his green eyes, always so brilliant and deep set, seemed to see only her. Yet before stepping out from under the building overhang into the bright New Orleans sun, he donned a pair of wire-framed sunglasses, which only further concealed his reaction.

She couldn't read him. The last time he'd locked himself down that way was when he'd put maximum effort into changing her mind about something she was determined she wanted more than anything

Don't make me choose. Do not do that to me. She'd thought nothing could destroy their love, but suddenly she was aware, with a mere sentence or two, he could tear it irrevocably to pieces. She couldn't bear that.

How could she carry the man's soul within her if he shredded hers around it?

He was everything to her. And to ask her to give up something she considered part of him...it was like he would be asking her not to love him with everything she was, to only give two-thirds of herself to him.

No. She wasn't ready to face this. She'd been wrong.

She got up and fled.

She caught the flash of surprise on his face, the creased brow, and then she was moving through the random wandering tourists, shoppers, and the forward marching office workers. She was moving as fast as she could go without breaking into an outright run, but still, her pace and expression earned her more than one startled look, a turned head.

It didn't make any sense; she knew it didn't. They were married, they lived together. Where was she running? But sometimes you just ran because you weren't strong enough for the truth.

"*Marcella.*"

He was calling her using that Master's voice that said, *What the fuck? Get your ass back here*, but it had another layer to it as well. Tenderness, concern. Like he anticipated having to comfort her over a loss, over a hard decision.

Fuck it. She broke into a run, nearly bowling over a knot of teenagers on a field trip from Baton Rouge.

She'd run the night at the pond, with Mikhael and Raina, letting Ben chase her down to the water. Though she had the satisfaction of knowing she'd made him work for it, he'd still caught her. He always could, no matter how many workouts she did to increase her running speed. But then, she'd never had to run for her life. He had.

He caught up with her two streets over. She knew it a second before it happened, because she was bearing down on a lady with a twin stroller, but the woman's wide-eyed look wasn't directed at the crazed-looking woman charging toward her, but something just behind her.

A strong hand clamped down on Marcie's wrist as he pulled even with her, brought her to a halt. She could have fought him, struggled, kept dragging them forward, but instead she just stopped. Went still as a bird in the grass, staring straight ahead, though she was breathless, panting from the exertion.

His other hand went to her waist, gripping, the palm conveying heat. His breath, also faster from chasing her, was on the crown of her head.

She'd gone over a hundred different things to say to him, but now, she had nothing, even though she knew she needed to have something. She had to have some kind of persuasion, some kind of argument to change his mind. Even as she knew the *need* to convince him would shatter her.

As he always had, he held everything, had all the answers, that mattered to her. That could end her.

Then he turned her toward him. Not gently, not an easing around. Like how he'd spin her toward him when they were dancing, yanking her up against his muscular body, letting her feel the pleasure of it from breast to hip.

His hand went under her hair, taking a firm grip in it, and then his mouth was on hers.

It was the kind of kiss that would make jaws drop, including the mother with the stroller. It was the kind of kiss that broadcast *"I would totally fuck you right here if we wouldn't get arrested."*

She kissed him back. With desperation, with anger. She was holding him at the same time she was clawing at his shoulders, whimpering in his mouth, a soft, angry, needy protest.

When he lifted his head an eternity later, she was sagging in his arms, held up by his strength and the power in that firm mouth, brilliant green eyes.

"Don't you ever run from me again," he said. "Your only option is to run to me."

She swallowed. "I'm so scared."

The tightness of his jaw eased a fraction. He stroked her face, traced the outline of it, touched her nose, her mouth, as if learning her face anew. And the whole time, he kept looking at her with that penetrating look. It seemed the universe went on a long time. She almost wished it could pause right here, not go forward or backward.

"Me, too," he said at last. "But it's okay. You're going to be the best mother that's ever been, so if I fuck up, the kid's not going to be ruined."

At first, she thought she'd misheard him. The time it took for the words to register told her just how hard she'd been bracing for a fight, for things to go the wrong way.

Watching her expressions, his eyes morphed from fire and concern to a touch of poignant amusement. Then regret.

She wasn't entirely sure she was steady enough for him to let her go, but he did. But only so he could drop to one knee, hands slipping to her hips as he leaned in, and pressed his mouth reverently to her flat stomach.

He held there as her nerveless hands came up, cupped his head, fingers twining in his thick hair. She was oblivious to any curious glances. There could be a million people on the streets of the Business District, or it could be as empty as it was at midnight. She wouldn't have noticed.

He spoke against her skin, since he'd pushed up her knit shirt to kiss her. Her Master would never tolerate a barrier of cloth between him and her flesh. When he spoke, his words were not for her, though they still spoke directly to her heart, hit her so hard it was painful. In the best way.

"When I married your mother," he said to that sleeping soul cradled inside her, "I promised to protect her with everything I am, and be the best Master and husband I could be. Now I'll make the same kind of promise to you, as your father."

Her eyes filled, the tears spilling out. Ben's gaze slid up to her face, and so did one of his hands, catching those tears on his fingertips as he rose. "And when he grows up, we'll both protect you."

He reached in his back pocket and came out with a folded handkerchief. "Matt," he explained. "He was wearing a suit, because he had a meeting this afternoon. He said he was pretty sure I'd need it more than he would. Most of his competitors cry in private, after he's left the room. Unless he wants them to cry in front of him."

She wanted to smile, but she couldn't. The past couple days had been too hard, too much of an emotional roller coaster. She felt like she was overflowing with feeling.

Ben wasn't smiling either, but his expression still had that tender look as he held her chin, carefully dabbed at her eyes. She expected there were women swooning around them, watching him do that, because it was mesmerizing her. The handkerchief had Matt's scent, which helped steady her as it perversely inspired more tears.

"How do you know he'll be a boy?" she sniffled.

"There is no other option. Girls are *so* much work," Ben seriously. "Look how much trouble you are. And girls can grow up to be giant dragons who try to drown the city."

"Like boys aren't just as much trouble," she managed. "Look at you." But then she put her arms under his so she could burrow, hold tight. "I thought...I thought you wouldn't want it. That you'd make me choose."

"Ah, brat." He put his head down over hers. "Since when do I ever give you choices? I won't even let you have a safe word."

He said it in teasing voice, her Master who knew how to comfort her, reassure her, build her back up. But he held her tighter. "Come here."

He drew her off the main sidewalk, over toward the lee of a building, where there was a small courtyard with a couple of stone benches, some artful landscaping. It was Richard Lewis's building, an affable competitor of K&A who was as much friend as rival. And who had been the owner of her McLaren before her.

Since the office was still closed in the wake of the storm surge, the courtyard was empty, so Ben was able to sit her down on a bench. He straddled it, facing her, but instead of drawing her closer as she'd expected, he held both of her hands, his expression becoming more serious. And that genuine regret was back.

"I'm sorry I put you through that. I could tell something was off with you these past couple days. Raina told me the magic had some side effects, and to just give you a little time." He grimaced, his eyes getting that glint she knew well. "She bullshitted me. I'll have to talk to her about that."

A lively conversation Marcie suspected would be entertaining to watch, but she regretted the deception, and told him so. "I'm sorry, too. I just..."

He shook his head. "I get it. It wasn't you. It was Matt."

Yes. It was. She understood better now what Matt had meant, about giving her time to be sure of what she wanted. Those days had given her a firmer foundation to stand up to Ben if they weren't in agreement on this. If he'd told Ben the same day she'd learned the truth herself, she'd have been too raw and vulnerable.

"He surprises you like that," Ben said, reading her face. His lips tugged in a grim smile. "He's so quiet sometimes, always watching, listening. We tease him about making us do all the really hard work, but no one is better at looking at everything involved and judging the best timing on a decision. Asshole."

She smiled, tentative, and he brushed her hair from her face, wrapping a curl around his fingertip. His thumb slid along the side of her throat, touched her collar, slipped under it. The provocative tug instantly focused her every nerve ending on that contact. He saw the reaction, an answering spark in his eyes, but he dropped his hand to lay it on her knee. He gazed around them, at the dark shiny leaves of the gardenias, the bright yellow frowsy sungold cypress.

"When I was a kid, I wondered why I was born, Marcie. Lots of times. Almost as many times as I thought about whether I should just give it up, let it go. It pissed me off big time, though, how shitty my life was. It made me mad enough that I was determined to live, just to spite Fate. It might have given me a crappy life, but I was going to survive, just to be a thorn in its ass. But even so...there were really low moments."

She saw it in the shadows in his eyes, those hints of the boy he'd been that she recognized in a way no one else did. She put her hand over his, fingers in between his spread ones. He brought his attention to the contact, then slowly turned his hand over, so their fingers linked, palm to palm.

"And then Jonas Kensington crossed my path," he said. "The guys, my brothers. You." He brought his green eyes back to her face as he repeated it. "You. Which made every bit of it worth it. No, don't start crying again."

It was one command she couldn't obey, particularly when he slid off the bench and knelt again, close enough he could wrap his hands over her hips, his thumbs slowly running over her abdomen. He adjusted his grip enough that he could tease the navel jewelry she was wearing. Today it was a tiny black cat, edged in silver, with green glittering eyes.

Ben spoke while looking at it, but she felt every word as if he'd delivered them straight to her heart. "If I reached that epiphany with the path I've walked, well hell, this kid's got it made. Because he'll have everything. You and me, that whole family we've built."

"Don't forget, his daddy is a really rich lawyer," Marcie sniffled. "He can have anything he wants."

Ben snorted. "Yeah, I also know about the dangers of being given too much, unearned. That kid is totally mowing the lawn for his hundred bucks a week allowance."

"We don't have a lawn," she said, thinking of their Garden District home with its tiny yard in the front. The back was shrubs, trees and pine straw. Plus a hammock, where they sometimes whiled away a Sunday afternoon, napping or reading together. Which gave her a wonderful image of the three of them there, the babe cradled in her arms as Ben held them both.

"We'll send him down to Texas on the private jet on weekends," Ben said. "To mow that ten acres of lawn around Matt's house. With a push mower."

She chuckled, shook her head at him. When he stood again, he drew her to her feet. Tipped up her chin, and then gave her a more even look. "I mean it, brat. Never run from me."

"But you like the chase," she said, despite the shiver his look gave her. "It's what predators do."

Instead of chastising her further, the heat in his eyes became something else. "I love you," he said roughly. "With everything I am, always."

She swallowed, put both hands on his face. "Same goes." She thought then of what Mikhael had said. *The two of you are proof that the universe sometimes knows what it is doing.*

"Or proof that even the blind squirrel sometimes finds the nut," Ben said dryly, when she shared it with him.

She sobered. "I'm sorry they weren't able to restore that piece of your soul, make you whole."

"Marcie, you made my soul whole a long time ago. And even if you hadn't needed it to survive, I wouldn't have wanted it back. Anything that might change the man I need to be for you, I'm not taking that chance."

"You will always be the man I need," she said. "Always."

Ben lifted her up on the brick wall surrounding the courtyard. It was about four feet tall, so after he sat her there, he leaned against it next to her, his hand curved over her thigh, her arm crooked on his shoulder. They sat there in companionable silence, thinking different thoughts, but she had to ask, because she did know him, knew he would have initially recoiled at the idea that she was pregnant.

"How did you...become okay with it?"

He curled his fingers in the waistband of her jeans, playing with the belt loop, a light tug. "Same logic that slapped me in the face with you. When I thought of someone else taking care of you, having you..." His jaw flexed. "I wasn't having that. Same thing with a kid we made together. Someone else raising him, someone else helping you every step of the way, being there for you... I'm sorry you were worried. Sorry you felt you couldn't come to me right off. But I get it. I wouldn't have wanted to hurt you in the first few moments of my what the fuck, terror down to my balls reaction."

"Did Lucas get it on video?"

"If he did, I will add that to my list of reasons to run his bike off the road. I'll borrow one of the company trucks so I don't scratch my car."

She swatted him. "You can't do that to my sister."

Ben curled a hand around her wrist, held her. "You're right. It's way more fun to get into his computer and hack his numbers so they're off by seven cents, then watch him go crazy trying to figure out what the hell happened. But I've already done that once and now he's password protected it with something like a NASA launch code. If fingerprints other than his touch his computer, it sets off an alarm at a local military base and they scramble the Stealth fighters."

She chuckled then. Her hand curled into the front of the shirt, fingers caressing him through the openings between the buttons. Her stomach, still doing flipflops, was nevertheless starting to feel better than it had the past couple days.

He stepped back enough to brace his hand on the wall, give her a direct look. "I'm sorry, Marcie."

She was about to tell him he'd already said that, but he shook his head, anticipating her. "About how this will affect you becoming a cop."

"You're not sorry about that at all," she began, trying to tease, but he knew her too well. He touched her face, the intent behind the touch taking away her ability to shrug it off. Which meant the loss showed.

"What do you want to do?" he said seriously. "You want to enter the police academy right after, I'll start working from home. Become a full time Mr. Mom so you only delay it a few months. I'm not going to be the misogynist asshole who knocked up his wife to keep her from pursuing the career she dreamed about."

Her eyes filled again, because she saw he meant it. What's more, she knew what it would cost him. Not the Mr. Mom part. She could see him doing that, easily, managing the legal side of things for Matt from their home, working it out however needed. No, the cost was in knowing how much, how deeply, her being a cop had worried him, and he was genuinely shoving himself away from the escape clause the pregnancy could easily give him.

"I thought about it a lot these past couple days," she said slowly. "Being a cop isn't a nine to five job. When I embrace it, I want to be sure that he's had what he needs from both of us in those first years of his life. So, we'll play it by ear. We're lucky enough to have the means to make that choice. I'm not going to throw away the gift of being with him during that time, for a career I can embrace a few years down the road." She touched his face. "Remember, I know better than anyone that waiting a few years for what you really want sometimes ends up being exactly the right time for it to happen."

He moved between her knees then. On the wall, she was a few inches higher than him, so he put his arms around her, drawing them together. His firm torso pressed between her legs, his head where he could tease her throat with his lips, which he did, but then he dropped his forehead to her breast. She curled her arm around his shoulders, her other hand curving over the back of his skull, her fingers tunneling into his hair once more.

It was a more nurturing position for him than he usually allowed. But he did it more often than he used to, laying his head on her breast in their bed in the early morning hours, letting her stroke his hair and shoulders.

Most of the time he was pure Dom in his interactions with her, but she cherished those moments, like this one. It was evidence that while he could always give her pleasure, meet her needs, he was opening up a part of him that would let her give him that as well.

He lifted his head to look her in the eye again, and now there was something in his gaze, a mix of the man she knew and something more vulnerable, from his past, that had her hands tightening on his chest, his waist. "You know, Marcie, there've been a lot of times in my life when I couldn't protect those I care about, even incidentally. A stray dog, a prostitute I exchange shit with in the morning, things like that. Then, with Matt and the others, I started thinking I could protect the things I care about again. But this brings it all back. The fear that I won't be able to keep him safe."

He gave her buttock a light pinch. "I thought worrying about you would give me gray hair. Overnight, I'll be turning instant white."

She smiled, but closed her eyes. She curled her legs around his hips and upper thighs, holding him to her with all available limbs. Joy was starting to brim over in her heart, because it really was going to be all right. He'd once again proven himself to be the man she needed him to be.

"You started thinking you could protect those you care about because you weren't alone in the world anymore. There were others who could help," she said. "Bad things can happen, do happen. Can't change that. But you can find and hold what you need to fix it, get past it. Survive it."

"Live with it," he said quietly. As he cupped her face in both strong hands, she nodded, folded her hands on top of his.

"Together."

~

WANT MORE OF JOEY'S PARANORMAL ROMANCE? How about vampires? Or maybe you want more of Joey's contemporary work.

You can start TWO new series for FREE!

If you found this book through the Arcane Shot series, you might be interested in the contemporary Knights of the Board Room series, Ben and Marcie's world. Book One, *Board Resolution*, is a first-in-series **FREE** ebook download, telling the story of how Matt Kensington won the heart of his business rival Savannah Tennyson.

He'll be there for her when she thinks no one will be...

Savannah was groomed from birth to take the reins of her father's empire. Business rival Matt Kensington knows commanding her submission is the key to breaking through her emotional armor. Calling on the unique sensual talents of his four-man management team, he engineers an aggressive erotic takeover, determined to rescue the woman he loves from the steel cage she's manufactured around her heart. Savannah will be theirs for this one night--and his forever.

CLICK HERE TO READ NOW FOR FREE
BOARD RESOLUTION

Reading this in print format?
Look for it at your favorite book vendor!

Or use this BookFunnel link for easy download to your preferred device:
https://dl.bookfunnel.com/ns4cw7rwsr

But maybe PARANORMAL romance is your jam...

If so, check out Joey's Vampire Queen series. Book One of that series is also a first-in-series **FREE EBOOK!**

His blood. His soul. His body. Hers for the asking...

Jacob, an alpha male and former vampire hunter, will protect a woman without thought. Submitting to her is a different matter. However, Lady Lyssa needs him. A thousand-year-old vampire queen, she is besieged by enemies, and haunted by past losses. Jacob may be the only soul she can trust.

In the vampire world, a human belongs to his Master or Mistress in every way. All choices belong to the vampire. But when love is involved, ownership becomes a tricky thing...

**CLICK HERE TO READ NOW FOR FREE
VAMPIRE QUEEN'S SERVANT**

Or use this BookFunnel link for easy download to your preferred device:
https://dl.bookfunnel.com/qnv6rl2rce
(books not free at Nook, but this link provides that format).

ABOUT THE AUTHOR

Having penned over fifty acclaimed BDSM contemporary and paranormal titles, which includes six award-winning series, *Joey W. Hill* has been awarded the RT Book Reviews Career Achievement Award for Erotic Romance. A submissive herself, Hill brings authenticity to her intensely emotional love stories.

She is grateful for the support of a wonderful and enthusiastic readership, which allows her to live on her beloved Carolina coast with her even more beloved husband and menagerie of animals.

- On the Web: https://storywitch.com
- Twitter: https://twitter.com/JoeyWHill
- Facebook: https://facebook.com/JoeyWHillAuthor
- Facebook Fan Forum: https://facebook.com/groups/ JWHMembersOnly
- MeWe: https://mewe.com/i/joeywhill
- GoodReads: https://www.goodreads.com/author/show/ 103359.Joey_W_Hill
- BookBub: https://bookbub.com/authors/joey-w-hill
- Amazon: https://amazon.com/Joey-W-Hill/e/B001JSCIW0

ALSO BY JOEY W. HILL

Arcane Shot Series

Arcane Shot

Arcane Madame

Arcane Chaos

Arcane Knight

Daughters of Arianne Series

A Mermaid's Kiss

A Witch's Beauty

A Mermaid's Ransom

Knights of the Board Room Series

Board Resolution

Controlled Response

Honor Bound

Afterlife

Hostile Takeover

Willing Sacrifice

Soul Rest

Knight Nostalgia *(Anthology)*

Mistresses of the Board Room Series

At Her Command

At Her Service

At Her Call

At Her Pleasure

Nature of Desire Series

Holding the Cards

Natural Law

Ice Queen

Mirror of My Soul

Mistress of Redemption

Rough Canvas

Branded Sanctuary

Divine Solace

Worth The Wait

Truly Helpless

In His Arms

Ignition Sequence

Naughty Bits Series

Naughty Bits

Naughty Wishes

Vampire Queen Series

Vampire Queen's Servant

Mark of the Vampire Queen

Vampire's Claim

Beloved Vampire

Vampire Mistress *(VQS: Club Atlantis)*

Vampire Trinity *(VQS: Club Atlantis)*

Vampire Instinct

Bound by the Vampire Queen

Taken by a Vampire

The Scientific Method

Nightfall

Elusive Hero

Night's Templar

Vampire's Soul

Vampire's Embrace

Vampire Master *(VQS: Club Atlantis)*

Vampire Guardian *(VQS: Club Atlantis)*

Vampire's Choice

www.ingramcontent.com/pod-product-compliance
Lightning Source LLC
Chambersburg PA
CBHW061130200626
46817CB00016B/591